In Search of Gods and Heroes

Children of Nalowyn, Book One

Sammy H.K Smith

www.kristell-ink.com

ISBN 978-1- 909845-33-6

Cover art by Raymond Tan
Design by Ken Dawson
Map by Hazel Butler
Typesetting by Book Polishers

Kristell Ink
An Imprint of Grimbold Books
4 Woodhall Drive
Banbury
Oxon
OX16 9TY
United Kingdom

www.kristell-ink.com

For Nanny and Granddad

"Chaeli, please! Chaeli, help me!" Acelle begged and cried, her pleas distorted by sobs.

"That's right Chaeli, stay where you are. Don't let me end it for her," the voice whispered, "please, let it continue."

Fear and bile forced their way up from her stomach. These creatures were not meant to be real, to exist in Ibea.

It must have been waiting for me.

She swallowed hard again and blinked back tears.

"Chaeli!" Acelle screamed, the desperation in her voice burning Chaeli like acid.

She shifted, blocking out the pain, and pushed open the door, rolling out onto the dusty kitchen floor. Pain seared through her leg and she cursed aloud, shoving a fist against her mouth in frustration as she scrambled to her feet, her left side sagging slightly with the effort of supporting her weight. The room was dark and musty, and her eyes took longer to adjust than she wanted. Gripping the side of the kitchen cupboard, she took several deep breaths to calm herself. She could hear movement in the room opposite, heavy bangs and short rasping breaths, which seemed to be getting closer. *Please, Elek, please help me*, she silently begged to the God of Chance. *It's not my time, not yet, please.* In her mind, she repeated the prayer over and over.

Nothing. No reply. Only the sharp agony in her leg. Metlina, Goddess of Pain, was taunting her.

Her strength and resistance ebbed away. There was no help coming and she was going to die at the hands of that monster. She moved towards the doorway, grimacing with each step as she tried to stop her leg from buckling. Thoughts and memories bombarded her mind as she prepared herself. Her parents, their deaths, Acelle . . . *oh gods, what's happening?*

She stood in the doorway, making no attempt now to hide or run.

"Where are you?" she called out, surprised her voice didn't waver. "Show yourself. I'm not hiding." Her voice didn't sound like her own; it was strong and resonated through the room. Warmth and strange languor caressed her, touching and commanding every inch of her skin. The heat spread and possessed her. A sweet intoxicating feeling of sheer . . . luck? Suddenly, Chaeli felt strong and alive. *Elek!* Smiling to herself, she called out again:

"Acelle, are you there?"

Even though there was still fear in her heart, divine energy from the God of Chance wove through her being. Bravery. Excitement. Power!

"Chaeli," the creature hissed, "I'm here, my lady. Will I do?"

She spun around, and finally faced the demon; she gasped at both sight and smell.

Limp in the arms of the creature was the body of Acelle, blood dripping from her torn throat, her eyes glazed and staring. Despite her horror, Chaeli let out a sigh of relief at the shallow but certain rise and fall of Acelle's chest; she was alive, just.

"Chaeli, will you come willingly with me? Come to my lord?"

"What are you talking about?" *Shut up, shut up!*

She tore her gaze from Acelle and stared into the black eyes of the demon. Tall and imposing, it seemed to fill the room. Although human in shape, the slick skin was mottled and bruised, the eyes cold and unfathomable. It was hard to stand her ground as the smell of the beast crawled around the space between them, searching and hunting for her.

"An answer. Chaeli, now!"

"Perhaps if you released my sister I would be more amenable to your offer," she replied, forcing herself to stare at the creature, her jaw set like stone and steel in her spine. As its odour intensified, Elek's blessing weakened. The demon's mouth contorted into a sneer.

"Of course, my lady." It dropped Acelle, her body hitting the floor with a sickening thud. Chaeli tensed and her throat contracted. She couldn't tear her eyes from the beast, refusing to look down at her sister's crumpled body.

"Are you ready?" The demon beckoned her forward with a claw.

"Where will you take me? What's going on?" Chaeli hoped her voice wouldn't betray the fear that began to envelop her again. "What do you want from me?"

The demon lowered an arm and grimaced. "Do not push me, I have been patient so far. We have all been so very patient."

"Patient!" Her eyes widened as the pain in her leg flared, preventing her from retorting further.

Chaeli stepped forward to kneel beside Acelle's motionless form, brushing the hair away from her face. Her chest was still now, her eyes unblinking. Chaeli cradled her, rocking backwards and forwards as silent tears fell. The pain of her injuries was nothing to the pain in her heart. Her only family in this world was gone because of her. Staring up at the demon she hissed: "I shall have my answers now, my lord."

The demon was unconcerned by the sudden edge in her voice. "Perhaps if you were to leave the human and come speak with me, you would come to understand that these sacrifices must be made." It grinned manically.

Sacrifices. Something inside Chaeli changed. Her confidence, and the presence of Elek, ebbed away until finally, with a jerk, it disappeared. Gently she laid Acelle down and kissed her forehead; the warmth had already begun to leave her body. As she stood to face the demon, Chaeli felt alone. Her legs were soft and unsteady, and the steeliness within her crumbled. Though tall for a woman, she didn't even reach the demon's shoulders. She gestured towards the dining area where the crockery from their abandoned meal lay on the table. The smell of ditari bread still lingered, scented water sparkled in the jug, and as she walked towards the great hearth, she noted that the fire still crackled heartily. The warmth whispered to her and she couldn't resist; she didn't know why, but she *had* to look at the fire. The flames licked around the logs, colours shifting as the heat permeated the grain. It was beautiful to look at and Chaeli felt her gaze drawn deeper into the flames, transfixed by the way they danced and twirled, the way they left nothing behind but ash, destroying everything in their path.

"My lady?" The demon leaned over her. The smell of the beast's breath churned her stomach and she recognised it as the scent of death.

"What?" she snapped. *Shut up! Don't provoke it. Idiot.* "What do you want from me?" she repeated. "Whatever it is, take it. I care not." She jolted; if she could escape, she could get help from the village, she just had to bide her time. The priest would know what to do; surely he would have something to repel this beast. But was the beast real? Had she finally gone mad? A half-sob, half-chuckle escaped her lips, and she clamped them shut, silently praying to the Kingdom gods for help and support. They had to answer now that she really needed their help. Closing her eyes, she forced a litany, calling on every god she could recall for guidance.

The demon moved a chair to face Chaeli, sat down, and pressed it's fingertips together. The smell of the beast overpowered her prayer, and the words faded, mixing with the screaming desire to run, to save herself. But liquid fear gripped her, and falling into her father's wingback chair she opened her eyes to stare into the creature's. For a moment it seemed to hesitate, and there was a flicker of emotion on the cruel face. Recognition, perhaps? As though it saw something in her eyes. But before she could think further, the thoughtful expression disappeared, and the sneer returned.

"You care not? Then tell me, why do you tremble so?" Extending a claw, he pressed hard against the cut on her leg; she screamed and her vision blurred.

"Get off me!" She lashed out, slapping the creature's arm. It laughed and pushed harder, gripping her flailing arms with it's other hand.

"Stop, please stop," she babbled, sweat sticking to her armpits and back. "For the gods' sake just tell me what you want." The

9

"Take care with your words, Shy'la. The walls are always listening," said Drenic, looking up and frowning. "You'd do well to remember that."

"Tell me, Drenic. Since when do walls hear? I fail to—"

Adley interrupted the God of Honesty with a loud cough, then lowered his head in apology. "Forgive me, but time is precious. I ask for permission to show her our world."

A voice thundered about them, silencing the chatter in the room. "Are you quite sure that's necessary?" The gods swivelled to see the huge shape of Vorgon, God of Water, forming in the air like a huge bubble. "The treaty may not be destroyed. Perhaps we can salvage something from this." The god leaned forward and stared intensely at Adley.

"My lord, they were eating supper when he appeared in her home. Acelle tried to protect her, but Malo struck her down." Adley's voice was reduced to nothing more than a whisper. The gods glanced at each other in dismay as Adley pressed on. "Acelle attempted to distract Malo. When Chaeli tried to help her sister, Malo struck out, injuring her leg. Afraid and hurt, she ran to hide. Malo then slit Acelle's throat. I saw nothing else; it was then I came to you. Malo gave no reason for his presence, no warning, and didn't send an emissary to the protectors advising us that he intended to speak with Chaeli."

"But why must you reveal the gods to her, Adley? Chaeli is already a believer, she prays to Elek, to Denna, and others. She doesn't need to know more." The voice that spoke was quiet and reassuring. It was Igon, God of Honesty, who had chosen the form of an old beggar for the meeting.

"But she can't be expected to find her way unless she can see." Adley could feel anger bubbling within him. Swallowing, he closed his eyes in an effort to calm himself. "I beseech you. The Underworld has broken the treaty, and we must stop them." Adley looked around the tower room. The gods wouldn't make eye contact with him. He opened his mouth ready to vent his frustration when someone spoke.

"Adley, you have my support in this matter, but hear me well: if Malo has twisted her before you arrive, you must deal with the situation accordingly." The Goddess of Love looked straight at him, her amber eyes burning. "She must not be corrupted by the Underworld."

Adley bowered his head with deference to mask his dismay. If he lost Chaeli to the Underworld then he too would be damned. A protector who neglects was no use to any god. Redemption would be found in the stilling of her heart, and the breaking of his.

"Aye, you have my support as well," muttered Drenic. "We've waited patiently for the daughter of Amelia Von Ariseré to discover her potential, perhaps now she needs a push."

Adley held his breath. The others were too quiet and he needed more of them to back him; two deities would not be enough.

"All in favour of Adley accompanying Chaeli to Lindor?" said Penella.

"Aye," chanted a chorus of voices with varying degrees of enthusiasm.

"All opposed?"

There was no reply. Adley's heart leapt. He had the support of all gods present. This was more than he had hoped.

Penella looked at him and pursed her lips with dislike. "Go, rescue Chaeli. Do what you must, but remember who she is, Adley. I will relay the Council's decision to His Highness."

Adley backed towards the door, stopped, and bowed to the gods.

"Thank you," was all he said as he left their presence and headed toward the halls. He knew that whatever happened from this moment on could change the balance of their three worlds. As he approached the gatekeeper, his mind was full of thoughts of Chaeli. He had spent so long watching from the shadows, ensuring her guardians took care of her. It was only in recent years he had felt the strong pull of his own emotions. He was her protector.

screeching of the harpies echoed through the darkness, cutting the silence and forcing the prince into the present. The harpies' nest, made from bones and rotting flesh, filled his gaze, and he watched as the fighting siblings clawed at each other, flapping their wings in anger, the prize for the victor a cowering man. The largest creature cackled with glee as she approached the human, her wings enveloping him and drawing his body against her feathered breast. Eli saw the soul of the pitiful mortal wisp into the darkness where it was consumed greedily by the shadows. A gust of wind sent the sweetness of the dead river straight into his chambers. The tang of betrayal and lies from the stirring waters permeated his corporeal form, and he quelled his excitement, instead focussing his attention on a dark shape moving through the silent streets. It was the only movement in vision, but it was too slow to be a demon, too large to be a hellion. It appeared to be dragging something behind it. He stared harder; it looked like a mortal.

Bored, he looked away and across the cold, empty land, dead and hard like a sheet of black ice where nothing grew. He shivered. Eli refused to wear a mantle in his domain, and to succumb to the environment was to admit defeat – something to which he was not accustomed.

The Damnable Lord swivelled on his toes and returned to his quarters, slamming the shutters behind him.

"Metlina! Where are you?" he called, striding to the fireplace. Staring into the flames he became aware of a strange feeling. He knelt on the hearth and studied the mass of glowing embers and dancing blades. It was as though he was being watched – no, not watched, it was as though someone was attempting to connect with him, pulling at his energy, reaching through the blaze. As he concentrated on the flames further he could almost feel . . .

"My Lord, you called?" came a quiet voice behind him.

Jerking his head up, Eli saw Metlina looking at him with concern. For the Goddess of Pain, she appeared too caring and too gentle. The fire and its strange behaviour had made him uneasy,

18

not an emotion he was accustomed to feeling. Barely suppressing his rage at the interruption he got to his feet – after all, he had summoned her.

"Something doesn't feel right, Metlina. What's going on?" He towered over the petite goddess. She looked away, hesitating. Infuriated, Eli grasped her chin in his hand forcing her to acknowledge him. "Well?" His dark eyes bored into hers, exuding dark energy and pressed into her being. None of his subjects would attempt to keep secrets from him. He was her master, and he would punish her.

"Eli . . . please." A small trickle of blood rolled from her eye. "It's Malo, he . . . he's with Chaeli."

For a moment everything was still.

"Get out," he snarled, releasing her chin. Metlina gasped and rubbed her eyes. Eli delighted in her pain, his energy stronger than it had ever been. He had so many more followers now. "Did you not hear me? Leave!"

He grabbed the goddess by the arm and walked her to the door. She gave a small, gratifying cry as he threw her into the hall before he slammed the door behind her and leaned his back against it; he was surprised to find his breathing was uneven. As he closed his eyes a thousand thoughts swamped his mind. The treaty, his brother, Chaeli – and then Amelia.

He had never meant for things to go as far as they did with her, but he couldn't help himself. It was a shame he had never loved her the way she had loved him. Opening his eyes, he went to his bureau and removed a sheet of calf vellum and a quill. Perhaps he should write to Daro? It seemed only yesterday when they had laughed together over one of Drenic's terrible jokes. He hesitated, then placed his writing instruments back into the bureau drawer. No, he wouldn't write to his brother. Daro had neglected him in his time of need, neglected him for Amelia. Daro had blamed him for her unexpected infatuation, and no amount of protestations from Eli had swayed his mind. Daro refused to believe his brother, and instead had placed a mortal above all. Smiling sourly, Eli drummed his fingers on the desk. No, Daro would feel his pain; he would feel what it was like to be neglected and alone. Chaeli would ensure it.

He smiled. He would have Chaeli even if it meant sacrificing every one of his subjects.

"Good Luck."

Boda's words echoed through Adley's mind as he headed towards Chaeli's home. It was a good seven kilometres from the gateway and would take precious time on foot. He cursed the unpredictability of the portal and the keystones – why could he not have appeared at her home? Since the dragon wars and the arrival of Boda as gatekeeper, the portal fluctuated in accuracy. It seemed a mystery to the gods.

As he touched the arc of carved stones on the ground, he prayed Chaeli was alive and that Malo had not revealed the truth to her. The damage could be limited if the treaty was intact. Turning away from the large lake and quickening his pace to a job towards the village, he remembered the day of the signing so well. The princes had emerged from the council rooms in silence, each unable to look at the other. The Beings scattered around the halls had whispered to one other with agitated glances towards the two princes. There was a chill in the air and ice formed around the marble pillars.

"Leave us," Daro had commanded, staring at the Beings. Adley too had turned to leave, but stopped as Daro called out, "Stay, Adley, you will be needed."

Dismayed, the Beings ceased their communications and bowed to the princes, scuttling away towards the Great Hall. Daro looked defeated and worn, and the sneer on Eli's face suggested he had won the argument.

"Penella, bring my papers."

"What's wrong, brother?" spat the younger sibling. "Regretting your decision?" The look on Eli's face had been a mixture of hatred and triumph; there was no need for him to mask his true feelings any longer.

Daro turned to Eli with a doleful look in his eyes. "Eli, the treaty will be signed and the papers sealed with our divine sanction. Once this has been done, do not speak to me again."

With that, His Highness had turned away from his brother and sunk to the floor, cradling his head in his hands. Adley could see he was crying.

Moments passed – it felt like hours – then he heard Penella. "My lord, your papers." Her voice trembled. Snapping his eyes open, Adley stared at the goddess. She was pale as alabaster. "Please my lord," she whispered, "don't . . ."

"Thank you, Penella," replied His Highness, holding out his hand. Penella bowed and handed Daro a mass of reed paper and his gold quill. "Eli? Shall we?" He inclined his head towards the council.

"Ah, brother, do you take me for a fool? This display of unhappiness does not sway my heart. You have always treated me like one of your pets. Once this is completed, I shall be gone with my followers and will never enter this place again. Of course, if the child is to follow me . . . well . . ." Eli smiled maliciously. "Then you may see me once more."

Eli closed the council doors behind them with a loud, echoing bang.

"Hey, you!"

The tall doors were ripped from his mind, replaced with the blue hour hues bouncing on the dusty ground. Slowing down to walking pace, Adley saw a local patrol guard staring in his direction, his hand on his hilt.

"Yes, sir?" called Adley. "How can I help?"

The guard approached. On closer inspection he looked young, perhaps just entering manhood, with his face still showing signs of acne.

"Your papers," ordered the young guard holding out his hand. Adley saw the silver band encircling his wrist; the runes were the ancient common tongue, and he could read that the guard's channelling abilities were average at best. He had no proficiency or specialisation, but he'd passed the test: he had enough energy to channel and, most likely, enough to ward off some dangers or to attack. He wore the band above his uniform with pride, for he was part of the small proportion of mortals on Ibea who had an affinity with the natural energy and power of the gods. "Papers, *now*," repeated the guard.

Damn, thought Adley, *I don't need this now*. It was the first time he had shown himself to mortals in years.

"I'm sorry sir, I don't seem to have them on me." Adley shrugged, grinning good-naturedly. "I must have left them with my woman."

The guard narrowed his eyes and gripped his hilt tighter. "All persons are to carry their papers at all times, no exceptions, as decreed by King Stirm. You are now bound by law for the offence of non-citizenship. You have no papers, which leads me to believe that you are not a free citizen." The guard hesitated, then muttered, "The speed at which you were running leads me to believe you are an escaped slave. Law thirty nine, code four demands immediate acquiescence of all slaves."

With the last few words, two more men appeared and flanked Adley's sides. Groaning, he put his hands up beside his head and debated with himself for a moment.

"I'm sorry to do this," he said, ducking forward and sweeping the young guard's feet away from him with his left leg. The man crashed to the ground with a cry. The guard to his right shouted something, and with a sharp movement of his right elbow, Adley connected with his chin, causing him to stumble back. Adley leant forward and grabbed the first guard's sword from his belt. The guard stared at him, holding his chin, and after a brief hesitation, turned and ran. Adley turned towards the third guard, and saw the fear in the man's eyes.

"You can run like your comrade, or fight and die," said Adley. "Make your choice quickly, son, I am a busy man."

The guard looked at his colleague on the floor and back at Adley, seemingly weighing up his chances.

"Do you have a family, son?" asked Adley.

"That's no concern of yours, *slave*."

"I think you'll find it is. If you stay and fight, you will lose." Adley weighed the sword. "Good weapon, sharp too." The guard unsheathed his sword and stood his ground, but the weapon shook in his hand.

"Run, lad. You don't want to die."

Adley lunged and connected with the guard's sword. The guard blocked the blow, but only just. Adley struck again, and this time the block was weaker. Dropping his sword, the young guard turned on his heels and followed his companion into the distance.

"Thank the gods for that," groaned Adley. He was in no mood for mortal bloodshed. He was a protector, not a slayer. Throwing the sword to the floor, he broke into a run towards the village, ignoring the burning of his lungs and the crunching of his back. He didn't have time for this.

Staring into the darkness, Prince Eli considered what Metlina had told him: Malo had broken the treaty and contacted the child. What had possessed him to do that? He hadn't seen Chaeli since she was a babe, small, chubby and helpless. Nothing like her mother. Was she still helpless? Or had talents emerged? He struggled to think how many mortal years had passed—was it fifteen? Twenty? He couldn't remember. Time passed differently here.

He sighed and sat beside the fire. He would wait for Malo's return. He would make the treacherous beast explain his actions. Gazing around his quarters, he thought back to his time in the Kingdom before the treaty. Although he wouldn't admit it to anyone, a small part of him was contaminated by regret. And regret was a weakness.

The fire softly illuminated the room and the shadows on the walls appeared to move and communicate with each other, their dark shapes creeping along the stone expanse.

"Be gone!" roared the Damnable Lord. "How dare you spy on me in my sanctuary?" The shadows scurried along the walls and slipped out under the door. Though loath to admit it, even to himself, he was anxious to see Chaeli; he had been preparing for the merge for such a long time. If she was indeed his child, the possibilities were endless. He would rule all three worlds and she would be the arrow to his bow—an arrow to pierce the heart of his brother Daro, crippling him and forcing him to bend his knee to Eli. If, on the other hand, she was Daro's child, then Eli would kill her himself.

He was surprised to realise this thought of killing made him uncomfortable. He had ordered the murder and torture of thousands of mortals, why should this be any different?

Because if she is not yours, she is still your blood, the daughter of your brother, your niece, a voice in the back of his mind whispered.

Eli concentrated on the flames and licked his lips with more than a little trepidation and excitement. The movement of the fire was exquisite, the licking, twirling, spinning, and finally, the consumption of the logs as matter transformed into energy. Eli opened his mind to the beauty of the blazing light.

He began to hear and feel, then see the music of the flames as they worked in harmony and chaos. The way each log was devoured with no mercy shown was exhilarating. But . . . there was something else. Frowning, he blended his energy further and deeper into the fire, channelling a link across the flames. It was there again, but now it was becoming clearer. He could see a girl, no, a woman staring back at him. A young plain woman with dark hair and huge eyes. She stared straight at him. He felt the stir of curiosity, but as realisation hit, her eyes widened and she opened her mouth to scream. Gasping, he broke the link and leapt away from the fire. Eli's shaking hand gripped the marble mantel as he poured a jug of water across the fire. Smoke poured into the room, wisping up to the shadows.

Her face . . .

He stared at the cooling logs and breathed deeply, re-absorbing his energy and quelling the unease. A mortal seeing him, really seeing him, in a fire-merge made no sense.

"Metlina!" he roared. "Come at once!" In an instant there was a flash of yellow light and the goddess appeared. There was no concern on her face this time, only resentment at having been thrown from his chambers earlier. She was his courtesan when it pleased him, and his vassal when it didn't.

"Master, what is it?" she asked, a sensual and yet false smile playing on her lips.

"When was the last time you melded with a natural entity?" He feasted on the memory of Melina when she had first given obeisance to him, his cat of nine tails caressing her skin in thanks. She looked up at him, but the face of the mysterious woman looked back, invading his memory, and he rolled his shoulders as though to shake the face away.

Frowning, Metlina replied, "A while. I meld only when I wish to feel the pain of one of my victims. A delicious feeling."

"Has a mortal ever felt you in the meld?" he asked, moving behind Metlina.

"No, my lord, why do you ask?"

She turned to face him, but he grabbed her shoulders. "My Metlina," he whispered, "I have not given you permission to face me." He breathed heavily and felt her unease. "I saw a woman in the fire. She was young and she stared straight back at me." He

25

loosened his grip and began to caress her shoulders, his fingers light, yet strong as they kneaded the flesh.

"My lord! Are you sure? Only the gods possess that power, I can't see—"

"Do not doubt me, woman! I know what I saw," he hissed, grabbing her hair. Metlina bit her lip, refusing to cry out.

"What did you require, my lord?" she asked cocking her head to one side and moving onto the tips of her toes to ease the pain and quell her desire.

"I want you to ensure Malo comes straight to me when he returns. He is to speak to no-one and go nowhere before communing with me, is that understood?"

"Of course, Eli." Metlina reached up and eased his hand from her hair. Turning to face him fully this time, she appealed to his vanity and lowered herself to her knees. Taking his hand, she kissed his palm, and in a glare of yellow, she was gone.

"I want your fealty. I want your everlasting obedience and unquestioning loyalty," the demon said, stroking her leg with long, sensual movements before beginning a quiet conversation with himself in a tongue that Chaeli couldn't understand. He spoke harsh, grunting words, and then laughed and chuckled before slapping his hand on his own thigh.

Not likely, you fucking monster. Chaeli clamped her lips shut to remain quiet, but the pain from her wound ate at her resolve. "Anything, please, just let me go," she said finally, the words sticking in the back of her throat, "please." *Coward.*

The demon smiled and sat upright, his face contorting and his lips peeling back to reveal blackened stumps that oozed green pus down his chin. Then the smile faded, and he slapped his hand onto her injury, causing her to scream again.

"I expected more from you. More courage. More heart. But you're *pathetic*. So weak and disappointing." He poked a claw into the wound and twisted, laughing as another strangled cry echoed around the room. Her back arched in pain and instinctively she slapped the beast's arm away again and cursed.

"So there is a little fight left. You'll make this fun for me then, yes? Like that sister of yours? She was a feisty one."

"Don't talk about her!" Anger burned through the fear as Chaeli glared at the creature. The smile returned, and he leaned over her, the heat of his body suffocating her as the stench of decay and degradation made her nostrils flare in disgust.

"She tasted so very sweet. Of life, love, and all things pure." He mimicked Acelle's cries, touching himself with mocking, lascivious moans.

Revulsion and horror rose in Chaeli's chest, and she turned away.

"She bored me. It all ended far too quickly," the demon said, searching her gaze for a reaction.

"Just tell me what you want from me," Chaeli said, her back still to the beast. A great pressure crushed her chest and pounded at her temples. A blend of rage and despair seemed to battle with her fear and force a strangled sob of frustration into the room. Gratefully, it went unnoticed.

"So rude! Does the Kingdom not demand manners now? Firstly," – he stopped and sat back down, holding up a claw – "you didn't address me correctly. In future, you will refer to me as 'my lord'. Secondly," – he held up a second claw – "you haven't even asked my name, and thirdly, no more mention of your sister." She knew he looked at her, the only sound between them the splitting, popping and hissing of the logs on the fire. His eyes bored into her back until she could no longer bear it; she turned and raised her eyes to his.

"Who are you . . . my lord?" she asked, forcing the words out through the pain and humiliation and biting back her angry words. Drained, a tiredness pressed down on her like a chainmail shroud,

Running her fingers over her bare wrist, she thought of the testing. Her parents and sister had stood by the benches in the church dressed in their finest clothes. Her mother had been so excited, and Acelle had grinned from ear to ear. Their hopes had reflected onto Chaeli, and she had been so very nervous. As the priest of the Kingdom approached, her heart sped up and she chewed at her bottom lip. He had placed his stars against hers and stared deep into her eyes. His white robes seemed to merge into his pale skin, but his eyes burned with the hunger of the Kingdom. Chaeli felt nothing but his cool skin on hers. She glanced at her parents, who nodded their encouragement. The priest narrowed his eyes in puzzlement and raised a well groomed eyebrow. He frowned and shifted, pressing his palm harder against hers. She sensed a rush of power from the gods and her hopes soared; it enveloped her and then slowly moved to the priest. His facial expression changed to one of excitement, then ecstasy, then to confusion, followed by realisation and resigned calm.

"You are no conduit," he called out and moved to the next child.

Chaeli's heart had dropped, the blood rushing to her face. She had failed her family and couldn't bear to see the disappointment in their eyes. Her mother had held her close and whispered words of comfort, but Chaeli did not hear them.

Until today. The events of the previous evening flooded her mind and pushed the memories away. She tried to stand, but her leg buckled, the pain excruciating. She lowered herself back to the ground and examined her thigh. The slash was long and deep, and though it had stopped bleeding, the skin was tight and swollen. She removed her outer blouse and ripped the sleeve away, then tied it around her thigh.

"Damn you, Metlina," she said. The Goddess of Pain would no doubt be thriving on this. After binding her leg, she stared at the blouse. Tears formed again, and she stroked the material, remembering how her mother had embroidered the delicate flowers on the arms. She had spent hours by candlelight diligently and lovingly stitching each lily, Chaeli's favourite. She remembered receiving the blouse and squealing with delight; it was a work of art and she wore it often. Closing her eyes, Chaeli thought of Acelle, she was gone, just like their parents.

She was alone.

But hadn't the demon said Glin and Nina weren't her parents? She pushed those thoughts to the back of her mind; she needed to move. She was cold, thirsty, hungry, and in pain, but where could she go? Not home. The demon might still be there, or that man who had fought with the creature. No, she would head towards Trithia. It was large and she could hide, disappear, sort this all out and find out exactly what in the gods' names was going on. She stood and braced herself, the bind helping to ease the pain. With no money, no pack, and no idea what was going on, she began the trek to the city.

Hana shivered and curled into a ball, first covering her face with her hands and then twisting strands of limp red hair around her fingers as she moaned softy. She was so very tired and wanted nothing more than to sleep. The howling of the wind and the jeers from the guards outside her cell prevented her from resting. They were playing moylona again, and when the game finished, the loser would attempt to console himself by beating her. She couldn't bear to think of it. A single tear slid down her face – she wanted to go home. She was hot and felt like she wanted to explode. She balled her little hands into fists and tried to control herself. The feeling bubbled inside her and made her want to cry and shout. She didn't even know where her home was now, not since the man had killed Danny and her guardians. But this cell wasn't home.

"Oi, you!" shouted a voice.

Hana scurried to her feet. Embarrassed at how her threadbare garments barely covered her, she twisted her body and stood with her hands behind her back, her head bowed. Closing her eyes, she could hear the click of the lock opening, the familiar creak of the door, followed by heavy footsteps. Hana knew the smells of all her guards, and this one terrified her. He was cruel and dark, and made her inner guide cry. Keeping her eyes tightly closed, the smells of sweat, dirt, and mead invaded her cell.

"Captain wants you in his office now, c'mon," he growled.

Hana opened her eyes and looked up, shocked: she was leaving this cell? Truly leaving?

"Ye gods, you stink," said the guard.

Hana stared at him. He was massive, his face glistening with sweat and his beard matted, with bits of food buried deep in the hair. His uniform was ill-fitting and he wheezed as he spoke. He caught her eyeing him and licked his lips.

"Like what you see, little one?" He ran his hand down her bare arm and she shivered but made no noise; she hadn't spoken in months and didn't trust her voice.

"Nothing to be afraid of, seer, I won't hurt you." He shuffled even closer and Hana's nostrils flared. His odour was so strong! She swallowed quickly to delay the inevitable retching. She shook her head, still staring wide-eyed at the guard. He curled his lip in disgust and stopped stroking her arm. "I wouldn't waste my time on a stinking runt anyway." He pushed her to the cell door, following behind, then continued to shove her along the corridor, making a game of it, jeering when she stumbled, and cursing when she didn't.

Hana's hopes rose; perhaps today she would be allowed to leave. After several shoves she reached the end of the corridor and climbed the winding stairs to a heavy wooden door. The guard wheezed his way to the entrance and grabbed her by the arm again, pulling her roughly behind him.

He knocked twice. "Sir, I have the seer." His voice was respectful now. Fearful.

"Enter," came the cool reply.

Hana held her breath as the guard opened the door. She followed him into the room and stared in awe, vaguely registering the door closing behind her. The room was large, warm and clean. It smelt of lavender and bread, and she began to salivate. The walls were light and she could almost smell the paint; it had been decorated, she guessed, within the last few months.

"Seer, come here." A man sat behind a desk in the corner. The desk was massive and at least the width of her cell, yet the man seemed to dominate it, commanding the space. She moved closer and gasped as she felt the softness between her toes. She wiggled them to let the gentle threads weave between them, tickling her. She smiled with delight and looked up at the man, beaming. A small smile played on his lips.

Hana stopped at the desk and examined him cautiously: he had grey flecks at his temples, and his eyes creased when he smiled – but they were cold eyes, blue as ice. She shivered. Her inner guide told her not to trust this man.

"Are you thirsty, seer? Would you like a drink?" He indicated a jug on his desk. Hana licked her lips and nodded. He poured a cup of water. "Take it. Drink. In fact, sit, take your ease. Are you hungry? Are you cold? Would you like a blanket?" He bombarded her with questions while she grabbed the cup and drank deep. Forgetting to breathe, she spluttered and water ran down her front, making the man chuckle. "Sit, seer, be comfortable."

She looked around and saw a large chair by the fire. Still wriggling her toes as she walked, she curled into the chair. It was blissfully soft.

"My name is Hana," she whispered, her voice cracking as she spoke.

"Yes, Hana," he said, the smile widening, "what a pretty name."

She smiled shyly. *Don't trust him*, her guide whispered, *he wants you, he wants to keep you.*

Shush! she hissed back in her head, the temptation of food and drink too much.

Nathan stepped back, and helped the man behind him to his feet. Reedy and thin with yellow-tinted skin and buckteeth, his face reminded Chaeli of a rat, and his eyes darted around, eyeing up the soldiers, Nathan, the men chasing him, Chaeli, and then the crowd that had gathered to watch. He trembled and wrung his hands together as Nathan asked him to share his story.

"I just needed . . . it weren't . . . they owed me. I took what I were owed! I worked all day for nothing, and they didn't pay," was all he eventually managed to say.

The two men stepped forward and he flinched. Nathan held up a hand and shook his head in warning, pointing to his soldiers. The traders glowered and clasped their hands behind their back to show passivity. Chaeli almost didn't see the tall man lunge at Nathan in a blur of black; as the blade slid from his wrist sheath to his hand, she tensed up and shouted out. Nathan, however, was ready for it, and in one movement he grabbed the man's wrist, twisted it behind his back and pushed the arm so far up that there was a loud popping sound, accompanied by a high-pitched scream. The knife fell to the ground where it stuck fast in the mud. The smaller man stepped back and shook his head wildly. The trader fell to the ground, his arm flopping at his side. His skin was pale and clammy, his right hand a deep, dark red.

"You bast—"

"Enough, Timle! Shut your mouth," hissed the short man, hauling his friend to his feet. "Idiot. You saw his band."

Nathan said nothing, but a flicker of sadness crossed his face before it returned to his usual grim determination. "You're lucky I didn't slit your throat. I suggest you leave." He picked up the knife and handed it to the trader, who stared at it in confusion. "You'll need to see a medic. Your shoulder is dislocated and needs putting back in place." The trader didn't move, so Nathan slipped the knife into his own belt. "Where do you think you're going?" He turned to the rat man who was trying to slip away unnoticed.

Adyam grabbed him, searched him, and retrieved a small leather-bound box. Inside were vials of spices and several silver coins, along with handwritten receipts and several copper trens. Adyam held the man still and, once satisfied, Nathan thrust the box to the short man. "You've got what you were owed."

"What about my face?"

Nathan gave a short laugh, "Don't push it. Your friend here tried to attack me. Consider yourself lucky that either of you stand. If you don't leave now, I'll make sure neither of you walk again." His voice grew lower and more menacing as he leaned over the man and slowly pushed them between the horses and back into the Sink. The crowd dispersed and Nathan approached the rat-man and drew his knife.

Holding her breath, Chaeli watched as he turned over the man's palm and cut into the skin as the rat-man wiggled and squirmed. Adyam held him fast, and as the blood pooled to the surface, Nathan pressed a large silver coin onto the wound and closed the man's hand over it. Instead of shouting, the rat-man held his bloodied hand to his chest and then held a finger to his lips, thanking Daro for Nathan's generosity. Adyam stepped back and released him; the rat-man scurried away into the outskirts of the Sink.

After Nathan re-mounted his horse and took back the reins, Chaeli went to speak but then closed her mouth. She had seen a thief be cut in her village before, but never the offering of silver afterwards. It made no sense. He punished the wrong-doer but then rewarded him.

Chaeli's heart, already heavy from the loss of Acelle and the knowledge of her own plight, felt a thousand times heavier by the time they reached the stone wall separating the Sink from the city.

"To the west, the guard on the city is easily bribed with coin. I can guarantee us entry there," explained Nathan, breaking the silence. Neither had spoken since the incident with the thief. "Once inside the city, I have . . . friends. We'll get that leg of yours sorted."

When they reached the west entrance, Nathan spoke quickly and quietly to the guard, and Chaeli saw the glint of silver passing from hand to hand, followed by a quick glance in her direction. The guard beckoned and Nathan handed over more silver with a sigh. Chaeli cringed and felt the redness creep up her neck; it was because of her.

"Come," called Nathan. Chaeli urged the horse forward, and the men followed, milling round Nathan.

"Time to dismount, my lady, the horses need to be fed and watered."

Chaeli dismounted awkwardly, trying not to aggravate her leg further. She passed the reins to the guard, who stopped and grabbed her wrist. Their eyes met. His stare seemed to penetrate her mind, and he slowly looked her up and down, checking both her wrists for a sign of a band.

"What are you doing?" she demanded, holding her voice as firm as she could.

"Making sure I have a good image of you should anyone come asking. Your man there paid good coin for you. Makes me think you're worth something." He grinned, a gold tooth glinting in the sun.

Chaeli shivered. She could think of no reply and the malice in his tone cut into her. Nathan noted her shivering and reached into his bundle, removing a mink-lined cloak. It was exquisite and clearly very expensive. He wrapped it around her, and Chaeli didn't have the heart to explain that she was not cold, but frightened. His gentleness touched her.

"Thank you."

He nodded and turned to his men. "Lads, I have business to deal with. I shall take Lady Chaeli to Anya, and I'll see you by The Trout at sundown."

The soldiers murmured their replies and scattered in different directions. Nathan turned back to Chaeli. "They've been on the road for some time. They have friends and family to visit."

"Will you tell me what's going on?"

"Soon, I promise." With this, he began guiding her through the crowds. He didn't rush her, knowing she was still in pain from her wound. Chaeli drank in the city; it was so different to the Sink. The stench lessened with every step she took further from the wall, and with every step she tried to block out memories of home.

The city was huge: the main thoroughfares were constructed from great flat stones, the smaller roads cobbled. The buildings were a mixture of stone and wood, solid and old; the people were cleaner, less menacing, and the desperation was absent – though there was an inexplicable tension in the air.

Chaeli inhaled deeply, and at once the smell of crackling and apple had her full attention. She was aware that Nathan was talking to her, but she couldn't comprehend what he was saying – her stomach was screaming to be fed. She looked round the busy marketplace hungrily, but too many traders and residents blocked her view. She could smell it, dammit, where was it?

"Chaeli, what's wrong?"

"Can't you smell that?"

"What?"

"*Food!*"

Nathan stared at her "That's what has your attention? Food?"

"I haven't eaten since last night." She recalled how she'd wolfed down a handful of raw mebeya berries from her neighbour's crops. The bitter taste had given her stomach pains, but she had needed something.

Nathan shook his head in wonderment. "If you can wait, Anya does the best broth in the whole of Trithia," he said.

"Broth. Yes. Lovely," she replied miserably, still sniffing and allowing the sweet glorious smell to taunt her.

Nathan navigated expertly through the city; they passed through more marketplaces and along alleyways, which snaked away at all angles. They passed a store full of exotic animals and Chaeli had to pause and stare. A small dark rodent scurried from the shoulder

"Unlikely. I grow weary, demon. You bring me nothing, and you risked war between our worlds for nothing." The creature grunted and clutched his shoulder. "I do have a use for you though," said Eli, nodding suddenly. "Yes. I will still the poison."

He rolled up his sleeves, exposing runes and spells etched on his arms. He pinched the demon's wound with his fingers and began to chant, using the ancient language of the gods. The demon, unable to understand the words, shook with fear as the chant grew louder and faster. He sensed the shadows lean forward in interest. The ink began to move, the marks snaking around his skin, pushing and prodding for escape. Then one rune slid from Eli's arm onto the demon, writhing on the forearm above his injured hand. Eli stopped chanting and released the demon's flesh.

"That rune will prevent the poison from moving any further. It will not last indefinitely, the poison will wear it down. You must return to me when the ink starts to fade." He paused. "I *may* replace it."

"Thank you, master." The demon stared at the stump where his claw had been; the wound had healed, but nothing would grow there again.

"Let that be a reminder of your insolence."

"Yes, master."

"Go, show the others the mark of your disobedience, but wear it with pride. Not many are allowed to live following such blatant disregard for my orders. Take comfort in the fact that this is because you are the best." They looked at one another for a moment. "Now leave."

Eli returned to his comfortable fire. The chilling darkness of the world outside his castle spread through the glass doors and shutters on his balcony, and now he wanted warmth. The demon moved slowly to the door; the once proud creature now humiliated, angry, and fearful.

"Oh, Malo?" Eli looked up from the fire.

"Yes, master?"

"Whose child is the girl?"

The prince stared at the demon, trying to disguise the interest, and the insatiable hunger.

"She's yours, master."

The prince smiled. "Yes. Yes, she is mine." He stood and strode decisively to his desk.

"Think, Hana. Try harder."

The cool insistence chilled Hana. She wanted to please him, but the headaches filled her as though she might burst, making her physically sick; she was sweating and trembling more with each word from Kerne.

"I can't do it," she shrilled. Her body slumped in a curled heap on the floor. She could feel the warmth of the candles around her, but it did nothing to ease the ice inside.

"Little seer, you must understand how it is, you really must. If you can't connect to the blood, I can't guarantee your safety." He paused. "The King will find you," he whispered. He knelt down and stroked her hair.

Hana shook violently with fear and strain, dragging herself up to squat like an obedient dog at his side. The seduction of food and warmth had worn off, and with the cursed clear-sight of her kind, she could see the evil that surrounded him. She needed to escape. Her inner guide agreed but what could she do?

"Little seer, you can't leave me," he murmured, running his hand down her face, a gesture that, for all its intent to comfort, might as well have been the cut of a knife. "You are mine now." He moved closer and kissed her cheek, running his tongue over her skin. "I don't like to share."

For a moment, all movement ceased. Then he pulled her closer, burying his head in her hair and inhaling deeply, greedily. She could feel the closeness of him. She squeezed her eyes shut.

If I can't see him, maybe he can't see me.

She tried to pull free, but he grabbed her hands. Something about her hands had caught his attention and he turned them over to stare at her palms.

"Interesting, little seer. You have not been marked."

Her face betrayed her confusion. He held up his left hand, and she saw a circle of seven stars inked into his skin.

"All mortals of the land are inked. So where have you come from?" He spoke more to himself than her, but Hana felt obliged to respond. She shrugged. "You are a mystery, my sweet Hana, my very own seer."

He let go of her hands. As she rubbed her numb wrists, Hana realised she had been holding her breath; now the blood beat in her head and her ears roared. She hadn't been this uneasy since the day she had been dragged to the castle dungeons – after *he* had come for her. She knew *he* was coming, knew that he was going to kill her when he threw back the mattress and stood over her, so when he had left her alive, she hadn't known what to do – had simply waited for the guards to find her. She hadn't resisted when they gagged and bound her, nor when they'd kicked and beaten her. She took each blow and absorbed the white hot pain deep inside.

Looking around the pleasant room and then up at Kerne, she didn't know which was worse, the dungeon or Kerne's protectorship.

There was a faint murmur. Adley's head was throbbing and he wasn't sure if the sound was inside or out. The murmur grew louder and louder until it became a roar.

"For the love of the gods, be quiet!" He groaned as he rolled over. The cool surface underneath him jarred his body and pain coursed through his neck and shoulders, as though knives were being pushed into his spine.

He opened his eyes, and immediately regretted it. The dazzling light nearly blinded him, and he closed them again. He repeated the exercise more cautiously, then, squinted and looked around. Several pairs of moon-like eyes stared at him, and he realised the murmuring was coming from the Beings. He was back in the Eternal Kingdom.

Struggling to think, Adley recalled the fight with Malo; he remembered the beast's claws in his shoulder, and then darkness. He sat up, crying out as he did. The room spun and his head ached. He touched the back of his head, found a clammy wetness on his fingers. Blood. So he had been injured. The cold realisation hit him: to awake in the Kingdom meant he had died on Ibea. He struggled to his feet and slid off the bed.

His military training kicked in and he began to examine himself carefully for injuries. His lower half seemed fine, but as he got to his chest and shoulders he noticed several fresh wounds already scarring and itching like the bite of Mischlan fire ants. Angry red skin puckered from his left shoulder to his right, continuing on to his back.

Ye gods! What did that beast do to me?

Tracing the cut, he found it went behind his right ear up to his scalp. He touched his neck gingerly; it was hot and sore, and with each movement he felt the damaged tendons strain. He grimaced. Never a vain man, he still had some pride, and the cruel marks humiliated and taunted him. The Beings scurried to offer their help, a rare honour, but still Adley waved them away.

"Leave me alone," he muttered, attempting to stride purposefully out of the chamber into the corridor, hiding his pain. He realised he was in the higher gods' dwelling, a place he had only been permitted to enter a handful of times whilst in service as a protector. The walls shimmered and danced in the sunlight beyond; the tall elegant marble pillars reaching to the domed ceiling rippled with vines. A soft, cool breeze kissed his skin and he closed his eyes, enjoying the crisp wind of the heavens. He opened his eyes and

73

looked down from the long hallway and balcony to the grounds and gardens below: he was above the fountain, in the hall adjacent to Penella's wing. Hesitating, he made his way to her quarters.

"Adley! You're up and about," she called in her sweet voice.

Adley turned and Penella approached him serenely, almost gliding along the white floor. She always managed to take his breath away, and this time was no exception. Her simple gold gown was loose, matching her hair and eyes perfectly.

She smiled and grasped his hands, her touch so cool it startled him. Penella had never been this familiar before, and her touch electrified him.

"Goddess," he mumbled, embarrassed at how close the Goddess of Love was to him. He felt the heat rise in his cheeks.

"Come with me, protector. The council is assembled." She smiled, letting go of his hands and turning back down the corridor.

"Council?"

She returned and looped his arm in hers. "Yes, we will explain everything. Please hurry." Together they walked on in silence. Through the floor-to-ceiling windows, the sun streamed and light bounced along the corridor. A mural decorated the wall, designed by the Goddess of the Arts, Denna, who had drawn the Mother and Great Father at the inception of time, followed by the birth of Daro, then Eli, then the creation of mortals and the birth of the remaining deities. Each shape contained and expressed the power of the goddess, the lines soft but firm, fixed for eternity on the wall. She needed no colour for her craft.

He glanced out of the windows to a carpet of blue; outside the palace walls, a sea of bluebells spread away into the horizon. He knew if he searched long enough, he would see the Mother, singing to her buds as they bloomed. Everything was so calm here, so right. The scent of flowers and grass filled his nostrils and the songs from the birds soothed his pain.

As Penella opened the council room doors, Adley's heart hammered like a thousand anvils being struck. The gods inevitably had that effect on him, a millennia of awe and belief would do that to a humble man. On entering, he gasped and stopped in his tracks. Prince Daro was present – he met Adley's eyes, which welled up as he drank in the vision of his lord, appearing now in common form, the form mortals sought to represent in pictures and tapestries: tall and muscular, preternaturally youthful, his long, sandy hair tied back in a band. But his blue eyes, so like Chaeli's, were tired and full of knowledge. No joy came from him. Adley's prince still mourned.

"Adley, my son, please sit," said Daro.

Adley approached a space at the large circular council table near to Vorgon and Elek.

"No, please, sit here with me," said Daro, placing his hand on the delicate glass chair beside him. Adley could barely breathe, but he nodded and took the empty seat, exhaling with relief that the glass didn't shatter. Penella took her place at Daro's left, shooting an enquiring glance at Daro as she did so. He nodded, and at this signal she spoke:

"Brothers, sisters, we call this meeting for the benefit of all, especially our dear Adley, who has suffered once again for us." A chorus of approving voices rang out, and Adley sensed the gentle waves of sympathy from the assembled deities – quiet, brief, and temporarily overwhelming.

"Adley fought the demon, General Malo, in service of this Kingdom, striving to protect Chaeli. Malo prevailed, and our protector lost both the battle and that mortal life. By the grace of our prince, however, Adley was brought back to the Kingdom to become a protector once again, blessed by Daro himself. Truly a miracle."

Daro smiled. Though the sadness remained, it was a smile of love and kinship. Adley didn't feel worthy of his lord's blessing and the shame of his feelings for Chaeli hung heavy like the weight of a noose. He lowered his head.

"Daro has received word from Prince Eli—"

At these words the council members roared, gods and goddesses alike speaking out; some stood and shouted, others began to cry. Daro leapt to his feet and immediately the assembly quietened.

"My friends, do not be disheartened! Eli has written to me and informs me that Chaeli's parentage is now clear." His voice became unsteady for the briefest moment. There was an expectant silence while Daro gathered himself to make the announcement. "Chaeli is Eli's daughter." He raised a hand in anticipation of an outcry, but the room remained silent. "She may be his daughter, gentle ones, but that does not mean she is like him. She is part of this Kingdom as well. Amelia's blood runs through her veins and she worships Elek. She prays at the temples, she observes the rites, she honours us." Daro scanned the room, ensuring that all took note of his words.

Adley's blood pounded so hard that his ears roared in protest. He didn't want to hear any more and involuntarily he started to shake: she was the daughter of the most abominable Prince Eli. An abyss opened within him.

"I have decided that Adley should return to Chaeli. She needs guidance, and she needs protection. I trust Adley to return and guide my . . . my niece with honour and integrity."

Penella caught Adley's eye and smiled at him secretly. The Goddess of Love understood his heart; how could she not?

"But he will not be alone," added Daro. "Sheiva returned to me some time ago, bringing news from Salinthos. He has asked my permission to tread upon Ibea for his own quest. He will therefore accompany Adley and report to me on Chaeli's progress. I will not leave my niece to be seduced and corrupted by her . . . father. I will do all I can to keep Amelia's child safe."

Daro's emotion was not lost on the gods. They understood the pain their prince had suffered. His brother's betrayal, seduction, and eventual abandonment of Amelia had wounded, though not destroyed, Daro's spirit.

Sheiva, the Salinthos fae, had arrived years prior and earned the friendship of Daro. A smart talking creature who spoke his mind plainly and without fear or flattery, he had left the Kingdom in the service and calling of his people. His impending return comforted Adley; it would be good to have such an ally.

Time passed strangely in the Eternal Kingdom. It might have been hours, it might have been days; in truth, such measures had little meaning here. The gods communed in their own language, entrancing Adley, though he could not understand. This was music indeed. It hypnotised him, dancing through his soul, the song eternal, infinite. Until suddenly he was brought back to awareness as several of the lesser gods disappeared. Vorgon, Elek, Penella, and Igon remained, moving closer together and talking in low voices. Daro was nowhere to be seen. Adley couldn't leave the room without passing their gathering, but he didn't want to be suspected of eavesdropping.

"Nonsense, Adley, this involves you, come!" called Igon, reading his thoughts.

Adley rose and joined them. His mortal form seemed harsh and cumbersome next to their divine perfection. His scars seemed like blasphemies in their presence, though they had been earned in the service of the gods.

The gods were discussing the meeting, and Adley soon realised he had missed several vital points. The Underworld had been busy: new temples were being erected at incredible speed, and the darkness was spreading throughout the land. The balance was tipping, and not in the favour of Daro and his gods. As a mortal, Adley understood only a small fraction of the gods' sanctuary, but he knew that all gentle gods drew their strength from the Pool of Power, the source of their very existence and a gift from Nalowyn, the creator of all. When the gods were honoured and revered by mortals, the pool was plentiful; when war struck the lands and the mortals were preoccupied with killing and survival, the pool diminished. Recently it had begun to drain away; the power was not being replenished as quickly as before. None of the gods knew why; even Daro had no answers.

"Adley, we wish to ask a small favour." Penella spoke softly and touched his arm. "As well as protecting Chaeli, listen and watch for us. Be our ears and eyes on Ibea, for we cannot walk with you. Our power drains and we must find why."

Adley nodded. "Of course."

Igon rested a hand on his other shoulder. "Daro couldn't remove the scars, son. He tried, but the beast is not his domain. Only Eli can fully heal your flesh."

Adley stood tall and held his head high. "I would gladly wear these scars as a sign of my commitment and faith."

Igon nodded and lowered his hand. "Good luck, son."

Elek gave a sad smile. "I will guide him as best as I can."

"It's an expression, Elek."

Penella gently clasped Adley's hand in hers, and he looked at her with tenderness. She smiled and kissed his palm as though he were the god and she the supplicant.

Kerne sat considering the most tantalising of offers while the temperature dropped in his office, the fire having gone cold hours earlier. He enjoyed the cold, however, and the way it embraced his body; it kept his mind clear and sharp.

He had been promised the realm of Trithia so long as he had the powers of the seer. Granted, there was the small problem involving her control over coercion and blood-binding, but he knew that she had the ability, and he knew she could hone her talent. But achieving this was proving tiresome and difficult, the simplest of readings producing negligible results, and he was growing restless. Failure was neither something he had experienced, nor something he expected.

Kerne had always been a loyal supporter of the Underworld; as a true believer, his first loyalty was to himself. Born and raised in the harsh pits of Velen, the faith had been taught to him from birth, and so successfully that when his parents had proven no longer useful, he disposed of them and travelled the realms, preaching to all who would listen. His religious fervour and unwavering commitment had caught the attention of his gods, and he was instructed to go to Trithia to join the King's Guard. Their captain had been stripped of rank and declared an outcast, leaving the King vulnerable and alone. Kerne's cold, hard efficiency and sharp wit – allied to prudent diplomacy when necessary – meant he rose through the ranks quickly. Within five years he controlled the King's Guard and had the King's ear: captain and confidante.

Whispers of a captured seer had reached him years before, but as he had not yet been elevated to the rank of Captain, he had not been privy to the details. On the night of his promotion, King Stirm called him to his private rooms and told him about the seer and her capture the morning after the betrayer's failure. DeVaine had failed his King; he had failed the Underworld; he had shown weakness. Stirm, having not the strength or courage to face her, ordered her thrown in the dungeons, never to be released. This was her punishment for corrupting his friend. Then Stirm had revealed to Kerne his own alignment with the Underworld; together they fed their dark desires with the sacrifice of a white mellin dove to the Damnable Lord.

Stirm was a weak and malleable man – Kerne would set his plans in motion and enjoy the rewards. Trithia would be his, no matter the cost.

Chaeli couldn't sleep. The quiet noises of the city sounded like an ill-tuned orchestra to a country girl and made her wince, tossing and turning. Voices hollered in the street below, some argument over monies borrowed and owed. The high-pitched cries of a baby cut into her; the soft giggles of two lovers glided through her. It was worse when she closed her eyes, for a vision of the demon leapt into her mind. She stared into the darkness around her, wishing for an escape from the darkness inside.

She flung off her blanket and stood. It was hot and stifling in the room, and even though Anya kept the small window open, she needed fresh air. Anya lay snoring on her small bed; even her snores were delicate, making Chaeli smile. Nathan lay silently on the floor at her side, facing the bed, his body rigid even in sleep.

Chaeli tiptoed past them and down the stairs to the healing room. She lowered herself onto the bench, held her head in her hands, and began to cry. Sob after sob, her tears flowed until her eyes hurt, her throat burned, her head ached, but she couldn't stop. She cried for her parents, she cried for Acelle, for herself. Her grief, a stone she had carried her whole life, had grown even heavier these past few days. But with each tear the stone felt lighter; she knew it would never leave her, and a small part of her didn't want it to disappear, however much it weighed her down.

She was so lost here in Trithia. She had no money, no papers, no direction, and no friends. Her pride made her hate the fact she had to rely on the good graces of these strangers. She had always been an awkward child, never quite fitting in, always on the edge of social gatherings and forever watching the world go by. Even on her eleventh birthday, she had sat in the corner of the main room while the other children played with the toys her father had bought from the city for her. There had been a red-dressed doll she had admired and wanted for what had seemed like forever, and when one of the other girls had unwrapped the gift and started playing with it, Chaeli had stood to protest, only to sit back down again with knocking knees and trembling hands. When the girl had taken the doll to her friends, Chaeli took herself outside and sat listening to the adults' talk of trading, money, new homes and celebrations.

But now she truly was alone and yearned for belonging.

Chaeli was so exhausted, caught up in grief and memory, that she didn't hear the footsteps. She jumped when a warm pair of arms enveloped her; she pulled back, flicking her face away from him and brushing her hands across her face as she tried to even her breathing and stop the gut-shaking sobs that rattled through her. The closeness of him was a balm that soothed the scalding reminder that there was no one in her village who missed her.

"Shhhhhh," hushed Nathan. He held her from behind, pulling her close. Chaeli sobbed harder as Nathan rocked her gently, carefully tucking her damp hair behind her ears. The warmth and touch consoled her and she allowed herself to sink into his embrace.

Nathan looked down at her. She was a strange one, this girl. There was something which marked her out – oh, she was attractive enough, but he'd seen and known plenty of attractive women in his time. No, it was something more. Unless that was just him, trying to find that spark he had thought long dead.

He hated seeing women cry. Ironic really, considering the amount of pain he had caused the countless women he had enjoyed and discarded. Assassins couldn't form attachments, it became messy. Anya was proof of that.

As he soothed Chaeli, he said a silent prayer to whoever might listen, no longer able to afford the luxury to pick and choose among the deities. He was empty inside; no rush of happiness, no warmth. The gods were not with him. He was damned.

He closed his eyes and thought back to the day that had finally defined and doomed him.

Please, oh gods, please no, don't, sir I beg you, please don't kill me!

The boy was on his knees. Tears streamed down his face and he clasped his hands together as he gabbled hysterically. He had soiled himself and the pungent smell irritated Nathan. The woman and her husband had been easy, quick; he killed them skilfully as they slept. Less chance of the alarm being raised that way. He hadn't been prepared for the boy though. Nathan grabbed him by his hair; the begging stopped and gave way to a brief silence. Then came the screams. Nathan clasped a gloved hand over the child's mouth and snapped his neck with a single, deft movement. The body tightened then fell limp. Nathan laid the lifeless thing on the floor. Cursing aloud, he moved to the window. He would have to leave quickly. The boy's screams would undoubtedly have raised alarm. Not his most efficient mission.

One leg on the window ledge, a movement caught his eye. Under the bed. He climbed back in and dashed across the room to lift the mattress. Huddled in the corner was a girl. She was tiny, but even in the darkness her shocking blood-red hair blazed. Immediately he knew she was a seer, rare and prized. He had never encountered one such as this, so small, so delicate, and with such vivid hair. But her blood sang to him, and her erratic energy betrayed her nature. The King had told him he was to kill all in the house, that none should be spared. Such a command was not unusual, but this time the King had been flustered. Nathan usually reconnoitred a kill with meticulous care, ensuring that there were no surprises when he came to act, but His Highness had forbidden any prior contact. He claimed the murdered family would know he was coming, and they mustn't have a chance to run. Nathan had not understood at the time, but he understood now.

As he stared at the girl, something changed inside him. An incredible tiredness threatened to overwhelm him, a burning pain beginning to spread over his chest, and he wanted nothing more than to return home to his sister. The girl didn't move; she remained curled in a foetal position, staring at him unwaveringly. He guessed her age to be around ten, but he couldn't be sure. Seers always appeared young and they lived for three to four times the age of an average mortal. She made no sound, only continued to stare at him. Suppressing the burning sensation, Nathan moved smoothly to grab her arm, dragging her to her feet.

Even unfurled, she was tiny, barely reaching his waist. She stood slumped over, staring at the ground. Still she made no sound. The stillness and silence unnerved Nathan. She had known he was coming; she had known and hadn't run. Did that mean she had not seen her death? He took his dagger from the sheath; it glinted in the moonlight. The seer looked up and stared, not at the blade, but once again into Nathan's eyes, no fear in her face, only pity.

Nathan paused. He tried to raise his hand, tried to picture slicing her throat, but he couldn't move.

"What have you done to me, witch?"

The seer continued to stare at him in unnatural silence, her wide eyes burning into his own.

A flash of the boy he had killed filled his mind; the boy was brushing her hair. Another flash of the two children playing, the seer running across the market with a headscarf billowing after her. Glimmers of her memories poured into him and he sensed her crawling around in his mind. He couldn't think or see clearly. Summoning up his power, he threw everything at the tiny girl, who blinked in response and released her mental hold on him.

"You're so sad," she said, her small voice so matter of fact and calm. His knife hand itched, though he still couldn't raise it. "It's all right." She closed her eyes; Nathan's fingers twitched and he stepped towards her. There was a small plait on the side of her head. That boy, he had sat plaiting her hair earlier that evening as they ate spun sugar and sung folk songs. Staring at the braid, Nathan cursed and dashed to the window, throwing himself through and dropping to the ground outside. He ran, stopping for nothing, thinking of nothing but the pitying eyes of the seer.

A clinging wetness across his chest pulled him back to the room. Chaeli's sobs had quietened, but Nathan's shirt was soaked with tears, but he didn't care. She glanced up at him, her eyes red raw and swollen, her nose pink, cheeks blotchy.

"Sorry," she hiccupped. "I di-didn't mean to wake you." She pulled away from him and wiped her nose with the back of her hand. "I'm just so . . . I don't know . . ." She waved her arm and looked exasperated.

"It's okay, Chaeli, a good cry helps now and then." The comforting words came awkwardly to him. He stood up, his chest tacky and hot from where she had pressed against him. Ye gods, she really had drenched him. He stepped back and pulled it off.

Chaeli's eyes widened as Nathan removed his shirt, and even more colour rushed to her cheeks. His chest was broad and sculpted, his skin smooth, the colour of dark honey. She had only ever seen her father and boys of the village shirtless before, and they had certainly not looked like this man. A large inking covering the lower part of his chest and stomach, stretching around to his back: two serpents entwined. She gasped and backed away. She knew – *everyone* knew – this mark. It was the symbol of the Underworld church. Panic filled her and she glanced in panic at the door. Nathan hadn't noticed her interest or alarm; he folded his shirt and placed it neatly on the bench, turning to face the balms and medicines as though he was looking for something. The inking continued up his back. Chaeli's eyes widened in shock as she saw the scarring; he had been whipped with extraordinary savagery.

He turned, a jar in his hand. "I think this will help you sleep, I—"

Chaeli made a dash for the door, fumbling frantically with the handle, but the door wouldn't open.

"Chaeli? What's wrong?" In a moment he was behind her, gripping her shoulder. He turned her around to face him ands he pulled away, and pressing her back firmly against the door.

"You– you're–."

He let go of her shoulder and stepped back, frowning. He followed her gaze down to his mark and shook his head. "I told you, I was the King's assassin. I was the best, Chaeli, the very best killer in Trithia."

"But . . . but the Underworld?"

He grabbed his shirt and pulled it back on. "That's in the past. If I could remove the serpents I would. I'm not that man anymore."

"But why would you get the mark? *Why?*" Her lips curled and her brows knitted as she crossed her arms and hugged herself.

He was part of the faith she had been taught was the eternal enemy: evil. Yet he had cared for and comforted her, held her just moments ago with gentleness as she cried, and yet he had killed people, many people. The thought made her feel sick.

"It was the route I took, the route given me. I rose through the ranks quickly, I was proud, arrogant and foolish . . . I didn't understand, didn't think." He stood by the table with his hands pressed on its surface, his head low and shoulders slumped.

She kept her eyes on him and when he finally turned his head towards her, she shrank back and stiffened, forcing herself to keep his eye contact and not look away.

"I am not that man anymore, Chaeli. I renounced the Underworld and began a new life. When I disobeyed the King, he punished me using my only weakness against me."

Chaeli squeezed her eyes shut. She didn't want to look at him and see sadness there, he didn't deserve pity, but the pain in his voice began to chip at her resolve.

"Anya," she said, her voice as flat and hard as she could muster.

He nodded. "Anya. Her scars are my own fault. Whenever I look at my sister, I am reminded of my weakness, my arrogance, and the stupidity of my former life. She was stunning, Chaeli, every man wanted her. The King himself resolved to make her his only mistress. He was utterly infatuated. When he found out I had run from a mission, like a coward, he was furious. And he vented his anger on her." Nathan whispered this confession as though to himself. "She is ruined because of me. No respectable man will touch her for fear of the his wrath. And all know of my defection, of my weakness." He fell silent for a moment and looked back at the table. "She was so very beautiful."

"She still is, Nathan." Chaeli hadn't expected to say anything, but the words came out of their own accord, and she knew them to be the truth.

But Nathan shook his head. "I live for her. But I was dishonoured and banished from Trithia. I couldn't be with her when she needed me the most." He looked up, searching Chaeli's face for some sign that she understood, that she might believe. "It was four years before I was able to enter Trithia without being recognised. When I did get into the city, I saw Anya and . . ." He sighed, and slumped onto the bench, his back to her.

Chaeli couldn't move; she didn't know what to do or say. She recognised the flutter of warmth inside, the presence of a god, but she couldn't decide who it was. Not Elek, at least. Chaeli went to Nathan and put a hesitant had on his back. It was hard to touch him now she had seen the mark.

He grunted. "You'd best get some sleep. I'll stay down here."

Chaeli went back up the stairs in silence and lay herself down on the floor. Exhausted, she closed her eyes. The godly warmth pacified her and she fell into a deep dream of snakes, swords, and blood.

After the council meeting, Adley returned to his own chambers. He stood in front of the mirror and observed Malo's handiwork: his neck, chest, and back were a mess, there was no other way to describe it. Long, ugly scars twisted around his entire torso.

He'd worried about Chaeli constantly since he'd awoken in the Kingdom. He had no idea how long had passed in the mortal realm, and prayed it was only minutes rather than days, and he could transport back to her and explain what had happened.

Securing his wrist blades, he pondered over the meeting with the deities. He grabbed his swords, sheathing one on his back and the other in the scabbard at his waist.

"Adders, my fine friend!" crowed a familiar voice from the doorway.

Adley smiled and responded without turning. "Hello, Sheiva." Something weaved around his legs and, looking down, he saw the mass of silver fur, a pair of feline eyes staring up at him. "Why do you insist on being a cat here? You can be yourself amongst the gods."

"I like being a cat," he replied, sitting down and raising one leg in the air. He began to clean himself. "This gorgeous form is revered on Ibea as much as the gods'. Truly loved."

"A cat, Shiv?"

"To know a cat is to know godliness, and besides, it's fun."

"You like teasing the Beings, more like," said Adley with a snort, and began to lace his boots. "Godliness, indeed." The cat purred in response and continued his grooming.

"We're leaving shortly. Penella will meet us at the gates to bid farewell."

The cat stopped grooming. "Can't we just go without all the fanfare?"

"I'd love to, but I dare not turn down the good graces of the gods."

"I guess not," muttered the cat, who got to his feet and wandered from the room, not waiting for the protector to join him. Adley jogged after him, and they walked through the corridors in companionable silence. When they reached the courtyard, both noticed it was eerily quiet.

"Where are they all?" he asked.

Sheiva shrugged with feline indifference. "Daro requested attendance as we were leaving. I guess they have convened."

Adley didn't respond. He knew that his prince would be confirming Chaeli's heritage to all.

As they reached the gates, Boda grinned and flicked his tail. "Penella can't make the meeting, she sends her apologies."

"Not to worry, Boda."

"Be well, Adley. " Sheiva meowed loudly and looked indignantly at the dragon. "Yes, yes, you too, Sheiva," he added hastily.

Together, Adley and Sheiva stepped through the gates and into Chaeli's home. It was dark and smelled of blood. The door still stood wide open. Sniffing the air, Sheiva stalked the room, exploring, assessing.

"Smells of death in here," he remarked.

"Acelle," whispered Adley. He drew his spine sword, and took a fighting stance. Moving slowly, man and cat scanned the house; Acelle still lay where she had been discarded by the beast, her glassy eyes staring into nowhere, her skin mottled grey and green. Her once heart-shaped face now bloated and dotted with blisters that continued down her body. The scent of her clung to Adley's skin and filled the air.

"We have to bury her," said the cat, gently sniffing the dead girl's face. "She's been dead for nearly seven days."

"I was gone too long. Why so long to return me?"

"We'll tackle that later, Adders." He considered his companion. "More importantly – where's Chaeli?"

Adley finished searching the bedrooms and returned to the hallway, sighing irritably. "Her papers and pack are still in her room. Where in all the worlds has she gone?"

Sheiva didn't answer. He moved out of Adley's sight and a flash of light filled the house.

"Sheiva!" Adley cried, gripping the hilt of the sword tighter and moving with slow, cautious steps. The flash reminding him of the fight with Malo and the hooded creature that preceded it.

"I'm all right."

Adley hurried to the breathless voice and was surprised to be met by a silver bloodhound. "You've changed."

"You're observant." Sheiva yawned and a string of drool dripped onto the floor. He backed away in disgust. "Eurgh! I hate dogs, such simple creatures." He stopped and sniffed the air hungrily. "Good sense of smell though."

"Why did you not tell me you were changing? I thought you were unable to on Ibea."

"Well, you thought wrong. Not for the first time."

"Fine, but why not a horse, Shiv? We could cover more ground that way." Adley scratched the fae's ears, pushing his unease aside.

"Horses don't have the best sense of smell. A bloodhound is the way today." He began to circle the room, sniffing deeply. "I need something of the girl's, something that smells of her."

Adley went to her bedroom; on the bed was a small, tatty homemade toy lion, well-worn and stained. He had seen her hug it when she cried, and whisper her secrets to it. He couldn't leave it.

"Will this do?" he asked, holding out the lion.

The dog sniffed excitedly. "Yes, yes, perfect!" With the scent now memorised, he began the track. "This way!" He barked in excitement, his tail wagging.

"Wait! What about the girl?" Adley pointed at Acelle.

The dog's tail stopped wagging drooped between his legs. "Oh, yes. Of course."

Adley sheathed his sword and put the toy lion in his pack. He would keep it, in case Sheiva needed a reminder of her scent. He hoisted Acelle into his arms; rigor mortis had come and gone, and she was now limp and ice cold. He tried hard to quell his anger; her death had been needless. He carried her out to the rear of the house and as he began to dig a grave next to those of Glin and Nina Dresne, he thought back to their deaths. They had caught the hack, and the fever had taken them both suddenly. Chaeli's sorrow when she had returned from the three-day church vigil and found their bodies still haunted him. She had dealt with all the funeral arrangements alone while she waited for Acelle to return from her own vigil. It was then that Adley realised just how much he cared for her. She wasn't like his previous charges, who took more than they gave. For when Acelle had returned, she had comforted her with a calm façade, then quietly cried herself to sleep. The constant stream of mourners were met with gratitude and open arms, when

Adley struggled to maintain his footing, stumbling back and breaking contact with the daggers. "I'm . . . sorry. It wasn't . . . meant . . . to—"

"Enough false apologies. We all died because you refused to listen." Andy spat on the ground and raised his dagger. "Your pride and arrogance killed us all. We should have known not to trust you. You were never one of us."

Adley attacked again with a vertical cut followed in quick succession by three downward swings, but they were blocked easily. *Where's Sheiva?* He didn't want to hear any more, and so spun to face Andraes, who flicked his blond hair from his eyes and laughed, his face just as Adley remembered it. Adley shook his head and tried to concentrate; he couldn't afford to be distracted my memories.

"I've waited many years for this, crusader," Andraes said, and advanced, his serrated blades glinting. "I've dreamt about this, over and over again. It's the only thing that kept my mind intact in that place . . . the thought of you on the end of my blade." Adley noted a slight movement in his hands, and Andraes moved to a palm grip, his fingers flat on the ricasso.

Sensing the onslaught Adley attacked, aiming for the man's left thigh, and at the same time he released a blow of energy to Andraes's head, temporarily blinding him. The younger man cursed and stumbled, and Adley struck deeply and twisted his blade into the flesh. His blade hit bone, and he pushed deeper until a satisfying *crack!* pierced the air. Andraes screamed and swiped wildly at Adley's arm. There was a snarl and the silver fur of Sheiva flashed into view. The changeling bared his teeth and growled, the deep sound rumbling through the morning air. Andraes sagged slightly, blood flowing freely from his thigh – Adley had nicked the artery, a fatal blow.

"You have killed me again, crusader. Did you not already have enough of my blood on your hands?" The hate in his voice burned as he collapsed to the ground. "Finish me, Adley! Or do you lack the courage?"

Adley looked round for the second man, but he was gone.

"Sheiva, there is another – find him!"

While the dog searched, Adley knelt next to the dying man.

"How, Andraes? How did you come back?"

"Desperation."

"Desperation?"

"We all do desperate things for love, crusader. My desperation overrode my sense. The price was worth it." He coughed and Adley touched his pale, clammy forehead. All was silent, not even the birds sang.

"What price?"

"My soul. My prince has my soul and calls upon me when needed."

"Your soul?" Adley whispered.

"She was worth it, Adley. "

Adley tried to pray for the fallen man, but Andraes grabbed his wrist. "You can't pray for me now. There is only one place I will go." His voice cracked and grew quieter. "I'll see you again, crusader. I'll have . . . my . . . vengeance."

"Why were you here?"

"For . . . his daughter, she's so like him, but . . . she was gone." The words gave way to more coughing. Andraes closed his eyes, and the shallow rise and fall of his chest became erratic. Then there was silence.

Adley slowly stood and picked up his sword. Already the body of Andraes was disappearing, recalled to his master. Guilt rose in Adley, but he swallowed his eternal shame. He cleaned his sword and replaced it, then scooped Nina's jewellery into the box and put it back inside the house.

The bloodhound in the doorway eyeing him curiously. "He's gone, Adders. I can't track him. What was that all about, anyway?"

awareness of what had been stolen away from them all, and what had been given willingly.

Chaeli's thigh was immeasurably better. The skin had already scabbed over, and she could walk and run without pain. Each night she prayed to Elek, and he bestowed his blessing upon her. His touch would stroke along her skin, soothing the pain in both her wound and her soul, gently consoling her.

With no clothes other than those Nathan had found her in, she had tried to sew the trousers, however when Anya found her patching them up, she tutted and sighed, declaring that she needed new clothes for the city. In the interim, and with a little persuasion from his sister, Nathan gave her a pair of his own trousers to wear. She tried them on, much to the amusement of her hosts, for they were huge and slipped from her waist constantly.

After that, Nathan brought her dresses, for which she was grateful, even though they were gaudy and unfashionable; they proved comfortable and flattering, and that was good enough. Chaeli was used to trousers – her mother had spent years trying to cajole and persuade her into dresses but she steadfastly refused. The village seamstress had been unaccustomed to designing clothes for women of Chaeli's height, and the one time she had made her a frock it fitted badly across the chest and was far too short. She hated wearing dresses, much preferring the freedom trousers gave her, though it had pained her mother to see her dressed that way. "*It's like I have two sons!*" she would say with a sigh and a shake of her head.

When Chaeli woke on her sixth day it was still dark, but Nathan was gone; lately he had taken to leaving earlier and returning later each day.

"Don't worry, Chaeli, he has business," Anya had said when Chaeli asked his whereabouts.

But his serpents had burned their own mark on her, and she found herself wanting to know more of him and his time in Trithia. She wanted to believe Nathan truly had severed all ties with the

Underworld, but she knew too little about him to be sure, and each time she tried to ask, the scars on Anya's face silenced her.

After the lowsun prayers, she found it difficult to concentrate on the archaic language and lay on the bed reading. The demon had mentioned scriptures when she had boasted to him her knowledge, and he had smiled at her knowingly. She pictured the black-cloaked figure who disappeared when the man entered. She couldn't remember seeing the face, but she did remember white hands – it had white hands, she was certain. It had taken her blood, but what did the demon want with that? And why hadn't it taken Acelle's? It was said that blood rituals were performed in the Underworld, and accusations of such practices were often levelled against minorities who aroused distrust. She remembered the stories at her small village school of how souls were captured and controlled through blood. Surely they were nothing more than childish whispers? She remembered then the school mistress chastising another student with her switch when they had dared tease and scare the miller's twin daughters with such a story.

Restless on the bed, she moved to the table and began to read another dry, old and very dull scroll. The fading ink and rough handwriting made it difficult to understand, but just as she opened her mouth to call Anya for help, the tinkling of the medicinia door distracted her.

"Can I help you?" There was something in Anya's voice that prickled Chaeli, and so she backed away quietly, to slide under Anya's bed. She stared through the metal grate in the wall down into the main room. Anya stood by her shelves, a towel in her hands and her headscarf covering most her face. Flitting her glance across the room, Chaeli took a sharp intake of breath; four King's Guard stood by the door, the red of their jackets out of place in the white room.

"By the order of King Stirm, we're here to ask some questions, ma'am. Do you mind if we sit?" The older, and obvious commander vegetable buried under a pile of turnips. Her mouth watered. Cret'cha! She hadn't eaten the spicy vegetable for months, and it was a rare find.

"How much for the cret'cha?" she called over the cries of other traders.

"Three silver."

"Pull the other one," she shouted back, laughing. "Three silver for one cret'cha? Have the decency to wear a mask if you intend to rob me!"

The trader roared with laughter and wagged a finger at her. "For you, two silver and a kiss!"

"How about I give you four coppers and we'll shake on it?"

"A silver and five coppers! Cret'cha is out of season at the moment and I'm the only trader in Trithia with a supply! Feel free to try elsewhere, but I'll not drop a copper below."

"Agreed, but only if you throw in a handful of those ratatta herbs and six good sized 'tatoes."

The trader chuckled and nodded. "Aye, but you drive a hard bargain."

She handed over the coin, excited at the thought of surprising her hosts. The bartering had revived her further, bringing a small part of her lost self back. Weaving through the stalls, she stopped to admire the jewellery – a weakness of hers. Many summer nights had been spent with Ven, the artisan who lived across the fields. She was fascinated by his skill, and when her parents died she found comfort in hard stones and cold metal, twisting and shaping them into unusual trinkets. Ven had often enthused over her natural talent, but she had dismissed his words as flattery; though his offer of an apprenticeship had arrived the morning the demon attacked. She hadn't the time to tell Acelle the news. Not before what had happened.

The jeweller's stall had felt mats spread on the tables, each laden with sparkling stones and precious metals. Chaeli selected a delicate filigree ring in silver and yellow gold, and slipped it onto her finger.

Whoever had crafted this piece had skill. Reluctantly, she took it off again and held it in her palm, gazing at it admiringly.

"That would look well on a beautiful woman such as yourself," an amused voice remarked from behind her. "Though it would be flattered by the association." Chaeli turned to face the man who had spoken. He was of a similar height to her, with deep moss-green eyes, messy dark hair and an open smile. She stepped back. Why was he staring at her so? Did she have something in her hair? Running her hands over her head, she hesitantly returned his smile and placed the ring back on the mat, nodding to the merchant, who stared at her suspiciously.

The young man leant forward. "I don't mean to offend you."

"No offence taken." She noted the expensive leather shoes in the traditional Algary style. His coat was stylish and understated, but undoubtedly had cost a small fortune, and he wore a huge solid gold signet ring. Thinking back to her school lessons on civility and courtesy, she recognised the symbol as being one of the royal houses of Algary – but her ignorance bested her again when she couldn't identify it. She could almost hear the voice of the school mistress. *Why does it not surprise me, Chaeli? Never listening, always dreaming. How do you ever expect to rise above the status of trader if you can't identify the regalia of your betters?*

"My name is Kee Dala," he said, "and after looking into your eyes, I am forever at your service." He bowed and reached towards Chaeli, gently taking her hand and kissing it as though she were royalty and he a commoner. She turned scarlet and pulled her hand back more roughly than she intended. "May I have the pleasure of your name? Or will I have to beg?"

"Chaeli Dresne," she replied, then immediately regretted her openness.

"Chaeli! What an enchanting name, I shall arrange for the chief balladeer of Algary to sing of your eyes and the way they have bewitched me."

She couldn't stop her cheeks from flushing and found herself unnerved, unable to respond coherently. She knew she looked dowdy and plain in his company, dressed in a simple shift dress paired with her cumbersome boots. "I…have to go. I'm sorry I can't stay and talk, I'm running late. Time, you know. Going."

She started to leave, but her admirer feigned shock and hurt. "My charms must be failing! Othos, help me!" he called to the God of Song, spreading his arms like the most hammy of balladeers. She was worried now; perhaps she had misunderstood, perhaps this man was unwell. But all she could see was a young man with a full and simple smile and an honest face. She glanced around for any signs of deceit or ambush, or a suggestion that there was some audience watching, but she found none that explained his interest in her.

"I'm really sorry, but I must leave, thank you, it has been very . . . entertaining."

"Alas, I know when my time is up, and when I have been denied. Oh, cruel Penella!" he cried, gripping his chest. He bowed deeply. "Farewell, Chaeli Dresne, may Drenic bless your path and Elek shower you with good fortune."

Turning with an attempt at some dignity, she smiled despite herself. Hurriedly she began walking away. She could feel his eyes still on her and she looked back at him one last time. As she did, he turned away and stared pointedly at the jewellery.

She took her time walking back to Anya's. The sun was setting and the cool air passed over her, caressing and calming. This place was so full of variety and life. She hoped she could stay. She considered asking Anya if she could lodge with her, perhaps even become her pupil, create a new life, a new Chaeli – anything to forget the horrors and block out the lies of that demon.

As she entered the house, the strong aroma of cleaning balms stung her eyes again. Anya greeted her briskly and continued to scrub the floor.

"I've got something special for supper," said Chaeli. "Do not disturb me and I shall create a wonderful soup that will tantalise your taste buds."

Anya laughed and agreed to leave her alone. Chaeli bounded up the stairs to the kitchen and busied herself with dinner preparations. She needed something familiar, something comforting.

"Why does Father insist on keeping us in this god forsaken city?" complained Fyn. "I miss home . . . and the pretty women."

Dal looked up from his letters. "Ah, dear brother, our father trusted me with his reasoning but not you." He tapped his nose. "I am sworn to secrecy."

Fyn threw himself onto the sofa. "Why does Father never charge me with one of his missions? I long for action and excitement. It's not fair."

"He probably doesn't trust you." Dal raised a hand before the youth could object. He was in no mood for an argument. "No, trust is perhaps the wrong word. Father needs someone older to handle his affairs. Be grateful I'm his lapdog and not you. I yearn to chase pretty women instead of pompous diplomats, and drown each night in wine instead of ink."

"I just don't know why Father doesn't even ask me. We're not so different, you and me."

Dal stopped writing and raised a quizzical eyebrow. "Fyn, you and I are exceedingly different in height, age, colouring, and blood – we even have different mothers."

"We all have different mothers, but that doesn't stop Father sending Nyla on missions, and she's a woman!"

Dal sighed. "Enough, brother, your time will come. Father knows us well and plays to our strengths. Nyla's happen to be on her back, and mine involve my handsome looks, wit, and charm." He waved his hand airily.

So the old captain was back and in hiding! Interesting. That was something he would have to send to his father, earn some longed-for and overdue praise. As he followed the source of the information, a woman caught his eye. He watched her as she haggled with a merchant, and was bewitched. She began to laugh, and he caught himself staring at her mouth and neck and then, almost without his will, he started after her, following her through the market. His breath caught and his heart quickened. Never had a woman raised such a reaction in him away from the bedsheets, and yet, though pleasant on the eye, she was rather plain. When she stopped, he stopped too. Her eyes ran covetously over some jewellery, and instantly he approached her.

What am I doing? Dal suddenly reminded himself of his father's court fools. He spoke, then immediately regretted it, thinking of the bottle that now lay empty in his apartments. He was nervous, and tried to be clever, then wished the ground would swallow him up. Still, she had smiled at him in response, though it was a guarded, un-encouraging smile. He adored her eyes, their unusual shade of blue, a blue which surely had never been seen before, never been matched before. They seemed to stare right to his core and strip him bare.

Like I should do to her . . .

Wait, what was he thinking? Damned wine! He caught her looking him over from top to toe and he became even more self-conscious. The weight of his house ring was a constant reminder of his station and responsibilities: she saw the ring but looked away. This apparent indifference intensified the thrill of her presence. He kissed her hand and begged her name.

"Chaeli Dresne," she replied and pulled her hand away. Before he could ask, she bade him farewell and left. He watched her walk away. She turned back for a moment, and he pretended to admire the rings she had desired. "How much for the filigree one with the gold inlay?" he asked, idly playing with the silver band on his left wrist and trying to look sideways at her. But she was gone.

"It's the first time the Games have been held in Trithia for nearly one hundred years, Nathan. We're not missing them because you don't think it's safe. Gods, you're one to talk." There was a pause. Chaeli slid down to the grate and watched as Anya scribbled in her ledger for the tax collector, sitting at her workbench, head bent and back hunched. Nathan leaned against the shelves with his arms folded, frowning at her. He sported a fresh bruise on his cheekbone and grazes to his knuckles.

"What if people see? They'll want to know who she is and why she's with you. I told you, Anya, people are talking. We can't have attention drawn here, not again."

"Am I not to have friends? I am forbidden to men, Nathan, not women."

"I'm sure Stirm won't care for the difference," he replied drily. "The next stage of the Games are held in Lindor, perhaps you could—"

"I told you, I'm not leaving." Anya was angry; her voice wavered and Chaeli involuntarily tensed.

"Why are we having this discussion? She's not going."

"Who are you to decide?" Anya stood and poked her brother in the chest with her pen. "This is my home, my business, and the decision is Chaeli's."

"Chaeli is my responsibility."

Chaeli opened her mouth to reply, then snapped it shut. She wanted to say she was no one's responsibility, but the truth of those words cut too deep, and instead the thought of someone caring for her warmed her. She stifled a sneeze, and the floorboards creaked as she jumped, causing Nathan to stare straight at her through the grate. Without speaking, he turned and left the medicinia, the small bell tinkling as he slammed the door shut.

"You might as well come down," called Anya.

Guilt stabbed at Chaeli as descended, and tried to apologise, but Anya held up a hand to silence her.

"Don't worry about it. He's a stubborn ox and needs to walk it off." Filing away her books in a drawer, she turned back. "The Principal Games are on tonight and tomorrow in the city. Algarian knife dancing, Sheeman archers, Porton defence form, and Trithian fist-fighting in the docks."

A thrum of excitement hummed through Chaeli. The underground competition between four of the realms, old as time itself and held every ten years, was always an exciting event. The prize, gifted to the greatest fighter who scored the highest in all events, was a golden chainmail sash handed from winner to winner believed to have once been part of a dragon's armour in the great war.

"Trithia is hosting an event this year."

"Which event?"

"Fist fighting, of course." Pushing a piece of folded parchment across the bench to her, Anya grinned. "Two nights, no holds barred, all with an invite welcome, anonymity god-sworn."

"I've never seen the Games," Chaeli murmured wistfully.

"Neither have I, not properly at least. I was a child last time."

"And this is our invite?" Tapping the parchment, Chaeli raised an eyebrow at the older woman who nodded. "And are we going?"

"Yes, I believe we are."

"Dinner can wait for another night, then," Chaeli replied, and both women grinned at each other.

An hour later, dressed in her too-large dress and boots, a loosely knitted shawl cinched around her waist as a belt, Chaeli followed Anya through the streets to the wharves. The smell of putrid fish filled the air, causing the younger girl to gag every so often.

"It gets better, I promise," said Anya, lifting a flap of material and ushering her into a tin-roofed building.

As Chaeli's eyes adjusted to the dark, a mountain of a man moved to stand almost immediately in front of them. His gold earrings gleaming in the black. Silent as the dark and twice as frightening, he held out his swarthy hands. Dropping the parchment invite in one, and two gold pieces in the other, Anya grabbed Chaeli's hand and pulled her close. The giant stepped to the side and pushed open the heavy metal door, revealing lantern-lit steps leading down.

"Where does this go?" Chaeli whispered, her voice startlingly loud.

"A sanctuary of sorts. You'll see."

Chaeli found herself staring open-mouthed at the stories etched into the hard stone of the walls. Dragons and fae, demons and men, arm in arm they marched towards a triptych inscribed with the vows of spirit and time, the foundations of life on Ibea. The deeper they walked, the louder the music and shouts from below grew. Chaeli could smell boar and apples, and her stomach sang happily to her, sounding more like a growl to the outside world.

The steps ended and the room opened up to a huge subterranean space filled with people, food, music and dancing. There were stands of sweetbreads and sugarlicks, and drums with thick and juicy slices of boar and fresh bread offered freely.

Dear gods, she thought. *I could grow fat and happy here.*

"Chaeli, come," called Anya, beckoning her through the throng to a roped ring in the middle of the room. "We need to get a good spot."

Anya's scarred cheeks were flushed with excitement, her eyes dancing. No one paid any attention to her broken beauty, however, and the ability to breathe easily without fear of detection lifted the heavy weight she carried. Chaeli could see that Anya stood taller, glowed brighter, and had shed the look of sadness she usually carried. Unsure exactly what to do, Chaeli found herself watching the people who weaved and bobbed through the crowds. There were sharp, short shouts, and jeers, and cackling retorts that cut above the hum of conversation. Two soldiers were heckling a group of Algarian traders. It seemed good-natured enough, but before she could join in the banter and betting, something prickled at the skin on the back of her neck. Turning, she caught a glimpse of a pale-skinned woman staring directly at her: one eye, milky and dead, the other a piercing green. Raising a finger to her lips, the strange woman indicated her silence and nodded towards the ring. Chaeli glanced at the empty fighting space and frowned with confusion. When she looked back, the woman was gone. Surely she hadn't disappeared? Craning her neck, Chaeli searched for her, but the crowds closed in tighter now and obscured her vision with their bodies.

"Chaeli, are you all right?" asked Anya, watching her with a frown.

"I'm fine. Would you like something to drink?" She dragged her gaze down to the small woman and forced a smile.

Anya smiled. "Mead, thank you."

Chaeli nodded, then squeezed herself through the crowd, hunting for the strange woman. Unable to understand why, she knew she needed to talk to her. For once, she thanked the gods for her height. Standing shoulder to shoulder with the men, she was able to navigate a path to the food stalls with ease. At the end of a long line and waiting for drink, she hunted for the pale woman again, but just as she thought she saw a glimpse of white-blonde, the musicians put bows to strings and filled the room with music. Momentarily distracted, Chaeli laughed and clapped as acrobats flipped and turned from the corners of the room towards the ring. The acrobats were from Agassia, she was sure. Small and lithe, with blue soles and palms, they lived on an island miles from anywhere but Porton. Fascinated, she failed to notice the long, thick, red rope drop down from the ceiling, and the rope weavers that followed. Shrieking as two of them dropped a garland of flowers around her neck, the crowd roared in laughter and stamped their feet in approval as the scantily clad women turned and twisted on the rope, touching and tantalizing all. The room rumbled and Chaeli reddened at the intimacy displayed to and from the weavers. Tempering her breathing, she forced a smile and admired the flowers. Tiny rainbow buds and white lilies plaited together into the shape of runes: prosperity, luck, joy and . . . the last one couldn't be right. Blood? Confused, she grabbed two tankards of mead and wandered back through the crowd to Anya.

On her return, she almost dropped the mugs at the sight of Anya laughing and chatting with a tall reedy-looking man. She had never seen her so carefree.

"Chaeli, this is . . . Erik?" She raised an eyebrow at the man, who nodded.

"Erik will do." He clasped Chaeli's forearm in greeting, and she immediately noted the band around his wrist: mathematics, obedience, and song. "I'm a tax collector for the guild in the southern quarter." Sharing a secret smile with Anya, he added, "And I sing at the Golden Trout once a week."

"Erik's got three trens on Merlon Derrick winning the first round. I've just doubled my bet in favour of his competitor."

Chaeli remained quiet, letting Anya and Erik share a laugh. The music petered away, and the dancers filed out. Then, a new sound flared up, a drum, heavy and deep with a slow beat. Soon the crowd was clapping in rhythm. Chaeli downed her mead, and Erik immediately handed her another; soon the warmth of the air, and of the alcohol, had her swaying and clapping in time with the others. The richest of the observers sat on a raised dais, their demeanour and clothes betraying their high born status.

"My lords, my ladies," cried a preternaturally loud voice. Standing on tiptoes, Chaeli spied a small man balancing upon a stool in the centre of the ring. He radiated a presence that screamed of power. Bowing to the nobility present, he turned back to the crowds. "Sirs and madams,"—he winked at the prostitutes who flashed leg and chest at him, and their customers for the evening, who doffed their caps good-naturedly—"welcome all to the first stage of the Principal Games."

He fought with power and strength of the Underworld – whether he wanted its influence or not, it was there.

The crowd continued to shout and groan, yell and cry, and eventually a loud buzzer declared the end of the first round. Nathan stood in the corner, drinking water and scanning the crowds in desperation, his gaze finally resting on Chaeli. He shook his head, and it was as though he knew her thoughts, but under the heat of his stare, it suddenly meant very little. The announcer shouted again and the second round started, but with her back against the wall, Chaeli saw and heard little of the fight. Instead, flashes of the demon and Acelle's body seared through her mind. Her throat started to close and her lungs ached. Bending over she breathed in deeply, gulping at air with a rabid hunger.

"Are you quite all right?" a cool voice asked. She twisted and glanced up, and saw cold ice blue eyes staring down at her. She noted the red of his soldier's tunic hidden under a brown cloak. The gold thread and piping warned her that he was of military rank.

"I'm fine, thank you." She straightened, standing taller than he, but he carried himself with such authority and power that their height difference was negligible. Looking her up and down, he nodded just once and then stared at the ring.

"DeVaine fights well. There's passion in his movements."

"I suppose so." She tried to sound enthused, but her voice was dull and low.

"Are you not a fan?" He didn't look at her, but placed his hands behind his back, the gap in the cloak displaying his daggers in the black leather sheaths.

"I've not seen anything like this before."

The stranger fell silent and Chaeli found herself drawn to him as he watched Nathan. His look was predatory, his eyes following each movement the fighters made.

"DeVaine has this fight, or he should do. I have seven gold pieces on him." He spoke calmly, and without conceit.

Seven gold pieces? That was more than Chaeli's father had earned in a year. Transfixed on the fight, the stranger didn't notice when she edged away and rejoined Anya.

"Round three and Nathan's two rounds up!" Anya gabbled, placing a hand on Chaeli's arm. "Oh! Are you all right? You look so pale."

"I'm fine."

"Do you want to go?" Anya asked, flitting her gaze to the ring where the announcer declared the start of the next round.

"No, no, I promise, it's fine." Smiling weakly, Chaeli forced herself to watch the fight as Nathan pummelled the ribs and kidneys of his opponent. The skin stretched and rippled under the power of his blows. Finally, he maneuvered himself into position and caught the top ribs of the Porton's left side, driving his full weight into the larger man's chest. Nathan braced for a return blow, the muscles in his shoulders tensing, but none came.

Merlon Derrick screeched, bending over, gripping his ribs. Nathan growled and punched his opponent in the face. Derrick hit the dusty floor hard, spitting up blood. The crowd howled as Nathan rained down blow after blow from all sides, blasting the breath from the man's body and rattling his bones. Before long, he was limp and the countdown started. Chaeli found herself holding her breath, both in anticipation and in fear.

"We have a winner!" the announcer cried, stepping over the Porton and throwing his small arms in the air, then flapping them at Nathan. "Nathan DeVaine!"

Anya darted through the crowds, small and lithe, and jumped through the now smoking ropes to hug her brother. Alone on the sidelines, Chaeli hugged herself and watched as several of the nobles made their way down from their stand to shake his hand. He greeted them as though they were old friends, and with a wry grin, Chaeli realised that most of them would be. And, it seemed, old lovers too; an elaborately dressed noblewoman leaned in close and whispered in his ear, her curled hair momentarily sticking to

"Did you not see me squash the feet of the Agassians?" She sipping on her mead and grinned back, tapping her feet. "I'm as graceful as a tree bear."

"But twice as pretty, and"—he paused, looking over at Nathan—"it would lessen the sting of my loss if I got to dance with a pretty young woman."

Chaeli smiled into her cup. Nathan was deep in conversation with his sister and a lord, and her two dinner companions were off dancing, their attention purely on one another.

"One dance."

Merlon was light on his toes, and as charming as a Porton sailor could be. His humour gentle, his touch gentlemanly, he told Chaeli of the many secular islands he had visited, and about his life on Lysena Rock – the black sand and sulfur that permeated everything was as welcome to him as rain in Mischla. He guided her around the dance floor, and she relaxed his arms and told him of her dream to visit Porton, to stare at the dark skies from the top of Lady Volcano. By the time the third dance ended, she suddenly noticed how close they now danced, and how his hands rested on her waist and shoulder with ease.

"Thank you for the dance, or should I say *dances*. I shall be the envy of every man in the room," he remarked.

"I think not. Most men are grateful to you, for you've saved their toes from being ground into mincemeat by a woman my size."

"Gods woman! You're half the size of me," he teased, pinching at her waist. "We like real women in Porton, not like these inlanders." He jerked his head around the room and grimaced. "All skin and bone and worrying 'bout what they eat. No wonder they don't smile." One woman heard him and scowled, dragging her partner to another dance space and muttering about Porton rudeness.

Chaeli bit her lip and shook her head in mock exasperation. "Merlon, hush!"

"My grandmamma, she was a tiny thing, but ate for all of Ibea. 'Have a little of what you want, when you want', that was her saying. She's as old as a dragon now, and twice as scary, mind. Anyway, she says women need not worry about stupid things like weight. You, Miss Chaeli, are a delight. We're all made different. Nothing we can do about that. It's the gods' will."

Gods' will, Chaeli echoed silently, thinking again of Acelle, and the man she had left at the hands of the demon. Shame engulfed her; while she danced and laughed with this man, her sister lay cold and dead.

She faltered, and Merlon gripped her a little tighter. "You all right, Miss Chaeli? You've gone the colour of a sea eel."

"I'm fine. I just . . . you just reminded me of something." And just like that, she found herself telling him about the death of Acelle, carefully omitting details of the demon and instead concentrating on the horror of finding her body. Merlon listened in silence, his dark eyes connecting with hers. It was unnerving to be able to speak so openly and freely with a stranger, but the words wouldn't stop until she confessed her guilt at enjoying the company of others and the feeling of happiness.

"It's no sin to celebrate life, Miss Chaeli. Your sister wouldn't want you miserable. Sometimes we need to cry and feel, because if we don't it will eat us alive."

With these words, a tear slid down her cheek and he brushed it away gently with a calloused thumb.

"See now, your tears honour her."

The back of her neck prickled again, and when she looked over her shoulder, the strange woman stood by the band, flickering in and out of focus as dancers crossed Chaeli's line of sight. She turned back, trying to ignore the woman, and smiled at her partner again.

"It's been four dances now. I've done good," he said, clearly proud.

"Thank you, Merlon, for listening to me." She smiled up at him, and spoke gently with warmth.

"Pleasure. But it looks like I'm about to be replaced."

"Sorry?"

The sailor wasn't given the option to reply, for Nathan appeared, slapping Merlon on the back and thanking him for the fight. Merlon stopped dancing and stood in the middle of the dance floor; Chaeli found herself smiling uneasily as the men discussed the technical aspects of the first round. She tried to slip away, but Nathan grabbed her wrist and stopped midsentence:

"Chaeli, wait."

Chaeli thanked Merlon once more, who bowed to them both and kissed her hand before departing. Nathan pulled her closer.

"Shall we dance?"

"I *was* dancing," she replied, still angry with him though she struggled to recall why. Ah yes, the fight. And the note.

"I'm sure there are other women who would be flattered to dance with the champion of the evening," she said, and though she protested, he held her close and she found her hands on his waist.

"I'm sure there are." He glided them around the room now. "But I would be flattered to dance with you."

"And why's that then?"

"Because you don't want to dance with me."

He made no sense, and irritated that she didn't understand him, she clamped her lips shut and they danced in silence. Her back was rigid and she stumbled often, crushing his toes and causing them to stop and start over and over.

"Relax, Chaeli. I won't bite."

"No, but *they* might."

Though they were covered in a white linen shirt, the tail of a serpent disappeared under his neckline. She pulled back, widening the space between them. The smell of blood and sweat still lingered when he moved, and she found herself half-wishing that she still danced with Merlon.

"I'm sorry. I didn't want you to come," he said, noting her unhappiness. He stopped and let her go. "I'm in control of them. I have to be."

He turned and strode away, not looking back as the bear- and lizard-adorned lady made a beeline for him, hooking her arm through his and leading him out of the room.

The following morning, with her tongue stuck to the roof of her mouth and a pounding headache, Chaeli woke late to find both Anya and Nathan downstairs reading. As she took a seat on the bench next to them, a smile tickled her, followed by a giggle, for Anya had covered every bruise on Nathan's face with a purple paste that smelled of vomit and pears.

"It'll speed up healing," Anya explained, sipping at her fruit tea with a straight face.

Nathan muttered under his breath and continued to read, hunched over the bench with an air of both indignity and resignation. Chaeli poured herself a cup of cool tea and grimaced as it mixed with stale mead and washed down her throat.

"Someone had a little too much to drink last night," Anya remarked, not looking up.

With a grunt, Chaeli pulled over the plate of sugar bread and nibbled. "Didn't think it would be that strong," she said in between mouthfuls.

"Well, Merlon seemed to love the attention, and if you ever proclaim not to be able to dance again, I shall cut out your silver tongue! You were the talk of the night. Where did you learn to jig like that?"

The hazy memories returned in broken pieces: dancing on the table, dancing on Merlon's shoulders, singing along to the Porton sea-tunes and then . . . oh no . . . she groaned and shook her head as she recalled climbing the Agassians' rope. Anya deliberately refused to make eye contact, but Nathan stared at her, though it was clear he fought a smile.

Her feet sank as she hit the mud on the other side of the wall and she crouched down. Pitch black at first, it was impossible to differentiate the shadows and the buildings. As the hairs on the back of her neck stood up and the wind carried whispers, Chaeli looked around for the voices, waiting for them to pounce, but nothing came. Exhaling in relief, she dragged her feet from the sludge and jogged towards the flat plains and the road. Here, she started running, her feet slapping the ground as she moved. Soon she felt as though her lungs would explode. She was exhausted. She couldn't even shout apologies to the people she knocked past. The constant battle against the resistance of the mud worked muscles she didn't know she had. She paused, leaning over to catch her breath, and wiped the sweat from her eyes. The buildings around her were tightly packed; she had wasted precious time weaving in and out of huts and tripping over debris on the path.

She scanned the route as far as she could see: dark outlines of people marred her view but as her eyes adjusted and the black gave way to shades of grey, she tightened the pack on her back and started off again, uncertainly this time. She was lost; she couldn't see the wastelands, and the smells of the Sink were beginning to make her feel sick. She slowed and held a hand to her face in a vain attempt to staunch the odours, but it did nothing to block out the sounds of weeping and begging that carried on the wind.

She prayed for guidance, for Elek, but there was nothing. Suddenly she screamed as she was shoved to the ground, face first in the muck. Her attacker lay on top of her, heavy and crushing, and Chaeli sank further, stones digging into her skin. Fear gripped her and silenced the cry inside.

She thrashed and heard a deep grunt as her heels connected with her assailant. The weight shifted and, grabbing at the mud, she dragged herself forward and rolled onto her back. The straps from her pack pinched her skin as she pulled herself to her feet.

134

Each breath and movement seemed to take an eternity. Then she saw him.

His face was covered with scars and fresh wounds, his hair matted and knotted. As he rolled to his feet it was clear she was taller than him, but that did nothing to ease the palpitations that rocked through her. She wanted to run, but couldn't turn her back on him, so she stood rooted to the spot. He laughed and launched himself at her again, his hands grasping at her skin. The smell of him, the closeness of him, violated her senses. He pulled at her dress and she could do nothing to stop him. She was weak, useless. He pushed her to the ground again and she winced as he collapsed on top of her.

It was then her body chose to respond. Her muscles relaxed and she felt blood rush to her limbs. She clenched her fists and in one swift movement she punched him in the head. His fumbling ceased as she hit him over and over again using both fists now. He scrambled off her and she leaped to her feet, kicking out at him.

No longer laughing, he groaned and sobbed as her foot connected with his stomach. Her fear gave way to anger and the rage roared and coursed through her veins. As she reared back to kick him again she paused and faltered. What was she doing?

"Forgiveness is an attribute of the strong. To seek revenge shifts the deserved right into a great wrong."

The words of her scriptures echoed in her mind and she drew back. The man tried to pull himself to his knees before falling back and crying. Giving up, he started to crawl towards the sludge and mud, apologising over and over again. Trembling, she turned and ran away, passing the last scattering of homes before she hit the wasteland. There she stopped, and bent over, her hands on her knees, gulping in deep breaths. The stench of the land seeped into her and she could still hear the thrum of voices from the Sink, the howling of the dogs. Ye gods!

The touch of her attacker still crawled along her skin. She could still smell him, feel him. She shuddered.

Nathan actually returning for her, or even finding her. She couldn't rely on him forever. With some trepidation she made up her mind.

He held out his arm. "I am Danven. Come, meet my girls."

"Chaeli," she replied. She took his arm and smiled. What in all the hells was she getting herself into now?

Eli smiled to himself. The rats had provided him with some useful information: Chaeli had run from the city and was now with Danven. Wonderful. He had sent Malo to the King, and according to the beast, Stirm was tripping over himself to help. That maggot was always trying to gain favour with the Underworld.

The shrieks and moans of the condemned pushed through the many doors and corridors that led down to his dungeons. Kings, peasants, farmers, lords – mortal hierarchies had no meaning in his Underworld, all were equally damned. Their cries formed a sweet chorus, a proclamation of love to him. Each blow they received from the whips and chains of his demons was a gift to him. Each death they relived, a hundred deaths of agony and pleasure, a sacrifice and declaration of loyalty to him.

The years of the truce had worn him down, but now he felt refreshed and alive. Sipping from a crystal goblet, he reflected on the letter he had sent to Daro. His brother hadn't acknowledged it, of course, but still Eli revelled in disclosing that Chaeli was his, that she belonged to him. Not only had Eli owned Amelia, he now had Amelia's daughter, her flesh and blood.

Amelia . . .

From the moment Daro had introduced her to Eli, he had wanted her. His jealousy towards his brother intensified, washing through him, burning and growing into an unquenchable fury. Not only was Daro the oldest and most revered, he had the purest and deepest love of Amelia. Now, the memory of her body, the touch of her skin, distracted Eli; he needed a release.

"Metlina, come!"

Within seconds he could sense her energy pulsing through the room. She appeared and knelt in front of her lord with her head bowed and arms outstretched.

"Rise."

She stood, keeping her head low, and he stared at her tight copper curls. Today she wore a blood-red gown with a black bone diadem; he was sure the jewellery had been a gift from him many years ago, though the memory was hazy.

"Kiss your liege," he demanded. She raised her head and leaned towards his face. He embraced her with a vicious passion. Their mouths met, lips and teeth clashing together. He loved mortal senses, the fragile life which brought the constant awareness of danger. He pulled her closer, running his tongue along her bottom lip. She whimpered, and he bit down hard. The Goddess of Pain yelped and he tightened his grip on her hair. Metlina touched her mouth, her fingers coming away with drops of red; a gentle moan of pleasure escaped her lips. Eli brushed her cheekbone with his thumb, then licked the blood away.

"Kiss me again, my beautiful Metlina," he whispered. He was hungry for her and as she reached up to him, he shook his head.

"Not there." He began to unlace his trousers. She dropped to her knees in anticipation.

"Adders, please, I need to stop," whined the dog. They had been walking for almost two days and he was exhausted. His paws were covered in debris from the road, and the pads were bruised; worse – his stomach growled. They had at last reached the rolling hills and green countryside of Trithia after crossing the wastelands; the surrounding woods were plentiful in small wildlife, but Sheiva's ability to transform only stretched so far. He could sniff out the food, however the ability to stalk their meal while it moved still proved a challenge and Adley's hunting skills were rusty, for he hadn't the need to eat or drink for centuries. So far, they had survived on an elderly rabbit that had needed hours of cooking to be edible and a handful of apples stolen from a farmer's field.

"Look, we're nearly at the city," said Adley, pointing, the relief almost overwhelming him. He, too, needed to rest, and to eat. He was still stiff and sore from being healed, and he felt *old*.

The dog wagged his tail. "Well that's good – the sooner we find her, the sooner I can change out of this mangy mutt suit."

"But you're so cute as a dog, Shiv."

"Careful, I might just bite you."

Adley chuckled. "It's almost sunrise, people will start to trade soon. When we hit the city I can't talk to you other than to give commands."

"Charming," snorted the dog. "But I understand." He took a couple of sniffs at the ground. "She's been here."

"Good. Hopefully we'll find her in the city." Adley jumped from the small ledge on which he stood to the scrub below. Sheiva followed, sniffing at the wind and snapping at wasps that hovered too close to his muzzle.

As they hit the Sink, Sheiva growled. Adley soothed him with a pat to the head.

"I know, Shiv. It gets better, I promise." The cool breeze from the sunrise soon disappeared. Adley saw the sick and the old, saw children scurrying around filthy huts searching for any scraps they could find. Two young lads beat each other for a half-loaf of mouldy bread. There had been a time when a philanthropic king ruled, when no one went hungry, and all were equal in his eyes. Children had been educated by the scribes and those unfortunate enough to be homeless were offered lodging in return for work at the castle. The equilibrium had been maintained, the people happy. Where had it all gone wrong? In truth, he knew: when House Windthorn had taken the throne by force at the time of the signing of the divine treaty four hundred years ago, Trithia had fallen into disarray. The gods were too busy, too distracted to grant their grace, and so the land and the people had suffered, were suffering still under the rule of the last of the Windthorn line.

Sheiva cocked his head and indicated the west gate. Adley nodded and the pair made their way over the mud, passing a tatty whorehouse with a makeshift nursery, little more than a lean-to, tacked on the side. The calls from the women and the groans from the customers could be heard clearly through the paper-thin walls.

"Papers," said the bored soldier at the gate. He sat staring into the distance and holding out his hand.

Adley removed his pack and dug out the papers. "Looks like it's going to be a nice day," he said.

"What?" The soldier stuck a finger into his ear and scratched. He pulled it out, sniffed it, then wiped the wax on his stained tunic.

"The weather, it looks good. Nice day and so forth."

"I suppose. I'm stuck here though, aren't I?" The soldier gave the papers a cursory glance and handed them back.

"Well, good day," Adley said, and they walked into the city. The solider paid no attention and went back to his staring. Sheiva sniffed and began casting about, moving in widening semi-circles. Eventually he found a scent that led them both deep into the city.

When Nathan returned to Anya, he fell upon her, hugging her in relief.

"Is she safe?"

Nathan nodded. "I said I would meet her and accompany her to Lindor." Anya said nothing but squeezed him tighter. "I'll miss you, little sister."

"Miss you too." She let go and freed herself from his embrace. "Do you think Stirm will know you were here?" she asked, her voice a whisper as she lowered herself into a chair, her golden hair hanging over her shoulders disguising her face.

arrived, there were too many civilians around, and too many guards. Weighing the coin in his pocket, he approached the guard.

Four silver pieces it cost him. Four silver pieces he handed to a weasel he could have flattened with one hand, and who, just a few years ago, would have quailed at the mere mention of the name DeVaine. He was furious, but was in no position to negotiate.

Making his way through the Sink was simple enough. Once out of view of the gate, he weaved and bobbed his way through the crowds with ease. He still had skills from the Underworld; his past as an assassin equipped him with the arts of concealment and disguise, while his life as a renegade had taught him to blend in amongst others. He could feel the sweet intoxication of his gifts and hear the call of the Underworld once more, but he pushed it to one side and concentrated on leaving. As the dwellings thinned, he searched the horizon hoping to see Chaeli near the road to Lindor; but there was nothing.

As he strode across the wasteland, caravans to the east caught his eye; they moved along the royal road to Lindor in steady convoy and he could just make out the name *Danven* in ornate lettering on each caravan.

Nathan sneered. He remembered this troupe: prostitutes in the guise of exotic courtesans and performers, the dancers whored out to rich men paying extortionate amounts of coin for one night of pleasure. He didn't despise the art of whoring itself, but the way these women were used to gain political status and were offered as gifts and prizes sickened him.

Where was she? He had left her almost three hours ago; he'd spent too long with Adyam. She could be a few kilometres ahead by now and he couldn't be sure she would follow the road. He gazed at the horizon: the road to Lindor was straight and stretched out as far as he could see, lined with hundreds of Trithian lehai trees. Their canopies shielded the road from the sun, allowing only bolts of light to stream through in golden bars. He re-arranged his pack and set off along the road. The caravans, smooth and well-maintained, were fast, and by jogging he managed to keep pace behind them. If they stopped, he would see if he could perhaps groom and feed the horses to earn a seat upfront with one of the drivers.

After an hour, Nathan was breathing heavily and a sheen of sweat covered his brow. He had kept a good pace, but knew he was tiring. There was still no sign of Chaeli; unless she was running, he should have caught her by now.

The caravans had started to pull away, appearing smaller as they moved ahead. He slowed to a walk, knowing he would need to conserve energy. As the sun bounced off the branches overhead and onto the ground, the light danced off the last droplets of dew. The world around him seemed so at peace, yet he found himself considering places for ambush and concealment. Swinging his pack around to his side, he removed an oat treat and smiled; Anya had packed his favourite, cooked oats rolled in honey and sprinkled with aritha vanilla. Chewing and savouring each mouthful, he considered his situation. He had rations for four days. The next village in this direction was six days, possibly five if he pushed hard. Could she have walked this fast? He thought back to their parting; she had been angry with him, to his regret – he hated the way his temper always seemed to get the better of him. Years of trying and he still couldn't control the rage inside. Pathetic. Perhaps she'd decided to return home, or move on to another city. Nathan hesitated, then sank to his knees.

"Praise be the Eternal Kingdom," he prayed, feeling as uncomfortable as always when asking the gods for help. "Divine Ones, I ask for your blessing and support. Please help me, I need to find her, I need to make sure she's well."

Nothing. Emptiness consumed him. Familiar feelings of pain, loneliness, and rage began seeping into him, spreading, filling the void. The rage was a thousand times stronger than any other emotion. Nathan recognised the signs that the Underworld wanted him to return, and despair wailed deep inside.

Not now, please, *not now*. He didn't have the strength, nor clarity of mind, nor purity of heart to fight the Underworld. He closed his eyes and felt the serpents moving on his back, and as the furious torrent of darkness began to overwhelm him, it was as if a gust of ice cold wind stilled the serpents and froze him from the inside out. Then unfamiliar warmth exploded within him. Every inch of him burned, uncontrollable love and happiness dousing the rage, but then there was silence and nothingness once more.

He tried to stand, but staggered and fell back to his knees, as though forced to return to prayer. It was then he heard the voice on the wind: "*For her.*" There was a pause, and then: "*Lindor.*"

He didn't have the strength to hunt for the source of the voice, and deep down he knew he wouldn't find anyone nearby. Nathan had heard the accounts of those who were touched by the gods. Indeed, his own sister had tried often to describe her experience, but every time Nathan had silenced her, from disbelief and pain.

He knew the truth: the gods were watching and they did listen. But somehow it didn't help. He felt worse, for he'd prayed to the Kingdom and begged for redemption, but received nothing. Today the gods had listened to his pleas – not for him, but for another.

He stood, his legs like jelly and his breathing ragged. His back burned as the serpents returned to their resting place and, re-arranging the pack, he walked on.

Chaeli struggled to keep her eyes open. Where was she again? She made herself sit up and look around. Three beautiful women lay next to her, their eyes closed. One look at them and Chaeli was transfixed – *who were they?* A rocking motion disoriented her for a moment before she realised she was in some kind of wagon with colourful silks covering the wooden walls and floor. As though peering through fog, she remembered meeting a strange man and being introduced to these women. The memory didn't reassure her and she began to panic. What was going on? Why couldn't she remember anything? The stale air of the caravan was beginning to make her feel sick; the mix of the perfumes and sweat from the women was too much for her to bear. She looked around, seeking a way out, or at least the chance to open a window. It was then that Chaeli was distracted by her clothing. She was wearing billowing, almost transparent yellow trousers. She ran her hands along the material, marvelling at the silk but then frowned, where were her clothes? Her breasts were covered by knotted cream silk wound around her and her stomach was bare. Her mouth parted and her cheeks burned, pulling her hair away from her neck she tried to cool herself down. It was too hot. Far too hot. Involuntarily, she covered her chest with her hands, even though there was no one to see her. This wasn't right. Not right at all.

Something niggled at her, some memory. Something important she had to do. She tried to focus but the fog remained.

"Chaeli," purred one of the women, opening her eyes. "Come here." She held out her tattooed arms and Chaeli wanted to do nothing more than sink into them and sleep. The pull proved irresistible; she moved into the woman's arms and lay down. The woman gently stroked her hair, and Chaeli fell back into a deep dreamless sleep.

When she woke, they had stopped moving. Shivering, she rubbed her arms as the women stood up and the rear of the caravan opened. She squinted as the sun streamed through the open doors. Chaeli realised the figure at the doors was the strange man that she hazily remembered.

"Where am I?"

The man smiled and stroked his clipped beard. "My rose, you are with Danven. Come."

Chaeli felt no fear, and clambered to her feet, walking into his open arms.

He held her close to his chest. "Chaeli, so pretty. My rose, Danven has a gift for you."

lock and realised it had been sealed with a holding rune; there was no way he could get through it without the man knowing – as soon as he broke the charm, the conjurer would be alerted.

He moved back out of sight while the slaves started the convoy moving. He jogged alongside under cover of the greenery, and once he knew the slaves were focused on the road, he silently darted out and grabbed the back of the last caravan. He lifted his feet on to it, hanging on the footstep as they moved, and thanked the gods for the small mercy that Chaeli's was at the rear. After a few minutes his arms and fingers began to ache, so he swung down and looked beneath the caravan: solid. Cursing, he crawled back. He would have to break the rune and hope he could get Chaeli out of there before all hell broke loose – perhaps literally, judging by the Underworld stench. He held on with his right hand and placed his left over the rune. Drawing from his energy and reciting the charm, the inking on his palm shifted, the seven stars moved into a circle and enclosed the rune. His hand burned, but he couldn't stop; slowly, the rune began to dissolve.

"Faster, damn you, faster!" He moaned and drew on more of his energy, jeopardising his grip on the caravan to push through the magical ward quicker. With a final, agonising flash of heat through his hand, the rune vanished. He breathed a sigh of relief and pulled on the door handle, but as he did so, all three caravans stopped and he was jerked forward. He had been detected. With no time to waste, he flung the door open to find Chaeli lying on a profusion of cushions, her eyes closed.

"Chaeli!"

Her eyes snapped open and the comprehension dawned. "Nathan!" she cried, scrambling to her feet to run into his waiting arms.

"We have to leave. Now!" He jumped to the ground, Chaeli right behind him.

"Can you run?" he asked. She nodded, and he grabbed her hand. Shivers danced over her skin at his touch, though she couldn't tell their nature. In any case, she had no time for that now; the three slaves surrounded them.

Chaeli panicked. Not now, not Nathan! What would Danven do to him? She stared at Kia who looked at Nathan with pity. Chaeli knew that Danven wouldn't allow him to live, but she couldn't let him die because of her. Nathan let go of her hand and drew his sword, but the slaves stood firm.

"Move," roared Nathan channelling the energy into his voice to make it wild and commanding.

"My rose," called Danven, "what is this?" He approached and the line of slaves parted for him.

"She's not your *anything*," growled Nathan, taking Chaeli's arm and pulling her behind him.

Gods, the smell of him, the scent of his power!

Danven smiled and Chaeli saw sharp pointed fangs. "She is mine. Come to me, Chaeli," he commanded, crooking a finger at her.

Chaeli was rooted to the spot, her legs refusing to move and her mouth dry. Danven dominated her sight; all she could see when he spoke were flashes of the fangs. She shook her head, drawing strength from Nathan and his protection.

"Never," she whispered, her voice broken and low. She cleared her throat and took a deep breath. *"Never!"*

Danven growled, and the three women appeared alongside the slaves. Chaeli and Nathan were trapped within the arc of enemies. Chaeli reached down and drew a curved blade from the sheath at Nathan's side; she would die before Danven would claim ownership of her again.

"My master won't allow you to be hurt, Chaeli. We won't hurt you, come, leave the mortal, come to Danven and embrace your father. Come, embrace his love."

"Not. A. Fucking. Chance."

Danven roared and his form changed. He grimaced as his clothes split and dark red and black flesh swelled in lumps along his

165

few days ago and I haven't been able to stop thinking about her, it's as though I'm enchanted . . ."

"By sweet Penella, Dal, you, lord of the bachelors, the royal singleton, have been snared by a woman in the *market?*" Fyn doubled over in laughter while Dal grinned wryly. "So then, brother, who is she and why does the King want her?"

"That's just it, Fyn, I don't know. I can find no record of her in the city archives. But I'll tell you one thing, I was captivated at first glance, and if I'd been in her thrall any longer I would have thrown away everything for the chance to be with her."

"Strong words."

"She raises such strong emotions in me, I can't explain it. Never have I felt this way. So, is the guard any closer to finding her?"

"No, no sign of them. We've taken DeVaine's sister into custody and she's in the dungeons awaiting interrogation. She'll crack soon, no doubt."

"If she does, let me know, brother. I must find . . . Chaeli." His pleasure in saying her name was marred by the knowing expression on Fyn's face.

"Of course," his brother. "Now, are we going to play molyona or are you going to pine for this seductress all night?"

Dal laughed, feeling it better to conceal how little he felt like humour. He nodded. "Get on with it, Fyn. I long to relieve you of your purse."

Chaeli found Nathan in the morthon's caravan. He had been searching through boxes and chests; parchments, paper and vellum covered the floor while he sat reading.

"Nathan?" she called from the doorway.

He looked up. "The morthon kept good records, very clear and detailed. He's been using his succubi on the richest and most influential men in Ibea. The women fed on the men at night, the victims becoming addicted to their touch." He stopped reading. "Chaeli you're hurt." He dropped the papers and rushed over, kneeling in front of her to examine her wounds. "They're deep, but they'll heal." He looked up at her.

She gazed into his eyes and realised they were the same colour as her pendant. Involuntarily she touched her neck.

"She heals fast because of who she is," stated Adley with cold certainty from behind her. He stood refastening the blades to his wrists; he didn't look up.

"Who is she?"

Adley looked up now and scowled, the hostility clear. Nathan straightened his stance.

"So who is she?" he asked, making it less of a question and more of a demand. Chaeli turned to face Adley, confused by his statement and by the animosity all around her. Adley stood silent, his hand now on the hilt of his sword. At last he nodded. "She is the daughter of Prince Eli, Lord of the Underworld. Her mother was Amelia Von Ariseré, the mortal lover of Prince Daro." He turned and walked away from the caravan and back to Sheiva's side.

"Smooth, Adders, really smooth," the cat muttered. "Been practising that in a mirror?"

Chaeli stumbled out of the entrance and fell. Nathan lifted her up and she pushed him away, running her hands through her hair. She needed to be alone. The demon had spoken the truth. The memory of its smell and touch made her shudder and she tried to concentrate on thoughts of her parents and Acelle but they faded in and out of her memory. She wasn't her sister, they weren't her parents. She wasn't anyone. She needed to breathe, but now the choker felt tighter, too tight. She clawed at her throat. "Get this thing off me," she gasped.

Nathan moved behind her and lifted her hair. "There's no clasp. How did you get this on?"

"Of course there's a clasp!" she snapped, grasping at the anger. But she couldn't hold onto it, and began to feel light-headed. She closed her eyes as nausea washed over her.

"Chaeli, there isn't a clasp. It's a single silver band, I can't remove it."

She couldn't breathe. The tightness of the choker and miserable resignation that everything she knew was a lie was trapped inside her wouldn't let her take in air; her eyes closed and her body went limp.

CHAPTER FIVE

"**M**ERCY, MASTER! GREAT one, forgive me," begged Danven.

The prince watched poison from the dagger dance into his morthon's heart.

"You failed me. You had her within your grasp." He cut the morthon's glistening chest again, leaving a blossoming wound. The creature howled in agony and Eli delighted in the sound. "Your task was simple. Wipe her memory and plant the charm. How much easier could I have made it? *She is a mortal!*" He kicked the huge creature hard, again cutting with the cursed blade.

"The charm," moaned the morthon. "I did . . . the charm . . ." His speech slurred as the poison began to take hold.

The prince burst into laughter. "Ah, *now* you please me!"

"Master," wheezed the creature as it fell to the floor, twitching and convulsing. The room fell still, punctuated by the slow dripping of blood.

Eli ignored the creature and went to his private chambers. "Shadows, remove the beast," he commanded, playing with a small black stone in his right hand. He held the stone to his lips and whispered in the language of the gods.

Chaeli screamed and Adley and Nathan had to pin her to the ground, leaning heavily on her arms to keep her still.

"What's wrong with her?" cried Nathan as she thrashed and jerked, she was dripping with sweat and mumbling incoherently between spasms, sometimes calling for her mother, other times singing songs and complaining of the heat.

"I don't know," Adley replied, grunting with the effort of holding her. She grabbed his hand, their inkings touched and the realisation hit him. "It's a charm," he said.

"A charm? How can we remove it?"

"I don't think we can, she needs a priest of the Eternal Kingdom. We have to get to her to Lindor and quickly."

"And if we can't? Lindor is three weeks by foot, a week even by carriage."

Some of Adley's hatred for the man dissolved as he heard the despair in Nathan's voice. "We can ride the horses from these carriages and be there in three or four days."

"Can she ride? And will that be enough time?"

Chaeli cried out again, calling this time for her parents and sobbing apologies to Acelle and Nathan winced.

"I hope so. I can sedate her for the time being with one of my own charms."

"Do it. Quickly." Nathan stared at Chaeli. Her face was chalk-white, her lips almost blue. Her choker glinted in the sun. "The necklace!" said Nathan. "That's the charm!"

"I think you're right; can you see here? The silver is engraved. I can't read what it says, can you?"

Nathan peered at it, then shook his head. Adley closed his eyes and entwined his fingers with Chaeli's. Her hand was clammy and cold; she had no strength to hold his hand. He drew on his energy; the love he gave his gods and his link to the Kingdom made him stronger than ordinary mortals and he poured this strength into Chaeli in an effort to supplement the flow of her energy with his own. He threw as much into her as he could spare. Gasping, he broke away. "I can't do any more, that'll have to suffice."

178

Nathan stared at him in wonder and mistrust. "I sensed your energy. You have more power than any person I have ever met."

Adley grimaced. "I hope it was enough."

Chaeli was silent now and her breathing had levelled. Blood was returning to her cheeks and lips, but still she didn't wake.

"Is she really the daughter of Prince Eli?" whispered Nathan, stroking her hair and moving the sweat-soaked strands away from her eyes and lips.

"Yes." Adley was drained. Although he had been linked in with a god before, he had never been required to give his own energy to a deity; the experience was both terrifying and exhausting. And he still burned with shame at his insensitive way of revealing her identity.

"Who are you, Adley?"

Adley lay down beside Chaeli, closing his eyes once more. "I was a man, like you, but a man who has seen many things and lived a hundred lifetimes."

Sheiva approached. "We must leave. The slaves will take one horse and one caravan, leaving us with two horses. I can change, but I'm tiring. I don't think I will be able to change again for some time."

"What are you, then?" asked Nathan, staring at the cat.

"I'm about to become her ride," he replied, and transformed back into the silver horse.

The men lifted Chaeli onto Sheiva's back, and using silk from one of the caravans, they tied her to the changeling. Chaeli was limp and difficult to manoeuvre, but they secured her as elegantly as possible, with her legs and head dangling on either side of his flanks. Unhooking the caravan from the remaining horses, Nathan dismissed the slaves who stood bewildered and bowed repeatedly at the former soldier as he repeated over and over again that they were free. Eventually, he walked away from them before he shouted and lost his temper.

"So, who are you?"

"My name is Nathan DeVaine. I was King Stirm's captain, and now . . . I travel."

They rode the horses hard in silence, one either side of Chaeli, their hands poised and ready to catch her if she fell. As the sun set, they reached the market town of Delani, a small place that neither man had visited before. The hand-painted welcome sign identified the community, the colourful, mismatched buildings invitingly simple. The horses were tired, and as the men dismounted, Nathan checked their hooves and legs. They felt strong and he could detect no sprains or bruising. Adley lifted Chaeli down and carried her like an overgrown child. She was awkward for him to hold, as they were of a similar height, but he would have walked himself into the ground for her, both from duty and love.

Nathan pointed to a large white building in the centre of the town. "Local inn," he observed. Adley nodded and together they approached it, Nathan leading the horses.

As they entered the building, they were met by the sounds of laughter and music. An upbeat jig was being played on a badly tuned lute but it had the men and women up and dancing, unconcerned by the off-key notes. It was a well-known rhyme from the Algarian lands; centuries old, the lyrics had changed over the years but Adley recognised the melody and nodded his head in time to the beat. In the corner, a group of young lads exploded into a fit of chuckles as one of their crowd fell from his stool whilst eyeing up a pretty dancer. The inn radiated warmth and cheer, and ordinariness.

Adley stood in the corner holding Chaeli while Nathan spoke to the innkeeper, a stocky man who frowned at the girl in his arms.

"The people round here can be a bit funny when it comes to women," said the innkeeper.

"Oh?"

"A woman travelling with two men might be considered . . . indecent. I'll have to tell people you're family. People round here, well, they ask questions, see? I'll be having to answer questions for days." He stood behind the bar with both hands flat on the wooden surface. The voices were low, but Adley leaned in and continued to listen. The innkeeper glanced at Chaeli and then back to Nathan, shaking his head.

"I am sorry for the intrusion," Nathan said and produced a handful of silver, but still the innkeeper refused to budge. Eventually Nathan slid a gold piece across the bar and the innkeeper nodded.

"I think I have two rooms, one for the girl on her own." He grinned. "Nice to see you, cousin."

Nathan nodded once and turned to Adley. "Let me carry her upstairs, it'll be easier," he said.

Adley looked him over: DeVaine had several inches on him and could navigate the steps more easily with Chaeli. He passed her over with care and followed behind.

"The owner has his wife heating water for a bath and preparing a meal. He seems a good man. Honest."

Chaeli's room was small and clean, a bed nestled in the eaves, a washbasin and chamber pot discreetly hidden behind a screen, and a chair under the window. As Nathan placed Chaeli on the bed she stirred and murmured. It was the first noise she had made since Adley shared his energy with her. Her clothes were damp with sweat and the jacket was open; the silk top left little to the imagination.

"Is she all right?" Adley stood in the doorway, watching.

"I think so," Nathan replied, pulling the jacket closed and buttoning it from waist to throat. "I'll stay with her tonight."

"No, I am her protector, I will stay."

"About that . . . who says you're her protector?"

Adley understood the jealousy and suspicion; he shared it. Adley undid his shirt and lifted it over his head. His skin was badly scarred but Nathan could still see the inking that covered his chest: a dragon, wings spread and ready to fly, the sign of a crusader and soldier of the Eternal Kingdom.

now. She had always been enchanting to him. Of course there had been village boys that stole kisses from her by the lake, but none of them truly *saw* her. Even when she celebrated her majority, the Alingale innkeeper's son had to be cajoled to dance with her at the party, complaining she was too boyish to dance.

She was cool to the touch; her temperature had dropped quickly once the fever broke. He held her hand and traced small circles on the palm, following the stars with his fingers. He couldn't understand how she was not a conduit of the energy; she was closer to the gods than any mortal. Closing his eyes he connected his palm to hers and concentrated.

He felt the connection and her calling immediately; sensing her presence, he delved deeper and searched. Her own energy was a huge expanse, like nothing he had ever felt before, and he teetered, then toppled, falling down a deep, bottomless cavern. Unbelievable strength. Caught off-guard, he staggered.

Falling still further, he searched for the origin, but there was nothing. He felt another blow, a push so strong and powerful as it swept over him that it left his own energy tingling. He dropped his resistance and let their energies combine.

The realisation hit him: she was not a conduit, she was a source! What he could feel was not the energy shared by mortals, but her own power, the power of the gods. He tried to gauge her strength, but there was too much. Adley pulled away and drew himself to the entrance of the cavern. As he released their spirits, his mobility returned and he dropped her hand.

He stared at the sleeping girl: there was no mistaking she was a demi-goddess. He understood now why Eli wanted her so much; the power she held was immeasurable, vastly different to that of Prince Daro and his gods. It was brash and harsh, ever poised and ready for attack where the gods' power flowed and meandered like a river.

He heard footsteps outside the room, and grabbed the hilt of his side sword.

"It's me." Nathan pushed opened the door. He nodded at Adley, then looked over at Chaeli. "How is she?"

"Better. She sleeps naturally now. I think I have stilled the charm, though I can't remove it. But she should wake in the morning, though she will need gentle hands."

"I suppose *you* will be her gentle hands?" said Nathan with a thinly veiled sneer.

Adley looked up, surprised. "I am her protector, Nathan."

Disbelief flashed across his face. "I've seen the way you look at her. You want her."

"Nathan, I've watched Chaeli from the shadows, visible to no one, since she was a child. I care for her more than I care for any other mortal." The older man closed his eyes and leant back against the bed. He ran his fingers through his unruly hair and continued, "I lost everything to the Kitaani in the Dragon Wars. My father disowned me, my wife and son were murdered, my home destroyed. My love for the gods saved me. I was rewarded with the role of protectorship, the greatest honour a soldier like me could have hoped for. But, however great the honour, I missed my family. I couldn't be with them in the gardens of the Kingdom. When I was finally granted time with them, they had gone. Their spirits had merged with the pool of power in the Kingdom. I returned to Prince Daro and begged him to allow me to join them, but he told me that I was still needed. I've spent centuries in the halls of the Kingdom. I saw my prince fall in love, and the Kingdom bloomed. I saw him betrayed, and the Kingdom withered. He sent me to look after her, and she is my reason for being. And yes, she evokes something in me I thought dead a long, long time ago." With his last words he looked at Nathan. "She represents the very best and the very worst in the mortal world, Nathan."

The former assassin walked to the window and opened it wide, remembering the cat. "You said your love for the gods *knew* no bounds. Past tense," he pointed out.

189

Chaeli staggered back to the bed and collapsed next to the cat. Soon the nausea dissipated, and she reached out to scratch his head, making him purr. "Nathan is out finding me some clean clothes. I don't know where Adley is."

The cat stopped grooming and rolled over onto his back with his legs in the air, exposing his soft belly. "Would you mind . . . ?" Chaeli smiled and obliged, rubbing his tummy and scratching under his arms.

She reflected, though she still couldn't think about Acelle: it hurt too much, even more when she recalled how she had run and hidden. She pushed her pain deep down inside again, and instead let the memories of Anya's kindness lighten her. And then thoughts of Nathan invaded her mind.

She had spent the majority of her youth around boys and men; they had treated her as an equal, cajoling and challenging her into joining them in tree climbing or tomb-stoning. Nathan was nothing like those men, and the feelings he aroused in her were new, though she wasn't so naïve as to be entirely confused. To her, he was complex and intense, and where many in her village had been tired from work in the fields, his weariness came from somewhere deeper. He was hard and battle worn. Her cheeks flushed at the way her heartbeat quickened when she remembered his shirtless form that night in Anya's home.

She could picture every scar on his chest and back, how the two serpents wound their dark paths across his body. The serpents. These thoughts of his earlier life, so far as she could imagine it, brought her back to reality. He was a trained killer who had worshipped the Underworld.

That doesn't mean he's unattractive, whispered her inner voice.

She frowned to herself. No, it didn't, and that was the problem. But his past both scared and intrigued her.

The cat bit her hand gently and meowed, and Chaeli realised she had been rubbing him too hard.

"Chaeli, while we are alone, is there something on your mind?"

Embarrassed that the cat might suspect she had been thinking of Nathan, she forced him from her mind. "Tell me about Adley. Who is he, where is he from?"

The cat gave her a look, but curled onto her lap and told her about the role of a protector; he said little of Adley's life beyond the fact that he had lost his family centuries before.

"Is it true what the morthon said? Is my father really the Prince of the Underworld?"

"Yes, that's true. Prince Eli is your father."

Chaeli fell silent. Everything she had known since she was a child was false. But instead of the anger and betrayal she knew she should be feeling, her heart was empty. It might have been the persistent headache dulling her senses, or the charmed choker numbing her emotions, but she felt nothing.

"So . . . my father, Prince Eli, rules the Underworld," she said slowly, as if trying to convince herself that this was true.

"Yes," said the cat, and closed his eyes.

"Does that mean I'm a goddess?" she asked in wonderment.

"Half-and-half," said the cat through his purrs. "Mortal mother, divine father."

Chaeli sighed. She couldn't hide from this forever. Her emotions rushed back, and suddenly she was angry at herself, at the world, and at the gods themselves. She didn't want to be a puppet, she wanted to live a normal, quiet life without the meddling of divinities.

"So what happens now?"

The cat opened one eye. "We go to Lindor. You need to learn more from the scriptures. Hopefully the knowledge you gather will allow you to see things in a fresh light. There is no precedent for you, no clear prophecies to guide us. You are unique. We, Adley and I, that is, are forbidden from influencing the path you take." He yawned and stretched, then added, "Lindor also has the best medics and healers in all of Ibea. We need to remove that charm from your blood."

193

"But what exactly am I supposed to learn in Lindor?"

Sheiva blinked. "The very reason for your being, Chaeli. There are no documented demi-bloods in the history of Ibea, and Daro feels that, should you learn your heritage, you will understand your reason for being."

"So, in other words, the gods have no idea?"

"Well, actually, there are plenty who have ideas. That's the very cause of your problems at the moment."

Chaeli reached up and touched her throat. "This was a gift from the morthon."

"I don't think you can remove it, Chaeli. I can sense evil, and that thing is undoubtedly evil." With this, the cat drifted off into a peaceful slumber, and they sat in silence until Adley returned, clad only in a towel about the waist.

"Chaeli, you're awake!" he spluttered grasping at the towel.

She reddened, what was it with her where men and their bare chests were concerned? Still, she could not help but stare at Adley; the huge dragon inking on his chest was glorious. It stood tall and proud on two legs, wings spread as though ready to soar. The golden scales seemed to shine in the moonlight. This man was truly a warrior for the Kingdom.

"So beautiful," she murmured.

Adley stared at everything other than the young woman before him. Chaeli gathered the blanket around her, approached him and with a tentative glance up at him, she reached out; she needed to feel the dragon, the ink called to her blood, urging her forward. He held his breath as her fingertips traced the outline of the beast. The dragon stirred and she gasped, snatching her fingers back.

"It moved!"

"It's part of me, a link to the gods."

"But how?" She blinked at the dragon as it started to stretch and yawn, her eyes widening with confusion and awe.

"All inkings are linked to the emotion of the bearer. They feel what we feel." He swallowed, desiring her touch again, the warmth of soft skin on skin. He ached for it and the dragon started to pace.

"It's amazing, it really is." She looked up, her face full of wonder. He took her wrist and placed her left hand on the dragon, his heart beating strong and hard beneath. She tried to pull her hand away but he held it firm.

"Stay. Feel," he whispered linking his fingers in between hers.

"I don't—"

"Feel with your spirit, your energy."

She shook her head. "I have no affinity. I was tested—"

"I've seen your energy and your spirit, Chaeli. I've tasted your power. Try, please . . ."

"I can't . . . I failed the testing." The memories of her humiliation, of disappointing her family, ebbed into her again, making her cheeks red, her gaze drop to the floor.

"You can. Trust me."

She looked up at him then, and he offered a reassuring smile. She closed her eyes and concentrated. The steady beat of Adley's chest set the pace so she matched her breathing to his; it felt natural and right.

"You have to fall into yourself, into your very core," he whispered. "Keep your eyes closed, and picture opening yourself up, your mind, your body, your emotions."

"How?" The fear of failing made her tremble.

"I picture an opening. You can imagine anything you like. A hole, a window, a door, anything that symbolises entering somewhere new. Once you have decided on your trigger, it will forever be the catalyst for your energy."

Chaeli breathed deeply, and emptied herself of all thoughts and emotions. A host of images ran through her mind: her tree house as a child, the stained glass window at the Kingdom church in her village, the front door to her home, the cupboard where she had hidden from Malo, Anya's opaque glass door, the caravan,

The power thrummed and pulsed. There was more energy, she could sense it lingering outside of her skin. It pulled at her from the inside out, and as the falling sensation slowed, she reached out for it, eager for more. This was what she needed.

"No, Chaeli!" Adley's voice was sharp. "Don't seek the energy, let it find you."

Why? I want it. All of it.

"Too much can destroy a god; it can destroy you." Though his words were gentle, his voice was firm.

But you don't have this power, you said that.

"No, but I have tasted the gods' power before. Trust me, please."

Disappointed, she stopped searching and allowed herself to drift; now she could control the speed of her falling.

"How do I leave here?" she said aloud, hating the way her voice cracked and squeaked. She wanted to stay there with her power, forever. Why shouldn't she? But before she could contemplate any further, Adley spoke:

"Just think about the very first door again. Go back through, and close it behind you."

Unwillingly, she walked through the door and felt the warmth of Adley's skin against hers. She allowed herself a few moments to gather her senses. Though its intensity had waned, she could still feel her energy inside, pressing to be released. She wanted more, she wanted to taste more of it, swim in its depths, but her eyelids drooped and her limbs ached. She stifled a yawn.

"You have an indescribable amount of energy."

She drew her hand away, lost for a moment in the gold of his eyes. He cocked his head and smiled sadly; a tear rolled down his cheek as his eyes crinkled. She remembered the despair he held inside. When she reached up to touch his face he closed his eyes. Her power moaned in delight and anticipation, surging within her. At the very thought of taking his pain away, her energy responded like a warm fluid, flowing from core to extremities. It moved along her arm and into her palm, resting there like a small, silver ball.

Chaeli opened her eyes. The silver orb travelled to her fingertips like a drop of water, then spread across his dragon, who greedily absorbed it. Adley opened his eyes; the pain was still there, but it had lessened, softened. A small flickering tail of his energy seemed to resonate and linger within her.

"What did you do?" he asked quietly, calmness in his voice.

"I don't know," she whispered back, lowering her hand.

The energy still pulsated down her arm, and she glanced at her palm to see that the stars had moved. Seven stars had moved into a spiral.

She burst into tears and laughter at the same time. She had something, something special that was just hers. She wasn't some broken thing that nobody wanted. She had *power*. Adley looked at her for a moment, then smiled. The smile turned to a chuckle, and soon he joined her in full roaring laughter. She bent over and tried to compose herself but as she did, her blanket slipped showing a large expanse of skin. She squealed and desperately tried to cover herself, managing only to lose grip on the other corner.

Adley bent down to help her but their heads knocked, causing him to stagger back and stand upright, rubbing his forehead. From under his hand, he caught a glimpse of her breasts, her stomach, the curve of her hips. His laughter stopped immediately and he turned away. She fumbled with the blanket and covered herself again.

"It's— I'm fine now," she said, stumbling over to the chair. Adley turned around, his cheeks burning crimson and his dragon hiding its face under its front talons.

"I'll just go and get dressed," he mumbled. But when he opened the door, he found himself face to face with Nathan.

"Sorry," Adley muttered, then brushed past Nathan and hurried into their bedroom further along the corridor. Nathan frowned. He glanced at Chaeli and saw the flushed look on her face, the blankets in disarray. Scowling, he dumped a pile of clothes on the bed.

"Clothes. Your bath is ready," he said curtly, then turned to leave.

"Nathan, wait," she called, but he ignored her and strode to the other room, slamming the door behind him.

Adley had already pulled on his trousers and was reaching for his shirt. Nathan couldn't contain himself any further.

"What were you doing in there with her?" he raged.

Adley turned in shock, the dragon on his chest shuddered. "I beg your pardon?"

"You heard me, what were you doing with her?" Nathan stepped closer to Adley and pushed him hard in the chest. Unprepared, Adley stumbled back.

"What the hell? What are you doing?" Adley gained his footing and fell into a fighting stance.

"You, and her! Naked. Together!" Nathan struggled to control the darkness; his serpents hissed and slithered around his chest, rage worming into his heart.

"What? No, you've got it all wrong. I showed Chaeli how to channel her energy, nothing more."

"LIAR!" Nathan clenched both fists and threw his weight into a punch. It connected with Adley's chin, the a sharp crack echoing about the room.

Adley refused to fight back. His opponent was mad, out of control. He blocked the next blow easily, and the next. Nathan was fighting like a wild man, all thought and form missing.

"Nathan," grunted Adley. "Calm down man!"

But Nathan ignored him. The serpents were murmuring to him, coaxing him. He needed this, the sweet, exhilarating haze of rage. It pulled at his mind and thrilled his flesh; the Underworld wanted him, and the Underworld would fight for him.

Adley sensed the change, could feel the evil weaving into his adversary. Something was wrong; this wasn't just a jealous fury. He waited for the next blow and, sidestepping it, grabbed Nathan's wrists. The larger man struggled, but Adley kicked him hard in the stomach. Nathan bent double, coughing loudly. Adley released his wrists and struck him with a stinging slap. Nathan staggered and fell; Adley pounced upon him, pinning him to the ground.

"Let me up, you filthy piece of shite," snarled Nathan.

Adley's dragon roared, writhed, prowled impatiently across his flesh, yearning for release.

"Fight me like a man!" Nathan cried, bucking under Adley's grasp.

"*His chest*," whispered a voice.

Adley let go of Nathan's wrists and ripped open his shirt. He stared in horror at the serpents, which had moved entirely to Nathan's chest. They hissed and spat, fangs visible and ready to strike.

Taking advantage of Adley's reaction, Nathan moving to his feet, but Adley kicked him back down and pressed his starred palm over the serpents. They bit hard, and the burning pain of their poison shook him. He grimaced and ground his teeth, fighting to keep Nathan down as he thrashed on the floor.

"I'm sorry." The protector bunched his hand into a fist, punching Nathan squarely in the face. Nathan sank back, unconscious, leaving Adley to concentrate on the snakes. Pressing his hand harder to Nathan's chest, he pierced deeply into the spirit within.

Whirling black mist clouded his path, stinking of betrayal, bitterness and hatred, and in the background, threatening and deep, was the rage. Adley searched on. This man had promise; his energy had sparks of hope, love and redemption, but the positivity was drenched in the repugnant stink of evil. He focused his energy on the hope, letting it pour into the centre of this tortured spirit, though it cost him. He had already given so much to Chaeli.

But the mere thought of her sparked something in Nathan, and suddenly the two men were connected. One. The tenderness of the younger man's emotion squeezed at Adley's heart and he moaned aloud in despair and wretchedness. It was the beginning of love; Nathan cared for the girl with purity and selflessness. With a sinking feeling, Adley fed that emotion as much as he could,

Without touching it, she knew the choker was there. It seemed to burn into her skin.

Penella closed the observatory doors behind her and turned to face the gods who had agreed to the meeting. The light from the domed glass ceiling fell around them, touching the glow from the auras of the corporeal forms they chose, while the white walls pulsated erratically with stored energy. The building held a special significance for all the gods; it was a place where they could watch and anticipate the return of their own creator, and thus reminded them of their birth and The Beginning.

"Penella, what is this all about? Why the secrecy?" asked Drenic in bewilderment. "Why here and not in the council rooms? Where are the others?" He stood with his hands clasped behind his back, his habitual smile lost in the firm line of his lips.

"Drenic, let me sit before I speak ," she replied, walking to the plain wooden bench in the centre of the room and indicating the others to sit. She arranged her skirts and shot Shy'la a knowing look; the Goddess of Fertility nodded in response.

Clendian, the God of Learning, consort to Hytensia, the Muse of Knowledge, strode around the circular room, deep in thought. "I, too, am concerned with the furtive manner in which we conduct this meeting. Away from the Beings, the other gods and, most importantly, our lord Daro."

"Before I go further I must ask, have you or Hytensia discovered why the Pool drains?"

"No. It remains a mystery." Clendian sighed. "Hytensia works from sunrise to moonset to find the answers." He stopped by the spiral glass staircase leading to the second observation balcony and sat on the steps, trying in vain to hide his ink-splattered robes.

"And Eli's daughter, what path does she travel?" Penella looked around, catching the steady gaze of Vorgon, who shook his head.

"Do any of us know what she is capable of? We must be wary, brothers and sisters. I worry that Daro does not see the danger—"

"What are you saying, Penella?" interrupted Drenic. "You know as well as I that Chaeli prays to the Kingdom."

"She has followed me all her life, she will not wander from my guidance," agreed Elek.

"She is half goddess, Elek, whose bloodline shows a history of betrayal and deceit on both sides. She was never meant to be! Daro himself decreed no god may create life with a mortal. With our power waning and her allegiance unknown . . ." She stared Elek down. "No matter how much you protest otherwise, Chaeli is a threat. We must prepare ourselves."

"It was you who brought Chaeli to us, Penella, and now you warn us to be wary of her? What game is this?" Vorgon's eyes bored into hers.

"I brought a babe to the Kingdom, an innocent child, one who was possibly the daughter of our prince. I love her as much as the rest of you, but we must be prepared."

"What are you suggesting?" Igon's soft voice carried through the room. "I will not harm her."

"I would never suggest such a thing." She stood and walked around the bench. "I wish to walk on the mortal world, I want to touch my devotees with my grace, show my face to the loyal. Inspire faith to grow and nurture love from its inception."

"The inception even I cannot ensure any longer," added Shy'la. Penella smiled her approval. "The birth rate among the mortals has dropped. Their numbers are dwindling and still they do not pray for me. They have forgotten the ways of the Kingdom." Shy'la stood and took Penella's hand. "Our sister speaks the truth, you must know that."

"Daro will not allow it," said the Goddesses of Joy and Trust in unison as they plaited each other's hair.

"Daro need not know," Penella murmured.

"Hush, Penella! You cannot mean to deceive our prince?" Igon stood. "I want no part of this." He made to leave, but the Goddess of Love stood in front of the doors and held out her arms to him.

"Igon, please listen. Surely you have felt us start to slip into the void? There will be no power to bring us back, no matter the strength of Daro's grace. Do you want that, Igon? Do you want to see your children trapped for all eternity?"

Igon, the God of Honesty, glanced over at Joy and Trust, their young faces staring at him in horror, and shook his head miserably.

Penella loosened her grip. "Will you stay, Igon? Will you help us regain the power of the Pool through prayer and worship on the mortal world?"

Igon hobbled to the bench and sat with his head in his hands.

"I beseech you. No, I beg of you! Think back to before the treaty, remember how powerful we were, how happy the mortals were. The Pool overflowed with our grace and power. We were respected, worshipped, *loved*. The treaty has made us weak. We are fading, and in another four hundred years we will be nothing more than myths, fanciful bedtime stories for children in a barren world. Everything I ask of you is for the good of the mortals. While Daro locks himself away, his children are slowly destroying the world he gave them. They need us, they need our guidance. I am asking that you allow the mortals to remember why they pray, show them to whom they pray. Relight the fire of faith in the Kingdom." Penella looked around her. Joy and Trust had moved to either side of their father, consoling him as he wept wretched tears; they glanced up at Penella and nodded. She looked around the room; Drenic, Vorgon and Elek all nodded at her and lowered their heads; Shy'la smiled.

"Igon, will you help save us?" Penella asked softly. He nodded. "Then it is agreed. We will walk the world of Ibea and inspire the mortals." Penella threw open the doors. "But what we have discussed must remain among us."

There were two interesting paintings on the far wall of Stirm's banquet hall that he simply had to see. According to Fyn, the artist had despised Stirm's grandfather with a passion, and so had painted the King's loyal dog with a pained expression on its face and sad, pleading eyes. Dal scanned the room and negotiated a route through the dignitaries who milled about, gossiping and waiting to pander over the King with their birthday gifts and promises of fealty.

"Ah, Prince Kee Dala! You have decided to honour the King with your presence! He will be thrilled the royal house of Algary has finally sent its emissary," said Kerne, his cool, oily voice making Dal smother a grimace.

He turned to face the King's most trusted man. "Captain, I do apologise. I have been in Trithia for some time, I confess. I have lodgings in the city. Modest, but then, I like my privacy – I'm sure you understand." He signalled to a servant and took a large glass of wine.

"Indeed, but when the Crown Prince of Algary graces our city, your safety becomes my responsibility. I can't allow you to remain unescorted in Trithia. I shall arrange for guards to accompany you at all times. I would see you safe." Kerne kept a level stare and Dal wondered if the man had any emotions at all. His reputation suggested not.

"Captain, while I accept your kind offer, I must request that my brother Fyn is assigned to me. If he were to hear that I had given permission to you and not requested this, I truly would be in trouble." He took a gulp of his wine.

"Your base-born brother? Of course, Kee Dala, though I wouldn't have thought you would want to . . . well, is he not a constant reminder of your father's infidelity, and a dishonour to your mother?"

Sighing, Dal caught the eye of the captain again, who raised his glass in acknowledgement. Dal reciprocated, smothering his discomfort with another deep gulp of grape.

As he scoured the room, he finally saw a face he recognised and a smile of delight crossed his face. He moved purposefully through the guests, though he was accosted several times by those wishing to negotiate use of Algarian mines. He had to remind them as delicately as possible that his father still controlled these, and their requests would need to be addressed directly. But his words became increasingly brusque and undiplomatic, rapidly losing the ability to care who he insulted; the grape was doing its job.

Eventually he reached his goal. Bending down, he murmured, "What's a maiden such as you doing at a dull gathering like this?"

"Fulfilling a bet, my dear prince. If I remain all night without offending any dignitaries, then I win one hundred gold lucs from my father." The Princess Ilene turned to face him.

"I shall add fifty gold lucs to that pot." Dal smiled and then added, "In support of your father."

Ilene threw back her head and laughed. "Oh Dal, how I shall enjoy relieving you of your purse tonight."

"It's a sure bet, Ilene. Your temper is legend. Why, there isn't a man here brave enough to come and talk to you – look around!"

She glared up at Dal. "Are you telling me that none of these fine men have the courage to converse with me?"

"After you turned down suitors from every realm? No, I don't think they have. And I don't think the Grand Maji has forgiven you for sending her son home with bruises covering his backside."

"He shouldn't have challenged me to a race! Those arrogant beasts from Mischla believe they are the only competent horse riders in Ibea. It wasn't my fault he couldn't control Princess."

"Princess? You gave him *Princess* to ride?" Dal laughed, catching the attention of several guests. "No wonder the poor lad got thrown. That mare is more of a handful than you are."

"Serves him right, thinking he could come to my father and demand my hand in such a manner. The sheer arrogance!"

"So what brings you to Trithia? You avoid these gatherings as much as I do." He was intrigued as to why King Cobey had sent his only child to such an affair when so many other emissaries would have sufficed.

"Father is joining me. Stirm requested his presence. I believe there is marriage proposal lurking." She sneered and downed her glass of wine in one slug. "If Father tries to marry me off to this pig, I shall run away. Why should House Myrrian join with House Windthorn? The idea makes my blood run cold."

"A handful of suitors in a year, Ilene. I think I'll have to join the pot." She glared at him and he winked.

"Don't you dare, Dal. Father would just die of happiness if you were to propose. The joining of Porton and Algary is something he harps on about constantly."

"You are looking very pretty, Ilene. I think it's time I made an honest wife of you." He loved teasing his cousin; he could feel her energy building up ready to attack. He had a small amount of energy himself, and used it to draw a shield around his body. "Play fair now, Ilene, I was only joking." He looked at her with a mock-pained expression. "I couldn't face the humiliation of you besting me in public."

She didn't smile. "If Stirm does propose, I think Father will accept and force me to marry. I'm scared, Dal." She grabbed another glass from a passing platter and took a deep swig.

"Do you really think your father would force you to marry? You're his pride and joy. Powerful, independent, sharp witted – you're everything he could ask for in an heir."

"Apart from having the right equipment dangling between my legs," she retorted, causing Dal to spit his drink out and cough loudly.

"Ilene! Such language from your lovely lips!"

"It's true! I know Father would prefer it if I was a man. He won't let me rule. I know he will expect me to pass on my birthright to my husband. Can you imagine Stirm controlling Porton and Trithia? The very thought makes my blood run cold."

Dal considered this and sympathised. He loved King Cobey like a father and had spent many summer days with Ilene on the oceans, travelling the coastal waters in her cutter. He would marry her if it meant she would be free, but he knew it wouldn't be that simple. The love they shared for each other was the love of brother and sister, not man and wife. No children would come from their union, and they would eventually make each other unhappy.

"I don't know what to say other than this: if your father tries to make you marry Stirm, then get word to me and I will marry you. And I will never take your crown."

His cousin looked up at him and smiled warmly. "My dear sweet Dal, I could never condemn you to such a depressing life as my husband." He smiled and she continued: "Now let's get back to socialising, I have one hundred and fifty gold lucs to win tonight and I'm not in the mood to lose, so stop trying to put me in a bad mood. Leave me be."

He kissed her lightly on the cheek and walked away, promising to come and visit her before her trip was over.

After several more hours, Dal was reasonably drunk and exceedingly bored. This was a celebration of King Stirm's birthday, and the guest of honour had yet to appear. He'd lost count of the glasses of wine he'd downed, but the spinning room and tilting floor led him to conclude it was definitely in the region of too many. Slowly he made his way to the halls and caught the attention of a passing soldier.

"Good man, bring me Fyn Miner. I need to see my brother." The command came out slurred, and he stumbled as he spoke. But the guard saluted and hurried away regardless.

Dal stood swaying in the hall; his head pounded and he suddenly felt sick. Even the shadows started to crawl and bend with the

212

moving walls. Gods! How much grape had he consumed? Breathing deeply, he clung to a nearby chair and sat down, putting his head between his legs. He had to close his eyes: he couldn't face the spinning anymore.

"Brother, can I not leave you alone for a few hours?" Fyn's voice boomed through the hall, making Dal wince.

"Shh!" He groaned. "Not so loud." His brother heaved him to his feet and Dal looked at him blearily.

"Gods, Dal, how much have you drunk this evening?"

"Too much, little brother. I need sleep. Take me home."

"Alas, brother, the captain has already assigned you quarters here, and I am to be your personal guard. Imagine that, the two of us together causing mayhem in Trithia! Ladies beware!"

Dal just wished he would be would be silent. "Fine, take me to wherever it is the captain has arranged for me, I don't care. I just need to sleep."

Staggering and swaying, his younger brother heaved him through the castle to a wing on the east side, the furthest from Stirm and Kerne, much to Dal's drunken delight. Groaning, he collapsed onto the bed. He could hear Fyn talking in the background, but within seconds his only response was a light snore.

Nathan groaned and opened his eyes, immediately regretting it and grimacing in pain. Something stabbed in his stomach like a red-hot poker, and his face ached fiercely. A dim light illuminated the room and he realised where he was. He recalled the events of the evening, and a swell of shame threatened to overcome him. Glancing to his side, he saw Adley lying on the floor, ashen. Only the shallow rise and fall of his chest indicated he was still alive.

Nathan closed his eyes again. He couldn't face up to his behaviour.; he had shamed his family name again. It wasn't enough that he had been an *Assaké*, an assassin, but now he had attacked a

213

crusader, the very best of the Kingdom. Mortified, he clambered to his feet and left. He needed some time alone.

Hetes, God of Disease, shuffled through the open pit, his head bowed as he inhaled the smell of his prey. Mud and clay soaked his feet and he trembled in anticipation of his coming joys. Somewhere in this cesspool, the most deadly of his diseases bubbled below the surface, waiting to be released.

"Get to work, old man!" He felt a blow to his back and he swallowed a growl. His pride rose and he almost struck out at the impudent mortal. Simmering, he reached down, grabbed a pickaxe, and started to chip at the sides of the mine. He could sense the overseer behind him and for several minutes he appeared to work diligently. When he felt the mortal leave, he threw the tool to the ground where it stuck fast, the shaft quivering from the force of his anger. He shuffled further along, then reached out and sought the sickness – so strong, so near. Scanning the pit, he heightened his godly senses with a thread of power and blocked out the chattering mortals. A thin red haze emanated from a middle aged woman who struggled with two pails.

"May I help?" He gestured towards one of the pails.

She frowned. "Get yer own, these be mine."

"I don't want to steal them, woman, I just want to help!" he said, then regretted it. He had meant to woo her. Woo; incubate; nurture; capture.

"I can manage on me own." But she dropped one of the buckets and the lumps of rock scattered. Hetes cursed her stupidity as he knelt down and gathered them, replacing them in the pail. He looked up and her gaze softened slightly. Kindness was a rarity, but still treasured here.

"A'right. Mebbe ye can 'elp."

He took a handle and followed her across the pit; she smelled of sweat and excrement. As they reached the living quarters, he handed over the bucket and she thrust both of them to a gaggle of children who sat chipping at the rocks and releasing the slivers of precious metal.

Hetes glanced around the tiny hut, his attention was drawn to a narrow bed tucked into the corner, screened off with a thin and tatty sheet. There was no solid or level floor, only crushed rocks and mud.

"Ye want some liquor?" She offered him a filthy glass, and with a nod he accepted and gulped down the amber liquid. "Yer meant to taste it. S'just common, doing it like that." She rolled her eyes and sipped at her own glass. He watched as she looked him up and down: no, this woman would not deny him. He sent a thread of power into her and fired up her desires, transmuting them into desire for him. He flicked his eyes towards the bed and raised an eyebrow. With a slow nod, the woman placed her glass on a rickety table and started to unbutton her dress, paying no attention to the children.

"No need," he interrupted; he had no desire to see her naked. Guiding her to the bed, he dropped the screen and reached up under her dress. The smell of her intensified. He touched soft flesh and she moaned with desire, her breath sour and hot.

With a perfunctory thrust, he released the disease. *Lovers' kiss* had returned, and soon it would spread throughout this pit. Unrelenting, merciless and so very, *very* painful. He felt the epidemic yearnings respond, and his power base intensified.

She collapsed onto the bed and Hetes readjusted himself with a smirk. "I will be off. Thank you so much." He bowed slightly.

"Ye can stay if ye want."

"Oh no, my dear, I must decline. I have pressing business to attend to."

"Ye don't sound like yer from 'ere." She moved her hands between her legs and began to scratch.

The first symptom! Excellent, excellent . . .

"I'm just passing through," he said over his shoulder. He walked a few steps from the hut and disappeared in a pulse of lime-green light.

β

Blue fell to his knees, the hands of his enemy around his throat, still squeezing. He lifted his shaking hands and grabbed White's forearms, digging his fingers deep into the muscle in desperation. It seemed to go on forever, and the Watcher sighed out a pang of compassion. He stood and leant down to the side of his chair, staring at the objects scattered on the sand. Finally, he threw an item into the arena. It landed soundlessly at Blue's knees. Blue groped at the ground in front of him, the hands of his foe still encircling his throat.

The figures continued to shuffle and tussle. The Watcher's view became obscured, and he twisted his body in his chair to adjusted his field of vision. Blue now had a hold of the item and, with a sudden access of strength, he drove it deep into White's foot. There was still no sound from either warrior. White fell to the ground clutching his foot and curled into a ball. A thin splinter of bone protruded from his boot, and he slowly drew it from the leather and held it close to his chest. The Watcher could see the slow rise and drop of the fallen warrior's chest, and he glanced at Blue, who remained on all fours, breathing heavily.

The atmosphere changed; the temperature rose then fell in quick succession. Blue heaved himself to his feet and retrieved his sword from the sand. All the while he watched White curled motionless on the ground.

CHAPTER SIX

S UN BURST THROUGH the window and birds sang delightedly
to the dawn, but Chaeli groaned and pulled the blanket over
her throbbing head. There was a soft knock at the door, which
sounded like a drum roll to her.

"Come in," she called. The door opened and Adley entered. He
was fully dressed and carried his pack. He looked fresh and alert,
and there were no outward signs of the altercation with Nathan.
Chaeli thought back to the night before; after her bath she hadn't
dared to look back into their room and instead crept into her small
sanctuary, where she fell asleep almost the moment she lay herself
on the bed, barely having the strength to dress.

"We must leave early if we are to make good time," said Adley.

Sighing, she threw back the blanket and sat up. Adley coughed
and turned to face the door. Chaeli frowned as she glanced down
at her attire. What was wrong with him? Her shirt was buttoned
enough to conceal her modesty and it fell to mid-thigh.

"Oh, for the gods' sake, Adley!" She wasn't a good riser at the best
of times, and this certainly wasn't helping; Adley's piety irritated
her this morning. She pulled on the rough wool trousers Nathan
had brought her. "Where's Nathan?"

His shoulders slumped almost imperceptibly. "I don't know,"
he replied. "I woke up this morning and he was gone."

"You can turn around now," Chaeli said, dragging her fingers
through her hair.

"I have to go and saddle the horses," he replied, opening the door. He paused. "Did you, ah . . . hear anything unusual last night?"

"Nothing. Why?"

"No reason. I'll see you in a moment."

She stopped battling with her hair for a moment and listened to his footsteps on the stairs; chewing her bottom lip, she replayed the whirlwind that had been the last week. She didn't know what to feel or indeed if she was capable of feeling anything. This morning she felt empty again, no joy, no sadness, nothing. Slowly she resumed detangling. These two men were both dangerous, each in his own way. But they were the closest thing she had to friends.

Nathan had spent the night outside staring at the stars. He hadn't slept a wink thinking over his monumental mistake. He'd lost control, been bested by a crusader, and his pride was wounded. Throughout his life he had always been considered the best in everything he did, and to lose this fight irked him. The power Adley commanded scared him; the Kingdom had blessed him more than Nathan had ever been granted by the Underworld, and he felt belittled. But what angered Nathan more than anything was that they had fought over a woman. A woman he barely knew!

Nathan couldn't understand how or why Chaeli's presence affected him so. He wanted to treat her like a lady and shower her with flowers, while the baser side of him wanted to consume her, taste her skin, feel her wrapped around him. She had thrown him back into the games of the gods' with a renewed determination, and she made him feel alive again. Too long had he been in the shadows.

Anya . . .

He frowned. Taking Chaeli to her had been a mistake, he knew it now. The King would summon Anya and demand to know every detail of Nathan's visit. He was confident the King wouldn't harm her physically – he knew the bastard too well – but Stirm would get pleasure just from seeing her disfigured face. Nathan decided that once they reached Lindor, he would send word to Anya somehow to reassure her and request a reply. As the sun rose, he finally calmed, his emotions in check, the serpents stilled once more.

"Nathan!"

Chaeli strode towards him, a nervous, relieved smile on her face. He stood to meet her. There was colour in her cheeks now, and the dark circles under her eyes were all but gone.

"Where have you been? We're ready to go," she said.

He smiled down and brushed the grass from his trousers. "Let's go then, eh?"

Together they walked towards the inn.

"The sooner we get to Lindor the better, Adders. This is getting *hard*." Sheiva had transformed into horse form and looked disgusted as he stared down at his front hooves. "I mean, what are these? Why *hooves?* Why not feet? I don't *like* horses."

Adley chuckled and bound the packs onto the other, less talkative horses. "Not long, eh Shiv? A day, maybe two at the most if we ride hard. But I'm concerned that we'll push these others too much. These beauties are used to pulling carts and caravans at a steady pace with plenty of halts, not hard riding."

"But I'm having difficulty changing now. I'll have to stay as a horse for the rest of the journey, and it's the size of the beast that's the problem. It's taking too much out of me."

The fae was trembling. Adley soothed him with a brush-down and he whinnied in appreciation.

"So, are you going to talk about last night, or do I have to kick it out of you?"

"Nothing to talk about. Minor disagreement is all."

"Minor disagreement?" echoed the fae incredulously. "*Minor?* I sensed the power. I'm surprised either of you are moving today."

"So am I, to be frank, but I thank the gods. We need to get Chaeli to Lindor. I had no idea Nathan is an *Assaké*. It complicates things. He's a problem we don't need."

"Who is?" asked Chaeli. Adley spun around to face her. Nathan was by her side, looking resigned and tired.

"No one," replied Adley. "The horses are ready, we should go."

Nathan nodded. "We have several days' ride ahead. Have we got provisions?"

"Yes, I purchased enough for the journey. Some of us are prepared this morning."

"Chaeli, you'll ride with me again," said Sheiva, flicking back his mane. Chaeli grinned and mounted, while Nathan took the remaining mare. Together they rode away from the village and towards Lindor.

"I've got some information for you, brother. Are you ready? Are you awake? Are you alive?" Fyn's voice pounded through Dal's aching skull, and he rolled over groaning loudly.

"You can't still be sick? By the gods, how much grape did you drink?"

"Too much. I detest these large court gatherings." He struggled to sit up and peered at Fyn through bloodshot eyes. "Information?"

Well done, Dal, you sound just like your father.

He cursed himself for his lack of manners, but was grateful his brother hadn't seemed to notice.

"That girl you are so desperate to find? I know where she is."

There was a pause and Dal tutted irritably. "Are you going to make me beg?"

"Not at all, I just enjoy witnessing my calm and calculating brother unsettled by a woman."

"Fyn!"

"All right, all right. Rumour has it she's on her way to Mischla with DeVaine, and now the captain's sending an extraction company to bring them back."

Dal poured a glass of water and drank deeply. He thought of her face, her neck and then her legs as they strode away . . .

"What will happen to her once she gets here?"

"I'm not privy to that, brother. I think the King's priest wants her."

"Who? Who is he?"

"No one knows. Stirm's been behaving strangely these past months. Rarely seen in public and refuses all companionship other than the captain."

"What of Chancellor Bren? I've not seen him at court."

"Bren? Gods, Dal, he's been dead for over six months."

Dal sipped the rest of his water slowly, annoyed he had missed something so crucial, while Fyn continued:

"You missed the best bit last night! Ilene threw her drink over the emissary from Velen, and had to be escorted back to her rooms by her own guard. She refused to allow 'the dogs of Stirm' to escort her!"

Dal chuckled. "Looks like I'm fifty gold lucs better off. She'll be in a filthy mood today."

"Better still, her father arrives tonight and Stirm is hosting a private supper for the royals present, no emissaries or barons. Just you pure bluebloods."

"Sometimes I envy you."

"Envy my bastard status? Fyn Miner, Fyn name-of-no-consequence? I think not. I have no lands or titles, so the best I can hope to achieve is a distinguished military career. And that always carries the risk of being short-lived." Fyn was serious now and Dal didn't know how to reply. He squeezed his brother's shoulder and Fyn smiled thinly.

"Father would legitimise you in a heartbeat if he could; it's only his love for my mother that prevents him. I love you as a full blood brother, and I will never see you want for anything."

"And that's why you're my favourite brother."

Dal smirked and moved to his wash basin. "I'm your only brother. Any other news for me? What of DeVaine's sister?"

"She still won't talk. We've salted her food and withdrawn water, but nothing."

Dal stopped washing and frowned. "Such cruel tactics. Are they really necessary? This is the same DeVaine girl that Stirm mutilated, is it not?" Fyn nodded. "Hasn't she suffered enough? These ways of his are despicable – certainly not royal ways. Father would never treat a lady in such a way. He would insist on respect, not beatings and butchery."

"Oh, I agree. She was stunning as well. Tragic the way he cut her."

Dal dressed and escorted his brother into his living room. The apartments were too large for his liking and far too gaudy. "Any movements in relation to the DeVaine girl and I want to know immediately. Is there anyone in the King's Guard that can be bought into my service?"

"There maybe a few. I'll put the feelers out if you like."

"I also want to know more about this emissary from Velen. Why did the captain spend the evening at his side, and what did he say to anger Ilene so?" He paused, deep in thought. "This Maji from Mischla . . . what do we know about him? Find out for me, won't you? Something doesn't feel right."

"Is that your uncanny sixth sense kicking in, or your dislike for the Underworld?"

Dal ignored the sarcasm. "Both. Mischla and Velen representatives working together leaves a bad taste in my mouth."

"Bad taste, eh? Sure that's not the wine from last night?" Fyn grabbed a star fruit and strode to the door, chuckling. "Captain has me on your guard duty now. I expect you to dine at Mina's tomorrow at seven. You will also decide to stay for a few meads until very late, and then you'll want to require the services of a lovely young lady." He winked and left before his older brother could reply.

Eli shifted the black stone from finger to finger, rolling it fluidly across the knuckles, all the time staring into the fire. He hadn't seen the entity within the flames again, and he still had received no reply from Daro. These two things seemed linked by more than the anger they inspired in him.

"Metlina," he shouted, turning his hand and gripping the stone tightly in his palm.

With a flash the copper haired goddess knelt before her master. "My lord."

"Where is Hetes? I grow restless."

"I believe he is in Velen, Master. An opportunity arose."

At these words, Eli's attention was drawn from the fire to his goddess' eyes. "Oh? Tell me more."

"Lover's Kiss has returned."

The Damnable Lord smiled. "Wonderful." With a flick of the wrist, he dismissed Metlina and stared once more into the fire. Now that the truce was well and truly over, he intended to show his brother just how strong the Underworld was. If that meant the mortals of Ibea suffering, all the better. True, the three worlds needed equilibrium, but the time had come for either Daro or Eli to rule all three. Now it was time for the Sherai to rise and the Kitaani thrive.

Eli moved the stone to his lips and lightly kissed the smooth, gleaming surface.

The coolness of the morning had worn off and the heat of the day intensified. The trio had been riding hard for several hours when Chaeli felt a surge of power, as though something had burst inside her; a haze of pain enveloped her body.

"Sheiva, stop . . . please," she whimpered. The fae immediately slowed to a canter and then halted.

"Are you all right?" he asked, but as he finished the sentence Chaeli gagged, then violently emptied her stomach onto the ground. Tears sprang to her eyes.

"Chaeli! Ye gods, what's wrong?" shouted Adley, dismounting and running to her. He pulled her gently from the saddle and steadied her.

"I don't know, I feel awful. My head feels like it wants to explode."

Adley placed the back of his hand on her forehead; she was running a fever again. Frowning, he turned his hand over and rested the palm firmly on her skin. Chaeli winced at his touch, but soon she felt a steady flow of warmth surrounding the pain, reducing it again to a dull thud.

"I can't keep doing this, Chaeli," he warned, a sheen of sweat on his brow. "The charm is getting stronger and will soon be beyond my power."

Nathan looked thoughtfully down from his horse at the crusader. "Your power comes straight from the Kingdom, does it not? If the charm on the choker is stronger than your capabilities, then there are only a few makers."

Chaeli raised her head, grimacing at the pain. "Who?"

"If the charm is too much for him, then it must have been invested with power by a priest of the Underworld . . . or a god."

"No," replied Adley, "not a priest. I can remove charms cast by priests. It's the work of a god."

"Prince Eli. I can't see any other god casting this charm." Nathan slid from his horse and gently took Chaeli's arm.

His touch set a fire within her, and she wanted nothing more than to burn, to rest herself against him and embrace the serpents. She pictured Nathan enfolding her in his arms as she ran her tongue along his serpents . . . The suddenly realisation of what she was thinking struck her like a jet of ice water and she drew back, repulsed, revolted by her own desires. Where had this lust, this unnatural yearning come from?

Nathan pulled back as though slapped, his lips pursed, and he sighed. "I only wished to look at the choker," he said, unable to keep the edge from his voice.

Chaeli nodded. The heat of his body touched her and she became aware that, while sick with pain, she was also sick with longing for him; and it wasn't simply her own desire but something foreign invading her. Nathan moved his head closer to her neck until she could feel his breath. His fingers moved her hair from the nape of her neck.

"The charm is nearly complete, I can sense the darkness."

"Then we don't have much time," said Adley. "We need to keep pressing forward to the library, where there is one there who can help."

"I don't think we'll have enough time. The charm will complete its cycle before nightfall."

"What do you suggest then, *Assaké*?" asked Adley.

Both men could sense her power spiking at Nathan's touch, and her trembling body gave away her desires.

Nathan let go of Chaeli. "I am no longer an *Assaké*, Adley. That life is dead to me and has been for many years." He moved towards his horse, turning his back on them.

"There is another way to get to the library," Sheiva said, shifting his hooves on the dusty road.

"What?"

"Maybe one of Boda's companions can help . . ."

Adley snorted. "I doubt the dragons could interfere in this realm. They're under strict orders not to help either side."

"Daro lifted those orders, Adders . . . remember?"

"How do you suggest we contact these . . . er . . . the dragons?" asked Chaeli. She sat on the grass by the road now, cross-legged and trying to look as though she discussed dragons with fae most days.

"We need to see Boda in the Kingdom . . . um, the only way we can get there is um, if one of us is summoned or if, um . . ." The horse trailed off, scuffing his hoof in the dirt with a bowed head.

"Or if what?" asked Chaeli.

"If one of us dies," finished Adley, staring into the distance.

"What? No, hold on, none of us is *dying!*" She tried to rise, but didn't have the strength. She sank back down on to the soft ground. "There has to be some other way . . . ?"

"Perhaps, but we don't have the time to argue, nor to find other possibilities. I am the immortal here. We can't kill you, nor can we kill Nathan as obviously *he* won't be entering the Eternal Kingdom."

Both Nathan and Chaeli were silent, waiting for the axe to fall.

"Nathan, you will have to kill me."

"No! You can't *kill* him! Nathan, please, you can't kill him!" The pain in Chaeli's voice cut through the assassin.

Nathan nodded, as if it were decided. "He can't kill himself, Chaeli. Suicide is a sin. He wouldn't be able to enter the Kingdom. I must do it." He drew his curved dagger.

"No, not your tainted blade," said Adley. "Use my sword. I want an honest blade to run me through, not something used to spill the blood of innocents."

"I swear to you, no innocent has been killed with this blade. I relinquished all my weapons of darkness when I left my old life."

Adley stared at the man and tried to gauge his honesty. He still didn't feel comfortable around him; the stench of the Underworld lingered, but he knew Nathan's feelings for Chaeli would keep her safe while he visited Boda.

"Nathan, Adley, *please!* There must be another way . . . we have plenty of time." Chaeli gasped as a fresh wave of nausea swept over her.

"No. Quickly, now!" Adley stepped behind the horses. For the sake of her feelings and his own pride, he didn't want Chaeli to see him die. He barely noticed Nathan move. With one clean stroke across the throat, Adley was dead.

"Adley!" cried Chaeli, again struggling to get up. Nathan dropped his dagger by the body and ran to her, but she fought him off, kicking and clawing. "What have you done, you murderer?" she sobbed. "I told you to wait!"

Nathan made no reply, but held her firmly and gently, letting her hit and scratch at him until the pain from the charm became too much. Weeping, she broke free from his arms and rushed behind the horses to Adley. He was gone.

Mr Kerne had her concentrating all the time, and she was exhausted. Really, *really* exhausted. When he wasn't looking, Hana thought she connected with the soldier who sat patiently in front of her. She saw hints of memories that weren't hers, feelings that were strange and unusual; most of the time she was tired and frail, and it was hard connecting with the people brought to her.

Whenever Mr Kerne watched, she was too nervous to channel and she stumbled and stuttered. She couldn't concentrate and his touch unsettled her.

"Harder, seer, earn your keep!" he hissed. He was unhappy today, she could see it in his eyes and sense it; a dark shroud of evil covered his body.

"I–I can't."

He moved more quickly than she could comprehend, and with a sweep of his arm, he sent her flying. Her cheek flamed red and stung. She'd caught him with her nails and felt his blood thick and sticky on her fingers.

Instantly she saw flashes of Mr Kerne whispering with a creature so alarming she couldn't breathe. All his coldness and anger projected into her and she wailed. The beast was a creature from her nightmares, something she saw often and wished she didn't.

"Shut her up!" Kerne shouted at the soldier, who nodded and grabbed Hana. He shushed her and cradled her but she sobbed uncontrollably, burying her head into his chest. He was nice to her, this soldier, and he had a warm aura that soothed her.

"A monster, horrible, horrible monster!" she cried.

Kerne stared at the girl. "What did you say?"

She shook her head, terrified. 'Monster' was the only word she could form. He reached out to her, and she flinched as he traced the bruise on her cheek. He had hurt her and she wanted to shout at him, make him leave her alone, make him never touch her again, stop staring at her the way he did. Make him *stop!*

"My Hana, you do make me angry, you know. If you didn't make me angry, I wouldn't hit you. You understand?"

She nodded meekly; this man confused her. He wasn't well. His energy was all over the place, like a spilt box of marbles. He wasn't good.

"Tell me about the monster."

Her teeth chattered. "Big monster, talking to Mr Kerne, big claws, big eyes." She sobbed again, shaking.

Kerne smiled, his eyes tightening. "Well done, my little Hana. It seems we have learnt how to stimulate your talent."

She closed her eyes and blocked out his hard cold smile. She missed her cell, she missed Danny, but most of all she missed her long-ago freedom. She broke free from the soldier's embrace and ran to her bed. She heard the soldier move to follow, but then Mr Kerne spoke:

"No, leave her be. She's of no use for the rest of the day."

She hid under the covers and prayed for her freedom. Nobody replied. Silence mocked her and she cried. Her cheek hurt, and she was scared. Mr Kerne had been furious with her and she tried so hard to please him. Couldn't he see how hard she tried? Couldn't he see how much it hurt to do what he wanted?

The memory of his blow made her whimper, but it was the monster which really scared her. Mr Kerne shouldn't be talking to monsters, he really shouldn't; he was a soldier. He should be killing monsters and rescuing ladies. She smiled as she remembered the stories her guardians had told her, brave crusaders who fought for the Kingdom, riding dragons, fighting and slaying the monsters and saving the innocent. She adored those stories. Closing her eyes, she tried to picture her guardians, but their faces faded. Sometimes she hated her gift. All she really wanted to see was her true family, her mother and father, whoever they were. But what greeted her instead was darkness. She was blocked from her memories; it was a cruel sentence and Hana couldn't understand how she had offended the gods.

Yet, however hard she tried, she couldn't forget the face of the man who killed Danny, her only friend. She loved Danny. He used to play games with her and brush her hair slowly and so gently, making sure it never hurt. Oh, how he had loved her hair, even though her guardians used to hide it away under shawls and hats. She remembered how she had cried when they had cut it all off in anger. That was the day she'd used her energy to lash out and had smashed all the glass in their house with a scream, just one scream. They never cut her hair again after that, and Danny had always taken care of it when they went out. He always looked after her,– even when the man came, he'd hidden her under the bed and tried to protect her.

The soldier Mr Kerne had sent to Hana reminded her of Danny. She liked Adyam, but he was very quiet and when he talked he stuttered, which made him go red. But he had a big smile, and that made Hana happy. Adyam would smile at her when no one was looking; he never got angry if she couldn't coerce him, and he was so brave. He never cried when Mr Kerne cut him for his blood.

She snuggled down in her bed and went to sleep dreaming of Adyam on a dragon fighting the monsters. The lady he rescued was very small, with hair the colour of blood.

Malo sent gratifying news: the seer was excelling in her art, and Eli was eager to see more of her talents. The seers he had used in the past had burned out quickly, their fragile bodies and minds unable to cope with the pressures of his colourful demands. This one . . . now this one was special. He was intrigued by her, and he needed to know more about her. His General promised to find out her history, but he was restless and impatient and he needed to know *now.*

"Malo," he commanded. There was a short delay, then the demon appeared through a burst of white, kneeling on the floor.

"Master."

"Rise, Malo. What have you discovered about this seer?"

"She has spent the last six years in the dungeons of Stirm's castle. He blames her for the defection of the *Assaké* DeVaine. This particular seer was the target of his final mission, the one he failed before he defected."

"Interesting. Who is she?"

"I have been unable to find further information on her, Master."

"Acceptable. You have been busy. Tell me, how fares my dear, loyal, *pathetic* Stirm?"

Malo chuckled and the grating sound resonated through the room. "That snivelling creature would lick my arse and call it honey if he thought it would gain a flyspeck of your favour."

"Indeed." Eli was thoughtful. "He always has been short-sighted and weak. A stronger man would control all the realms by now."

"The replacement, Kerne, he is truly worthy, Master."

"Truly worthy, you say? Yes, I remember the pit boy from Velen who would honour me with sacrifices of his companions."

"He has been a constant and loyal servant of the Underworld."

"I don't doubt your choice, Malo. He is truly reverential and devout. I especially enjoyed his time in Mischla – some interesting sacrifices, truly inspired."

Malo nodded, pleased that his master was content; it seemed the perfect time to ask a favour.

"Master, my rune grows weak. I respectfully ask you to renew it."

Eli smiled slowly. "Of course, come here." The giant beast fell to his knees in gratitude once more and bowed low, holding out his arm in anticipation. Eli released a fresh rune and Malo grunted in pain.

"Thank you, my prince."

The Damnable Lord stretched lazily. "I have a gift for our most loyal supporter." He opened a box above the mantel and withdrew a collar. "My Empress holds the other half of the pair. Quite beautiful, is it not?" Holding the collar to the light he admired the black crystal sparkling in the glow of the flames.

"Yes, Master."

"This is the stone he must keep with him at all times. Should Kerne lose the stone, or another take hold of it, then the wearer of the collar will no longer obey his commands." Malo nodded in understanding. "Good. You are dismissed."

Dal had spent the day wandering around the city, while Fyn stayed behind. He needed space and time to think. His network brought him interesting news: Kerne had smuggled thirty thousand gold pieces out of the castle in the last forty eight hours. The cases had been loaded straight onto the Maji's ceremonial chariots and been escorted out by their warriors under the cover of darkness; the emissary from Velen had taken some outside the walls. Something was wrong in Trithia and Dal needed to know what.

He realised he had walked all the way back to his humble lodgings near the fish market. He had been in the castle for less than a day but already felt crowded and claustrophobic. He had no privacy there; the captain's spies were all around. Even Dal recognised those apparently unconcerned strollers and loiterers. He could only trust Fyn and Ilene, both as ignorant as they were young. He couldn't leave Trithia and return home though, not until he had seen the Dresne girl again. He needed to be free of her, needed to know why she haunted his thoughts, or if there was something else.

As he turned and headed back to the castle, he overheard snippets of a conversation.

". . . Malo visited him last night" ". . . war . . ." "I know, it's madness!" "weapon . . ."

Glancing up, Dal saw two soldiers from the King's Guard walking back towards their garrison, talking in low voices.

Malo. He knew that name, but where from? Dal tried to jog his memory but nothing came. He would have to instruct his agents again – more coin, more complaints from his father. At the castle gates, Fyn stood deep in conversation with a pretty young maid. The girl laughed and touched his arm; Fyn to winked and whispered in her ear. He looked up at Dal and winked at him too, then held up his hand. Dal nodded, standing back and watching his sibling. He envied Fyn his confidence with women, it was something that didn't come naturally to him and he'd never found a woman he was interested in courting. Well, until he'd met Chaeli Dresne. He even liked saying her name to himself.

Fyn bid goodbye to the girl with a pinch on her bottom, then strode over to Dal. "Apologies, brother, just sorting out my bed for the night. The barracks are awfully cold."

"Indeed. Kingdom forbid you should spend the night alone." Dal grinned back at his brother and indicated the castle. "Anything of note?"

"Not yet, King Cobey is approaching and should be here by dusk. He's brought most of his court with him. I think this is the real thing, Dal. He intends to marry her off to Stirm."

"Not unless I request her hand first. It might be enough for Uncle to reconsider. Ilene and I could have a long engagement and perhaps come to an agreement."

"Ilene would rather chop off your cock and eat it for breakfast! There's no way that woman will ever marry. Besides, what about this nymphette of yours, this Chaeli?"

"I barely know her. And my loyalty is to family." Dal didn't want to talk about Chaeli, but he fingered the ring in his pocket. "What of this Maji and the emissary from Velen?"

Fyn smiled at the unsubtle change of subject. "The Maji has left. He sends his regards and claims you swore to attend the Grand Maji's naming ceremony in the spring. The emissary from Velen disappeared last night after the gathering. His entire entourage has gone as well. Sometimes it's hard being your brother, Dal. No one tells me anything. They actually seem to think I might pass it on to you."

"I appreciate every morsel of information. Now, shall we see how Ilene is?"

"I don't have my armour! I'm not ready."

They heard her shouts before they reached her door and the brothers exchanged puzzled looks.

"Oh, for the love of the gods, Keri! No, I will not wear that dress tonight. I'll look like a gutter whore!"

Dal knocked on the door and called out, "I've come to collect my winnings."

He grinned at Fyn and opened the door. Ilene wore a pair of hunting breeches and a scruffy shirt. Her elfin-cropped hair was sticking up in peaks and she was clearly flustered. Hands on hips, she glared at him.

"I could have been naked, Dal! Wait till you're invited before entering a lady's chambers. Besides, you shouldn't be here, there will be a scandal. Two ladies alone with two men!".

"Naked? Now there would be a sight," Fyn chipped in brightly. Ilene scowled at him and he dropped his gaze to the floor.

"Stop being so ratty and hand over your gold, Princess."

Growling, Ilene stalked to her desk and withdrew a small pouch. She threw it over to Dal.

"Going to count it, Kee Dala?"

"No need, Princess, I trust you." He stared at her. "I think you'd look rather lovely in that dress. It would distract from your scowling face and terrible hair." Fyn snorted, then quickly moved to the corner of the room out of Ilene's reach.

"You be quiet or I'll make *you* wear the dress!" she snapped, pointing at Fyn. She flopped onto her sofa. "Keri, please bring Prince Kee Dala, Fyn and me some refreshments."

"What's wrong?" Dal asked, leaning against the door frame. She looked up at him, then over to Fyn, who was more interested in gazing after Keri as she hurried away.

"No, Fyn. Keri is off-limits. I want *some* maidens left in my service." She turned back to Dal and rolled her eyes.

"Don't change the subject. What's wrong?"

"Father is nearly here. He demands I wear a dress tonight and act 'with decorum, humility, and good grace'." She huffed. "Don't I always?" She tossed a roll of parchment over to Dal. "Read it. He intends to marry me off. Me!"

Dal grabbed the scroll from the floor and scanned it quickly. "Why?" Dal was genuinely perplexed. His uncle adored Ilene and had pandered to her every whim. He had taught her swordplay, *ashanasha*, politics, and points of sail. Most of all, he had shown her how to be independent and not rely on anyone.

"I know, it makes no sense. I never thought he would send me here under false pretences and then spring it on me." Keri returned and placed a tray of fresh fruits, a bowl of cream, and cool tea on the low table by her mistress.

"My offer is still open, cousin." Dal grabbed an apple and bit into it absentmindedly.

"And my answer is still no. I can't marry you."

He paced the room, thinking. Both Fyn and Ilene watched him expectantly. But Dal felt helpless; he didn't know what game his uncle was playing, and it unnerved him.

"Sometimes we can't control our destiny. Mine is in the hands of the gods now. If Father makes me marry Stirm, I'll make the beast miserable and live up to my ice maiden reputation. I'd rather a die an old maid than lay with him."

"Such a waste," murmured Fyn under his breath, but Ilene heard him and glared.

Dal nodded. "I don't want to see you with someone like Stirm. You deserve better than that."

"What's wrong with you, Dal? Are you turning into a romantic all of a sudden?"

Fyn looked up. "My brother mopes for a woman. An invisible woman who seems nothing more than a ghost or a dream."

Dal blushed and threw Fyn a dark look. Ilene caught the look and cackled. "Oh, my sweet cousin! Tell me more."

"It's nothing. I met a woman in the market and she caught my attention, but she disappeared and I've not found her yet. It's nothing."

"Are you coming to the supper this evening, then? Please don't leave me alone with my father and Stirm." The vulnerability in her voice was clear.

"Of course I'll be there. Are there any other royals hiding in the palace I'm unaware of?"

She shook her head. "I'm sorry to be a bore gentlemen, but I really want to spend the next few hours alone before father arrives. I have to control my temper and relax before I explode."

"Will Ilene survive this evening, Dal?" Fyn whispered as soon as they were outside the door.

"Ilene is a strong woman. The strongest I know. She'll survive."

"Well?"

The demon sat in front of the fire and the freshness in the air evaporated. The putrid smell of rotting flesh and blood permeated every pore on Kerne's body; it excited him, but the silent arrival of Malo also unnerved him. Still, he never let his cool exterior slip.

"It progresses well, my lord. She can coerce and possess the subject for in excess of thirty minutes. She has not yet mastered the art of manipulating their thoughts, but I anticipate results shortly." In truth, Kerne was impressed by Hana's grasp of her talent. Although her powers had bloomed late for a seer, she was extraordinarily powerful and needed only the smallest amount of blood to channel.

Malo eyed Kerne doubtfully. "Will she be ready in time?"

"Yes, my lord."

"And what of the other girl? Our *Assaké*'s sister?" The demon's huge eyes were focussed on the fire, and he appeared distracted and restless. Kerne noted that he rubbed his left forearm with his right claw obsessively.

"In the dungeons, my lord, sixth level, guarded by my most trusted men. None outside their circle know she is there."

"Good," the demon murmured. "Our master will be delighted."

"But what use is the girl to the prince? Why not let me deal with the problem?"

"No, the master has plans for her." He did not elaborate, and Kerne nodded in acceptance. It was not his place to question his prince.

"I have a gift for you." Malo extended a claw and beckoned Kerne over. "This is from Eli himself."

Kerne knelt at the feet of the demon. At Malo's signal he held out his hands and a black stone dropped onto his palm. The coldness spread through Kerne's fingers as he turned the stone over and over. The demon handed him a black collar, carved and decorated; it glittered like black ice.

"An obsidian collar. You will be able to control whoever wears the collar through the stone. They will become your slave." Kerne backed away from the general, gripping the stone to his chest. His mind reeled with the possibilities; he could control Stirm through such a thing and the seer would no longer be required.

"The prince is eager for the seer to progress. You will make this your highest priority. I will ensure that Stirm does not interfere."

Kerne bowed his head. "Thank you, my lord."

"If this fails, Kerne, you will still keep the collar," the demon said, pus from his mouth oozing down his chin as he flashed a rotten-toothed grin. "However, you may not like the way it feels around your neck."

"What have you done now, Adley?"

"My lady," he croaked, opening his eye. He almost cursed at the painfully bright light.

"What happened?" The goddess placed her cool hand on his head. Looking into her eyes, Adley saw nothing but beauty and love, and for a moment was overwhelmed by it. The events leading up to his death came out in a rush, and the goddess drummed her fingertips on the altar where Adley lay. She sighed and said, "I

239

must consult with Daro, but you must not tarry. I am eager that you get back to Chaeli and this Nathan quickly."

"Yes, my lady, but, forgive me, why the hurry?"

Penella hesitated and her eyes suddenly became guarded. "I won't lie to you, protector. The Father of Ages is gone. We don't know where and have no control any longer. Without him, a minute here is a minute in the mortal realm."

Adley moved to inspect his throat in the mirror behind the altar. Not a blemish; a shame the same couldn't be said of the brutal scar Malo had inflicted. As Penella spoke he turned and faced her. "Gone? Where would the Great Father go?"

"It is not known, but we can't feel his presence or power in the Pool." The goddess moved closer, her fruit and honey scent tickling his nostrils. "Have you managed to control your desires?" she whispered, catching him off guard.

Adley tensed. "There are no desires to control, my lady."

"Do not lie to me. I am the Goddess of Love. You think I can't tell?"

"I am in control," he conceded quietly. The humiliation of his predicament washed over him; now he even lied to the gods.

"Perhaps I can help you," she offered, laying a hand on his arm.

"How?" he asked, shifting his body slightly so the goddess removed her hand. The touch of her beautiful fingers flustered him, caressing without moving.

"Chaeli is young, and not in control of her emotions. She is inexperienced and needs guidance, a certain . . . expertise to point her towards love."

Adley slowly turned from the mirror and faced Penella. The silence between them screamed at him, and his blood pounded in his ears. "I'm not sure I understand what you're saying."

"Adley, Protector of the Eternal Kingdom," – she used his title deliberately – "I am offering reciprocation of the feelings you have for Chaeli."

Clearing his throat, Adley shook his head. "You overwhelm me with your offer, I don't deserve such generosity. But if Chaeli is to love me, then I need her to love me freely, without interference or persuasion." The words tumbled out; he knew if he didn't refuse immediately, then he would accept and be forever damned.

To have Chaeli's love would mean more to him than anything; he pictured her in his arms, imagined the warmth of her body against his, the feel of her breasts against his chest, her lips working down his neck. His dragon moved.

"As you wish," she replied. "It can be painful, loving someone from afar and watching them fall in love with another." Sadness filled the room, thick and cloying. "Chaeli and her champion await your return." Penella left quickly before Adley could reply.

He stared once more into the mirror at his scars and imperfections, the consequences of war, and it was like seeing them with fresh eyes; he felt repulsed and vain. He wished his nose was a little straighter, his hair not so wild. He should be taller and broader. Anger started to gnaw at his chest, both at his appearance and pride, and so he recited his vows over and over again until he was numb.

He strode through the halls to the courtyard. The Kingdom was eerily quiet. No Beings could be seen, and as he walked down to the gates, he realised that the Kingdom seemed to have wilted. The flowers were dying, the trees and bushes brown and lifeless. Birds sang, but not with the joy and love to which he was accustomed. He reached Boda and even the dragon seemed dull, his scales no longer gleaming in the sunlight.

"Boda!"

The dragon lifted his head from his paws and opened one giant eye. "What brings you to me, Adley? Normally you like to bypass the gates and the Kingdom's gatekeeper. I once again feel honoured to be in your presence, oh great one." The dragon closed his eye and laid his head back down.

"Boda, please, I understand you are angry with me. But I need your help."

The dragon didn't move. He was either asleep or pretending to be.

"Boda, I need your help, *Chaeli* needs your help. I must get her to Lindor. Today."

"Well, you best get back to her then! How can you get her to Lindor when you are here with me?"

Adley stepped closer and ran his hands over his hair in exasperation. "Boda, I need the help of the dragons or I can't get her to Lindor by tonight. On horseback, we are at least two, if not three, days away. I fear she will be dead by tonight. You are my last resort."

Boda opened both eyes and stared at Adley; the Protector couldn't gauge his reaction. "What of Sheiva? Can the fae not transport you?" The dragon's voice held no emotion nor hint of how he felt.

"Sheiva has had to transform too much in recent days. Please, Boda, for the Kingdom, for Ibea."

"We dragons paid dearly once before for interfering in the mortal realm, and many of my brothers and sisters were lost – some still are lost in the darkness. Tell me, protector, why should we help you?"

"Because you are honourable. Because whilst you are angry at me, you know it is the right thing to do. All treaties are off, old friend. If we fail, if *I* fail, then what do you think will happen to your kind? Please."

The guardian sighed, knocking Adley to the ground with the pressure of his breath. "Once you return, be patient. I will send Nitayla. She is a hatchling and very keen and brave. She will take you to Lindor. Be warned though, should any harm come to her I will hold you personally responsible! We dragons value our females above all else. If I could send you a male I would, but Nitayla is the only dragon within travelling distance who is a fast flyer. Honour her as you would honour me."

"I will protect Nitayla as though she were my own daughter."

A deep chuckle rumbled through the ground. "That I do not doubt, Adley. But remember, she is a female with a sharp tongue, so you be careful too, old friend."

With a hug of a claw, Adley thanked his friend and returned to the mortal realm, praying that the portal would place him close enough to Chaeli and that the time disparity wouldn't be too great. At the back of his mind was the question which occupied most in the Eternal Kingdom: where had the Great Father gone?

Chaeli sat shivering, weak and ill. How could Nathan have killed Adley so callously? It had frightened her how little he had protested, and his speed was phenomenal, unnatural. Sheiva had transformed back into a cat and curled himself tighter on her lap. The warm weight comforted her, but it was a small consolation, for his slow breathing and lack of purring worried her. The fae was drained and exhausted.

The midday sun beat down, but did nothing to quell her shivering and the cold clamminess of her skin. Nathan stood by the horses; he had said nothing since Adley had gone and he had left her to cry and grieve alone.

Chaeli truly hated him for what he had done and couldn't bear to look at him. After everything he had told her about renouncing the Underworld, he hadn't hesitated over killing Adley. Biting her bottom lip hard she willed tears not to fall anew. She had wanted to believe him; he had done so much for her, welcomed her into his life and, supposedly, shared himself with her. The frightened thoughts whirled around her mind. Nathan was still working for the Underworld; he was a spy, he might be her enemy. He belonged to her father.

She threw him an anxious glance where he still stood by the horses, readjusting their saddles and leathers. Scrambling to her feet, the cat tumbled to the floor.

Nathan turned, eyes narrowed, lips in a thin line. Chaeli backed further away, terrified.

"What's wrong?"

She said nothing, not trusting herself to speak.

"Chaeli, please, what's wrong?" He stepped closer, and with each step he took, she took two backwards. "Chaeli . . ."

"Stop it! Don't talk to me." Now the tears came. "You murdered him without a second thought! I believed you, I thought you were better than that. I thought you had renounced the Underworld, but you're nothing but a murderer."

Nathan shook his head quickly and rubbed his face with his palm. "Chaeli, you know nothing, you are ignorant in the ways of the churches. Adley isn't dead. He's an immortal crusader, your protector by name and right. He is in the Kingdom with the gods as we speak. Grow up, little girl! Things are not so black and white!"

Chaeli jumped at the change in his tone; she could sense an underlying anger, pushing and prodding at her core.

"Adley is not dead, trust me. That man holds the love and respect of the Kingdom's gods, and they won't let him die. He is an immortal."

Chaeli stopped backing away. Her skin warmed and a soft breeze enveloped her. "*Trust him,*" whispered the voice, the same voice she had heard in Danven's carriage. That voice had helped her then and so, for now, she must trust it.

"What was that?" He drew his dagger and adopted a fighting stance. "Did you feel that?"

"It was nothing, just the wind," she said, a little too quickly. Nathan narrowed his eyes and slowly sheathed his dagger, his face full of disbelief.

"I'm . . . sorry. I don't understand a lot of what is happening to me. It all feels like a nightmare."

244

Nathan smiled tentatively and beckoned Chaeli back towards the horses and Sheiva. "Come on, let's wait for Adley."

She walked to him and allowed him to put an arm over her shoulders. Her stomach contracted at his touch. She was embarrassed by her outburst, and her distrust in him. She tried to blame it on her fever, but a small part of her was still unsure.

"You two sorted out your differences?" the cat enquired without even opening his eyes.

Chaeli smiled sheepishly. "I think so. I was being stupid and over-reacting. Do you know how long it will be before Adley returns?"

"Not long at all," said a familiar voice.

Both Nathan and Chaeli stared as Adley strode towards them, smiling.

"Thank Elek, you're all right!" Chaeli shook free of Nathan's hold and ran to throw her arms around his neck. She barely knew the man, but was so connected and comfortable in his presence now; they had shared energy.

Adley returned her hug, squeezing tightly and breathing in her scent; for a moment he regretted turning down Penella's offer but, as he opened his eyes and locked his gaze with Nathan's, he knew he had done the right thing.

"Good to see you, Adders! Dragons are going to help then, eh?" The cat stood and stretched.

"Yes, a female hatchling will be joining us soon to fly us to Lindor."

"Female, eh?" Sheiva's interest was sparked. "Didn't think the old lizard would send one of his ladies."

"Apparently she is the closest, and the fastest flyer in this region, although I have been warned she can be a handful."

"All dragons are a handful, the females are just a little more . . . fiery." The fae snickered at his own joke.

"Any idea how long she'll be, Adley?" asked Chaeli, tilting her head and forcing a smile. She was pale and clammy, sweat soaking through her top, eyes bloodshot.

Adley's eyes lingered on the choker, which seemed to shine; the words were deep enough to see, though he still couldn't read them. "Not long. Perhaps you should sleep for a while." He smiled, nodding to a soft patch of moss just off the road. "We'll wake you as soon as Nitayla arrives."

She hesitated and opened her mouth to speak, but thought better of it. Resigned to rest, she curled up and closed her eyes. The warmth of the little cat and his gentle purrs soothed her into sleep.

"Well met, Uncle." Dal smiled as he greeted King Cobey in the traditional Porton way, grasping his arms firmly.

"Kee Dala, you look more and more like your mother each time I see you," boomed his uncle, his pearl earring glinting in the sun as they walked together from the stables to the castle.

"I'm sorry for pouncing on you so soon, but I have to ask what brings you to Trithia. If it is what I fear, I beg you to reconsider."

The King glanced at Dal with ill-concealed curiosity. "Bold words, Dal. Very bold and very inappropriate. It is not the place of a subject of Algary to criticise or question the King of Porton."

"Forgive me, Uncle, I apologise. I love Ilene like a sister."

"I want the best for my daughter and she needs security and protection. Two things I can't guarantee for her always. Now is not the time to question my judgement. Ilene means more to me than anything, and I would do anything to keep her safe."

Dal did not reply and understood the underlying message in his uncle's words. He thought back to the smuggled gold and the clandestine meeting in the night. "What dowry does Ilene bring with her?"

246

"One hundred thousand gold lucs, a fleet of twenty fully crewed ships and my fealty." His uncle spoke quickly and quietly. Dal whistled and looked up at his uncle. The big man, once a feared warrior, looked worried, and for the first time Dal saw just how old he was. His beard was now flecked with white and his usually carefree face heavily lined.

"Should my father be worried?"

"Things are moving quickly, Dal, and not in the favour of the gods we love and worship. Choose your friends and allies carefully, my boy." They walked in silence the rest of the way.

"King Cobey, Trithia welcomes Porton with open arms and an open heart." Kerne bowed graciously and presented the elite of the King's Guard, who saluted with a display of unity more threatening than welcoming.

"Porton would gladly accept the love of Trithia, Captain, should Trithia have embraced us as brothers, allies, and equals. I expected your master, not his servant." The King's voice was cold and clipped. The captain tensed, but remained courteous.

"Your Highness, King Stirm awaits you in his private apartments. Alas, he has been unwell these past days, and he begs for understanding."

Dal frowned, watching Kerne closely. No one appeared to have seen Stirm for over a week, and all the visitors from other realms knew something wasn't right. Kerne looked at Dal and nodded respectfully. "Prince Kee Dala, King Stirm is anxious to make your acquaintance this evening. He is eager to discuss a trade agreement involving your mines and our crops."

Dal offered a thin smile. "I shall gladly discuss a treaty with the King this evening, but I will be unable to agree to anything without first discussing the matter with my father."

"Your Royal Highness, let me escort you to your royal apartments. I have ensured that you are next to your daughter."

"How fares my Ilene, Captain?"

"She is well. Always charming, though her independence shines through."

"Independence." Cobey smiled. "How very diplomatic of you, Captain." He glanced at Dal wryly as they made their way towards the royal apartments.

Cobey left his guard by the stables and strode confidently through the halls. His large build dominated the space around them and he carried himself with sureness and a sense of power. Dal envied him, though he wasn't sure that such confidence was wise.

Chapter Seven

THE DARKNESS SCARED her, reminding her of the weeks she had spent blinded and bandaged whilst healing. The gods had visited her then and she had walked in the Kingdom and communed with creatures, spirits, and fae so majestic the pain of her injuries had dissolved in awe and her heart was soothed by the blessing of merely existing in that place.

This time Anya was alone in the dungeon. She tried to pray, but only the rats answered; they visited her often and she caught them staring so intently she truly believed they knew what was to come. Her back no longer hurt, she had blocked out that pain long ago, but nothing could ease the despair of isolation. She hung against the wall, shackles digging into her wrists, biting the wounded flesh.

They had come for her soon after Nathan left. They burst in and overpowered her, dragging her from her home to this place. Deep down she had known they would, known that this time there would be no forgiveness; Stirm was unyielding and merciless. She had refused to give up Nathan before and her face had been the punishment, this time she expected to lose more than surface beauty. But seeing Nathan again had been worth it – he was her brother and the only family she knew. She would die to keep him safe. A small part of her hoped he would come for her, but as time rolled by, she resigned herself to her fate. This cell would be the last place she could call home.

"Is she still alive?"

Anya struggled to lift her head to see the speaker.

"Yes Cap'n."

"Good. Let her down. Bathe her, feed her, and clothe her. Once she's presentable, bring her to my office."

Two guards entered and loosened the shackles. Gasping with pain and relief, she fell to the floor; the movement opened the whip cuts on her back, fresh blood seeping out and trickling over the wounds. Dazed, she fretted over the thought of infection.

"Get up!" snarled a guard, kicking her in the stomach.

She yelped and tried to push herself up, but her arms buckled and she slumped down.

"I said, get up!" Another kick.

"Leave it! Can't you see she can't?" This second voice was gentler, gentle as the cold hands that took hold of her arm and helped her to stand. Still it hurt, and though he tried to be careful, even the slightest pressure caused her agony.

"Thank you," she croaked, squinting to see his face.

"Don't thank me, miss, I'm no saviour," he replied with bitterness in his voice as he guided her to the door. Anya tried to focus, but the light from the candles was too harsh and made her eyes water.

She was taken along flagstone corridors into the mess room where she could smell food, sweat, and drink; after the barrenness of her dungeon cell, the odours and sounds overloaded her senses and she began to shake.

"The light isn't so bright here, miss," the gentle voice whispered.

Anya opened her eyes a crack and made out the shapes of tables and chairs; slowly her eyes adjusted and she opened them fully, fighting against the dry, crusted mucus around her eyelids.

The voices fell silent. Soldiers stopped their socialising and stared at her. She heard her name murmured several times, but couldn't pinpoint the source. Humiliation ebbed into her; she used to be friends with many of these men, but when Nathan defected, she was cast out. The very men she had laughed with, gambled with, and healed had dragged her from home, beaten her, violated her, and imprisoned her. The whispers became louder, but no man dared to speak up. She could feel their eyes on her.

"Take me out of here, please," she begged. "Please, someone."

The gentle guard coughed. "I'll take you to our bath house, miss. I'll make sure no one enters." Anya touched his arm. She couldn't bring herself to look him in the face; for the first time in a long while her scars embarrassed her.

"Get lost, Small, you prick!" the man who had kicked her jeered. "*I'll* watch Miss Anya."

Anya recognised the lust in his voice, and gripped the guard's arm a little tighter.

"Perhaps I should tell the captain you kicked her?" suggested the gentle voice.

The other grunted and spat on the ground, then turned away. Small guided her from the room.

"I've no clothes to offer you other than a shirt and trousers, but I did manage to get some soap and salts," he said. Anya slowly lifted her head, her damp and filthy hair hanging like rat tails. She looked at Small. He was young, with a boyish face. He looked at her scars and frowned. "He was wrong to do that to you, miss. The King, I mean." He passed her the package of clothes and soap.

"He is the King. His word is law," she croaked.

"That just makes it law. Doesn't make it right, miss." He turned and went to the far end of the bath house, where he stood with his back turned. "I promise I won't peek, miss."

Anya removed her dress, which fell to the ground heavily, caked in filth and blood. The air hit her skin and her injuries felt like they were on fire. She staggered over to the bath, clenched her teeth and climbed in, gasping at the pain.

"Everything all right, miss?" called the guard nervously.

"Yes, thank you," she replied through her teeth, examining her arms and legs. The injuries were minor but several looked as though they were infected, the water too dirty to cleanse them. She couldn't see her back.

"Can you help me?"

"Miss?"

"Can you help me, please, I need to know what my back looks like."

The guard crept over, keeping his eyes averted.

"What does it look like?" she asked in as clinical a manner as she could muster.

"Um . . . it's not good, miss."

"Describe it to me, in as much detail as possible." He noted fifteen separate lash marks. Each had reopened, and from his description, she knew at least four needed stitches. "Touch the skin. Is it hot or overly inflamed?"

His fingertips gently touched her back and she winced. "Sorry, miss, sorry. No, it feels warm, but not hot."

"Thank you."

The guard stood awkwardly and returned to the other side of the room. Anya washed and scrubbed her body and hair, her teeth gritted throughout. She had no concept of time and didn't know how long she had been in the dungeon. Not that it mattered; all that mattered was he had escaped. She prayed for her brother.

Dressing in the clothes the guard had provided, she was grateful that they swamped her small frame.

"Need to get you some food and drink, miss, then the captain wants to see you."

Anya nodded. "Will you be with me?" She didn't need the physical support any longer, but she didn't want to be alone.

"As long as the captain allows it," he replied.

She followed him back into the mess room. This time she looked around, recognising several faces; when she caught their eyes they looked away, ashamed. She pitied them – they only followed orders. The ones who didn't look away stared at her scars, and she saw a mixture of fear, disgust, and fascination on their faces.

"Someone get Miss Anya some food! Or are you all just mannerless pigs?"

"Get it yourself!" someone shouted back.

"Yeah, bugger off, Small!" called another to a chorus of laughter.

"May Hetes rot your cocks!" shouted Small. "Begging pardon, miss."

She smiled and lowered her head again. He took her arm and sat her at an empty table. The cook came and slopped a serving of foul smelling stew and over-cooked potatoes into a bowl with an indifferent shrug. Small pushed it gently to Anya, followed by a glass of water and a tankard of watered-down mead. "Didn't know what you'd prefer," he explained, sitting beside her.

"Thank you."

She ate slowly, and in silence, wanting to delay the inevitable meeting for as long as possible. When the soldiers realised she wasn't going anywhere, and that she wasn't reacting to their taunts, they turned their backs and ignored her. In the cell, she had fully believed she was going to die there, but now, freshly bathed, fed, and clothed, there seemed a tiny chance she might live – unless this was merely a cruel trick, one more stage in her punishment.

The price for her life was Nathan's life. She knew that, but she wouldn't betray him. If the sudden change in treatment was a way to win her gratitude and support, they would be sorely disappointed. Thinking back to her time with Stirm, even now she had fond memories. He had treated her like his queen even though she was only Anya DeVaine, daughter of no one. When Nathan had first introduced her to him, she had thought him a handsome man, though aloof and arrogant. After their meeting, the King summoned her to court and she was proclaimed his ward. She had never realised Stirm wanted her, and looking back now, her naïveté embarrassed her. The constant dances, the gowns, the education, it had all been for his gain. He wanted to be envied, and he would have the perfect courtesan.

But Anya wasn't under any illusion anymore. She knew now he had never intended to make her Queen. He wanted to own her, rule her, never allow her to be his equal. She chewed the gristly food slowly, thinking back to the moment her life had changed.

Standing before her screaming, ranting King, she had trembled and cowered. She was just sixteen years old, but he beat her bloody, and with each punch and kick, he denounced her brother. When she could take no more, he took out his black dagger and sliced her face. The memory of the blood, and the smell of copper, the soaking of her skin still haunted her. On the final stroke, he declared Nathan an outlaw, and the DeVaine family traitors. Everything Nathan had worked so hard for was taken: their home, lands, horses, all gone.

He wasn't finished with Anya though. When she was healed, he had her brought to his chambers where he stole the last scrap of innocence from her. For some reason, her scars excited him and she couldn't fight him off. The last time she had seen Stirm, he had publicly proclaimed her 'forbidden', and any man seen alone with her would be executed.

"Are you ready, Miss Anya?" Small asked. He had stood and was waiting patiently for her. She nodded, and he guided her out of the mess and up into the tower. She recognised the route: she was going to Nathan's old office. When they arrived, Small knocked on the once-familiar door and waited.

"Come."

He paused and allowed Anya entry first. He held the heavy oak door open for her, and she hesitated a moment before walking through and looking fondly around the room. Very little had changed: the King's banner still decorated the chimney breast and the coats of arms of the former captains circled the room. She noted with a pang that the DeVaine family arms had been removed.

"Sit." The captain indicated a heavy chair by the fire. She lowered herself gingerly into the seat, careful not to allow her back to make contact with the chair.

"Do you know why you are here, Miss DeVaine?" The well-groomed man before her was impeccably dressed, his bright red tunic fit perfectly and his black trousers were immaculate. But the way he held himself and his hard exterior chilled her. Anya answered with a small shrug. The captain held her gaze and smiled. "Let's not play games, Miss DeVaine, I know your brother entered the city, I know he visited you, and I know he was in the company of a young woman. What I don't know is where they went. That's all I want from you, Miss DeVaine. To know where they went."

She looked away, staring into the fire. "I don't know. He wouldn't tell me."

"I see. That makes things very difficult, Miss DeVaine. I have been instructed to find your brother at all costs, and I always follow my orders. I always succeed." Kerne moved to the fire. Standing by the chair he, too, looked into the flames. "I think perhaps I have a solution." He strode back to his desk and opened one of the drawers to produce a black band. He paused, weighing it in his hand and looking thoughtfully at her. "My dear, I really would like to know where he is, without having to resort to extreme measures."

"Captain, I can't tell you something that I don't know. And I don't know where Nathan has gone."

"What about his young travelling companion, the girl? Where is she?"

"She disappeared the night Nathan did. I have no idea what happened to her."

The captain walked back to Anya with the band his hand. "Time is being wasted. I dislike waste." The band opened.

She could see it was a collar and instinctively pulled away, gasping as her back hit the chair. Using her moment of disorientation from the pain, he reached forward and snapped the collar around her neck, muttering the words of his holding spell. The stench of the Underworld assailed Anya, and a deep and thrilling agony washed from her neck down through her entire body.

"What have you done to me?" she gasped, scratching at the collar.

"You have done this to yourself. I tried to be a reasonable man. I will have your brother's location, Miss DeVaine. Once I have your brother, you may go. Until then, you belong to me."

Anya fought the collar's grip, tearing her nails to the quick in her desperate attempts to be free, but she could barely feel the pain through the torture of her own panic. What had this monster done? Inwardly, she tried to pray to the Kingdom, but a searing pain shot through her as though in response, and she screamed.

"Ah yes, Miss DeVaine, a side effect, I'm afraid. There will be no praying to the Kingdom whilst you wear the obsidian."

"I told you," she rasped, "I don't know where my brother is. Take this off me!"

"Let me explain the collar to you, Miss DeVaine. It was a gift from my prince, and it allows the owner of the collar to control the wearer. Soon you will not be able to defy any request that I make of you. You will do anything, tell me anything . . . including the location of your brother and his little friend." He paused, his cold blue eyes drinking in her pain, delight in his gaze. Though she could barely think, she realised it was not her pain but the power that pleased him.

"So I ask again, where is Nathan and the girl?"

Anya gritted her teeth as the collar burned and itched. She would never tell this devil where Nathan was, *never!*

"Velen, he went to Velen!" Instantly she regretted this attempt at deception as the collar tightened and she felt the oily slip of the Underworld ooze around in her blood, contaminating her. "Lindor, he went to Lindor." The words slipped out before she could stop them.

"Now that wasn't so difficult, was it? What about the girl?"

"She went with him." What was she doing? Why could she not fight this compulsion? Each time she fought it, the Underworld tightened its grip. "Please, take this off, I've told you what I know!" She began to sob, pleading without restraint. She closed her eyes, ashamed that she handed her brother over so easily.

"Not yet. I'm sure there will be plenty more questions for you." The captain sat at his desk and started to write. Without glancing up he summoned Small. "Take Miss DeVaine to my quarters. Ensure the room is guarded at all times."

Anya panicked as Small approached. She saw the unhappiness on his face, but he was a soldier of the King's Guard and he had to obey.

"Oh, before I forget," came the cool voice again, "you will not scream, you will not run, you will not attempt to harm yourself in any way. Do you understand?"

"Yes," she whispered.

Eli's eyes closed. He could sense Chaeli, her life force almost within his grasp. Excitement rushed through his soul as adrenalin pumped around his corporeal body. He was alive, he was *strong!* He focussed harder on his child, his daughter. He wanted to see her, wanted to see what he had created with Amelia, and know her with these human senses. A dark expanse surrounded him, cold and thick. He recognised the tang of a charm in the air and was pleased that it held steady even in the dream state.

He moved quickly, the foggy darkness giving way to dawn mist. It recognised its master, and with recognition came submission; the mist cleared. There she was, curled on the ground, sleeping. But she looked nothing like Amelia. Disappointment mixed with anger oozed from him like black oil. With them came a small, puzzling amount of relief.

Kneeling, he brushed the hair from her face. She wasn't ugly, but she certainly wasn't beautiful. No king would battle for her hand. She could do with losing some weight, too; fleshy folds ringed her stomach, and her adolescent face was soft, with little definition. She had his colouring though, dark black hair, straight

257

and glossy, though she was curled up, he could see she was tall. He tilted his head.

Am I supposed to feel attachment to her? Fatherly love?

He tried to summon up an emotion, any emotion, but could sense none that might be associated with kinship; certainly nothing like the feelings he had once held for Daro or Amelia. She was just a tool, a means to an end, something with which he could destroy his brother and the sanctimonious Eternal *loving* Kingdom.

It had been *her* face he had seen in the fire, for she had the ability to meld with flames; the thought caused a flicker of apprehension. If she mastered her control, the gods of the three worlds should be watchful in her presence. He placed his hands around her throat, the warmth of the silver reacting to his burning ice touch. The charm was strong. Good. When she was dead, he would intervene and stop her entry to the Kingdom. The hellions would take her body to the Underworld, and he would guide her soul back to him. When she was dead, he could work at obtaining loyalty and support, possessing her completely.

He removed his hands from her skin and wiped her sweat on the ground, not wanting to sully himself with the earthly smell of her. He stood and backed away into the returning mist.

Slowly Eli opened his eyes, so *that* was his daughter. The dream touch of her was encouraging, and she clearly had power – much like the power of his gods, but at the same time a power that radiated with something he couldn't touch or comprehend, though there was a strange familiarity. He touched the black stone. It was nearly full; she would be dead by nightfall. Cruel pleasure filled him; his brother would be heartbroken at the thought of Chaeli dying, and his vision of Daro broken with yet more grief made him shiver in anticipation of some greater ecstasy.

He rolled up the sleeves to his robe, his powerful arms covered in ugly, vicious runes. Black and dark, they wormed under his skin.

"Metlina," he called.

Almost instantly the goddess appeared, her copper curls dancing. "My lord." She knelt at his feet and kissed the pale robe reverently, the Sheeman snow wolf's fur gentle on her mortal skin.

"Metlina, it is time the mortals of Ibea understood their place. I want discord in the streets. Famine, rape, plague! I want them scared, disorientated, desperate." His voice seared through the chambers, though it grew no louder. "Rally the others. I give permission for the dreams of damnation to flow. Send Malo to Ibea! Stirm is the weakest and most greedy. Once Trithia is under our control, I want their armies ready for battle and then they march with Velen to Algary. One by one the realms will submit to my authority, and I will control this world as well as Sheranshia. The balance will be in my favour and then we shall see who is victorious."

Nathan stared at Chaeli as she slept, her body shivering in the sun. He could sense the evil around her. It excited the serpents, and they writhed and hissed in pleasure, wanting to taste her. Every time he closed his eyes, the snakes moved closer to the surface; he knew the Underworld wanted him still. Denial was a constant battle, and one he feared he was losing. The intensity of his longing peaked, and he dug his nails into his palms, the pain forcing his attention back to the here and now, to the dusty road and scrubland, the snorting horses and the cool breeze. His skin and soul burned, but within minutes the sensation had subsided and he was left feeling only a little queasy.

As he moved around their makeshift camp in an attempt to shake away the discontent, he considered his earlier actions. The speed with which he had killed the protector had left him feeling uncomfortable; whilst he was naturally quick, without the powers of the Underworld he would never have been that fast. His own power was strong enough for the glamour of speed; he had specialised in lock picking, shields and sleight of hand, and mirage. As an *Assaké* his repertoire had been extensive and speed had been one of many of the extra boons that Prince Eli had granted him – but still he shouldn't be able to command such lightning quickness.

He was so alone. He knew he was losing control and nothing could stop it. Chaeli shook his defences, but he couldn't leave. He had promised to protect her, and he was a man of honour. He had to be a man of honour. He couldn't leave.

Couldn't or wouldn't? The effect she had on him was intensifying, thoughts of her filling almost all of his waking moments. He pictured her lips on his, imagined running his hands across her body.

A whimper broke him from his thoughts and he and looked down. She was sweating now and scratching at the choker. Adley had noticed too.

"I hope that dragon of yours gets here soon, crusader."

"Me too."

Sheiva had woken and gently licked the sweat from Chaeli's face. "Tastes of death, Adders."

Kneeling down beside her, Adley placed his palm on her forehead and chanted the healing incantation, but he sensed no change. He poured more power into her, but still nothing quelled the fever. "I can't alleviate her pain. The charm has taken too much of a hold."

The two men stared at her, each as helpless as the other. They sat in silence as the sun continued to glide across the sky. No other travellers crossed their path, and the horses grazed contentedly.

Eventually, from either pain or tiredness, Chaeli stilled. Adley leant down to check her breathing, and once satisfied, sat by her side with his eyes closed and held her hand while Nathan tended to the horses, rubbing their ears and brushing them down. The horses twitched and whinnied, stomping their feet and looking up. Nathan followed their gaze and gasped.

A dark silhouette approached, growing larger with each second that passed. Nathan stepped back, his hands hanging limply at his sides. A cool breeze spread through the camp, and the form became clearer: a flicking tail, two large, scaled wings that rarely beat as the dragon glided towards them. Turning effortlessly, it started to descend; the breeze grew stronger and the trees rustled, sending the birds scattering in the opposite direction. Approaching the ground, its large head dipped and tilted, as if considering the landing.

"Adley," called Nathan, indicating the dragon.

"Looks like the gods were listening. Our carriage has come." Adley shook Chaeli. "Wake up, time to go," he murmured. Chaeli stirred but remained unconscious. "Nitayla is coming, we're off to Lindor!" He tried shaking her a little harder. Nothing.

"Nathan!" The protector couldn't hide the alarm in his voice. "She won't waken." Immediately, Nathan was at her side. "What can we do?"

"When Nitayla arrives, lift her onto her back. I'll carry our packs."

Nathan nodded. He closed his eyes and squeezed her hand. *Please, gods, hear me. Don't take Chaeli. Take me, not her. Please . . . She's needed, the worlds needs her, I'm nothing compared to her.* He begged in silence, too proud to let the protector or the fae hear him.

"Nathan, move!" cried Adley.

Nathan opened his eyes to see the dragon crouched next to him; he had been so absorbed in his prayers that hadn't felt her land. She was a deep bronze colour, her hard scales gleamed and reflected the light like diamonds; there was no doubting she was female. She was the size of two caravans – tiny compared to her older male counterparts, but daunting nonetheless. Her tail was covered in hard spikes and quills, quivering in the breeze, razor sharp and deadly.

"Nitayla, it is an honour." Nathan scooped Chaeli into his arms.

"Ooooh the big strong man *honours* me," said the dragon with a giggle. The sound resonated through the air, and as she laughed Nathan caught sight of her fangs. "Hatchling teeth." She smiled, showing her sword-sized teeth and running her rough tongue over them. "I can't wait for my dragon teeth."

"Nitayla, please sit still," begged Adley as he bound their packs to her back using bridles from their horses tied around the underbelly of the dragon. She giggled again as he touched the soft, vulnerable scales.

"I'm sorry, I'm sorry, I'm just so excited! I've never been given a mission before."

Adley climbed onto her back and held out his arms. With more than a little reluctance, Nathan handed Chaeli over. She mumbled slightly, but the words were incomprehensible. Adley cradled her close while Nathan turned to release the horses, but they were already gone. With a frown, he jumped up behind Adley and gripped hard on the dragon with his knees.

"You can pass her back now, protector."

"No, she's quite safe with me."

Nathan said no more; this wasn't the place for a debate. Sheiva jumped up behind, startling him.

"I'll sit with you, if that's all right." The cat didn't wait for an answer and snuggled into his lap. "The horses bolted the moment Nitayla came in to land. It wasn't exactly graceful." With a miniature roar, Nitayla flapped her wings and her legs pushed hard against the ground, sending her soaring into the sky. Nathan grabbed at her scales until they dug into his hands and his knuckles turned white; he already disliked flying. The air was cold and the gentle sway of the dragon made him feel nauseated.

"It's a long way down from here," Sheiva murmured. Nathan glanced down and immediately regretted it: the thin wisps of cloud hazed his view, but he could see the rolling hills of Trithia's countryside pass by, the dipping, curving of the land flowing beneath him. The streams and roads reminded him of the veins on a leaf, twisting and reaching as though they had no purpose, but touching all the land and nurturing it. They flew over the north-easterly area of the realm and Nathan recognised the large market town of Sitori, overshadowed by Arthon hill where locals believed the God of Earth lay sleeping, waiting for his love to return. Nitayla banked abruptly and Nathan found himself gripping tightly again as he slid to the left. He pressed his thighs tightly against the dragon and screwed his eyes shut.

"Ohhh the big strong man doesn't like flying," sang the dragon. "Never fear, big man, not long now."

Nathan thought longingly of solid ground, but the minutes were agonisingly slow and his stomach continued to roll and churn. He allowed himself a quick glance to the ground and saw the patchwork colours and shapes of the farmers' fields. The orange and red squares meant they were close, for the fields of bothon wheat and 'tatoes bordered the city of Lindor. He shut his eyes again.

Suddenly the dragon dived and Nathan's head whipped back. He opened his eyes and they immediately began to water. The cold blasted his face and the fae dug his claws into his lap. Grinding his teeth, he ignored the pain.

"Nitayla!" shouted Adley.

"Nearly there," she sang, and with a bump they hit the ground, mud and dirt spraying up around them as she skidded, creating two long, deep tracks. "Oops, not used to carrying people. Sorry." Nathan's head snapped forward with an uncomfortable thump of chin against chest.

"I bith my thongue," meowed Sheiva, shaking his head and rubbing his face with his paws. "Ow."

"Lindor," declared the dragon proudly. Nathan looked to where she pointed a claw. Tall delicate stone pillars filled his view; the city was walled with creamy limestone, decorative not defensive. Tall blue and grey spires rose from the centre of the enormous city. So light and inviting, Lindor was very different to Trithia.

"The greatest library in all of the realms lies in there," Nathan murmured. Many times he had considered visiting, but his skills had always been needed elsewhere.

"Thank you, Nitayla, without you we would never have made it." Adley slipped to the ground with Chaeli clutched tightly to his chest.

"A pleasure, protector. I should really thank you, though. Flying in the mortal realm is a great honour." She cleared her throat, a wisp of black smoke puffing from each nostril. "Ahem . . . big strong man? You can get off now. It's quite safe."

Nathan, who had not moved, was still breathing deeply and gulping in air. The sickness had subsided, but he didn't trust his stomach. "Just a moment please," he said weakly.

"Your big strong man's not much of a flyer, is he?" She flicked her tail, causing Nathan to topple off and hit the ground with a bump and a curse. "It'll go in a bit, big strong man, don't worry— Hey! You get off too!" Sheiva, who had dug his claws into her scales, refused to be shaken off, and instead walked slowly and deliberately to the dragon's haunches, then hopped nimbly down to the ground.

"See you later, protector! Bye-bye, big strong man." Her eyes narrowed and she gave a grudging nod. "Cat." The dragon soared into the sky, disappearing into the falling sun and sweeping clouds.

"My Lord, the gods have been summoned and await you." Metlina knelt at the door to Eli's chambers. Her prince moved into the candle-lit hallway and his shadows scurried from the room. They had brought him interesting news and he had relayed new instructions. Metlina could feel the closeness of his touch and tremors of longing rushed through her.

"Excellent. Accompany me, my Metlina." He offered his arm and she took hold. He placed an ice-cold hand on her arm. They walked slowly through the many hallways to Eli's council chambers, their footsteps echoing on the stone floor, while the shrieks of the damned wailed in the background. The slapping of a whip across bare skin, followed by a groan of pain, excited her. With each slap, a hum of power and a thrill of satisfaction dripped into her energy. She bit back a moan of pleasure and concentrated on the floor. Eli demanded that the windows and wooden shutters remained constantly closed and the candles barely cast enough light. The ever moving shadows followed quietly behind. Metlina was surprised Eli had requested her company; he rarely seemed to want her anymore and she found herself growing desperate without his touch.

Eli did not respond to her comment, and the silence continued until they reached the council chamber. Finally the awkwardness seemed to dissipate, and Metlina was once again able to revel in his company.

He turned to her. "Things are progressing slowly, my Metlina." He gestured for her to open the door.

The stench of the room hit her first and she swallowed. These were her brothers and sisters, and she mustn't appear weak, not now. Scanning the circular room, her gaze caught the attention of the dark gods who nodded in acknowledgement of her presence. Each stood by the designated alcove, separated by dark panelled wood stretching from the low ceiling to the stone floor. The walls were bare, the room windowless. Eli walked to his own alcove and sat; his bench was a smooth expanse of obsidian and his alcove pitted with the eyes of thousands of mortals that had passed to him. Metlina moved to the space on his right and sat on her stone bench, smoothing her skirts. The eyes in Eli's alcove followed her and the hairs on the back of her neck prickled. Eli's energy surged, and the candles flickered into light, scattering shadows of varying shapes and sizes around the floor.

The rasping breaths of Hetes filled the space. He had been the first to arrive and was now the first to speak. "My lord, I—"

"Silence! There is no time to waste and I care not for grovelling or simpering to gain my favour. I require you all to honour me and attend to your temples. I have sent Malo to rally all those he can. I want the streets of Ibea to run with blood and my hellions to have a plentiful choice of hosts for the Sherai witches. I yearn to hear the cries of pain and despair, to hear the weeping of the weak sweeter than the melodies of the choirs of Lyensa Rock." He looked around at Kry'lla. The great brutish form raised his head and his pockmarked face twisted into a depraved smile whilst his gaze swept around the room. "You are not to fail me, Kry'lla. From this moment on I give permission for you appear in mortal form and walk the lands. Your whispers and bitter rage will spread the wretchedness I crave. Go now, and scatter these insects for me. This is my thirst, my hunger, my *desire!*"

Kry'lla pressed his fingers to his heart, then his forehead, saluting his prince. With a flash of green, he was gone. The other gods sat quietly – Metlina could sense the hunger and anticipation in the air; it had been too long since they were free. For centuries they had been denied the pleasures of flesh in the mortal realm, for centuries they had seen their energy levels seep away almost to nothing. Now they were to be reinvigorated, renewed, . A wave of arousal swept through her at the thought of drinking in her energy directly, and the desire to inflict pain in another was a need she could no longer deny. She longed for it, longed to taste each tear shed in pain, savour the scent of mortal blood as it flowed in her name.

"My daughter grows weak in her mortal form and she shall soon be joining us. I wish to present her with a glorious throne of blood and bone. She will be my slave and regent on Ibea, and I desire her reign to be rapturous. You are all to ensure this will happen. If any of you fail, you will discover new levels of suffering. Leave now and spread your gifts to all. I shall soon break free from my prison and join you."

Tregan stood and bowed deeply. "I shall not fail you, my prince. I shall feed on all I meet, from the children who fight in the streets, to the husband who beats his wife and slaves. My skill and fury shall know no bounds. The earth of Ibea will madden and become yours."

"As will I, my prince," said Nishka. "Forgiveness will soon be a word confined to history. My revenge will breed discontent and disharmony in your honour." Nishka bowed and shot a glance at Metlina, the distaste evident in her black eyes.

One by one, the gods and goddesses pledged their allegiance and left. Avarice, hatred, envy, famine, plague – so many eager deities disappeared to the once forbidden world, ready to release their gifts.

Hetes stood and bowed, ready to pledge when Eli spoke: "I do not wish for you to spread your ailments across the world, Hetes. Too many would fall too quickly. For now, you are to concentrate on nurturing those diseases already spreading and no more. I will not deny you forever, but for now I will not overwhelm my hellions, for they will surely have enough flesh to feast on."

Hetes' wrinkled face curled in disgust and disappointment, but he nodded obediently and left. Only Metlina remained. She could feel the joyous rage in her master and it pleased her. She wanted to feel him within her once more, to experience him biting her flesh and tearing at her throat. She wanted ecstasy.

"Metlina, my goddess of agony and suffering . . . I do not wish for you to leave me. You will thrive and bloom from the events the others set in motion. There is no need to leave. You are *never* to leave me." He held her gaze. "You are to stay and respond to my every desire and wish."

With a pang of regret combined with a flash of lust-sick hope, she prostrated herself before her prince. "Of course, my lord."

"It's quiet outside this evening, even the foxes are silent."

"When the foxes are hunting, a predator must be silent around its prey," Dal replied coolly, pouring a mug of mead for the stranger. He had grown accustomed to the presence of this silent, hooded man, though part of him wanted to jump over the table and reveal his face. He snorted at the thought, gulping his mead in an attempt to smother the laugh he could feel bubbling to the surface. *Gods! How much have I drunk this evening?* He lifted the jug and peered to the bottom. It was almost empty. *Surely not . . . ?*

"The visitor your father arranged is dead. The inn he stayed at midway was burned to the ground."

Dal lifted his gaze from the bottom of the jug and stared at the stranger. What did he just say?

"Why? . . . I mean, who? . . . What happened?"

"It appears the bachelor's only friend is aware of our movements. I suggest you arrange a replacement and return home."

"The bachelor's friend? I don't understand . . ." This couldn't be right. Lendin was the best, the most thorough of his father's men. He would have double-, no, triple-checked the inn. How could this have happened?

"I have arranged for mutual friends to examine the remains and report back anything of note. The ravens are quiet and returned to their nests. Our friends in the west are still cold. May I suggest a gift of friendship?"

Dal nodded. He couldn't concentrate. All he could think about was Lendin. True, he had resented the thought of the man visiting, but he was one of the few Dal could truly call friend. *Was – already I'm using the past tense.* Without Lendin's help, he would never have known how to start creating his own networks. This was bad, very bad. In the background he could hear the stranger talking, but nothing made sense. He forced himself to focus.

". . . more slaves than expected."

"Wait, repeat that last bit."

"I said our friend in Lindor has received a copy of our bachelor's slavery records. There seems to be a rise in the number of slaves and purchased indentures. It appears our bachelor's friend has amended the law on slavery to include debtors who owe more than three gold, and petty crimes such as larceny and damage."

"You know he's not exactly a bachelor anymore, don't you?" Dal said, although not sure why he felt the need. He glanced at the almost-empty jug – maybe that was why.

"What?"

"He's to be engaged to Princess Ilene." There was no reply and Dal coughed. "How did we miss this slavery?"

"The laws were given assent in secret and filed at Lindor, with papers relating to the Farmer's guild. It wasn't easy to find."

"Unacceptable! What are we paying you for?" He glared at the man, then sighed. "I'm sorry. This isn't a good time." He glanced at the man's full mug. "You must be thirsty, please drink."

"I must decline."

Dal shrugged. "Oh well, up to you. Same place, next week. I must know what happened to Lendin, and who was responsible. Arrange for a suitable gift for our friends in the west. Perhaps forest leopard furs from my estate in the north. Bring me word from the far south, there is an arrival expected in spring. I need to know details. And I want more on the slavery."

The stranger stood and left. Dal pulled the discarded mug of mead towards him and downed it in one. This wasn't good, wasn't good at all. He left the inn and signalled to a cloaked Fyn by the door. His brother nodded and immediately moved to his side.

"News?"

"Yes, and not of the pleasant kind. I need some decent wine."

"Mina's?" Fyn didn't ask about the news; Dal never discussed the intelligence he received with his younger brother.

"No, I think . . . I think I need to be alone. I shall return to the castle. There's no need to accompany me, I'll use the servant's entrance. Enjoy the night, brother." He nodded absently to his sibling, then made his way through the streets, digesting the information from the stranger. He felt sick and didn't know if it was to do with the mead or something else. As he wound through the backstreets to the castle, he thought back over the last week. Velen had increased production in the pits, Trithia wanted more oil, and had amended slavery crimes. Mischla . . . ? Mischla was an unknown, as was Sheema. His uncle spoke of fealty and ships passing hands. But why? What was going on?

CHAPTER EIGHT

THE MEN WALKED through the city, with Sheiva winding in and out of their legs, threatening at times to trip Adley as he marched determinedly on with Chaeli's limp body in his arms. The sun was setting and streams of dying light glanced off the walls and half-lit the streets, the rays flooding the roofs with the gentle touch of old, forgotten magic. Heat was absorbed into the stone walls, warming hearths and homes; nothing was wasted.

People glanced at them with curiosity but none stopped to enquire nor to question their right to be there. Nathan had never seen so many people apparently at ease with their lives, so relaxed and happy. No guile, worry or fear showed on their faces. It took him a while to realise there were no guards in the city, that there were neither beggars nor thieves, and that the streets smelled sweet and clean. It was the most calming place Nathan had ever visited.

"Adley, where are the guards?" he inquired.

"Lindor needs no guards; all the realms have agreed this is a place of learning and growth, not power."

"There is no discord here? No arguments that require settling, no thievery or bloodshed?" asked Nathan, his disbelief clear.

"None. Lindor houses some of the most powerful priests, healers, and energy users in the world. If even one person was to commit a crime, the consequences would threaten all."

Nathan said no more, but thought deeply about this. Could he live in such a place? Could Anya? Could they find happiness here? Deeper and further into the city they walked; their road was straight and Adley led without hesitation. At last they reached a small building encircled by a smooth pavement of blue quartz. The white front of the building was adorned with friezes depicting the gods of the Eternal Kingdom, and at first Nathan thought it was a temple. Story upon story was carved into the stone: Nileen, the Goddess of Wind, and the story of her reluctance to remain in the Eternal Kingdom, her corporeal form melting into the stone; Arthon, the God of Earth, stood behind her with his arms outstretched, waiting for her return. Above the doors, the form of Hytensia stood staring down at the entrance – scrolls in one hand, a quill in the other, her companion, the Austellius bird of scholars, perched on her shoulder. As they crossed the threshold of the library of Lindor, Nathan felt lightheaded and calm at once.

"There is a cleansing charm soothing all who enter, creating a state conducive to contemplation and study," Adley whispered.

The entrance hall was spacious and lit with a warming glow, which seemed to emanate from all sides; candles were arranged behind semi-transparent screens in between the high marble shelves along the walls. On these shelves, extending from floor to ceiling, were thousands of books. The smells of dust and parchment, of ink and paper, filled the air along with the more recognisable smell of the Algarian forests' Braunwin trees.

Their steps echoed on the marble floor as they continued slowly towards a great table in the centre of the hall. Passages led away and down either side, curving and giving the sense of unending knowledge preserved between leather boards and in rolled documents.

Adley saw Nathan staring. "It twists and turns and is always logical. Have you ever seen inside a honeycomb?"

"Who enters my library unannounced?" an old voice called out, followed by a bout of dry coughing.

"An old friend, one who has been away for far too long," said Adley with a laugh, tears of joy in his eyes. As Adley kissed Chaeli's forehead in happiness, Nathan shrunk backwards, swallowing hard, to watch.

"There are many that call themselves my friends, but few who are in fact my friends, stranger. Is the title yours to give, or merely to propose?" The voice became louder and at last an elderly man appeared, shuffling towards them from a corridor at the far end of the hall. He approached unhurriedly and stared at Adley with milky eyes. His wispy white hair lay ragged around his shoulders, his thin frame covered in a white linen robe. He leaned heavily on a staff fashioned from dark walnut and covered in symbols burnt into the wood.

"I recognise you, but I fear I must be losing my mind. You remind me of a very old friend, someone I haven't seen for . . . well, for what feels like an eternity." The old man shuffled closer and touched Adley's face. Suddenly, in a wondering, plaintive tone he said, "Is it you, old friend? Have you finally come to set me free?"

"Yes, Mickalos, it is I. But I have not come to free you, I have come to request your help and knowledge. This girl," he continued, brushing the hair from Chaeli's forehead and showing her face to the old librarian, "is Chaeli, the daughter of Prince Eli, niece of Prince Daro. Amelia's babe."

"Ahhh . . . the scriptures are true then, the reckoning has—" The old man began to cough again, dry and rasping, and he turned his face away. After a few moments he collected himself and looked back from Adley to Chaeli. "What's wrong with her?" The old man peered at her face and sniffed her hair. "Ah, she smells of death. Eli and his malediction."

"You sense the curse on her?" Nathan stepped forward eagerly. "Can it be removed?"

"What, who speaks here?" Mickalos turned and realisation filled his face. "You! I have seen you before! You are the harbinger of death, and your arrival has been written for hundreds of years. *Assake*!" The old man chuckled darkly. "You just don't know it yet."

273

"You speak in riddles, old man. All I want to know is if you can cure Chaeli."

"Yes, yes, I can remove the charm, but Chaeli will have to cure herself. She must want to return to us."

Adley cleared his throat. "Mickalos, old friend, we should begin immediately."

Mickalos looked at them all for a moment before turning and leading them back to the corridor from which he had emerged. A short way in, he indicated a room off to one side and under his guidance, the three men began the preparations. Nathan followed the instructions of the protector and the librarian while the fae watched. Incense cones and candles were lit and encircled Chaeli on the floor; she was soon surrounded by runes made of an ash wood tree. She no longer murmured or moved, and her breathing was shallow.

Mickalos called acolytes from their cells and instructed them, designating duties to each man. Nathan was surprised to see the youngest acolyte was close to his own age. It was unusual in Ibea to see older acolytes, in most realms they were young boys and girls, rich in power but poor in coin. They would sign their life over to the church and in return receive hot meals, education and safety. Here, however, it seemed any age was considered, any background acceptable. Those he observed wore sandals and tunics cut from the best leather and cloth; clearly these were men of money and status in the outside world.

Mickalos rolled up his sleeves, revealing rune upon rune tattooed across his stringy arms. The symbols were a brilliant ghostly white that glowed in the candlelight.

"Nathan, I need you here," called Adley. "You must ensure all these candles remain lit. Don't allow even one to go out, do you understand? Not one."

Nathan nodded and took the taper and tinderbox from Adley, who grasped his hands as they stared at each other. "She'll come through, Nathan. Mickalos is a healer like no other in history."

"Adley! I need you here. I need your dragon," commanded Mickalos. He suddenly appeared years younger, the shuffling movements gone and the raspy voice loud and clear; he had not coughed once since entering the room. "Remove your shirt and summon the dragon."

The acolytes stopped their incantations and stared, eager to see the crusader's inking.

"Continue!" snapped Mickalos. "Idleness will not be tolerated!" The acolytes looked at one another guiltily and resumed their chantings, but their eyes remained fixed on the crusader.

Adley removed his shirt and his dragon roared to life. Nathan sensed his serpents stir, but, to his relief, they remained asleep.

As Mickalos closed the door, suddenly everything felt real to Nathan; all his senses came alive, and his feeling of being an outsider vanished. He could hear every tiny noise, could smell the myriad scents of spices and oils and the harsher odours of his own and Adley's bodies, but he could also smell the bitterness radiating from Chaeli. It was a familiar smell: the stench of the Underworld. Mickalos moved his acolytes behind him and they removed their robes, fastening them around their waists. No runes decorated their skin, only brilliant white stars.

Mickalos spoke words Nathan could not comprehend, chanting in old Trithian, a language not used for hundreds of years but familiar to those educated in the hidden and esoteric arts. The spell picked up pace; the acolytes joined in, their stars moving towards their forearms. Nathan recognised the constellation they formed: the star of Salinthos and the third world. He was enraptured. Mickalos unpinned his own robe and exposed his chest, scrawny and wrinkled, and the stars moved from the acolytes onto his own skin, writhing and moving within the runes. The way to the third world was mapped out on the healer's chest. Nathan tried to memorise the constellation but it wouldn't stay; Salinthos was the world of dreams, the world where all could be cleansed of sin and past misdemeanours by the pure energy flowing through the land and by the grace of the monarch who ruled there.

"Nathan, the flames," whispered Sheiva, slinking from his quiet corner. Nathan hastily re-lit the dimming flames and nodded his thanks to the cat.

Mickalos motioned Adley forward and placed both hands on the dragon. Again, the constellation moved but this time onto the dragon, into the beasts open maw. The flames from the candles surged and the room became hot. Mickalos spoke in old Trithian and, with an acknowledging nod, Adley took hold of Chaeli's upturned hand. Her stars visible to all, he placed her palm on his dragon's mouth and the beast roared, flames erupting from the dragon's flickering tongue and engulfing Chaeli. Nathan sprang up ready to pounce, to fight, to spend his own life in order to save hers.

"Stay!" hissed Mickalos. "Stay where you are!" He held up his hand against Nathan's chest firmly. "See how the flames consume her!"

As Nathan stared at Chaeli, the flames burned from red to white and spread across her body. She began to shriek and thrash on the ground. He closed his eyes, blocking out the sight, but he couldn't block out her voice.

"Nathan, help me, please! Don't let them kill me, Nathan, it hurts so much! I don't want to die. I'll be alone, Nathan. I don't want to be alone again. Please!" Her pleading voice cut into him and he swallowed thickly.

It has to be done, she has to be healed.

"Don't you care? How can you let them do this?" Her voice lowered to a hiss. "It's your fault, Nathan. All this is your fault. You left me alone, left me to the morthon. And now I'm dying, they're killing me." There was a pause and he heard a sob. "Why are you letting them do this? Save me!"

He opened his eyes and stared at her again. The flames still licked over her body but she was silent, no pleas, whispers or accusations. But he knew she screamed.

"No, gods no! You're killing her!" shouted Nathan. "Please, Mickalos, you have to stop!"

"Foolish, ignorant *Assaké*! The flames are purging her, cleansing her of the evil her father inflicted! Just watch the candles, boy, do your job. Do not listen to falseness."

Nathan resumed his post and watched only the candles, his eyes straining as he forced himself not to look at Chaeli. He couldn't watch as she was consumed by fire. Slowly the shrieking in his heart subsided to whimpers, and then to sobs. Once again she spoke to him: "You've failed me again, *Assaké*. Your promises are meaningless. You are nothing. You are weak." Then, with one last soul-cutting scream, she was silent.

The air in the room was stale. He needed to breathe, he needed space, needed to get out of this torture chamber. But he couldn't leave.

"Nathan, open your eyes," whispered Sheiva, "look!" Nathan glanced at the cat, who nodded towards Chaeli. "Look!"

He looked. The choker had disappeared from her neck and lay discarded beside her. The skin where it had gripped was red raw and weeping, but she was free from the cursed jewellery and already her cheeks had a healthy pink tinge, her breathing deep and even.

"It is done, the charm has been lifted. Chaeli will choose when to wake, we have done what we can," said Mickalos. He sounded tired and old once more.

Nathan moved to her. Gently, nervously, he touched her skin. She was warm and dry. And so smooth.

"Adley, look," he whispered in awe. He traced the constellation on Chaeli's shoulder and arm. The stars had permanently engraved themselves on her skin. The acolytes stared in disbelief; the skin of each of them was now empty and unmarked.

"Impossible!" Mickalos stared at his chest, bereft of the many runes and spells which had enveloped him.

Adley looked down at himself; his dragon slept. His own skin and inkings were intact.

"She's sucked our energy into herself! How she can do that?" cried an acolyte.

"Why would she do this?" sobbed another.

"What *is* she?"

"Silence, you simpletons! Let me think!" The old man hobbled towards the door and opened it; Nathan felt the welcome rush of cool air. "The girl needs to rest. Everyone out," Mickalos shouted. The acolytes fled first and disappeared to their cells, bewildered and upset. "You did well, *Assaké*. You remained strong." Without another word. he left the room. Adley slowly replaced his shirt and followed him into the main hall where they conversed earnestly in low, worried voices.

"C'mon, Nathan, you heard what the wizened prune said. Let's go get some fresh air!"

With a flash Sheiva transformed again and Nathan gasped; a silver-haired boy stood in his place, thin and delicate, with a wolfish grin and knowing eyes. His skin gleamed with a golden hue, and he seemed no more than twelve years old. "You asked me what my true form is, well, this is pretty much it. One of them. Boring, huh?"

"Sheiva? You're human?"

"No! Please, don't insult me! I am a fae, a fairy in simple terms. *Your* simple terms, that is." The boy stretched out his arms.

"Do you . . . have wings?" Nathan blurted out, thinking back to the stories of his childhood.

"I do not!" The boy gasped and put his hands on his hips, screwing his face up in disgust. "Ah, I forgot what this feels like. I don't like it, I'm changing back."

"No, wait, please, stay in this form for a while. I don't want to talk to a cat at the moment."

"Humph, fine, fine, fine!" Sheiva moved to the door. "But I need some clothes."

"Well done, Hana!" Kerne enthused, a thin smile spreading across his face like a wound. She was progressing. He had known all along she was too precious to leave languishing in that fetid cell.

Sweat beading her face and tracing patterns on her body, Hana beamed up at him. She had managed to coerce Adyam into thinking her pillow was a baby, and he sat cradling it in his arms and cooing. She still couldn't bring herself to do the cruel things to the young guard that Kerne commanded, and had taken several beatings for it, but he finally relented and allowed her to work at her own pace, using coercions of her own choosing.

She released the hold on him and abruptly Adyam stared in confusion at the pillow and then up at Hana. Realisation hit and he winked at her; her heart flipped and her inner guide laughed. She grinned back at him and then, cautiously, at Kerne. He noticed the looks they gave one other, and scowled at Adyam. Hana's insides went cold and shivery.

"Hana, try to do something with me." He walked to a side table upon which stood a bowl of fruits. Taking up the fruit knife, he sliced his thumb. Blood dripped onto a small platter and he passed it to her. He showed no sign of the knife having hurt him.

Using two fingers, she smeared the blood on her forehead and closed her eyes. Kerne felt something pushing into his skull. The burrowing creature poked and prodded, yet curiously it wasn't an unduly uncomfortable sensation. The room start to change and distort, the swaying of shapes and shifting of colours making him feel sick, but he couldn't fight the change. Ivy wove around the furniture and flowers spurted from the rugs, hundreds and hundreds of flowers; he could smell almonds, nutty and rich, mixed with the freshness of lemons. He reached out and plucked a rare orange starflower found only in the rich mineralised walls of the Velenese pits, it was like nothing he had ever smelled before, more vibrant, more intense than his childhood memory. He crushed it in his hand and looked around. The flowers faded and the ivy withered.

Dazed, Kerne looked down at his seer. His blood had burnt away from her forehead and she was looking up at him expectantly.

"Very good, Hana, very good indeed." He stroked her head thoughtfully; her hair was very soft. "Try again, but this time I want you to force me to do something against my nature." He sliced his thumb again and she wetted her forehead with his blood.

Kerne blacked out.

Upon awakening, he saw Hana grinning over him while the idiot boy soldier simply looked worried. He was sitting on the sofa in Hana's rooms. He felt no different; his energy was his own and physically he was fine. Hana giggled and passed him her little hand mirror. He raised an eyebrow, then looked at his reflection. His face was painted garishly with rouge and lip-stain, a simple-minded prank but something she clearly thought daring and bold.

Her innocence fascinated him. She was improving, and quickly. He hoped she would learn to conserve the blood and allow the coercions to last longer, but he couldn't complain. Yet. Since he had beaten her, she had moved along at a pleasing rate. Her giggles faded and she stared at him with those challengingly innocent eyes.

"Mr Kerne . . . ?"

He could see the fear now. "Well done, Hana," he said. "How long did it take?" He remained calm. She had tried to humiliate him with the rouge, but it was of his own doing and, for the Underworld, he had suffered worse. She screwed up her face trying to think. The captain looked over her head to Adyam. "Well?"

The boy stammered and stuttered. "A-about an hour," he finally spluttered.

"Excellent." Once his face was clean, he stood and walked to the door.

"You'll earn your keep soon enough, seer. Keep practising."

Dal bent down and flicked a speck of dirt from his trousers. He had to look perfect tonight. He started to tie his neckerchief and snorted in disgust at his reflection in the mirror. He looked like a jester in his green jacket and yellow tie. Appalling, simply appalling.

He had spent the afternoon leading up to the supper alone in his room. Things were starting to fall into place and the cryptic rushed words with his uncle had supported his conjectures – and confirmed his worst fears.

The realms were preparing for war. With Velen and Mischla bought into the service of Trithia, and with Porton to be joined to Stirm's house in marriage, only Sheema and Algary remained apart. King Derrin was the richest ruler of the Seven Realms and his mines were brimming with gold and precious gems; whoever controlled Algary could buy enough loyalty and support – and enough mercenaries – to take control of all Ibea, should they wish.

Finally Dal managed a modest Algarian coat knot, tucking the creased ends into his waistcoat. The heavy wool already made him uncomfortable and with the warmth of the castle and lack of fresh air, he knew he would suffer. He sighed. Tonight he represented his father and the realm of Algary. He snatched a jug of wine and poured a large glass, drinking deeply to drown his nerves. As he left his room, he saw the King's Guard lining the halls, each soldier dressed in ceremonial attire. Stirm was certainly intent on making an impression this evening.

He mopped his brow, it was going to be a long night. Approaching the double doors to Stirm's hall, he saw his brother stand to attention and salute. Dal stopped and nodded to Fyn, who glanced at him without moving his head, but instead winked and turned sharply to open the door to the dining hall.

"His Royal Highness, Prince Kee Dala of House Montareon, Duke of Alim, Duke of Tyrin, Earl of Bornholm, Commander of the Algarian army and High Steward of Neinhelm."

Dal grimaced. He hated pomp and ceremony, and his ludicrous official titles embarrassed him. On entering, he saw that Ilene and his uncle had already arrived. Ilene stared at him, then looked down at her dress. Personally, Dal thought she looked stunning; her maid had teased her short hair into twists and fastened each one with a crystal slide. She had even coerced the headstrong princess into applying a slick of rouge to her lips. Ilene reminded Dal of a porcelain doll, dressed and ready to be presented as a gift.

"Kee Dala, how wonderful to see you." Ilene addressed him first, the sarcasm dripping from her voice. Her father glared and she pinched her lips into a thin, prim line.

"King Cobey, Princess Ilene." Dal bowed. "You look beautiful, Ilene."

She smiled, though it did not reach her eyes. "Thank you, Dal. You look hot, sweaty and uncomfortable."

"Ilene!" her father said sharply. "I apologise. Ilene is feeling a little unwell and forgets her place." King Cobey glanced at his daughter, then smiled a broad, false smile.

"No apologies necessary, Uncle. I can sympathise with Ilene's . . . illness. I feel a touch of it myself."

"Indeed. I pray you recover quickly. Our host and his lapdog have arrived." Cobey nodded towards the door.

"Who is the lapdog and who the host?" Dal murmured to no one in particular, which set Ilene to giggling.

"Ah, King Cobey, Princess Ilene and Prince Kee Dala! You honour me with your presence!" King Stirm, ruler of Trithia and Keeper of the Royal Courts of Ibea had finally graced Dal and his relatives with his presence. Dal acknowledged the King with a bow. Stirm looked older than his thirty five years, his once golden-blond hair streaked with grey. He was thin and his skin stretched tightly over his bones. Weary and worn, the good looks and broad build of his youth had withered away. He leaned heavily on a gold-topped cane.

"I apologise for not greeting you earlier, Cobey, but I have been unwell." Stirm signalled for Kerne to join them. "I trust Captain Kerne accommodated you whilst I was recovering."

"Indeed." The Porton King looked at Ilene and she gave a sickly smile.

"As do I, Your Majesty. You have been most courteous and kind."

Dal was impressed; Ilene sounded sincere, and if he hadn't known her better, he would have thought her a demure and dutiful daughter.

"Princess Ilene, I hope it is not too forward of me to say, but you look exquisite tonight, like unto a goddess indeed! The mere sight of you lifts my spirits more than the tonic from my healer."

Dear gods, thought Dal. *Stirm really does not know Ilene.*

"Oh, you are too kind, Your Majesty. Your health is paramount, and I would urge you to continue with the tonics rather than stare at me." For good measure, Ilene added a girlish laugh and touched her hair coquettishly.

Stirm chuckled. "There is a spark in your daughter, Cobey."

"Not all rumours, Stirm. Ilene does indeed possess a fire, but she can be docile, gentile and considerate. I have taught her humility."

"I'm sure, I'm sure. She is exquisite, a rare jewel for any man to possess."

Anger flared in Dal. He hated the thought of Stirm possessing Ilene – she wasn't a prize pig! A few years in his company would surely crush her spirit.

"Prince Kee Dala, how fares your father?"

"He is well, Your Majesty. He sends his apologies for being unable to attend. Pressing matters of state required his attention." Dal's thoughts flitted to the latest serving woman with whom his father had become infatuated. Irritatingly, he also saw Chaeli, but that was quite different; he was not his father.

"Apologies are not necessary. Your company more than makes up for the absence of your father." Stirm paused and considered Ilene once more. "Lovely Ilene, I would very much enjoy a walk in the gardens with you. I feel we should get to know one another." He held out his arm and smiled. Hesitating for only a second, she took his arm and smiled warmly back at him.

"It would be my pleasure. Father?"

"Nothing would delight me more."

Stirm nodded once and turned to Kerne. "Please entertain my guests, Captain."

He escorted Ilene towards the glass doors leading to the gardens. Dal could see him whispering in her ear; she giggled in response, ever the actress.

"King Cobey, I am delighted at the joining of our two great nations. I hope Trithia and Porton will enjoy many years of peace and prosperity."

Cobey shifted irritably and stared at Kerne. "I too look forward to the day that Trithia and Porton are joined. And to the joining of all the realms in peace and prosperity."

"Indeed, Your Majesty, Trithia is eager for all of the realms to be of equal standing."

Dal couldn't hold his tongue. "Captain Kerne, I have noticed you speak for Trithia quite often of late. Has King Stirm raised your status to that of First Minister or High Steward?"

Kerne cocked an eyebrow and stared at him, as did his uncle. "Please accept my apologies if I have offended Algary. Sometimes I forget my place. I am content to be Captain of the King's Guard and Commander of the Army of Trithia. I have no desire for higher political office." He bowed graciously. "Forgive me."

"Nothing to forgive, Captain," said Cobey. "Young Kee Dala here also sometimes forgets his place."

The public rebuke in front of the captain infuriated Dal. His uncle treated Kerne as an equal and spoke of Dal as though he was a young pup, still wet behind the ears.

"We are all passionate, Your Majesty. Perhaps I can offer you both a drink? We have some excellent wine from Mischla." Kerne bowed and left.

Cobey grasped Dal's arm. "Learn to hold your tongue, boy! This is a serious game we play."

"A *dangerous* game. Am I to stand here while Kerne taunts Algary under my nose? He is aware that I know of the games Trithia plays, but he expects me to do nothing. I am here playing dutiful little prince while my father remains in ignorance. I have been manoeuvred into the castle, my letters are screened both in and out, and I have received word my last missive to my father was intercepted as it reached Lindor. I am a virtual prisoner here."

Cobey looked at him, his face unreadable, and frowned. "Although Trithia and Porton are to be joined, I would never allow harm to come to Algary. You are as much my family as Ilene."

"Are you so naïve? Ilene will be queen in name only. Stirm will hold her to ransom and demand you do his bidding. If he threatens Ilene, will you truly be able to protect Algary? Will you choose my family over Ilene?" King Cobey remained silent. "Uncle, I request that after the wedding celebrations, you leave Trithia and take my brother Fyn with you. He will relay everything to my father. Whilst he remains in the King's Guard, he is only another hostage."

"Son, I would rather *you* leave with me. You are the Crown Prince of Algary."

"Exactly. I am the heir to the throne. Fyn is nothing more than a bastard. In the eyes of the royals, he is expendable."

"You may be in danger if you stay. By Vorgon, you need to leave!"

"I intend to leave, Uncle, but I must make my excuses believable and timed to perfection."

The Porton King sighed and patted Dal on the back. "I hope you know what you're doing, son."

"No, Uncle, I hope you know what you are doing. Marrying Ilene to Stirm will be the greatest mistake you ever make. You have sentenced her to a life of unhappiness and handed Porton to the Underworld on a platter. Stirm will erect temples of copper and obsidian in the streets of your realm faster than you can blink. You have shamed the Eternal Kingdom." Dal breathed deeply; he didn't know where his sudden courage had come from.

"I will forgive you your outburst, Dal," said Cobey through his teeth, "but do not forget to whom you speak. I may be your uncle, but I am also the King of Porton and Lord of the Seas. I have seen and done things you can only imagine in your nightmares." Dal sensed his fury rising.

"I meant no disrespect, Uncle. I hold Ilene as dear to my heart as my own siblings."

Before Cobey could reply, Kerne approached followed by a servant carrying a tray laden with wine.

"King Cobey, Prince Kee Dala, I apologise if this is presumptuous but I would be greatly honoured if you would join me in a game of molyona?"

Cobey laughed too loudly. "I would be delighted to relieve you of some coin this evening. I do believe Dal here would revel in emptying the coffers of both Trithia and Porton, however, and we shall have to be sharp to beat this lad." His tone was jovial, but Dal could sense the anger radiating from him.

"Indeed, Your Majesty. Algarians have always been adept at gathering coin."

"All this talk, gentlemen, and no deck. Kerne, lead us to the cards and my inevitable winnings."

The men moved to an alcove by the fire, away from the dining table. Dal was thankful that it had not been lit this evening. Sitting down, he noted that Kerne didn't drink with them, but dismissed paranoid thoughts of drugs and poison. The captain wouldn't be so foolish as to try anything this evening, not before Ilene was bound by marriage.

As Kerne shuffled the deck, they made small talk, discussing the weather, the garrison, military life and the comings and goings of the elusive Sheeman Queen. King Cobey commented lightly on the dancing troupe that had left a few weeks prior and his dismay at missing them. Something in his voice caught Dal's attention and he looked up to his uncle to see the wistful lust clear on his face.

"Uncle, you seem rather fond of that troupe, perhaps you should invite them to Porton?"

"I'm seriously considering it, Kee Dala, very seriously indeed. The women are the most sensual creatures you could ever hope to meet. Have you ever seen them lad?" A bead of sweat rolled down his face.

Dal shook his head. "Who are they?"

"Danven's Dancing Delights, and those women are indeed delightful."

Dal frowned to himself; he had heard the rumours that they were little more than selling their dancing to the crowds and then their bodies between the sheets, exploiting the richest and most influential men of Ibea. He remembered his father receiving a request for their attendance; it was the only time he had ever seen his mother, Queen Freya, explode with rage. Derrin had spent days placating her, promising to refuse the troupe access to Algary. At last she was mollified – and considerably better off in jewellery – but her reaction had disturbed Dal.

"I believe they are headed towards Lindor, Your Majesty, so perhaps you can arrange for them to meet you in Porton on your return," suggested Kerne dealing out a fresh hand.

"Maybe I will," mused the King. "Or I could always taste the delightful women that young Stirm has to offer. I hear they are beyond compare." The wine had clearly loosened his tongue.

Dal sipped carefully at his own glass; he could taste the strong Mischlan grapes and the undertone of cinnamon, but detected nothing suspicious.

"My King doesn't have other women, Your Majesty. He only has eyes for the Princess Ilene."

"By the gods, man, do you think I was born yesterday? All men have their molls. I don't expect Stirm to be any different. I do, however, expect him to be discreet and courteous towards my daughter. I am not naïve and don't expect him to love her as he did that ward of his, but perhaps that is a good thing. Perhaps my daughter will keep her beauty. Perhaps, with Penella's help, love will grow between them."

"King Stirm is always discreet, and he forms no emotional attachments to his . . . women. The incident with Anya DeVaine was poorly handled and not something that will be repeated."

"Indeed. She was the most alluring woman I've ever seen, a goddess in mortal form." Cobey sighed.

"Whatever happened to her?" Dal asked casually.

"She still resides in the city. Stirm allows her to run a medicinia, but she has been declared forbidden."

"What of her brother? The traitor has surely been dealt the King's justice?" Cobey signalled for another glass of wine.

"Alas, Nathan DeVaine still eludes us. However, gods willing, he shall be in custody soon. I'm afraid I can disclose no more at this time."

Cobey nodded. "Shall we continue to play, gentlemen? I feel Elek's blessing on me already."

Metlina heard the roars of anger from Eli's chambers and flinched. Something had gone wrong, and her prince was furious. As she stared at his door, paralysed with indecision, something barged past her and barrelled towards the dark ebony door.

"Careful, fool!" she spat and the mass turned, revealing itself to be a Kitaani warrior. It stared at her. Between them lay the corpse of the mortal man he had been dragging behind him.

The warrior said nothing, which was to be expected. The Kitaani were resurrected mortal men and controlled by the Sherai witches, servants to the Underworld. The Kitaani were plentiful and easily obtained, but dumb as cattle. Metlina sneered at the inferior creature and paid no attention to the corpse it held. The warrior turned away from the goddess and entered the chambers beyond without knocking.

Metlina hesitated, her interest piqued. Eli had obviously summoned the Kitaani, but she had no idea why. The door closed with a thud.

She stalked to her apartments in a temper; she was the greatest of their deities and should be by Eli's side for all important matters. She should know all that passed in the Underworld; she should be his equal, his lover. His Queen.

Slamming the door behind her, she forced the shadows to leave and sealed the room. She threw herself onto her bed and closed her eyes in an attempt to calm her anger and fear.

Eli was her world. Blinded by love, she had disregarded her family and followed him from the Kingdom to this loathsome pit. He thanked her by using her body and disdaining her emotions. He debased her and she thanked him for it; she cherished his contempt. She, the Goddess of Pain, whose power was self-sustainable through her heartache, was a pathetic creature indeed.

"I offered to help him love you years ago," a familiar voice said, soft as a caress. "But you were too weak to accept."

Metlina sighed. "How did you get in here? I sealed the room." She wasn't in the mood for a family reunion.

"That would be telling."

Metlina rolled onto her side away from her sister's voice. "You shouldn't be here. Leave." A warm body lay beside her and a soft arm hugged her close. Blonde curls mixed in with her copper ones.

"I hate seeing you so upset, sister. Does he still not love you?"

"What do you care?" Metlina's voice was flat and emotionless. "Haven't you got your own unrequited love to wail over?"

"Oh, you're so cruel." The embrace loosened and Penella sighed.

"What do you want? Why are you here?" Metlina got up from the bed and stared down at her twin, as light as she was dark. Penella was transcendentally beautiful and made even Metlina feel plain in her presence.

"Can't a sister visit her family without an ulterior motive?"

"No, not you."

"Very well. I want to know what Eli's next move will be. I have information for him that may . . . tip the scales, so to speak."

Metlina narrowed her eyes. "Why would you do that? What of Daro? You don't belong here!" She didn't trust her sister. Everything Penella did was for her own gain, yet no one ever saw it. Metlina had always been the one to be scolded and frowned at for telling tales, whilst Penella had been fawned over and rewarded for her truthfulness. It had never been fair, never right. The Mother had never seen the darkness in the sweet Goddess of Love.

"I want to be with my sister. I grow lonely. Daro does not commune with us and I want to be one of the victorious."

"You've never wanted to be with me, *Penny*. Now is no different. You just want to bask in the glory of victory, to be lauded and hailed above all others – but do you really think we have a chance of defeating the Kingdom?" The Goddess of Pain snorted in disbelief. Penella's presence somehow always made her act in a more ugly manner than usual, as she sought the furthest extreme from her sister.

"With all the other gods sanctimoniously preaching what we can and can't get involved in? With the gentlest persuasions then yes, you – or, should I say, *we* – can be victorious." Penella stretched out on the bed and smiled lazily.

"You're the Goddess of Love, Penella. You're supposed to stand for all things good."

"Metty, love is everywhere regardless of who is in control. Mothers love their children, women love women, men love men, they all love each other. Even if Eli wins, he can't eradicate love. It's like breathing."

"Don't call me Metty, you know I hate it." The copper-haired twin pursed her lips. "I don't trust you."

"You never have little sister, but this isn't up to you. I want to see Eli, so make it happen. I'm not leaving until I do." Penella stood up and faced her sister. Matched in height and strength, they were a formidable pair. At last, Metlina sagged, crushed under the weight of her own inadequacy.

"Very well. I will approach Eli and formally request a meeting. If he refuses, you will have to leave. No one can see you here."

"Agreed." Penella went to the divan and stretched out, pulling a soft woollen throw around her shoulders. "I don't like your bed, the cushions are too soft." Metlina grunted. Just like old times.

As she left, Metlina heard the shouts from Eli's room. He was still screaming and ranting. Her pulse quickened, fear filled her and she began to shake. She didn't know how Eli would react to her request as long as he was in this mood, but the thought of him beating her filled her body with terror and desire; perhaps there might be fulfilment, a brief moment of completion. Still trembling, she knocked on his door and the shouts instantly stopped.

"Come."

Metlina opened the door and entered. The room smelled of blood and bile, making her nostrils flare. Eli stood by the fire, his eyes wild and his hands covered in blood, while the Kitaani loomed silently in the shadows. The corpse he had carried lay on the ground.

"You dare disturb me, whore?" spat Eli. "I did not summon you."

Metlina winced. "No, my Lord, I come with news from the Kingdom. One of the gods requests an audience . . . to offer services." Metlina fell to her knees and placed her forehead on the cool floor. She waited for the kick, but instead a laugh erupted from her prince. "A traitor! Why would one of Daro's precious lapdogs want to desert him?" He paced back and forth before the fire. "The charm failed. My daughter is free." Metlina heard him move and braced herself. "Do get up, you pathetic creature," he said. "It's embarrassing to see one of my gods writhing on the floor, behaving like an animal."

She slowly climbed to her knees and stood. Eli glanced at her as he washed his hands in a bowl of water.

"Which god is it? Who would be so deliciously duplicitous?"

Metlina hesitated. "Penella."

There was a silence and then Eli chortled in delight. "Your sister? How wonderful! She is a creature beyond beauty. And yet you are twins." Metlina looked up at him and he licked his lips. "I've always wanted to taste her. I imagine she tastes like honey from the starflower. So very sweet." Pain filled Metlina. "My Metlina, do my words hurt you so? You know you will always be my favourite whore."

Eli moved closer and cupped her face in his hands. Staring into his deep blue eyes, she knew then why she loved him. He made her feel alive, and the pain to which he repeatedly subjected her made her powerful and strong, brought her to ecstasy. His hands were cold and soft, and her breathing quickened as she sensed his power surge – he was aroused. Gently, she moved her hands up and touched his fingers.

"You are like a dog, Metlina. The harder I kick you, the keener you are. Always so loyal. Why so?" he whispered, searching her face. "Why do you not leave?"

She couldn't answer. How could she tell him she loved him? Here in this place? "You are my master," was all she could say.

Eli raised an eyebrow and ran his fingertips down her face. Slowly he planted a simple kiss on her lips. She closed her eyes. No pain from him now, just a kiss. It was the first time he had shown her anything but derision and humiliation. When he withdrew his lips, disappointment filled her.

"Go get your sister, Metlina, and once you have shown her to my rooms, I wish you to bring refreshments. The Goddess of Love is to have only the best."

"Yes, my Master," she replied.

"Oh, and Metlina?" he added. The goddess turned to face him. "Close the door on your way out."

"So much for Elek's blessing, Uncle," chortled Dal as he scooped the pile of coins into his purse an hour later.

"Vorgon's arse, boy! Have some humility," grumbled the Porton King as he slumped in his chair, looking dejected. "Do you ever lose at this damned game?"

"It's a game of patience, Uncle, patience and good timing. I am lucky enough to have both."

"Indeed, the gods were surely with you this evening," said Kerne.

"The gods are always with Dal when he plays molyona. The boy never loses."

"Another game, Uncle? Captain?"

"I shall have to decline, Your Highness. My modest purse is no match for yours, and my King approaches with the Princess Ilene." Kerne nodded towards the glass doors and stood ready to greet the King. Cobey turned around and stood also, gesturing to Dal to follow suit.

"King Cobey, your daughter is beyond compare. I do believe I am smitten."

Dal looked at Ilene who smiled benignly in return.

"Stirm, you are but a man. My daughter enchants all."

"I would be honoured to ask for your daughter's hand in marriage and a formal betrothal." Stirm smiled gently at Ilene.

"I would gladly accept such a request, and I rejoice at the joining of our houses."

Stirm let go of Ilene's arm and the two kings embraced. Dal thought he saw a hint of derision on Ilene's face, but he blinked and it was gone.

Stirm beamed at everyone. "Let us go to supper. I have arranged for dishes from Porton, Algary and Trithia to be served this evening."

Dal loosened his neckerchief and undid the top button of his shirt. The fire had been lit in the dining hall and the air was thick. The humidity was too much for Dal. The sweat beaded on Cobey's face, and the Porton King loosened his own shirt buttons. Dal could see even Ilene was suffering with the heat, but Stirm appeared unaffected. As they sat down to eat, the conversation flowed; Stirm could be a gracious host when it suited him.

Dal considered Anya DeVaine. He remembered seeing this girl years before when he accompanied father on a visit to Trithia, a girl with unnaturally beautiful features, delicate and symmetrical. Indeed, his first crush had been on Anya DeVaine. Without thinking, he compared Anya and Chaeli, polar opposites in looks, yet there was something about the mysterious girl with no heritage he couldn't shake. She had become another obsession to juggle. He had to get her out of his head . . .

. . . *and into your bed*, the voice in the back of his mind whispered.

He had tried to throw away the ring he had bought, but each time he withdrew it from his pocket he stopped. He had deliberately placed the ring in Fyn's rooms only for it to reappear in his own apartments next to his bureau. He had thrown it into the garrison twice, and twice it reappeared in his room. He didn't understand what was happening, but had decided that until he knew more he would hold onto the ring; perhaps eventually whoever kept returning it to him would explain its significance.

"Kee Dala, are you listening?" King Cobey looked at him quizzically.

"Sorry, no, I was distracted."

"I asked if you had plans to stay in Trithia."

"Actually, I've grown accustomed to Trithia and would like to stay longer, if that would be acceptable to His Majesty?"

Stirm smiled blandly and nodded.

"Excellent. I am intrigued with the workings of the King's Guard here. My father has his own regiments, but none quite like these. I would like to learn more and perhaps observe some training sessions? It would please my father to know his bookish son was capable of something more than writing and reading." Dal laughed self-deprecatingly and the others politely joined in.

294

"Prince Kee Dala, I would gladly show you the workings of the King's Guard. Fyn Miner will undoubtedly advise you of our training schedules in more detail," said Kerne.

"Ah yes, Fyn Miner," said Cobey, with an almost imperceptible glance at Dal. "With your permission, Stirm, I would like to take the boy back to Porton with me after the ceremony. I promised his father that he'd have an attachment to my navy. I would consider it a personal favour."

"I'm sure we can arrange something. After all, you are giving me your most precious treasure." Stirm smiled at Ilene and patted her hand. She smiled back.

Kerne sipped his water carefully and stared around the table. "It will be a shame to lose Fyn midway through his training. He has great promise and I feel the remaining few months would shape the boy into a man. Could I arrange for him to travel to Porton later?"

Ilene stood and the men followed suit.

"Gentlemen, I fear that perhaps I have consumed too much wine in my excitement. I shall be retiring for the evening." Dal smiled and he could sense his uncle's displeasure.

"Princess, I do hope you feel well in the morning. I shall send a messenger to you early in the day and we shall announce our engagement tomorrow afternoon to the court." Stirm took her hand and kissed it.

"Thank you, Your Majesty." She turned to Cobey. "Good night, Father." She kissed his cheek and then glanced at Dal. "Kee Dala, are we still to ride tomorrow morning?" Dal hid his surprise and nodded.

"Ride?" Stirm enquired, narrowing his eyes at Dal.

"Yes, Your Majesty. I arranged for a short ride with Kee Dala in the woods surrounding your city." She flashed him a brilliant smile.

"Indeed," said Stirm, tapping his fingers on the table. "Then I will have to insist on Kerne escorting you. You are my betrothed now, and your safety is my primary concern. I couldn't bear the thought of something untoward happening to you." He looked up and matched her smile in both brilliance and insincerity. Ilene nodded and withdrew from the room.

As the meal progressed, Dal undid his jacket and waistcoat and mopped his brow. The heat in the room was becoming too much for him, and even Kerne had loosened his tunic. The food was exquisite and the needs of the guests had been considered carefully, but Dal still couldn't shake his feeling of discontent and unease. Neither Stirm nor Kerne had given him a reason to feel so out of kilter, yet he did; he needed guidance and silently planned to visit the temple of Igon at the earliest opportunity. Dal's thoughts were drifting this evening; he knew he should stop drinking but he couldn't.

The night wore on and the men moved to the study where Stirm personally poured glasses of Velen liquor, a rare delicacy. Dal swirled the green liquid around and sipped it slowly, closing his eyes. It was said that the liquor tasted different to each who savoured it, and to Dal it tasted of aniseed, cinnamon, and oranges. He finished the glass and the room began to spin. The conversation was relaxed but still Dal fought to remain alert and hold his tongue. He knew it was time for him to leave and he got unsteadily to his feet.

"Your Majesty, Uncle, Captain." The pause was long and uncomfortable. "I'm afraid I will have to leave, please forgive me."

He didn't wait for acknowledgement, turning on his heel. He focussed on the large doors and walked briskly towards them, praying he didn't appear too drunk, and fearing with each step he would trip over his own feet. As he closed the door behind him he heard someone laugh softly. Looking to his left he saw the blurry image of Fyn. He closed his left eye and Fyn appeared much clearer. How odd. What was the meaning of this? He would have to write to his tutor, ask him to explain, see what magic was occurring here, what strange . . .

"Dal, how much have you drunk, man?" Fyn took his arm.

"Enough," Dal replied, suddenly fascinated with is own feet.

One foot in front of the other, simple really.

Fyn guided him back to his chambers and placed him on his bed. Dal was too tired to undress, and sprawled on the bed in a twisted heap of clothes. He closed his one open eye and dreamt of home.

"Such charming views, Eli, you really have come . . . down in the world," said Penella staring out of his balcony at the cold, dark streets. Eli grimaced into his glass and downed the nectar. "I see my sister still fawns over you like a lovesick fool. You are so cruel to her."

"Metlina and I have an understanding, Penella. Our arrangement is none of your concern. Have you come solely to anger me, or is there more to your visit?"

Penella stretched her arms behind her, then grasped the balustrade. Her gown clung to her and Eli examined the contours of her exquisite body.

"Do you like what you see, Prince?"

"Don't flatter yourself," he replied, placing his glass on his bureau and stalking to the balcony. The gods stood within inches of one other, one smirking and wetting her lips, the other scowling in reply. "Enough games. I grow bored. If you've come to pout and thrust your chest out in the hope of seducing me, you'll be disappointed."

Penella laughed coquettishly. "You're not my type. I like men, not boys." She sashayed past him and sat in his chair by the fire. Eli clenched his fists, his body rigid, her scent lingering around him.

"Penella—"

"Very well, very well. I've come to offer some vital information to you. Something of which only I am aware," she declared, inspecting her fingernails with every appearance of nonchalance.

"Oh?" Eli didn't turn back, concentrating on the streets below, watching as two of his beasts tore apart the remains of a condemned soul, flesh shredding as easily as parchment. They fought over the last piece, beating their wings and howling in anger.

"Yes, it has to do with your daughter and her two love-sick suitors."

"Chaeli? That plain creature has sparked the interest of *two* men?"

"Indeed. It seems she has her father's gift for enthralling all she meets. And yes, two suitors."

Now Eli turned and entered the room. He stood behind Penella, his hands on the top of the chair. "Continue."

"Well, her two suitors are unique and pivotal for the contest. Of course, before I can supply more information, I need assurances that, should the time come, I shall be safe with you."

Eli stared at the top of her head and said nothing; slowly he moved his hands onto her shoulders, causing the goddess to jump.

"You'll be safe with me. Please continue. I grow tired and restless." The goddess tried to shake off his hands, but Eli gripped her tighter.

"Her suitors are well known to us, and to you, Eli. Your former *Assaké*, Nathan DeVaine, and our very own protector, Adley."

Eli relaxed his grip and bent down towards the goddess, his breath in her ear. Her cool façade was gone; she was frightened and knew he could sense it.

"Tell me, goddess, how this is supposed to benefit me?"

"Do not underestimate the pull of love and lust. Many wars have been fought, won, and lost because of them."

"Again, how is it supposed to benefit me?"

"I've already offered Adley the chance to have Chaeli reciprocate his feelings, and I'm confident that he will eventually succumb. With Chaeli and Adley besotted with each other, you'll get your assassin back. He is close to losing control as we speak, and their love will be the final straw, the last little push he needs to send him over the precipice."

Penella shrugged free of Eli's hands and stood up quickly, turning to face him over the chair. "Believe me, Eli, splitting the group will give you a great advantage. You see, Chaeli is falling for Nathan entirely of her own accord, and that love is pure and undiluted. I can change the course of these emotions. Once Nathan is yours, I can release Chaeli from the thrall and she will be devastated. I want you to orchestrate a situation whereby Chaeli realises that Adley bought her affections. With the three of them divided, conquering her will be inevitable. She will be broken, weak, and so very vulnerable."

"You've thought long and hard about this, haven't you? But your plan is too simplistic. You place too much weight upon the two mortals and their feelings for one another. What happens if Chaeli and Nathan declare their love before Adley crumbles?"

"Nathan doubts himself. Being with the protector constantly reminds him of his failings. He won't admit anything as he fears rejection. He can't forgive himself his past life as an *Assaké*, and if he can't accept himself, he won't believe anyone else can accept him."

"Don't be too sure. Mortals can surprise us." Eli straightened and stared into the fire. Penella kept her face like a mask.

"Let me put it this way, Eli, what have you to lose?"

The Damnable Lord sighed. "Agreed. My charm has failed and she still lives. I need to exploit her; I *need* something that will cause her to lose control. All that power bubbling just beneath the surface is just too enticing for me to ignore."

"You won't regret this." Penella allowed herself a smile; Eli looked at her and realised suddenly how cruel she actually was.

"When did you become so twisted? What did Daro do to you to make you so bitter?"

"Your brother is weak. He allows himself to love these mortals too much. He needs to be shown that they do not deserve our unconditional love. They need to be submissive and loyal. We deserve to be honoured and obeyed, not ignored and only prayed to when they remember us and want something from us."

"And how will meddling in the course of love open Daro's eyes?"

"It won't, not when addressed as a single incident. Think, Eli, think! When you win, Daro falls, and the Kingdom will need a new leader, someone who will show the gods how to treat their followers. With the Kingdom and Underworld combined, we will be able to walk the mortal realms again – oh, imagine what we can do!"

Eli fell silent and mulled over what Penella offered. He would not reveal that he had already given his gods permission to walk the lands. If her plan succeeded, he could lead the gods, usurp his brother, and finally control the three worlds. Ibea alone was a great prize, but Salinthos and Sheranshia had always been neutral, one for the Kingdom, one for the Underworld. All three worlds. He would be unstoppable.

"What have you got to lose, Eli? You are already exiled."

"What of my brother? He will not hand over the Kingdom quite so easily."

"Let us cross that bridge when we come to it."

He snorted. "All right, agreed. When Adley comes crawling, let me know. Until then we shall continue plans as usual. I do not want to see you in my Underworld again. If you enter again without permission, you shall not find my hospitality so enjoyable. Now leave."

Penella bit back a retort. He was so arrogant, but he was also intoxicating. She knew now what her sister saw in him; he exuded power. She wondered what he would be like in bed and shivered – she didn't know if it was fear or delight, or if the two could even be separated. She wondered if he had a gentle side, and quickly dismissed the idea. If he had, then maybe Amelia would have fallen in love with him herself and not have needed Penella's helping hand . . .

CHAPTER NINE

CHAELI DREAMT SHE was home and preparing dinner. The front door opened and Acelle entered, carrying a basket of apples and moaning about the market crowds. Chaeli grinned as her sister dropped the basket on the table and shook the rain from her headscarf, switching from complaining to gossiping without pause. The dream faded, and another scene unfolded: they sat laughing at the table whilst the smell of pastry and fruit wafted through the house. Tears rolled down Chaeli's face and she clutched her sides.

"Why did you let me die?"

The laughter stopped and Chaeli stared at her sister, whose eyes were now full of tears of pain.

"I . . ." she trailed off, uncomfortable. This wasn't right. No. She didn't . . . no.

"You could have saved me, but you ran like a coward. I died for you. I thought you loved me."

Acelle's face twisted in pain. She coughed, and blood splattered the table. Chaeli rushed over to her side, the table now dripping with red. Acelle slumped in Chaeli's arms, her voice coming out in a rasp: "You let me die."

Anya hadn't seen Small since he had taken her to her captor's rooms three days earlier. The captain, or Kerne as he asked her

301

to call him, had spent each night in his office and thankfully left her alone with only books for company. But whenever she woke he was always there, watching her from his chair in the corner of the bedchamber. He insisted on joining her for every meal, and they would eat together in silence. She wouldn't talk to him unless commanded; when he did command, she would resist until she could take no more pain, but on the third day she realised that he took pleasure in seeing her resist. It was then she made it her plan to behave impeccably. To submit was to defeat him.

She sat at the window and stared out over the courtyard. This place held so many memories for her that she didn't know how to feel about it. She hated the situation she was in, but reminiscing over her time here paradoxically took the edge away from her pain.

"Miss DeVaine."

Startled, she whirled round. He was back, immaculately dressed as always; the black and red tunic suited him, but the gold embroidery was too ostentatious, too fussy on a man like him, a misplaced touch of the dandy. His face was, as always, impassive.

"Please join me for tea."

"Is that an order or a request?"

"Would you like me to make it an order?"

She followed him into his drawing room. Kerne escorted her to the table and pulled out her chair, before seating himself.

"Are you well?" he asked, pouring two cups of tea.

"As well as could be expected."

"How is your back?"

"As well as could be expected."

"Do you want for anything while you are here?" He sat upright, gazing at her, his hands knitted together in front of him. He swallowed heavily and coughed. With a shock, she realised he was uncomfortable.

"Only to go home."

"Unfortunately, that will be impossible for the foreseeable future. I was thinking more along the lines of embroidery, books . . . perhaps writing materials?"

"That would be pleasant, thank you." To thank him for these trifles made her want to throw up. Over him, preferably. But she kept the disgust from her face; he was still looking at her, always looking, watching, waiting . . . for something.

"Tell me, Anya, did it hurt when he disfigured you?"

"Of course it hurt!" She closed her eyes and swallowed, the smell of oiled metal and Stirm's lemon scented hands flooding her as she remembered lying on the throne-room floor, screaming while he slowly sliced the rows of cuts into her skin. The captain's interest brought her pain to the surface once more, and his voice was like salt in open wounds.

"Do you miss your beauty?"

"No. People saw my face, never me. Since he destroyed my face, people see what I can do, not what I look like." She opened her eyes and looked straight at him. He nodded slowly.

They drank the rest of the tea in silence. He asked no more questions, and she offered no more information.

Chaeli woke with a sharp scream and sat upright. She was soaked to the bone with sweat, her mouth dry, and she ached all over. Disoriented, she looked around the room. After a while, her eyes adjusted and she could make out hundreds of unlit candles around her; they appeared to have been extinguished for some time. The room had no windows, but she could see cracks of sunlight under the door. On her hands and knees, she breathed in deeply, sharp pain stabbing throughout her body. There was nothing for her to grab onto, so she pushed herself to her feet. Her knees buckled and she hit the floor. Cursing, she tried again, but her muscles were sore and tight, and it took several minutes for her to straighten her legs.

Rune upon carved rune adorned the walls; the floor, too, was covered in them, but these were made of wood. She rotated her arms, working the stiffness out of her joints, then her fingers travelled instinctively to her neck. The choker was gone, but when her fingers made contact with the skin where it had been, she winced as a sharp stinging pain coursed through her. She had to see, but there was no mirror in the room. Hesitating, feeling like an old woman, she crept to the door. The absence of her companions made her uneasy – was she in Lindor, or had something happened?

She took hold of the handle, drew in a breath, then opened the door. Sunlight burst into the room and she raised her hand to shield her eyes. With the sunlight came a wave of fresh air; Chaeli took a deep breath and savoured the sweetness.

"You're awake!" came a whisper. She looked down and saw Adley sitting by the door, his back against the wall, gazing up at her. He jumped to his feet and moved to embrace her, but hesitated, then stopped. Instead, he stroked her face with a calloused hand and kissed her on the forehead.

"Hello, Adley," she croaked, then swallowed, wincing. "I need some water."

"Of course." He guided her towards the main library. Her legs gave way several times and Adley caught her each time; when he touched her, she felt a hum of energy throughout her body and her left shoulder grew hot.

He sat her down at a table in front of a huge stained glass window. Bright blocks of colour streamed into the room and she watched the light dance on the floor as Adley brought her two glasses of water. She downed them both and gasped at the freshness.

"Where's Nathan?"

"With Sheiva and Mickalos, custodian of this library and one of my oldest friends. They are studying in the library."

"I take it we're in Lindor?" she asked, gazing round the room.

"Yes, we arrived three days ago. Mickalos removed the charm and you've slept since."

"Three days? Gods!"

"Mickalos said your body needed to heal and that you'd wake when you were ready. Your neck looks sore, but nowhere near as bad as when the choker fell off."

"I need to wash, Adley, I smell awful."

"I can arrange that," he said, jumping up. "I'll arrange for the acolytes to prepare the wash room for you. I'll get you clean clothes too. No hurry, take your time. We're safe in Lindor and we can spend time recuperating while we try to work out what's going on and what to do next."

"Sounds good. The recuperating part especially." Chaeli smiled and sat back in the chair. She closed her eyes for a moment and the next thing she knew Adley was gently shaking her arm.

"Bath's ready," he smiled.

"Gods! I must have fallen asleep again. Who would have thought I'd drop off sitting upright after three days of snoozing." They laughed and he helped her to her feet. A familiar dark figure appeared from behind a bookcase.

"Nathan!" The delight in her voice was evident. Lindor agreed with the man; he looked fit and well and his face was calm . . . and he was smiling.

"Chaeli," he said with a nod. "You look like shit."

She burst out laughing and gripped the table for support. "Ever the poet."

He grinned wider and shrugged. "Only telling you the truth." He came forward and pushed between Chaeli and Adley causing the older man to step back. He put his arms round her and pulled her against his chest. Chaeli closed her eyes and allowed his warmth to seep into her. His smell was so comforting and alive; she inhaled deeply and sighed.

"I missed you," he murmured.

"Was only three days," came her muffled reply.

"Yes, but in those three days not even Sheiva could irritate me the way you do." He pulled back and pressed a soft kiss to her cheek. The touch of his lips burned her skin and she blushed and felt giddy.

"You need a bath. You stink worse than the pits of Velen," he said, still smiling.

"Thanks," she muttered and turned back to Adley, who was staring at them, his face unmoving save for a frown. "I believe Adley has sorted a bath for me anyway," she added, smiling at the protector, who nodded.

She followed him to the wash room and he showed her the drying linens, bath oils, and a pile of clean clothes.

"Thank you," she said. "Adley, before, there wasn't—"

"Enjoy your bath. We'll be in the library when you're ready," he said, and left before she could speak again.

She stripped down to her bare skin and went to the mirror, but the shock of her appearance made her reel backwards. Her neck was scabbed and a dark livid red; dried blood coated the skin where the choker had been. Yet the injury was not what had caught her attention. A constellation of white stars covered her left shoulder and collarbone, trailing down to her breasts, and collection of white runes and scripts followed the contours of her rib cage. She traced six lines of runes, which quivered under her touch. The sensation made her weak; uncertain of what they were and why they were there.

She had become thinner, her face more defined, and she now had less of the soft double-chin of her plump childhood and her hips jutted out – how could she have lost so much weight in just three days?

The runes continued on to her back, though her arms seemed normal and unchanged. She checked her palm, and the seven stars were still there in the now-familiar seashell pattern. On her other palm, seven white stars twinkled up at her, identical in size and pattern to those on her other hand, except that one set was black, the other white.

306

Chaeli shook herself and made her way to the bath, sighing in delight as the warm water lapped over her legs. The bath was as large as her bedroom, and she walked in until it covered her shoulders. The water splashing gently on her neck stung at first, but she swam a few careful lengths and allowed the heat to work into her aching muscles. The sensation was glorious, renewing her strength and fortitude. Moving to the shallow end, she sat on the steps, picked up several bottles of oils and sniffed. Some were too strong, causing her to cough and hastily replace the stoppers, but one reminded her of cherry blossom and the honeysuckle roses her mother grew; this she worked through her hair, savouring the smell. Drops of the oil hit her neck and instead of stinging, they soothed, caressing her skin like a mother's hands. She dabbed more oil on the scab and gently worked it in; the pain subsided and she began to feel whole again. With the oil in her hair she dunked her head several times and swam under the warm water to the deep end, where she turned to float on her back, staring at the rune-covered ceiling. The whole room reminded her of the countryside surrounding her village; in tune with nature, the vines up the wall entwined with the statues and seemed to merge into one.

Closing her eyes, she entered her energy and delighted at the speed with which it responded. She no longer had to conjure a door and could tap into her reserves with a mere thought. The energy pulsed and hummed happily and pulled slightly on the runes and stars in the room. As time passed, she realised she was drawing energy from the room itself; the roof no longer sparkled and the stars had become dull and listless. Uneasy at this change, she touched her energy core and sensed the new additions. She couldn't access them but they were comfortable and . . . true. She would have to ask Adley about this, he would know what to do.

Calm. Chaeli was calm. She hadn't felt so safe and secure since the morning before the demon appeared, when she had been setting the table for the three of them, still mourning the loss of her parents, yet content with her life and considering the offer of apprenticeship. Had she been truly content, though? She thought through the events that had brought her to Lindor and deliberately shied away from the knowledge of her adoption, of being the daughter of the Damnable Lord. This whole series of events was simply unfair, as though she had been dragged into the middle of a celestial war, dumped on the battleground as a participant – or as a trophy.

A battleground. She thought of Adley, a warrior sent from the Kingdom to protect her from the Underworld. His dragon reminded her of the scriptures she had memorised at the Kingdom Church. Only the crusaders of the Kitaani and Dragon Wars over a thousand years ago had been honoured with such an inking, but he didn't look a day over thirty five.

Then there was Nathan, from the higher echelons of the damned. He had thrown away that life in search of the Kingdom, but he still so angry; she had seen the rage leak from him and sensed a malevolence so great it scared her. Thoughts of Nathan made her flush, especially as she lay naked in the warm water. She had thought him attractive from the moment they had first met, a feeling which had only deepened at the sight of him shirtless, the broad expanse of muscle corded and honed, the serpent and the scars from his lashings marring his otherwise flawless skin.

Adley, on the other hand, was an average-looking man, but the goodness radiating from him made him attractive. He was full of old fashioned – even archaic – sensibilities and manners, some of which annoyed her, but still others made her feel feminine and special. When he looked at her, she felt as though she was the most beautiful woman in the world.

As the water cooled around her, she stepped out and dried herself. The mirror showed her neck wasn't as bad as she had first thought, and with a start she realised the slash to her thigh was completely healed. A thin, red, puckered scar covered the area, unsightly but clean. The balms Anya had given her had been lost with Danven, yet it seemed they were no longer needed. The speed her with which body healed amazed her. *A bonus of my bloodline?*

Chaeli examined the clothes Adley had prepared for her. They were new and pressed to perfection. The cut of the white shirt complemented her colouring and she tied it in place with a sense of luxury. The trousers were a caramel colour, made from buttery soft leather, undoubtedly expensive; as she pulled them on, they stroked every inch of her skin and accentuated her shape. The boots were also leather, reaching to her knees and shining a deep black. She took her time lacing them, and as she gazed in the mirror once again, she could barely recognise herself. She had never been a vain girl, envying Acelle her looks. But, at that moment, she felt truly pleasant on the eye. The oil made her hair gleam and her complexion glowed like moonlight. Laughing aloud, she skipped from the room, for the first time in a long while ready for anything.

As she entered the great library, the scholars turned and stared at her. Chaeli was suddenly uncomfortable; everywhere she looked she was met by pairs of shocked, staring eyes, and from each corner, a hum of whispers followed. The heat rose to her cheeks as she searched for Adley and Nathan. She trotted down the aisles of books, searching left and right, but only strangers returned her gaze. Where were they? Her good mood began to ebb away, replaced by fear and burgeoning panic. She felt like an exhibit in some golden menagerie.

"Lady Chaeli, may I help?"

She turned and saw a young man in a long white robe approaching her. "How do you know who I am?" she asked, backing away.

"I was with Master Mickalos when he healed you. You bear my stars on your body." His voice was cool and dispassionate. Chaeli relaxed slightly.

"I'm looking for Adley and Nathan."

"They are with Master Mickalos in the courtyard. Follow me."

The young man led her through a maze of book-lined corridors to large glass double doors. He opened them and she stepped into the most exquisite gardens she had ever seen. It seemed so strange to be in a city, and yet have the colours, scents and wildlife from the countryside within her grasp. The garden was walled, but each wall was covered with climbing vines, and so there seemed endless vistas of the natural world. The scent of honeysuckle reached her once more, the freshness transporting her home; the sun beat down as it had in the summers of her childhood.

"Chaeli!" called a gravelly voice. "Over here."

She squinted into the distance and saw an old man beckoning her. The sheer size of the gardens overwhelmed her – at least twice that of the library itself. She approached him slowly and smoothed down her hair and then her shirt, the feeling she was being inspected stronger than ever. Then she caught sight of Nathan and Adley sitting at a wrought iron table in the sun. Both men were laughing and cups of mead cluttered the surface. The old man smiled as she approached and, despite towering over him by a good six inches, she felt small. Childlike. His touch was soft but strong as he hooked her arm in his and escorted her to the table. Both men looked up at her, grinning.

Adley cleared his throat. "May I say, m'lady, you look . . . you look . . . you look bloody gorgeous!" The words were slurred and his mead splashed in the mug as he tried to set it on the table, missing by some distance. "Bloody, bloody gorgeous."

"Aye! Hear, hear!" roared Nathan. "A nymph from Salinthos, a beautiful star . . . a . . . a—."

"Nay, she is far too beautiful for a nymph. She is more beautiful than the Goddess of Love, who, I might add, is a close personal friend. Close." Adley took a deep swig of mead and placed his mug theatrically on the table.

"She is a goddess, aye . . . Goddess of my heart!"

"Nay, *my* goddess!" cried Adley, raising his mug, which he clinked against Nathan's. The men downed their mead, splashes of liquid hitting their shirts as they guzzled. Nathan slammed his mug down first on the table and shouted in delight: "I win!"

"Just this once, *Assaké*, just this once."

"The old goat has been bested by the young lion!" Nathan playfully punched Adley in the arm. The protector chuckled.

The sight of them both relaxing and laughing together shocked Chaeli into speechlessness. She had grown accustomed to their disputes, their underlying antagonism and hostility towards one another. Only a short time ago there had been an air of discernible tension and yet now she sensed nothing but good will and positivity. Suddenly, she giggled; she caught the eye of the old man, who tried to control a smirk. This made her giggle harder, and within seconds she was doubled over with waves of laughter.

"The nymph laughs at us, old man," said Nathan, raising his eyebrows.

"The cheek of it! I think she needs to be taught a lesson, don't you?"

"Aye, a nice icy shower to cool off and scare those giggles away." Nathan moved around the table to a nearby well. He dipped his mug into the water and approached Chaeli. "Time to cool down the nymph."

"No, Nathan!" she shrieked whilst laughing. "No, please, I've just got dry! Don't!" She backed around the table while Nathan stalked her, stumbling into the old man.

"Don't you children get me involved, else you'll all get a tanning."

"Tell him to leave me alone," she laughed. "Tell him!"

"I'll tell him nothing of the kind. You're a big girl, you stop him."

Nathan lunged forward. Chaeli dodged to the left and fell into Adley's lap. The water hit the paving behind with a loud splat.

"Missed!" she cried.

Adley held onto her as she laughed, his swaying even as he sat making it clear he was drunk.

"Chaeli, there's something I have to—" he began, but before he could finish, she leapt to her feet and grabbed his empty mug. She dashed to the well and filled it with water, then turned on Nathan.

"Now look who needs cooling down!" She chased him onto the grass and lunged with the water; he feinted to the left and she missed.

Grabbing her by the waist, he pulled her to the ground and lay on top of her. Suddenly, Chaeli could feel the curve of his body, his heat and his strength. He was breathing heavily and his chest crushed against her; his lips were near and she could see the flecks of a darker blue in his eyes. He moved her arms and pinned them above her head with one hand, the other traced down her arm, along the outside of her breast, coming to rest on her waist.

"Chaeli" he whispered, then leaned in and kissed her deeply. She felt his tongue on hers and responded hungrily. He tasted of mead and honey, his lips unexpectedly, thrillingly soft. He moved his free hand to her waist, and she kissed more deeply, her fingers winding into his hair. Nathan broke away and pressed his lips to her throat.

"Sorry to interrupt, children, but your . . . demonstration seems to have affected my dear friend," called the old man.

Chaeli's blood turned to ice. She opened her eyes and broke free from Nathan's kiss.

"Chaeli—"

"No, Nathan, stop! We can't!" She scrambled up from under him and looked at the table. Adley was gone. The old man began to clear up the mugs.

"The honourable Protector of the Kingdom has left to give you some privacy," he said.

"I'm so sorry, forgive me!" Chaeli blurted out, wishing the ground would swallow her up. She had made a fool of herself in front of this venerable man mere minutes after meeting him.

"Not for me to forgive," he replied.

Chaeli glanced at Nathan. His eyes were unfocussed and he was clearly drunk. She felt sick. She had behaved like a common harlot, like the barmaid at old Wilyem's Inn. She could hear her mother's voice now.

"A lady who submits to a kiss will always consent to more."

She had taken advantage of Nathan when he wasn't himself. Mortified, she ran through the library after Adley. When she couldn't find him, she continued out into the streets of Lindor, calling his name. She had to make him understand, had to show him that it had been nothing but a kiss.

Adley stared at them, writhing on the ground, oblivious to any audience, the way Chaeli responded to Nathan, the way her body craved his. When Nathan traced the shape of her body with his hand, Adley wanted to hit him; when he kissed her, he wanted to rip out the warrior's throat. His dragon swelled and quivered in sympathy. He tried to move but couldn't, he had to stay, had to see how she responded. He was praying silently she would protest and shake free, but she didn't. She moaned with pleasure and kissed him back. He knew then that she was lost to him, that she could never love him the way he loved her, and he couldn't bear to watch any more. He stood up quickly.

"Friend, wait," said Mickalos, but Adley couldn't stand the pity in his voice. He swept through the library and out into the streets. He needed Penella, she would understand the ache in his heart that grew fiercer every passing day, that now threatened to break him. She had consoled him all those years ago as he scattered the ashes of his loved ones. It was her soft words of comfort and belief that had pulled him from the madness of grief. It was her cool touch that soothed the fire that had burned away his senses, bringing him back to sanity. Her guidance was needed again, for no other god understood the torment of love as she did. How could they?

313

So deep in thought was he that several people bumped into him, disturbing the Lindorian calm; one grumbled loudly, bringing Adley back to himself.

"Excuse me, which way to the temple of Penella?" he asked.

The man, taken aback, responded at once, and a knowing smile spread over his face. Adley made his way to the temple, sure of what he had to do. He entered and went straight to the altar, barely noticing the scores of people praying in the pews. Baring his wrist and taking his knife from its scabbard, he drew a line across his un-inked palm; blood dripped onto the marble floor. Closing his eyes, he drew on his energy and begged the Goddess of Love for guidance.

"Adley," came her sweet tones almost at once, "what is wrong, my dear protector?" His goddess covered approached, draped in a dark cloak, blending into the congregation of followers, most of whom kept their eyes down.

"My lady, you should not be here."

"I sensed pain in your summons, and could not wait for you to come to us. I can't allow our protector to be in such distress." Her touch on his face was like a thrilling warm breeze on his skin. "What is wrong, my champion?"

Adley shook his head, trying to clear the alcohol-induced haze. "Chaeli," he croaked.

"What has happened? Is she all right?"

"Yes, fine, she's fine. Wonderful, in fact. And . . . and she wants *him*."

"Adley," she said gently. "She's always wanted him."

"As I have always wanted her," he replied bitterly.

She stared at him thoughtfully. "You have suffered, and we have asked so much of you. Chaeli can love you Adley, but what will you do for me in return?"

The protector looked at her in surprise, swaying slightly on his feet.

"To alter the course of love is a delicate process, especially where one such as Chaeli is concerned. I need something from you in return."

"Anything," he blurted, no longer thinking clearly. All he wanted was Chaeli.

"I do not want war," said the goddess, "I want peace, tranquillity, a time of ease. My role is to nurture love. The option of peaceful negotiations between our princes needs to be explored. It is not for Daro to decide alone. Chaeli needs to meet her father, and Eli needs to embrace fatherly love and family – that is important too, is it not? For a father to see his daughter?"

Adley stared at the goddess. Surely she was not suggesting this? He shook his head hazily. "I don't understand." Something wasn't right. He would do anything for Chaeli's love, but his dragon was unhappy – and when the dragon was unhappy, it tortured him; the claws dug into his skin, pulling him in on himself.

"Just think about it, Adley. If you decide that love should prevail, then you need only call me in prayer. I will answer." The goddess kissed his bloody palm and was gone.

Adley stared at the empty space Had the Goddess of Love really visited the mortal realm so readily, at the first cut of his skin, the first call of blood? He stared at his hand. No sign of a cut, no sign of his blood on the ground. A slight dull throbbing filled his head. He really shouldn't have drunk all that mead. Never again. *Never again!* He sheathed his blade and stumbled out of the temple. By this time, the sun was setting and the shadows were long. He wandered through the streets, each step sending pain through his skull.

"What *are* you doing?"

Sheiva balanced on a wall above his head, matching his pace and staring down at him.

"Clearing my head," he growled. He was in no mood for the fae.

"Chaeli is worried about you."

"I doubt that."

"She is! She's looking for you, and she's very upset."

"Yes, she was being upset all over Nathan when I saw her last."

"You can't have her anyway. You do know that, don't you?" The cat was persistent, and the plaintive tone wormed into Adley's mind. "Don't you?"

"Leave me alone. I don't need lecturing, especially not from a cat!" He quickened his pace. The cat matched him, hissing with exasperation.

"Yes you do! You listen here, Adley. You are Protector of the Kingdom, remember? You are forbidden to love, you are celibate. That was your pledge and promise to the gods. Have you forgotten your oath? Does it mean so little to you?"

Adley stopped and stared at the cat. Sheiva's tail was enlarged and his hackles raised.

Adley crossed his arms, sighing through gritted teeth. "What about me, Sheiva? I've given *everything* to the gods. I just want something for myself. I want to be happy . . . I want a family, someone to love, someone who loves me." Even saying it, Adley knew it was selfish.

"The person you want doesn't want you, Adley. She doesn't love you the way you love her."

Adley scowled at the cat. "You don't know that."

"She's young. She's only twenty years old. You placed too much on that kiss, and now you have to get over it. You've seen her kiss boys before."

"Exactly my point, Shiv. I've seen her kiss *boys*, but not a *man*. She's never shown interest like that, never . . . been that way . . ."

"I come back to my point: she's twenty. Adders, do you remember what you were like when you were that age?"

The cat had a point. He was drunk, and not rational, and silently glad he now realised how irrational he was being. He looked away, relaxing his arms by his sides. "I love her. I've always loved her. These last few days with her, actually being able to touch her, have only served to intensify my feelings for her."

"I know. But she's not yours, and she never will be."

Adley nodded, though his heart was screaming.

Chaeli ran through the streets. She had to find Adley and explain that the kiss had meant nothing. Above all, she didn't want to hurt the protector. She had seen how he viewed her, seen the way he looked at her, but never did she truly think he wanted her. There were a million women more attractive than she, and besides, whatever he did feel for her was now surely damaged by that disgraceful scene.

But . . . did she *want* Adley to love her? Or was it only humiliation and sadness at the upset and disharmony she had caused that made her chase him through the unfamiliar city streets. Both men had risked so much for her over the last week, and she didn't want to be responsible for playing with their emotions like an immature child.

But the kiss was good, came a whisper in her head. Yes it *was* good, better than good. She blushed at the thought of kissing Nathan, and licked her lips; she could still taste him on her. She had never kissed a man like that before, firm and intense where the boys of the village were wet and fumbling. She slowed down as the streets became narrower. Where was Adley? For that matter, where was she? The sun was setting and though Lindor appeared a pleasant place, the idea of being lost in the streets scared her. The limestone walls and alleys all looked the same, uniform and non-descript. Even the runes etched into the stone were repeated themselves.

"Are you lost?"

She jumped and spun around. A blond-haired man smiled back at her; he stepped from the shadows and held his hands up in a placatory manner.

"Just looking for a friend," she mumbled, glancing to the next alleyway and screwing up her face in confusion.

"Where did you see him last?"

"At the library. He left suddenly."

"Lovers' quarrel?" He laughed gently and she shook her head.

"No." She paused. "Can you tell me the way back to the main streets near the library?"

"Oh, of course." He moved towards her and instinctively she stepped back. "I don't bite. Look – it's down there, to the left, then the third right. That will bring you out by the Merchant Square. You then take a left at the temple of Nishka, carry straight on to the arena and then right. You'll see the spires of the healers' university. A shortcut across their courtyard and you'll come to the council buildings, you can then—"

"Wait! Sorry, can you start again?"

"How about I show you? I'm staying not far from there." He put his hands in his pockets and nodded towards the alleyway.

"That would be good, thank you." She followed him as he started off down the alley.

"My name is Andraes," he said, glancing over his shoulder and grinning.

Chaeli considered this stranger; something didn't feel right. When she met Nathan and Adley, the gods had guided her with warmth and words. With this man all she felt was unease, the quietness of the streets only adding to her concern.

"My name is Nina," she said.

"Nice to meet you, Nina. What brings you to Lindor?" He slowed and she shot him a wary glance. He raised an eyebrow and grinned back.

"The library. I'm here with my friends."

He continued to talk as he led her through the city, telling her he was a fire juggler from Algary and was in the city for the spring festival. He spoke of his home in Baywen, the wettest part of his realm, but, he explained, the most beautiful. He described the lush green forests, rolling hills, and even the swamps. Chaeli hadn't realised just how much of the far northern realm was forest.

He intended to start his own troupe and hoped the pay from the spring festival would enable him to realise his dream. Mentioning the troupe caused Chaeli to think of Danven and she shuddered.

They passed the temple of Nishka and Andraes paused for a moment. Chaeli noticed his hesitation and wondered if he was an Underworld follower. But when he spat on the temple's threshold, she relaxed.

"Nearly there." He pointed up to where tall and delicate blue-grey stone towers filled the sky. The moonlight bounced off the stone and lit the building like a beacon. "That's Porton stone, quarried from the bottom of the Lady Volcano. Rumour has it the King of Porton gifted the remaining stone to Lindor's council for future development."

"It's beautiful."

"It's very rare and almost indestructible. It takes the most gifted of energy users to carve and mould the stone. Perfect for a hospital."

She nodded and they cut across the courtyard, carefully pruned bushes and well tended shrubs lining the walkway, the scent of mint and ratatta weaving through the air. Andraes started to whistle, and then changed to humming. The tune worked into her and soon she found herself replaying the melody over and over again in her head.

"Pretty, isn't it? Velenese, I think."

"It's lovely."

"You can see the library from here. How did you get so lost anyway?" He stopped suddenly and turned to face her.

"I don't know, not paying attention. Thank you for showing me the way back."

"I hope you find your friends. It was nice meeting you . . . Nina." She blinked slowly and smiled blandly back at him.

"Be careful," he added.

"Thank you. I will be." She turned and walked towards the library, shooting a glance over her shoulder, but the fire juggler was gone. Humming the tune to herself, she turned a corner only to find Adley walking along, talking to his feline friend who followed on the wall above. Chaeli ducked back behind the building and caught the end of a conversation:

"I love her. I've always loved her. These last few days with her, actually being able to touch her, have only served to intensify my feelings for her."

"I know. But she's not yours, and she never will be."

Chaeli gulped. So he did love her. Adley caused a reaction in her that Nathan did not . . . could not. Her skin felt alive when she was with him; the energy she produced with him was strange and powerful, and the link to his dragon was incredible. He just seemed so much *older*. Not merely physically, but emotionally as well. He was in control of everything; he never shouted or behaved rashly or childishly the way she did. Whilst she stood there musing, Adley turned the corner and stopped in front of her, looking twice to ensure he saw her correctly and then straightening his jacket in surprise before flitting his gaze to the cat and back up at her again.

"Adley!"

"Chaeli, before you say anything, let me speak." The protector swallowed and forced a smile. "I need time alone. I drank too much and . . . I thought a walk might clear my head. I'm sorry to have worried you. Sheiva just found me, you see, and told me you were looking for me."

"I see," she replied slowly. "How is your head now?"

"Much better, just a slight headache. I don't think the mead here agrees with me."

She smiled back at him. "Shall we go back before it gets darker? I have so many questions to ask you. I got caught up with seeing Nathan and you so . . . er . . . different. Relaxed. Jovial."

"I'll have you know I have a perfectly serviceable sense of humour. Some consider me rather amusing, in fact." He smiled as he offered her his arm. "Shall we?"

She thought back to the snippet she'd heard: *"I love her. I always have."* With effort, she pushed the memory away and looped her

arm through his, the heat flaring between them as they walked
back to the library.

Elek felt the pull on his grace: another request. Sighing, he closed
his eyes and concentrated on the prayer. It was an Algarian
desperately praying while losing a game of dice; he needed three
pairs of odds and he had six dice. Elek felt the heightened anxiety
of the player and realised the stakes. If the man lost this game, he
lost a finger for each die that fell on even. The God of Chance wove
his power into the believer; he was in no mood for severed digits.

As he sat back and smiled at the relief and exaltation of the
player, he felt another call, a summoning. The familiar signature
of Igon wove into him and he sighed again. No doubt the God
of Honesty wished to chide him for his interference yet again.

Igon was on Ibea, in Algary no less. Drawing his power around
him, he concentrated on the bells and colours of the Calling. The
music danced through him and sung to his very core, while the
colours roared around his form, the brilliance and clarity of the
rainbow wrapping around him. He fixed his attention on the
music and felt his corporeal body dissolve with the notes of the
bells as the harmony carried him to the mortal plane, whispering
and caressing him as he rode the colours. Elek guided the Calling
to the northern realm and sensed the power of Igon pulsating like
a beacon in the middle of the greyland swamps. He shut out the
Calling, swallowing with difficulty as he did. The intoxication
of the colours and bells had spread and, as his body formed, the
Calling was torn from him, leaving a gaping emptiness.

"Well met, Igon." He smoothed his robes and nodded towards
the old hobbling man before him, sensing the arrival of another
god as he did. "Drenic, you were summoned also?"

"Indeed." The grinning God of Happiness' voice grew louder
around them as his form solidified.

Elek glanced at both expectantly. "Well?" he prompted, standing with his hands behind his back. The smell of rotting leaves and damp never failed to make his mood sour. *Why the swamps, Igon?*

"Can you sense the change already, brothers? I feel uneasy with this subterfuge. My power base has increased two-fold since I began to walk the lands, and yet the pool continues to drain." Igon leant heavily against his staff and stared around. "I feel uneasy betraying my prince. I fear I cannot do this for much longer."

Elek exhaled and concentrated on the wisps of green and blue haze in the night sky shining and shimmering against the backdrop of Nalowyn's stars, the echoes of those who had been welcomed directly into her arms. The shades of the sky reminded the God of Chance of Denna's paint palette, the colours swirling haphazardly together, yet perfectly complementing one another. "I, too, have been uneasy. I've found it impossible to stay away from the betting houses."

"You jest, Elek, but I cannot do this any longer. I've watched Shy'la at her temples, and the dedication and hope her followers show her worries me. It is too much too soon. I *must* tell Daro."

"And consign us all to the void? Have you taken leave of your senses?" Drenic frowned and sat on a fallen tree. "We do this for the good of the Kingdom, for Daro."

"My daughters have grown petulant. They are never seen and do not listen to my guidance. I sense them in schools, in crowds, their grace intoxicating. The balance must be maintained!"

"What of Hytensia and Clendian?" Elek asked, partly distracted by the request of another gambler and follower who begged for his help.

"They remain silent, locked in study, away from all."

"You worry too much, Igon. I sense no unbalance. Ibea remains neutral," said Drenic. "I have been called to all Seven Realms, touched many followers, and have seen the pain they hide. Eli's Underworld still infects."

"What of Chaeli, Elek?"

"She prays. I sense no darkness, only calm." In truth, the God of Chance had not felt her call in several days, but his loyalty to her silenced him. All Elek could hear was the soft warble of nearby birds and the clicking of crickets and insects scurrying around the swamp.

"No darkness? A child of Eli's will always dance in darkness, Elek. And she is part mortal. We know they are fickle, wild and unreserved." Igon shook his head. "What will happen if she strays from the protector's side, my friend? If she embraces the blood of her father, imagine then what will be released. The creations of Eli's imagination, the nightmares of the mortals, the monstrosities who will hunt and destroy the land. This will become the playground for the Underworld and the balance will tip in their favour. The mortals will become enslaved, their love for the Kingdom will die, and thus will we." Igon rested his head on the top of his staff. "I worry for Daro. He is clouded when it comes to the child and his brother."

"Aye, I understand. He still mourns for Amelia. He will not leave his quarters." Drenic paced the small clearing. "We do this for him, do we not?" He sounded lost and Elek paused slightly before nodding in agreement.

"Adley will ensure she doesn't stray, my friends, and if she does, he will deal with the situation accordingly." Igon said this with confidence, patting the God of Happiness's back.

Elek remained silent; he doubted the protector would kill her, and knew if presented with the same ultimatum, he himself would also be unable to complete the task. He was assiduous to her wants and needs. She commanded his grace and he found himself joyously submitting to her requests, time and time again: he needed her to open herself to him, to allow him to possess her with his energy.

"Elek? You remain quiet, my friend."

Elek looked up and, dragging himself from his thoughts, saw both his equals staring at him. He forced himself to speak: "There is nothing to worry over, Igon. We walk the realms in Daro's honour, to preserve what he created for us and for the mortals. What we do is neither dishonest nor disloyal."

The God of Truth nodded unhappily. "Forgive me for calling you. I find this whole business leaves a bad taste in my mouth. I cannot control my daughters, and now I feel as though I am betraying my prince."

"I will speak to Joy and Trust," Elek offered. "We are protecting what Daro created and what he loves." He couldn't deny the uncomfortable feeling that engulfed him. "I will find your daughters now." He reached out to the Calling and summoned the bells and colours, allowing the power to take control and guide him away from the mortal world.

Nathan closed his eyes and tasted Chaeli, who was sweeter on his tongue than he could have dreamt. A moan of pleasure escaped her lips and he instantly hardened. He let go of her hands, needing to touch her skin, to possess her. She grabbed his head and kissed him deeper. Gods, *oh gods!* His serpents slithered quietly, their ever-jealous and hateful nature quelled momentarily by his desire and then, to his surprise, they reared up again, wanting her too. A cool breeze caressed his back, and he remembered then they had been play-fighting in the courtyard. He had been so enraptured by touching and kissing her that everything else had faded away. He heard the old man but paid no attention to what he said.

Suddenly Chaeli stopped and jerked free, horror plain on her face. It scared him; what had he done wrong? She begged him to stop, and he couldn't believe what he was hearing. He tried to reply, but she was already on her feet. He too stood, the world spinning around him, his stomach rolling with nausea. He kept his meal inside with a concerted effort, but Chaeli still stared at him in horror, which quickly turned to disgust. Then she ran.

He staggered to the table and sat down, clutching his head. What had happened? Had he pushed her too quickly? Placing his forehead on the table, he groaned. *Gods, but my head hurts!*

"Too much too quickly," grumbled the old man. "You need to learn how to handle your mead, boy."

"I'm a seasoned drinker, old man," he replied, then groaned again.

"Lindor mead is more potent than the hog's piss served elsewhere."

"Where is Adley? And where did Chaeli go?"

"Ah! So now you care about Adley! Didn't consider his feelings when you were rutting like a stallion on the floor with a girl half your age did you, eh? A half-and-half to boot." The old man frowned at him. "You're a disgrace, boy, you're not fit to be here and I only put up with you for Adley and the girl. It's all I can do not to spit on you, *Assaké* scum!"

"Now hold on a minute! I am not *Assaké*. Have a care with your words!" he replied, his voice growing louder and deeper.

"You wear the mark of the serpents, boy. I sense them. They slither and slide their way through the barriers you've built up. You pin a girl to the floor and mark her as your own in front of all. I don't blame the girl, but you, you know exactly what you are doing." He pointed a gnarled finger at Nathan and the younger man sat up straight. "You bring death with you, DeVaine, death and destruction. *Misery.*" With that, Mickalos hobbled back into the library carrying the empty mugs and shaking his head, leaving Nathan alone in the dying rays of the setting sun.

Nathan was numb. He didn't deserve Chaeli; he would ruin her, break her spirit, take her innocence. The old man was right, he was nothing but misery. He cleared his throat and wiped his eyes on the back of his hand. He would distance himself from her and hope that with time whatever feelings they had for each other would fade. He didn't believe the lie, but he needed something to cling on to.

"I had another dream," Hana whispered into the night as she hid under her covers with her candle and her drawing paper. "A silver lady and a gold man were dancing around the castle. Their faces were touching as they danced around and around. They were so very pretty – I'd like to go dancing one day, wear a pretty dress and pin my hair like the ladies in the court." She spoke aloud while sketching the dancers. It helped her empty her mind of the dreams and visions. There were so many that she needed to release them and the shadows were only too happy to help.

The faces of the dancers were darkened with charcoal for, like most of those in her dreams, their features had been hidden. She drew the circle in which they danced, drew the way they twisted and curved together again and again.

"A fire started in the castle, but the dancers ignored it. The flames burned them but they didn't catch on fire. They did start to cry though, and their tears fell from the ceilings and put out the fire." Hana paused and reached out of her cover, groping in for her pencil box, pulling it under and into her blanket before colouring in the silver lady. "They stopped when they got to my room and the man knocked on my door three times. But I wasn't there, I was watching them from above. Adyam answered my door and he took the dancers to another room in the castle, full of scrolls and birds, and there was a big tree with huge green leaves growing in the middle, and a snow leopard sleeping at the bottom. The dancers cuddled around the snow leopard and they all slept together."

She finished colouring the dancers and stared at the picture, tracing the figures and the sleeping snow leopard with her finger. She had seen the leopard before in her dreams. He – for she was sure the leopard was a he – had been muzzled and led around by a man with a crown. That had been a sad dream. When Hana had woken she cried for the leopard. He was meant to be free.

Throwing back her covers, she lifted her candle and peered around. The shadows stretched and shortened as she padded across the room and hid her picture under the loose material on the love seat. She didn't want Mr Kerne to see them. He would want to know everything about her dreams, but they were her secret, the only thing she could keep from him, the only power she could have over him.

This room, her room, was as suffocating as her cell. In the dungeons she had been forgotten, left alone, but here, here she had to work all day and it was so tiring. She touched the wall. The soft pink was deceptive, still cold stone under the wood panelling. Cold stone like her cell. This whole place was one big prison and she wanted to be free.

There was a creak and Hana froze. *Someone is in my room.* Her inner guide began to cry and Hana's hands shook, making the light from the candle flicker.

"Who's there?" she called. "I heard you, and I am not afraid."

There was no answer, only the sound of her own irregular breathing. After a few moments she spun round quickly with her candle, waving it to spread light into the corners of the room, but there was no one. She ran to her bed and blew the candle out before burrowing under the covers again. Closing her eyes, she said a small prayer to the Kingdom:

"Lord Daro, Keeper of Souls, lover of All, please take away my dreams. I know I haven't prayed in a long time, but that's only because Mr Kerne makes me work so hard, and I've been too tired to pray before bed. I don't want to dream anymore. The dreams make me cry and my head hurts so much afterwards. I dream during the day now, and it scares me. I forget things. I'll be working with Mr Kerne and then the next thing I know, I'm eating my dinner. I don't like it. Please stop them. If you do, I'll pray every day forever and ever. Light guide my way, darkness hide away."

She finished the prayer and snuggled down to sleep, hoping her god had heard.

γ

It had been too long. White didn't move and the Watcher rubbed his chin thoughtfully. Could this be it? Could it be over? Somehow it seemed too simple, too easy. He frowned as Blue stood over White, sword at his side. Even now, with the clear tactical advantage, he did not finish it. Instead, he reached down and pulled his companion to his feet and handed him his own sword, withdrawing his opponent's and arming himself with the new weapon. The Watcher stood, fascinated. This was new. He hadn't seen this before.

White threw the bone to the floor and grabbed Blue's right shoulder, pulling it down as he kneed him in the stomach twice. Holding nothing back and forcing his power into each blow, Blue lashed out methodically with his left fist, connecting with White's shoulder. It was then that it began to rain, a steady yet heavy shower, soaking the ground and the men. Water pooled in small sections of the arena, and as the men moved, their feet sank into wet sand. White struck out with his sword, but a flash of lightning, followed by a deep grumbling sound, filled the air. The bolt licked the sword, making the warrior drop it and fall to his knees clutching at his wrist and hand.

Again Blue refused to end the match, though he had the perfect opportunity to run his enemy through. Instead, he picked up and sheathed the scorched sword in his scabbard, throwing the warrior's out of the arena. He would not be fooled twice, however, and he kicked White, making his head snap back. He dragged him to his feet and then threw him to the ground again, kicking him repeatedly in the ribs and legs. The Watcher was unhappy. None of this should have happened. He shifted irritably; the rain had soaked even him to the bone and he was growing bored.

CHAPTER TEN

THE DAYS PASSED in a blur. Dal had heard nothing from his agents in days, and his fingers were permanently stained with ink from the many letters he had written to his family and associates, begging them to be wary of Trithia and prepare their defences. But he had no replies. Sure his post was being monitored, he hoped at least one might slip through Captain Kerne's fingers. He considered telling Fyn of his arrangement with King Cobey but decided against it. Fyn was well known amongst the guard for lamenting his position, and the time he was wasting in Trithia, and so a change in his demeanour would arouse suspicion. With the agreement honoured between Cobey and Stirm, Fyn was to leave for Porton after the wedding; this one piece of good news cheered Dal.

Fyn brought him word that the DeVaine girl had been moved from the dungeons and Kerne now hosted her in his rooms. No one was allowed entry, and when Fyn tried to access even the same level of apartments as the captain, the guards had politely prevented him. Dal wanted to know why Kerne had taken such an interest in this woman. Could she possibly be the leverage he was looking for? He sighed and picked up a bottle of Mischlan red. He paused. He had consumed far too much wine in the last few days.

As he reluctantly placed the bottle back down, the silver and gold filigree ring glinted up at him. He had taken to wearing it openly on the little finger of his left hand. The warmth of the metal reassured him and when he visited the temple of Igon, but his pocket had felt so hot that he had been forced to remove it. It was then that the inspiration to wear it came, and he felt better for it. He took it as a sign from the gods, and his efforts to find Chaeli were re-doubled, offering large sums of gold to his contacts should they find a tangible lead as to her whereabouts. He wrote to friends in all kingdoms asking them to instruct their own spies on his behalf, promising to owe favours and debts. If Kerne sought her, then Dal would find her first.

He sat at the small card table and shuffled the molyona deck absentmindedly. A plan started to form, but for it to be executed he would need Fyn and Ilene on board. It would be too risky without them but, if caught, Fyn had the most to lose. Both Ilene and Dal could claim diplomatic immunity, while Fyn would be fed to the wolves. Sighing, Dal placed out the cards and started a three lined solo game. He had to think on this one. There was too much at risk.

The days passed without incident in Lindor. Mickalos would often disappear with Adley for hours, their conversations muted, confidential. Nathan and Chaeli were put to work scouring the books for a sign or hint as to what they should be doing, and what exactly was expected of her. So far they had only found brief and cryptic references to someone who might be identified as Chaeli. The books were old, and often written in Old Trithian, something neither of them could understand, and which the acolytes spent hours deciphering for them. It was painstaking and tiresome.

The library overwhelmed Chaeli. She was captivated by some of the texts surrounding the elusive third world of Salinthos. She knew the stories, of course; everyone did. Salinthos was the home of the dragons, fae and other gentle creatures –that was the legend. Here, texts and old tales spoke of Salinthos as real and the more obscure stories spoke of the Star of Salinthos: one day the Star would be stolen and this was a sign that the end was near. Neither Nathan nor Chaeli could find what the star itself was meant to represent. They considered it might be Chaeli herself, and spent hours searching for anything they could cross-reference against, but there was nothing. However, some texts believed it to be a literal translation, and believed the star would fall from the sky and destroy the world of Ibea.

This star intrigued Chaeli and she would sometimes touch the stars on her shoulder as she read. She knew the marking was a sign, but could find nothing explaining the transference of the acolytes' power to her own. She heard the acolytes whispering and knew they resented her; more than that, they feared her. She tried to speak to them and apologise, but they coldly refused to converse with her unless ordered to do so by Mickalos.

She had also learnt a great deal about the *Assaké*, and the protectorship. Once an *Assaké* reached certain proficiency, he was inked by the head priest of the Underworld using blood believed to be from the Damnable Lord, and that inking would then forever hold the wearer to the will of the Underworld. The wearer faced a constant battle should he try to resist the call of his master. Most wearers were only given one serpent, only the highest were given two. Nathan caught her reading about this, but instead of objecting or attempting to defend himself, he silently handed her a collection of hand-bound papers titled, *The Dark Guardian Codex*.

"I had to learn every page of this, word for word. It became my doctrine. If you want to understand what it means to be *Assaké*, then read these pages. They explain the hierarchy and inner workings of the Underworld Church."

She accepted it with a nod and flicked through the pages. Incantations filled the margins, and hand-drawn images of young *Assaké* trainees kneeling in front of a human sacrifice disgusted and shocked her. But she couldn't stop staring. In the background, the image of a goddess had been imagined; she didn't recognise the form.

333

"The Goddess of Revenge," Nathan murmured. Chaeli turned the page. More spells and charms. She didn't want to look at them, didn't want even one to creep into her memory. Slowly closing the codex, she placed it on the pile of discarded books. They needed more. Leaning back and stretching, she glanced over at what Nathan was reading: *The Encyclopaedia of Myths, Legends and Faerytales of Salinthos*. She knew the book from her childhood; it was fanciful and full of childlike theories – yet Nathan read it as though it was a diary of truth.

Nathan hadn't mentioned their kiss, and she wanted desperately to explain away that afternoon. When she had arrived back with Adley that night, Nathan had already gone to his rooms, and the following day he was cold and distant with her. Chaeli was mortified but relieved that Nathan hadn't questioned her morals or the fact she'd taken advantage of a drunken man. He was a gentleman, she decided.

Adley also made no mention of her behaviour. The few times he wasn't locked away with Mickalos, he expanded on the channelling of her power, showing her how to tap into her energy for simple things, such as lighting a candle or warming the air around her. He demonstrated how to generate a defensive ward and how to attack. He only taught her a basic energy blast but promised they would soon move onto more.

She read about her mother, Amelia. It made her weep to learn how much Prince Daro had loved her, and how she had turned from him to Eli. Chaeli couldn't understand; they seemed so in love. Suddenly she felt the familiar pull of sadness. Nathan looked up from his reading and frowned.

"What's wrong?" he asked.

"I wish I had known my mother," she blurted out. "I know it sounds childish considering I had wonderful parents, but I still wish I could have met her."

"Everything I've read about her leads me to believe she, too, was wonderful."

"She was," interrupted Adley, striding towards the table.

"You met her?" Chaeli stared open mouthed. "Why did you never tell me?"

"I'm sorry." Adley pulled up a chair and sat next to Chaeli.

"What was she like?" she asked eagerly, closing her book.

"Kind, clever, gentle, witty, everything a man could want in a woman. Before she met Daro, she was a normal mortal girl living with her parents. You have to understand things that so many years have passed over. It was so different then. The gods would walk amongst the mortals and converse as you and I do now." He paused. "He met her one day at the local market. She dropped a basket and he helped pick up the apples, and the moment they saw one another they knew. They were soon almost inseparable. He told her who he was, and it never once affected their feelings. Daro is the most understanding of the gods, and he truly doesn't place himself above mortals." Adley looked at Chaeli and shrugged. "Daro made the mistake of introducing her to his younger brother, Eli, who became jealous. Everyone loved Amelia, but Daro most of all, and Eli couldn't understand how his brother could love her more than him. He stole Amelia from Daro in jealousy, wooed her. At first she wasn't interested, but eventually, somehow, he won her over. Daro was heartbroken, but he didn't interfere. He believed that if Eli loved Amelia, and she him, then he shouldn't interfere. When Amelia told Eli she was pregnant . . ."

Her face was expressionless. "What happened?" she asked.

"Eli was furious. He denied being your father, denied he loved her. He claimed she had been pregnant before she seduced him. Amelia was heartbroken; she left both brothers and disappeared. Penella turned up with you, Chaeli, and told the brothers Amelia had given birth, and then taken her own life. Daro has never been the same since, and he always hoped you were indeed his daughter." He glanced at her. "I'm sorry." He took her hand. "He wanted to claim you as his own from the moment he saw you, but Eli refused. As soon as Eli saw how much Daro loved you, he

335

put in his claim for you. Your birth sparked the war, but it was something that had been brewing for centuries."

Chaeli hadn't realised she had been crying until Adley touched her. She hastily withdrew and wiped her face.

"Thank you for telling me," she said, sniffling. Her mother had loved both of them, something Chaeli could understand, and even though her true father didn't want or love her, the love of Daro for her mother warmed her. When she thought of Eli, rage bubbled up inside, running thick through her veins and crawling over her body. She scratched her arms absentmindedly and shivered. The thought of being the cause of the war sat uneasily with her.

"May I steal you away for a moment? I would like us to practise with your energy some more."

Chaeli nodded. "Yes. Yes, that would be good. I'd like to understand defending and attacking simultaneously. I've tried to draw a ward and then attack at the same time, but I can't seem to grasp it."

Adley nodded. "I'll just be a moment." He wandered towards the old man and a quiet discussion took place. She looked over to Nathan again, who seemed tired and drawn; just looking at him caused an inexplicable tiredness to seep into her.

"Have you been sleeping well?"

Surprised, he looked up. "Why do you ask?"

"You look tired."

"Is this your way of saying I look terrible?" He raised an eyebrow playfully and smiled as he continued to flick through the books.

"You just look a bit weary, that's all."

"It's nothing to worry about."

She drummed her fingers on the desk and gazed around. After almost a fortnight in Lindor, she still marvelled at the beauty of the library. They had spent hours and hours trawling through books, but they hadn't even seen a tenth of the texts the shelves held.

It was a strange feeling, learning about her past, and whilst she had been a regular visitor to the Kingdom's Church, she hadn't realised just how many deities graced their world. They were a part of everything, and were immortal; she had often fantasised about living forever, but the dreams always ended the same, with sadness at the thought of living for eternity without anyone to share it. She would rather live one brief lifetime with someone she loved, than a thousand lifetimes alone.

She was alone though, with no family except for her father. The word stuck in her throat. *Father!* No, he wasn't her father. Glin had raised her and been the one to comfort her when she cried, chastise her when she was naughty, and he would always be her father. Eli hadn't even claimed her when she had been born, and only wanted her to infuriate his brother. She pushed the sadness down inside.

Nathan stood and closed the encyclopaedia. "I'll be back shortly. I have a small errand. Will you be all right?"

She nodded and he weaved his way through the shelves and out of view. Pulling the encyclopaedia over to where she sat, she opened the huge book and flicked through the pages, pausing on the image of a tiny white-haired woman dressed in a long white shift, sitting alone by a still and serene lake, her hand trailing in the water. She read the entry underneath the caption:

"The Wandering Children: Descendants of the mortal, Elissa, and the messenger god, Eremal, (see Eremal). The inhabitants of Salinthos carry the blood of the gods. Gentle, innocent, and pure, these are divine beings who see what others do not. Due to their mixed bloodlines, the Children are known to live long and healthy lives. Outliving mortals by several hundred years, they are paired for life with a Fae companion (see Fae).

Like Ibeans, the Children are ruled by a single monarch, a King or Queen who can trace their heritage back to the union of Elissa and Eremal. The monarch holds the ability to forgive misdemeanours and wash away sin (see Absolution)."

Chaeli flicked to the section on Eremal and read the story of the great betrayal. Nileen, the elemental Goddess of Wind, had fallen in love with Eremal, only to be spurned by the messenger god who took a mortal lover and hid her away on Salinthos; he continued to bring mortals to the gentle world in secret. As punishment, Prince Daro banished Eremal to the void and tied those mortals to Salinthos. They were never to leave, and their children would be tied to the land and the creatures that lived there.

Chaeli looked up, she couldn't concentrate any further. The skin on the back of her neck crawled and she turned in her chair, staring into the shadows of the room, between the shelves and bookcases. She was alone, but still the feeling wouldn't go away. She got up and tip-toed towards the first row of bookcases, peering around the corner. She continued to wander along the narrow corridors and into the different sections of the library, deeper and deeper into the archives. There was still nothing. No one.

There!

A thud echoed through the room and Chaeli jumped, then turned back towards the main room and her table and the colourful light that streamed through the window. A flashback to the Sink shot through her mind, the grasping of the man, his rotten breath, his grasping hands. She couldn't breathe and panic flooded her body. She ran, but as she skidded around a corner she collided full force with someone, sending them both, and a collection of books, flying. She landed hard on her stomach.

"I'm sorry," she blurted out as she rolled to her feet. An acolyte, one of the men who had been helping transcribe the writings, knelt to gather the tomes. Chaeli crouched down to help.

"I can manage." His clipped reply made her pull back, stung.

"I really am sorry," she repeated. He didn't answer, but after collecting the books, he looked her up and down before dumping the books haphazardly on a nearby trolley.

"What exactly are you apologising for, Lady Chaeli? For this accident, or for stealing my birthright?" He rolled up his sleeves to reveal pale, smooth, unmarked skin. "I earned that ink. For fifteen years I've trained here, researching and translating texts, learning the magic of the land, and for what? I cannot be re-inked. The stars have dissolved and disappeared, and now I am nothing." His voice cracked.

"I'm sorry! I don't know what happened. I didn't mean for it to happen." She could feel his pain, it travelled over the small space between them and almost suffocated her, invading her heart and wrapping itself around that heavy stone. The emotion flared within her, a hot, searing pain that beat against the surface of the stone, desperately trying to claw inside. It was another agony she could barely contain.

"What *are* you?" the acolyte demanded.

A demi-goddess, her mind replied.

"I don't know," she answered aloud, praying to the gods that the madness of pain would soon leave.

He rolled down his sleeves, and picked up his pile of books from the trolley. The top book slipped from the pile and landed face up, open. She knelt down and picked up the ancient volume, the hard, cracked leather rough against her hands. Each page was stained and loose, but it wasn't the condition of the book that caught her attention. She stared at the huge symbol in the centre of the left page; it matched one of the symbols in the script on her ribcage.

"What does this mean?" she demanded, turning the book to the man. He glanced down and then searched her face frowning.

"That's an ancient Tessian dialect."

"Tessian?"

He jerked his head towards the main room. "Follow me." They walked in silence back to Chaeli's table and the acolyte placed the books down and sat. She followed suit.

"Tessia was once Mischla and Velen. A single great nation, ruled by two families. The Dragon Wars split the nation through greed. The book you hold is an ancient diary from one of the Tessian royals of the time."

"What does the symbol mean?" She felt the agony subside, giving way to an alien fear at that clung to her insides, mingling with, and yet violating, her own feelings. The stillness and quietness of the library contrasted with the battle inside her, creating a whirlpool of emotions; her head started to pound and spin, the closeness of the acolyte too much. Chaeli pushed back her chair, creating space and a barrier between them.

He raised an eyebrow. "Where have you seen this mark?" He was staring at her now, and the fear she felt changed; curiosity wormed and poked at her.

She shook her head. "Just tell me, please. What does it mean?"

He held out his hand for the book and she passed it to him, watching as he stroked the fragile tome.

"Tessian hasn't been spoken for almost a thousand years. Translations are broad and must not be viewed as precise."

"Yes, but what does it mean?" She was desperate now, and the acolyte exhaled, closing the book gently and handing it back to her.

"Torture. It means torture."

"Prince Kee Dala, I thank you for this meeting, but I must admit I am somewhat perplexed. If you required access to my library, you only had to ask the captain. He deals with all my affairs nowadays." Stirm coughed and Dal could hear the wetness in his chest as he breathed. "I apologise for being so abrupt. I am a little under the weather and seem unable to shake this infection."

The King did indeed appear ill; his complexion waxy and grey, he had lost weight so quickly his eyes were sunken in his face.

"What do your medics say, Your Majesty?"

"My priest informs me that with prayer and the grace of the gods, my fate is in good hands. What can we do after all but trust in them?" He coughed again. "Now, was there something particular in the library you wished to view?"

"Indeed, Your Majesty, I wished to learn more of the ancient rites of the Trithian Council. In Algary, the head of state – my father – has supremacy over all military campaigns and decisions, but I believe Trithia has a somewhat different way of working."

The King struggled to sit up and shakily sipped at the cold peppermint tea. "Why would Trithia's war council interest the Crown Prince of Algary?" His body was failing, but today his mind was sharp. He drew his throw closer and signalled for his servants to leave.

"As I said at the engagement dinner, I am eager to learn more of Trithia. Your way is an example to the other realms. I feel I could take home useful policies and procedures for my father." Dal lied smoothly, appealing to the vanity of the King.

"You'll be after *The Precepts of War*. It's divided into twelve volumes." He was wracked once again with coughing, and placed his tea on the small table with a shaking hand. After a few moments he wheezed, "The first volume went missing some centuries ago, I don't know where it is. However, there are still too many books for my liking."

"Indeed, Your Majesty. My thanks. I am overwhelmed, though, at the size of your library. Could anyone possibly assist me in finding this book?" He held his breath and prayed to the gods for their intervention and support.

"Alas, no. The library is barely used nowadays. The last keen scholar left me some time ago in, ah . . . somewhat unfortunate circumstances." Stirm looked at Dal wistfully. "She was knowledgeable. She would help you in an instant."

"She?" Dal tilted his head to one side and held his breath.

"My ward and perfect woman, Anya DeVaine." the King was slurring his speech now as he sipped his tea. Dal willed him to down the cup.

"Anya DeVaine, yes, I've heard that name. I do believe she is in the castle as we speak, Your Majesty. Word has it that Captain Kerne has been entertaining her in the hope of gleaning information relating to her traitorous brother."

The King continued to sip and his eyes slid closed slowly. "Impossible. I gave strict instruction for her to remain in the dungeon. Besides, Anya would never betray her brother. Her loyalty infuriated me greatly a long time ago. So unreasonable. Surely her loyalty should have been to me?" He seemed to be talking to himself now.

"Even so, if this Anya DeVaine is in the castle, she could prove helpful during my research. Perhaps a change of tactics with her? Perhaps the lure of books and information will appeal to her more than chains and beatings? Any information I gain I can then pass on to Captain Kerne."

Drink the damn tea, Dal hissed to himself, but held his composure. On cue, the King took a deep gulp.

"Perhaps so, Kee Dala, perhaps so. I confess, I would like to see Anya DeVaine once more. Her face is my greatest regret, but also my greatest canvas. Very well, very well – you have permission for Anya to accompany you to the library. She is, however, to be guarded at all times. I will not have her alone with another man."

"Would a member of your King's Guard suffice, Your Majesty?"

"Indeed." The King sighed. "Indeed. Bring me ink and parchment, I will arrange for Kerne to bring her to you tomorrow morning."

Dal placed the pen and parchment within the King's grasp and watched the monarch scrawl a short note and seal the paper.

"Give this to Kerne. Now I need to rest." The King lifted his legs onto the footstool and at once began to doze. Dal left his rooms taking the teacup with him. Even the novice medic would recognise the soft smell of moon root, or 'sweetheart's whisper' as it was commonly known. Manipulation was an art, but even artists needed tools.

Torture.

Chaeli held the book tightly in her hands. Surely he was wrong? Why would her inking hold the word torture in the script? She opened the book and looked through the pages again; none of the other symbols were familiar. She went to close it, but a small scribble in the corner caught her attention. The swirling of patterns reminded her of something, but she couldn't remember what. Sensing someone approach, she looked up to see Adley returning, Nathan at his side. They spoke in low voices to one another; Mickalos directed six of his acolytes over to them, whose faces fell in dismay at the task. They didn't want to be near her. Why would they? She was an anomaly, something that was never meant to have existed, a problem that even the greatest scholar in Lindor couldn't solve. They hadn't learnt anything here, instead she was more isolated than ever. Immediately she felt guilty as the memory of her father chiding her floated into the forefront of her mind.

"Self pity is a terrible enemy. If we give in to such feelings, we find ourselves lost and without purpose. We become so blinded that we never achieve anything."

His voice in her memory made her heart physically ache, each beat reminding her that she was still alive, and her parents and sister weren't, reminding her she was alone. Glancing up at her companions as they approached her, she pushed the guilt away, swallowing it bitterly, and forced a smile.

She closed the book and slipped it into the pile on her desk. She needed to speak to the acolyte again and have him translate more. If that meant him reading her script, then so be it. She wanted to learn, wanted to busy her mind and body with the feel of her energy.

"Ready?" She was eager to press on. When she channelled energy, she felt alive, whole, and healed; she craved that feeling of completeness.

Adley nodded. "A walk, perhaps? I found a peaceful meditation garden a few streets away I'd like to show you."

"Definitely. Nathan, you don't mind, do you?"

He waved them away. "I'll keep researching here. There must be something in these books that can help us work out exactly what we're doing and why."

"We won't be long," said Adley, and he led Chaeli outside into the street.

It was so peaceful in the neutral city. She disliked seeing those loyal to the Underworld converse and trade with the Kingdom's followers, but at least they were civil to one another and showed neither distaste nor propensity for argument, let alone violence. The rest of the realms could learn from Lindor's example.

They walked side by side, Chaeli drinking in the sights. The architecture of the city was a marvel, each stone laid with extraordinary skill and purpose, the ringed levels of the city like a circular maze. Even now, the city expansion was carefully thought out, the architects even incorporating underground drainage. It was something Chaeli remembered Mickalos marvelling over one night; at the time she failed to appreciate his enthusiasm, but now she could see it was something unique to Lindor.

"Here we are." Adley stopped in front of a wooden gate. Looking around, Chaeli could see nothing but a huge expanse of limestone wall, until Adley opened the gate, revealing another garden inside; huge expanses of lawn spread away from the walls, with partitioned sections in which people practised their own channelling. Chaeli caught the eye of a young man, whose lip curled as he focussed a bolt of energy directly into her path. Panicking, she flinched and drew a shield, but the energy was absorbed into his partition and came no further.

"It's for safety," Adley explained. "The council devised a way of harnessing individual wards of energy. They need no bearer, and remain constant. However, these stones,"—he pointed to the rows of stones that separated each partition—"each have a holding rune etched into the surface. If the stones are moved, the wards will crumble."

344

She scowled at the young man who laughed and turned away; she caught a glimpse of a serpent band on his arm – a trainee *Assaké*! She wanted to throttle him, but she calmed herself by drawing on her energy. That word whispered to her again: *torture*. She gritted her teeth and counted to ten.

It was a mistake, a mistake. It had to be a mistake.

Adley looked at her. "Everything all right?"

Nodding, she moved into a section with him and began to dip in and out of her energy, allowing it to flow and channel, working its way through her confusion and anger. Exhaling steadily, she placed two fingers to her chest and pushed them outwards in a straight line, expelling her energy and feeling it ripple around her. Adley had explained that as she grew to understand her power, the channelling would come instinctively and movement would be limited, but for now, he wanted her to concentrate on her breathing and ensure her movements were fluid and in sync.

"Today we'll work on holding a ward whilst attacking. It's a lot easier than it appears." Without warning, he shot a blast at her ward. She stepped back, frowning but holding firm. "Always be on your guard, Chaeli. How many times have I told you?"

"Sorry." She heard a derisory laugh from the *Assaké*, which only made her concentrate harder. Adley stood with his arms crossed and threw another bolt at her, stronger and more powerful this time, but again her wards held. She concentrated on allowing her energy to flow naturally, it was so tempting to draw it into the ward and hold it there, but she remembered her lessons. The energy held its own consciousness and knew where to go; she had to trust it. Her role was merely guide to and form it into the reaction she required.

"Excellent, now ignore your ward and attack me."

She tried, but immediately her ward dropped and she was vulnerable. Adley sent a small shock at her and she yelped, glaring at him as she rubbed her arm.

"Again!"

Twelve times she failed, and twelve times he stung her. She was embarrassed and angry at him for showing her up. The *Assaké* had stopped his practising and stood smirking at her. She sensed Adley draw his energy again, and she knew he was about to attack. Her wards were in place, but this time, instead of allowing him to shame her again, she threw a ball of petulant energy at him. He staggered back in surprise and chuckled.

Chaeli grinned and dropped into a sparring stance, curving her fingers and beckoning him to attack, but he only threw steady, predictable bolts.

"Adley, please! Make it more complicated," she whined, growing quickly bored. But with her last word, two hits flew at her in quick succession. The first caused her to stagger, the other winded her with such intensity that she dry-retched before throwing energy into her depleted wards.

She threw a blast back at him, and he caught it, their energies crackling and dissipating. Before she could consider what had happened, another blast caught her – two at once! Sweating and shaking her hands out, she considered her next move. The protector glanced at her feet and she saw him start to smile. She pulled on a ball of energy and prepared to attack, but before she could, her feet slammed together and she fell on her face, her wards failed as her anger flared.

She pushed herself up on her elbows and glared. "That's it, I've had enough! Why did you do that?"

Adley shrugged. "You wanted it more complicated."

"Not *that* complicated." She looked over at the *Assaké*, but to her relief he was gone.

"He left a while ago."

"You knew I was watching him – why did you humiliate me?"

He shrugged again. "You concentrate better when you're angry." She got to her feet and stormed off towards the gates, but Adley caught up to her and grabbed her arm. "We need to use whatever advantage we can, Chaeli. I don't know what your father has planned for you, or what will happen next, but if making you angry is the only way you'll learn, then I'm sorry, but I won't pander to your ego if it hinders your development."

"My ego? I don't have an ego!" She was shouting now, tensing her arms and balling her hands into fists. *Gods, he is so arrogant!*

"Yes, you do. You hate being wrong and you hate being questioned."

She opened her mouth to object, but sensed that was what he wanted; he wanted to be proven right. Instead, she took a breath and calmed herself, cracking her knuckles and taking pleasure at seeing him wince at the sound. *Serves you right.*

"Let's leave it there. I'm sorry. Seeing an *Assaké* here upset me, that's all."

"I feel the same way, but this is Lindor. This is the way of life here." He shrugged. "I should have explained what I was doing, but I was afraid that if you knew, you wouldn't get angry and it wouldn't work."

They stood and watched the city pass them by; stopping had been a mistake, for every part of her ached and throbbed. It was refreshing to stop and relax with no worries and no thoughts of the Kingdom or Underworld.

"I suppose we should get back."

"Yes, we have another long night of reading and theorising ahead of us." Slipping her a sideways glance he added, "I can't wait."

She felt the corners of her mouth curve up in an involuntary smile, and they headed back to the library in companionable silence.

As they re-entered the library and went over to Nathan, Mickalos waved Adley to a dark, quiet corner. Chaeli caught the knowing look between them and shook her head – their secrets and skulking around was starting to wear thin, and she slammed a book on the table, the echo startling the studying scholars who looked up in both disgust and horror. Adley's jaw tensed and Nathan looked at them both, raising an eyebrow.

"What's going on with you two? Nathan and I have hardly seen you recently. Mickalos doesn't speak to either of us, and his acolytes are colder than the icecaps of Sheema."

"I can't tell you everything at the moment. Things are happening in the city. There have been several disappearances and Mickalos's camarilla believes Kitaani are involved. The disappearances started happening just after we arrived."

"Kitaani? Here? I thought Lindor was a sanctuary?" Nathan asked.

"Sanctuary in the Seven Realms but Sheranshia and the Underworld pay no heed to mortal agreements. But now I must go. I'll be around this evening, so meet me in the courtyard at dusk." He looked at Nathan. "Both of you." They nodded their agreement as Adley walked away, then Nathan moved his chair closer to Chaeli, making her pulse quicken and her skin prickle in anticipation; the response irritated and excited her in equal measure.

"If Kitaani are here, it means a Sherai must be close to the city to be controlling the Kitaani, and we don't want to run into her."

"Her?" Chaeli asked. She wanted to turn her head but he was too close.

"The Sherai is a race of female magicians who control Sheranshia. They're the most powerful mortal energy users. Some extend their life by consuming the blood of sacrifices." He opened a book and flicked through the leaves; finding what he wanted, he slid the book over to Chaeli and tapped the page. She looked down at the engraved image of an exotically dressed dark-haired woman with many piercings. The design showed her as scantily clad but with a veiled face. Her hands were covered in inkings, but none Chaeli could recognise from the engraving.

"I know very little about them, but I do know if you see a woman like this, you run in the opposite direction and don't stop."

"But what are Kitaani?" asked Chaeli.

"Kitaani are the servants of the Sherai. They used to be men. The Sherai made a pact with Eli that his hellions would relinquish the bodies of intact male corpses to them, and in return the Sherai would serve him. It ensures a fresh supply to the Sherai and adds forces to Eli's cause."

Chaeli felt sick, a cold nauseating wave crashing over her. "That is vile," she hissed. "Where do they get the bodies from?"

"Anywhere. The only condition is that the body must be intact with all limbs, since the Sherai magic holds better that way." Nathan moved his chair away slightly and sat upright. "I don't know anything more than that."

Chaeli stared at the closed book and an icy dread spread over her – was a respite from evil too much to ask for? Nathan reached over and took her hand, the rough calluses on his palm and fingers scratching her skin. She looked at him, but he continued to flick through his book, pausing to read passages now and then. The comfortable weight of his hand on hers helped her relax and she opened the nearest book again. A picture of Prince Eli stared up at her.

She snorted in disgust upon reading the passage: "Benevolent, loving, generous, gift from the stars."

Her eyes filled with tears again. 'Gift from the stars?' Who had written this? She pictured Acelle in the arms of Malo. The terrible image was imprinted on Chaeli's mind. She hadn't even been able to bury her sister, and she was eternally thankful that Adley had eventually given her the respectful burial and prayer of sending that she deserved.

Nathan squeezed her hand and let go. "I've still not heard back from Anya," he said. "I sent a courier the day we arrived. He was to wait and bring me a reply, but he hasn't returned yet."

"Maybe his horse went lame?"

"Maybe." Unhappiness rolled off him and wormed into her, clawing at her skin. She didn't know what to do, so she placed her hand over his and smiled encouragingly. He looked up, and the corners of his mouth tilted slightly upwards.

Sheiva, still a cat, arrived as the sun set. He spent the days exploring Lindor and reporting any unusual movement back to Adley. He was constantly hungry and tired.

"Found anything?" he asked jumping onto the table and sending books flying.

"Nothing really," said Nathan. "I'm convinced the Star of Salinthos is a sign though. I've searched through texts from five realms trying to link the Star to Chaeli, but if we presume the 'Child of the Brothers' is Chaeli and not the Star, then what, exactly, *is* the Star? Several have written of facing the kiss of a dragon as a test of purity. If you pass, the arms of Salinthos will open." Nathan put his face in his hands and rubbed hard.

"A kiss from a dragon? Who'd kiss a dragon?" said the cat, cocking his head to one side. "Apart from another dragon, that is."

"Do you have any news, Sheiva?" Chaeli asked, collecting up the discarded books.

Sheiva's ears went flat and his tail flicked in annoyance. "Not really. None of my contacts have any idea what the Star is, or if they do, they aren't saying."

Nathan stood and stretched his legs. "We've got a few hours until Adley wants us, Chaeli. Meet me in the courtyards." He strode away.

"Perhaps he wants to roll around on the grass again?" said Sheiva with a smirk, peeking at Chaeli from under a paw. "Another kiss maybe?"

Her cheeks reddened. "Hateful cat." She placed the books back on the shelf and followed after Nathan. Once outside, she closed her eyes and breathed in deeply. The air was divine, so quiet and calming.

"You're going to walk into that tree if you aren't careful." Nathan's voice was a murmur in her ear, and she opened her eyes and spun around, bumping her back against the tree. She stumbled and Nathan caught her, smiling. It was hot in the early evening sun; a trickle of sweat ran down the back of her neck.

"I want you to be able to use a sword. Adley can teach you how to use energy better than I, but I'm the better swordsman." He let go of her arms and in a blink of an eye had drawn his sword from the scabbard.

"I don't know the first thing about fighting," she protested.

"I'm going to show you." He held out his sword. "Take it"

"Wait, don't I get a practice sword first?" She gulped and glanced around. They were the only ones in the garden.

"No time. Lindor isn't exactly known for its forges, so we'll have to make do. Take it."

She held out a shaking hand.

"Take it, Chaeli." His voice was firm and low. She grabbed the hilt and Nathan let go. Her arm immediately dropped and the blade swung to the ground. He slapped her wrist and she dropped the sword.

"Ow! What did you—"

"Lesson one, a firm grip on the hilt. Don't be afraid of the sword. Pick it up."

She scowled and picked up the sword, holding it out defiantly and pointing it at Nathan, the tip inches from his face. He raised an eyebrow, and with the flat of his hand he slapped the blade. The sword swung away from him.

"Lesson two, a good stance. Your feet are all wrong."

He walked around in a circle. The sun beat down, and the sword was heavy. Her arm ached already. She kept an eye on Nathan but didn't turn to follow him. He stopped behind her and she felt a nudge to her left foot.

"This needs to be forward and pointing straight." He kicked her right foot. "This one further back, pointing diagonally. Balance the weight equally on the balls and soles."

Chaeli did as he instructed and he pushed her in the back. She stood her ground.

351

"Good, you see how you have better control, better balance? This stance will aid you regardless of what angle or direction the enemy approaches from."

He moved in front of her, and held up three fingers.

"Thirdly, relaxed breathing. Breathe from deep within, using your core." He tapped just above his stomach. "Deep breaths."

Chaeli breathed deeply.

"Now, I prefer a one-handed sword, it makes direct attacking easier, quicker and smoother. Unfortunately, it also means defensive moves are limited." He ran his gaze up and down her body. Chaeli noticed a change in his demeanour; he was more focussed and completely immersed in the training. "Your height and build lends itself to quick thrusts and strikes."

Chaeli arced the sword from right to left in an elaborate movement.

"No, wrong." He slapped her arm and frowned. "Short, strong strokes. Long strokes leave you vulnerable here and here." He poked her arm and chest. "You would be dead in seconds."

"Thanks," she muttered.

"Elbows bent, close to your body," he barked, circling her once more. "Think about your opponent. You have a short sword, so you need to get close and make it impossible for your opponent to parry." He stood in front of her. "Now attack me."

"But you have no weapon."

"Attack me!"

She found her balance and allowed Nathan to circle her. Several seconds passed, then she thrust quickly and fluidly. He twisted and she missed. He slapped her arm hard, and pain radiated up to her shoulder. She grunted, but held the sword steady.

"Good, you didn't waver. But when a skilled swordsman attacks, he will go for your arms or legs. If it's easier, he would watch you bleed out and weaken, and then deliver a killing blow rather than sweat it out in an active fight."

She thrust again and Nathan blocked easily. He used the back of his arm and somehow always made contact with the flat of the sword. She attacked again and again, but he danced around her, fluid and ghostlike. Several times she got close, and once she actually made contact with his shirt. She cried out in delight, but the euphoria was short lived; her small victory distracted her and he slapped her shoulder hard, making her drop the sword. She bent over and held her knees. Her lungs were screaming and she was sweating profusely.

"Not bad for your first time, especially since you're using a sword too heavy for you," he remarked.

"What?"

"Chaeli, I'm a lot bigger than you, and you won't be fighting with my sword. This was made especially for me."

No wonder it hurt. She rotated her arm and worked out the pain. "You hit hard," she grumbled, rubbing her shoulder.

"Don't be weak." He picked up his sword. "My gods, Chaeli, how sweaty are your hands?" He grimaced and wiped the hilt with his shirt. "I'm shocked you kept a hold of this and didn't send it spinning!"

"I was nervous! I've not used a sword before!" She clutched her arm. "I feel battered. How did you do that anyway?"

"Do what?"

"Slap the sword away and not get cut, you haven't got a mark on you."

Nathan smiled smugly. "Best in the King's Guard, remember? I'm not giving away all my secrets." She snorted in reply and flopped to the floor. "No, up."

"What?" She groaned. "I ache all over."

"You need to stretch out. You haven't done this sort of exercise before, and if you don't stretch out now, you'll barely be able to walk tomorrow."

"I'll take my chances."

"Don't say I didn't warn you."

She closed her eyes and let herself cool down. The grass tickled her back and she knew she needed to bathe, but she couldn't be bothered. Nathan hummed to himself and she sensed him moving around. Chaeli opened one eye.

Nathan stood in the fighting stance he had showed her and seemed to be blocking blows that weren't there. He moved his feet, then punched, keeping his body protected. With each blow, she felt the now familiar pull of energy. Nathan incorporated his channelling into his fighting.

Block, move, punch. Move, block, punch, kick, block. Move, punch, move, block, kick, kick. Chaeli recognised the sequence and repeated it in her head, but suddenly it changed and she could no longer keep pace.

"This is *ashanasha*," he said, his voice tight from the effort of his exercises. "A form of defence taught in Porton. It requires complete control and balance. Limited weapons, but the majority of the sequences use your power and body, and you need a disciplined mind." He didn't look around.

"It's beautiful." She rolled over to balance on her elbows and continued to watch.

"When I was exiled, I travelled to all the realms. The Porton King was the most accommodating. He sensed my anger, my pain, and my guilt. He knew who I was and ordered his personal steward to teach me *ashanasha*. It helps keep me balanced and focussed. I owe my sanity to King Cobey."

Chaeli couldn't keep track of the time; she was mesmerised watching Nathan. He changed the pace and moves at least four times, graceful as a dancer, more fluid than an acrobat. A film of sweat covered his face, but his breathing and speed stayed true.

"How long did it take to learn?" she asked.

"I studied every day for six hours and was in Porton for just over a year. I still only know a small fraction of the *ashanasha*. True understanding and mastery takes a lifetime."

"Gods!"

"No. Men." He laughed and finished the *ashanasha* abruptly.

She stared at him with the familiar longing as he lifted his shirt off to cool down. The snakes were still and coiled together; his chest heaved and Chaeli's breathing rate increased to match. She looked up and saw him regarding her with a strange expression.

"Does it still bother you?" he asked, pointing to the serpents.

"Yes, but not in the same way." Standing up she undid her shirt slightly and showed him the constellation on her chest and shoulder. "I abhor what the serpents stand for, but I know what it feels like to be permanently reminded of something you want nothing to do with. I know mine is nothing like your serpents, but it's still here and I have no control over it."

She thought back to the trainee *Assaké*, and then to the translated word, *torture*. With a jolt, the glaring difference between Nathan and her was so obvious that it was painful: Nathan and the trainee had both chosen to embrace the Underworld, both chosen evil.

Nathan hadn't seen the complete inking on Chaeli before. As he took a step forward she stepped back, a guarded look in her eyes.

"I just want to see it," he said, his voice low. She slipped her shirt down a little more, exposing the top of her breast. He traced the outline of the constellation with one hand, his touch so light and delicate that she shivered.

"I have others," she added, not wishing him to stop.

"Where?" He cleared his throat, heat surging throughout his body and reflecting onto Chaeli. She lifted the bottom of her shirt and exposed her stomach and ribs. He knelt on the ground and turned her body towards him, his head level with her navel, left hand on her waist. He moved his fingers across her ribs examining the runes and script. Every touch of him sent waves through her body and her stomach tightened. When he let go and stood up, she felt like screaming.

"These runes are very special. I've never seen anything like them before."

"Mickalos won't talk to me about them. I think he feels I've stolen them. I know his acolytes do."

"I doubt these are the same runes that graced his skin. Mickalos was covered in runes, but I could recognise many of them. These . . . these are something new."

Reluctantly, she let go of her shirt, and it fell back down to cover her. She imagined Nathan sweeping her into his arms and kissing her as he had before. She wanted his lips all over her body – she wanted him to trace the constellation with his tongue. She wanted much, much more from him, and when she looked into his eyes, she could see the same longing in him. She began to speak, but saw Adley striding towards them. She sighed and shook her head.

I must learn to control these feelings!

Chaeli waved to Adley and sighed.

Adley raised a hand in acknowledgement; he had seen the closeness of the two of them again and it pained him. He knew Sheiva was right, he knew he must not think of Chaeli as obtainable, but he couldn't help it. Penella's offer still taunted him. He had dismissed what he thought he'd seen in the temple and put it down to drinking too much, but when she had offered him his dreams in the Kingdom . . .He was a just man, a crusader. He could never agree to coercing Chaeli into loving him. If it was meant to be, then it would happen on its own.

"It is as we feared," he said. "Six men have gone missing in the last week, and what is believed to be a Kitaani warrior was spotted in the centre of Lindor last night. Two Sherai have been seen this morning in the temple of Kry'lla."

"We have to leave," declared Nathan. "We can't handle two Sherai and their Kitaani."

"Agreed. I've met with Mickalos's camarilla, and we're to leave tonight. We may take whatever texts we need with us. Horses and supplies will be provided – to be honest, they seem keen to get rid of us." Adley paced, running his hand through his hair repeatedly and muttering to himself.

"What about the missing men?"

"They are undoubtedly dead. We must presume they are now Kitaani."

"Adley?" said Chaeli, her voice small. "What will happen if meet these Kitaani and Sherai?"

The protector looked up to the skies and exhaled deeply, and then, looking straight into her eyes, confirmed her fears: "We will most likely die."

Chaeli's world spun, her legs buckled, though Adley caught her as she fell. If she died now, then her sister's death was for nothing.

"Being your sister is hard work sometimes, but I love you."

All she could hear was her voice. It was her fault she was dead. If only she had been somewhere else, if only she had been with Ven discussing her apprenticeship, or in the church . . . anywhere but home. Then Acelle might still be alive.

Adley pulled Nathan aside. "Her control of her power is still poor, and if they attack we must protect her above all things," he said in a low tone, hoping Chaeli would not hear. But she did, and flung back her hand and slapped his face hard. The protector looked stunned, though he grabbed her arm as she went to strike him again.

"I'm sorry, Chaeli. I know this is hard for you." He tried to stop her struggling but she kicked out, hitting him in the shins and making him release his grip in surprise.

"*Hard* for me? You know nothing of how I feel! I'm so sick of being lied to! You didn't even have the decency to talk to me about your concerns, you *whispered* them to Nathan, like I'm a fool who can't cope with criticism." She took a deep breath and held up a hand to stop Adley from speaking. "You are *not* my master, and you are *not* my father, brother or lover. You have no say over what I do, or what I know. Start treating me as though I am your equal or leave!" She glared at him, breathing hard. "Look at me, Adley." He stared into her eyes. "I heard you and Sheiva. I know what you said and how you feel."

She needed to know the truth, needed to know what else they hid away from her, and she instinctively knew what to do. She reached up and tore open his shirt with one hand, placing one hand on the dragon and the other hand upon Nathan's serpents. Both men stood still, in shock, neither understanding. She closed her eyes and drew on her power. She felt Adley pull back, but she opened her eyes briefly, and shook her head.

"No." Her voice shocked her. Deeper and darker than normal, it resonated with power.

Her energy washed over them, holding them in place. Breathing deeply and steadily she concentrated on their beating hearts, pulsing in time, the rise and fall of their chests steady. She slowed hers down to match.

She concentrated on Nathan first, and her stars tingled as they touched the serpents. The snakes moved but did not attack, and instead began to coil and weave around her fingers.

So much pain inside him, an ocean of hurt. She didn't know how he could stand it. Delving further, she sensed his rage and cruelty, and instinctively her fingers curled.

Gritting her teeth, she drew her energy and tried to calm the ocean, diving into its depths. Nathan gasped and she opened her eyes. Hundreds of small silver orbs, like the orbs she had seen with Adley at the inn, burst from her hands and into his chest. Nathan looked at her panic-stricken, and now she sensed his fear.

Spreading her fingers, she concentrated on this time on Adley, delving and tunnelling again. His cloud of grief threatened to suffocate her; though not as intense as Nathan's, it was older and more potent. She could go no deeper. Calling on her energy, the orbs descended into his dragon like a swarm of bees. The inking barely moved, save for opening one eye to stare at her.

Then, something changed. Suddenly she was drained and her energy levels dropped. Summoning the last of her strength, she severed the link and snatched both her hands back . . . but her energy was still being siphoned.

"Chaeli, what have you done?"

She stared at her hands. The orbs fell like tears and splashed onto the grass, disappearing into the ground.

Nathan stepped back and stared at his companions in confusion. "Adley, something's wrong! Can't you feel it? She's still expelling energy."

Adley touched her hands and felt power enter him. "We need to stop this. Nathan, take her other hand. No! Stars to stars."

"Do you know what you're doing?"

"Not really, but we need to stop the flow of energy. *Concentrate!*"

Both men threw every shred of their energy into stemming the flow, but instead they absorbed more. Chaeli was swaying, without even the energy to speak.

"She can't take much more, Adley, we need to change tactics. Instead of stopping the power transference, reverse it. Give her ours."

"No! I will not have her sullied by Underworld power!"

"She is part of the Underworld already, Adley! Please, we have to try something."

Adley knew Nathan spoke the truth, but he was afraid. To invade her body and blacken it with Eli's magic would only make her more susceptible to his control, his temptations and corruption. If she gave herself to the Underworld, he would have to kill her. Could he? And why would Nathan want that for her? Why would he want her to face the same struggles as he did? He stared at her, blinking, his mind full of a hundred unwanted thoughts and images of Chaeli at Eli's side, with Nathan.

Nathan didn't wait any longer. He released the serpents and they hissed in delight. His face remained impassive as he fought the urge to give in to the sweet seduction; he threw his power into Chaeli.

359

There were no orbs, but the serpents spat angrily and jumped from his chest, biting at her palm. Black poison spread into her veins, creeping up her arm and through her body.

"What have you done?" cried Adley.

"What I had to."

Adley felt the Underworld crawl and ooze under her skin, reeking of suffering and death, bringing tears to his eyes. But her energy visibly increased and the colour returned to her cheeks.

"You have to complete the circle, Adley," cried Nathan, "or the balance will be tipped forever in the Underworld's favour. I'm struggling to hold on."

Adley closed his eyes. "My gods, forgive me. Daro, forgive me!" His dragon sprang to life; wings beating, it rose from his chest and roared. Fire consumed Chaeli, white and blinding. Her body absorbed it, and the poison bubbled and finally faded.

"She's stopped spilling energy," said Nathan, sagging to his knees and shaking, drawing in huge gulps of air and looking around the gardens for witnesses; there were none.

Adley stepped back, head bowed. "Yes, but at what cost?"

Chaeli opened her eyes. She was no longer weak; she was alive and knew the power inside her.

"What in the gods' names were you trying to achieve, Chaeli?" demanded Adley. His voice was low, controlled, and full of anger as he knelt by her side and checked her temperature. "You could have died."

"I wanted to know if you were hiding more secrets."

Nathan's face was smooth as a mask. "Everyone has secrets. It's not your place to hunt them out. You maybe a demi-goddess, but that doesn't mean you have the right to violate me – *us* – in such a way."

He turned and stalked away towards the library without looking back. Chaeli turned to Adley.

"Don't look at me, I agree with Nathan. We all have secrets. To deny us our privacy is to deny us ourselves and our freedom. Be assured, however, that any secrets I keep from you are for good reason."

She hung her head to hide her own anger. They would have kept the truth from her, as if she were some untrustworthy outsider. Couldn't they see she had a right to know?

"You have a lot to learn, and I fear this transference couldn't have come at a worse time. I have no idea what channelling our power into you might have done. You're now more strongly connected to both the Kingdom and the Underworld. I worry that Eli will be able to summon you."

Chaeli balled her fists. *He can try, but I'd fight him all the way.* "Will I ever understand? Will I ever get things right?"

He gave her a weak consolatory smile and helped her to her feet. "You just need to start thinking before you act."

"You mean I'm an idiot, right? Just a stupid child."

"You are young, yes, but you're not stupid. You simply need guidance. I will always be here for you. I will help guide you, and I pledge my life, heart and my soul to you." He knelt as he spoke these words.

She placed a hand over his mouth. "Shhh! That's blasphemy!" Panic bubbled, and her gaze darted around.

Adley took hold of her hand, turning it over and pressing his lips to her palm. "These things are mine to give," he murmured, and placed her hand back on his cheek.

She looked down at her protector, the most noble of men, the greatest the Seven Realms had to offer. This man pledged everything to her and demanded nothing in return. He was immortal and yet was ready to die for her. She dragged him slowly to his feet and looked into his amber eyes. Whilst she cared for Nathan, this man was her protector.

Chaeli leaned in to kiss him on the cheek, but Adley couldn't control himself and turned his head at the last moment; her lips met his and for a moment she was too surprised to move. But when her senses returned, she tried to pull away. He only pulled her closer, working her mouth open with his tongue. A spark of *something* turned her insides to liquid and warmed her from head to toe. Soon she was kissing him in return. She was safe in his arms, soothed and calmed.

Adley broke away first. "Forgive me, I am cruel and unfair."

Chaeli pulled out of his arms. "No, I'm the cruel one. I'm greedy and selfish and I just don't know what I want! How can you love me when I'm so pathetic?"

Adley stared at her in silence for a long moment, then stepped back and turned away. "Come, we must leave."

Penella watched the afternoon unfold with the shadows. She was excited and shaking with glee. Things were more complicated with the trio than she initially thought – all those secret emotions and feelings for each other, it was too much!

Penella had always despised Amelia, the plain mortal who had bewitched her Daro and then, not content with Daro, she allowed herself to be seduced by Eli; a woman truly in love would never have strayed so. Penella remembered the sorrow Metty had endured watching Eli weave his affections around Amelia. It was then Penella had decided to interfere in the course of love at the cost of Metty's happiness. She fixed Amelia's love to Eli in the hope Daro would be released to love another. But he was not. To make matters worse, Eli spurned Amelia once her pregnancy began to show, and everything began unravelling in Penella's world. Her only satisfaction was in the moment she found Amelia, still raw and bloody from the birth; after a long and deeply gratifying conversation, Penella had watched as the broken woman slit her wrists, her cries for Daro and her baby weakening as her lifeblood ebbed away. Penella waited until the last drop of life force had left her before she snatched up the mortal babe and fled.

Now history was repeating itself: Chaeli lusted after both men, one from the Eternal Kingdom and one from the Underworld. Penella eyed Nathan and could understand the attraction, sorely tempted to bed him herself. Adley, on the other hand, had always been a bore; so pious and pure. Tonight, though, seeing him defy Daro and kiss Chaeli, had surprised her. She watched them walk back to the library and then, in a flash of bright light, she too was gone. She did not see the cluster of bluebells sprout where Chaeli's energy had fallen.

"Release him, Hana," commanded Kerne. He had taken to bringing the seer and Adyam to his office to work now; he disliked the way they had become close and wanted to keep a close eye watch on them. He had tried to separate them, but each time he did, the seer closed down and became almost catatonic. He suspected it was her version of a tantrum but didn't have the energy nor time to fight her. He needed her compliant and powerful as quickly as possible. But oh! How he envied their intimacy. She belonged to *him*.

Hana shrugged. At once Adyam stopped dancing and sat on the floor, his face sweaty and red. Kerne had noticed how little blood Hana now needed for coercions and was content. It would make the next phase easier. However, she still had trouble understanding and implementing the subtler threads of her art; full coercion, possession and visual manipulation came easily to her, but she needed to learn to pull back a little to pass undetected.

"Come here."

The seer's little face fell and she walked to his desk with a shambling, reluctant gait. He picked her up and sat her on his lap. Stroking her hair, he whispered, "I want you to make Adyam think he has a stomach ache. No possession, no full coercion, just plant the idea he has a sore tummy. Once you've put that idea in his head, come straight out – understand?" She was so small and childlike, he often forgot she was a young woman of sixteen.

Hana was upset, but could not let Mr Kerne see it; he would get angry and hurt her again. Besides, a tummy ache wasn't as bad as some of the things he asked her to do. She didn't want to hurt Adyam, but she reached for the vial of his blood anyway, placing a tiny amount on her forehead. She closed her eyes and entered his mind, easy as breathing now, and did as Mr Kerne asked, teasing his thoughts, snaking through and dropping the images and feelings of an upset stomach. Then out she came again.

Opening her eyes, she looked at Mr Kerne and nodded unhappily. Adyam was frowning and she desperately wanted to say sorry – but with Mr Kerne in the room she dared not. Hana felt so helpless. She regretted ever agreeing to leave her cell. In the dark and cold she had been safe – forgotten, but safe. Now she lived in constant fear of Kerne's wrath. She would lie awake at night and pray desperately for freedom, but each morning she awoke in the same rooms, the same routine ahead.

She shivered again and her skin pimpled. It was hot in the room, but the coldness wouldn't leave her. Her skin had become dull and listless, the cruelty asked of her too much for her gentle nature to absorb.

Adyam groaned and rubbed his stomach. Within seconds, he was pale and clammy and clearly in pain. For the next hour Kerne watched, fascinated, as the boy retched and groaned. Hana was devastated, the sight of her only friend in so much pain tearing at her, knowing it was her own doing.

"Mr Kerne, please can we stop now?" she begged, wringing her hands. Her keeper ignored her and continued to chuckle to himself. Breathing deeply, Hana closed her eyes and delved into Adyam; she removed the pain and released him from her coercion.

It took Kerne several minutes to realise what had happened. Scowling, he rose from his chair, grabbed her arm and shook her. The seer went rigid with fear.

"You never, *ever* relinquish control without my permission! Do you understand?"

Adyam stood and moved next to her, his gentle nature shielding her from Kerne's fury. He fancied himself her knight, her champion.

Kerne glared at him. "You, leave! Return to the guard for reassignment."

Hana looked at Adyam in despair. He couldn't leave her, not now, not her only friend in the world. The room grew cold, silence thickening the air.

"Please, Mr Kerne I—"

Her keeper held up his hand and she fell silent; she knew better than to disobey. "No, you have grown too fond of each other. It is detrimental to your training." His voice was colder than the icy air. A wave of his jealousy hit her, but it held a hint of satisfaction. He wanted her for himself. Hana bit her lip, tears filling her eyes.

Adyam said nothing, but caught Hana's eyes and gave a sad, knowing smile.

"Take Hana to her quarters, then you are released." Kerne dismissed them both. In a final act of defiance, Hana broke into Kerne's thoughts – he was thinking of the monster with the claws, and she shuddered, closing the connection as quickly as she had opened it.

She cried the entire was back to her rooms, despite Adyam's hand in hers; she barely noticed that he was gently running his fingers along hers to hush her.

"I'm sorry, Adyam," she sobbed, "I didn't want to hurt you."

Adyam blushed. "I kn-know Hana, I kn-kn-know." She looked up and he smiled back down at her. "You have v-very p-p-pretty hair." With a tiny giggle, her tears stopped and she smiled, touching her hair and winding a section around her fingers. He broke into a grin and opened the door to her room with flourish.

"M-M'lady," he declared, sweeping his arm out in a florid gesture and bowing low. She held a hand up to her mouth and giggled as she walked into her room, suddenly wanting to change her clothes and brush her hair to look prettier for him. Neither of them paid any attention to Kerne's men in the hallway.

"I w-wish I could take you away, Hana." Adyam spoke slowly, struggling with his speech. "N-N-Nathan wouldn't let p-people hurt you." He gazed wistfully out her window and across the city. "Everyone leaves m-m-me. N-N-Nathan t-t-told me he would be back, b-but he's n-not." He looked at Hana. "I won't leave *you* though." He concentrated hard on getting the next words just right. "Even if you can't see me, I can see you."

"But if I can't see you, how do I know you're there?" Hana asked, confused. Adyam's excitement bounced against her.

"Promise you won't tell?" He stood up taller, smile gone, eyes wide. She nodded. Adyam held up his palm and showed her his stars. "I have no affff . . . inity, but I can do this!" With the last word, he disappeared into the shadows. Hana couldn't see him at all, yet could feel him all around. Usually so silent, his energy now sang to her.

Gasping she turned round and round in excitement. "Adyam, where are you?"

"Here," he whispered, and the seer jumped. He was behind her, watching her with a lopsided grin on his face. She squealed with joy and clapped her hands, her sadness replaced by wonder. "N-no one knows, Hana. It's a s-s-secret."

She held her finger to her mouth and grinned.

"I ha-have to g-g-o," he said with a sigh. "I w-wonder where I will be p-p-placed."

"Will you come and see me like that, so no one else can see?"

He nodded and walked to the door. He was gone, but he would return. Adyam was special, just like her. Hana's inner guide sang for joy.

"So why is there a snow leopard on the House Montareon signil then? There are no snow leopards in Algary." The red-haired woman grabbed a bottle of rum from under her elaborate dressing table and pulled the cork out with her teeth, dancing over to Dal and kneeling between his legs. He took the drink from her and swigged.

"Actually . . . there are . . . ahh . . . many." Dal struggled to speak as she unlaced his trousers and slipped her hand beneath them. "It's a myth that the snow leopards died out in Algary. We have— oh gods!" He grabbed her wrists. "Mina, you wicked, wonderful woman." He pulled her up to him and kissed her, tasting the wine on her lips and inhaling the scent of her perfume. It was cheap and strong, burning the back of his throat, but he wanted more of it, more of her. She pulled back and grinned, running her tongue through the gap between her front teeth. Her elaborate coiffure had begun to fall, curls dropping around her face, bejewelled pins sagging. Dal trailed his gaze down her body, desperate to remove the tightly buttoned bodice and skirt.

Taking the bottle again, she wrapped her lips around it, running her tongue across the rim and maintaining his eye contact before drinking again.

"You are incredible," he murmured, running a hand through his hair and reluctantly relacing his trousers, momentarily of course. "I wish you would reconsider my offer and return to Algary with me."

She laughed and hiccupped. "And what? Be your mistress, Kee Dala? I think not. I love it here. I'm my own master." She stood and kissed him on the cheek as he reached towards the neckline of her dress and traced the ruffles. "My girls respect me, the guards respect me. In Algary I'll be nothing, remembered only as your whore."

Dal pulled himself further onto the grand oak bed and plumped up the silk cushions behind him. "If you want for anything, you—"

"Men say that to me every day. You're not the first, and you shan't be the last." Mina started to unpin her hair, the curls tumbling down her back to her waist. Dal regretted lacing his trousers and watched as she sat at the dressing table and ran a brush through her hair.

"If you're not here to let me play with your cock, then what are you here for, Dal?" She glanced over and raised an eyebrow.

Drinking more rum, Dal unbuttoned the top of his shirt. Her room was stifling, and he briefly considered opening the heavy drapes, but she would grow angry at such a thing. This was her room, and he was simply a guest. "What do you know of the Mischlan emissary in Trithia?"

She removed the rouge from her lips with a moist linen cloth and dipped a toothpick in a small vial before staring back in the mirror and continuing her routine. It was several minutes before she replied.

"While my tastes are somewhat exotic, they don't extend to the sand people. They find me too . . . bland for their tastes. They prefer the Sheeman and Lindorian whores nearer the Sink." Using a long strand of thick ribbon, she wound her wrists together and held them out, batting her eyelids. "Those that prefer more than just being bound."

Dear gods. Dal's ears burned, and he unbuttoned his shirt further. The image of Mina bound and bought unsettled him. He coughed and readjusted his painful erection. "The Velenese then?"

She laughed, winding the ribbon around her hair and weaving it through a thick plait. "Oh, Dal. You're not the first royal to ask me to spill my secrets between the sheets. What is it with you men? You think that because you buy my services you buy all of me? My female clients never ask such things."

"Never? I mean . . . never. I would never presume to own you."

"You say never, but you come here, we fuck, and then always I tell you what I know." Moving over to the bed, she crawled up between his legs on all fours and looked across to him, her faces inches from his own. "Now, remind me why I cancelled a rather

368

generous client for your visit today, Prince Kee Dala. Put that mouth of yours to good use and let it be silenced."

He sagged against the pillows. Everything of Mina's smelled of sex and perfume, and Dal kissed her, gently at first and then, as she ran a hand up his thigh, a guttural growl escaped. She moved and pressed her body against his, rubbing him through his trousers and tilting her head to the side, beckoning his kiss forward to her throat. He obliged, and fumbled with her skirts, reaching up and tugging at her undergarments.

Mina pulled away and straddled him, reaching behind and unbuttoning her bodice until it loosened and slipped down her shoulders, revealing an expanse of soft skin that called to him to taste. Removing his own shirt, he beckoned her forward and soon found himself forgetting about the Mischlans, the Velenese, and Kerne's manipulations entirely.

Afterwards, with both their desires sated, Mina lay on his chest, twirling his house ring around her own finger while he smoked a glass pipe filled with calona leaf. The smoke of the drug filled the room and Dal felt his senses lighten and the walls started to bend and melt.

"Trithia and Mischla are to be officially joined," she said without prompting. "Kerne and the Maji signed a bloodsworn contract at an Underworld church. With the sand people's support, Trithia has promised the support of the Velenese."

Dal exhaled and placed the pipe on the floor, struggling to stop the fuzz as it clouded his thoughts. He took Mina's hands in his own and sat her up. Her eyes were glazed, her lips still swollen.

"Why would Kerne promise what he cannot guarantee? Velen would surely refuse any Trithian order?"

She blinked several times and shrugged. "I know not. Only that my Guard Lieutenant overheard the Mischlan secretary dictating a letter to his Grand Maji."

He pried himself free and opened the drapes and window, a gust of cool air stinging his eyes and blowing away at the haze, enough to give him a few moments clarity. He stared down at the early morning streets, thinking. It was only when Mina's arms reached around him that he dragged his mind back.

"What is it that the Velenese want more than anything?"

"Sunshine? A relief from rain?"

"More than that."

She let go and breathed in the fresh air, coughing before adding, "more power."

"Indeed," he mumbled to himself before gathering his clothes and dressing. "Mina . . ." He trailed off and kissed her gently on the lips.

"Oh, you are Cobey's son, indeed," she replied with a guileless smile. The thought made Dal uncomfortable.

'I'm sorry I cannot stay."

"Be gone. I have things to do." She pushed him towards the door with mock outrage and slipped his ring back on his finger. "Don't leave it too long before you visit me again."

"I won't."

Walking down the stairs, he nodded at the man by the threshold, who crossed his arms in acknowledgement and opened the heavy wooden doors, checking first and then indicating Dal forward. A gentle thrum from the traders travelled on the air. He walked through the streets and reached the courtyard, a feeling of guilt dragging at his stomach as he recalled Mina's words of payment, ownership and information. Instead of returning to the castle, he entered the temple of Igon and placed a gold coin onto the altar. Save for the acolyte who stood patiently in the corner, it was empty.

He ran the sharpened stone blade across his palm and prayed.

"Igon, forgive me. I am not an honest man. I am weak. I lie to be strong. Accept this offering as atonement, my god."

There was no reply, and instead giggles broke the silence. Dal turned, two small blonde-haired girls sitting on the back bench holding one another's hands.

"You're funny," said the first.

"Why did you cut yourself?" asked the second. They spoke in unison and watched Dal with large eyes and curiosity.

"Because I honour the gods with the most precious thing I have – my blood."

"But why would a god want your blood?" asked the first, letting go of her companion's hand and walking over to him. "Wouldn't they want you love? Or your heart?"

"Well I can't cut my heart out, can I? They can have my love." He smiled as the child walked around him and admired his belt and rings, her sweetness and innocence enthralling him.

"You're rich."

"I am."

"How did you get rich?"

"My father."

The second girl came over and Dal glanced over to the acolyte who appeared uninterested in the two young girls; his eyes were closed and he leant against the stone walls, his chin resting on his chest. There was another giggle, and Dal looked down. They whispered to one another, their hands cupped to each other's ears as they stared up at him.

"We think you should give us this ring," said the second girl, pointing to a silver and topaz ring on his right little finger. He swallowed, a spark of loss digging at his insides.

"This belonged to my grandmother." Taking it off he rolled it between his fingers. "She gave this to me when I came of age."

"It's very pretty. I'd love a ring like that." The first girl again, her voice wistful. It was then that Dal noticed the bare feet and patches on their dresses.

"Here," he held it out to her. "You have it. I have my grandmother in here." He tapped his chest.

The girl took it and they whispered and giggled again.

"You can have this from us," the second girl said, crooking a finger towards him so that he was forced to bend down. Both girls kissed his cheeks and then ran from the temple and into the streets.

CHAPTER ELEVEN

"YOUR BROTHER IS not in Lindor."

Anya woke, startled. Scrambling to get away from him, her limbs caught in the bed clothes and she jarred her shoulder, making her cry out in pain. Staring round wildly she finally saw him standing by the bed, hands behind his back.

"Tell me where he is, Anya," commanded Kerne, his voice cold and crisp.

"I don't know." She didn't try to hide her fear. It scared her being unable to see his hands; a thousand images raced through her mind.

"Tell me!" he screamed, moving around to her side of the bed as fast as lightning. She cried out and tried to run to the door, but he caught her and spun her round. The pain of the collar paralysed her, shooting through her spine. She went limp in his arms and he carried her into the main room. The fire was crackling loudly and he placed her into the chair by the heat. She said nothing, her neck burning, swamping her senses.

"I dislike causing you pain, Anya. I gain nothing from it." He was calm once more.

Liar!

But she could not speak.

"Do you know who the girl is? Who she *really* is?" Kerne's voice sunk almost beneath human hearing; it held a quiver of excitement.

"She's a girl he found on the road," croaked Anya. She had grown skilled at half truths.

"She's more than that though, isn't she?" he murmured. In truth, she didn't know who Chaeli was other than a girl who had caught her brother's attention, though she suspected there was more.

"She's Prince Eli's daughter, and he wants her."

Anya gasped. "You lie!" She had fed Chaeli, cared for her and treated her like a sister; surely she would have known if she had been nurturing evil . . .

"Have I ever lied to you, sweet Anya? No. Lying is unnecessary and inefficient." He stood by her chair, his hand on the arm. "Perhaps it is time I told you the truth about Chaeli Dresne – or, rather, Chaeli Von Ariseré – and her celestial ancestry." Kerne sat opposite her and told her everything he knew.

Anya relaxed. So Chaeli had not deceived her, nor taken advantage of her. She had not known who her father was, and possibly still did not. Her heart filled with sympathy and concern, and she prayed for her. Pain set in immediately, and she stopped with a gasp. She thought of the demon and the hesitant way Chaeli had admitted the attack; she must have been terrified.

"You seem to have taken my revelations well," said Kerne, tapping his fingers absentmindedly on the chair.

"No. The thought of who her father is terrifies me."

Kerne leaned forward "Why?"

"I don't pray to your master, Kerne, I pray to the Kingdom, to Prince Daro and eternal sanctuary. For forgiveness, for love, for hope."

"You pray for forgiveness and love? Even after what was done to you?"

"How can I not? To seek retribution, pain, or suffering would achieve nothing other than to damn my soul to the Underworld," she replied.

"The Underworld can offer much, Anya, such sweet rewards. Your dreams and desires, your hopes, your pleasures. My prince could make you beautiful again."

"I told you, Captain, I don't want to be beautiful again. I want peace."

Kerne didn't reply. She thought she recognised a flicker of emotion on his face, but it was gone so quickly she might have imagined it.

"I am tired, may I be excused?"

"Of course." He stood as she did. His sensibilities puzzled her; he was the perfect gentleman – when he wasn't treating her like an animal.

"Anya," he called softly. She turned and looked at him. "I want you to kiss me. Kiss me like you would your lover."

A lump formed in her throat. It grew bigger and bigger until she wanted to explode. She couldn't fight his order, she could only go slowly, so slowly. The pain became quickly unbearable, her head feeling as though she had been beaten. With every slow step, a scorching, stinging tore at her. She stood in the shadows next to him, looking up, humiliated, degraded, and in agony. She realised what it was like to truly hate someone, and despised herself for it. She concentrated on the creature before her, and he gazed down, predatory eyes narrowing.

"Kiss me, Anya. Touch my face as you would a lover's. I command it."

Tears rolled down her face, and she couldn't hide her revulsion. But still he did not rescind the command. Her lips touched his lips, as cold as his heart. She hesitated and tried to fight the command, pulling away slightly, but he placed his hand on her back and pressed her closer to him. The collar dug into her skin, the stench of the Underworld coursing through her blood. Hating herself, she kissed him again, this time with closed eyes; his mouth opened and he responded. His kisses were regimented and ordered, no life or passion in them.

Anya was disgusted at herself and her inability to fight back; Kerne had taken that away from her, had taken her free will.

Eventually he pulled away and murmured, "Stop." He wiped her tears away with his thumb. "You may leave."

She wanted to run, but instead walked calmly and steadily to the bedroom. There she sobbed herself to sleep. Kerne sat by the fire listening to her cries, her birdsong. His delicate bird sang for him in her gilded cage.

Eli felt a gust of warm air envelop him. He looked around the room; all the windows and doors were closed – there should be no draughts. The warmth lingered and slowly dissolved into his skin, then something changed. A delicious sweetness erupted in the centre of his power, deep inside. He moved into the power and a hint of apples caught his attention. He frowned. Something new had been added. He tried to reach the apples, but each time he hit a wall. Whatever this was, he was blocked from touching it. Frustrated, he desisted and left the new band of power in place. He would address it later.

He returned to his chair and picked up the sealed missive he had received earlier. The seal was that of his brother. Eli had stared at the note for hours, unsure whether to open it or throw it straight into the fire. He hadn't expected Daro to reply, he thought his brother still too weak and grief-stricken to respond. Clearly he had grown a backbone. He snapped the seal and unfolded the parchment – his brother was too gentle to use vellum.

My Dearest Brother,
I beg you to reconsider the breach of the truce. We both have lost so much. I miss you.
With fond memories and love,
Daro

Eli glared at the short note. That was it? That was all his brother had to say?

He crumpled it up and threw it into the fire, watching the ends burn and curl until it was nothing more than ash.

'I miss you'? His brother had never *missed* him; he had neglected him for that woman! They went from doing everything together to never seeing each other, and it was all because of *her!* The rejection still consumed Eli. He couldn't forgive Daro and would rather destroy everything than change his plans now. Since Penella's visit he had been on edge, for the subterfuge of the goddess had troubled him. She conducted it with such ease that, while he appreciated her help, he didn't trust her. She didn't fear him like his other subjects, and that was simply unacceptable.

Malo had reported back twice, both times with cheering news. Kerne, the replacement for DeVaine, was doing well, and his work with the seer was impressive. Malo reported that Kerne had been attempting to tap into the seer's power to unlock the skill of blood coercion. His goal was to coerce the insect Stirm into becoming Kerne's puppet. But Eli had a better plan for the seer. Moving to his bureau, he withdrew a small glass vial and held it up to the candle. A small amount of blood swilled around the glass. Chaeli's blood.

He certainly wouldn't pin all his hopes on Penella's little plan; this was his insurance. He replaced the vial in the drawer and returned to his seat by the fire.

Apples. He really fancied some apples.

"Your gods seem to have heard your prayers, Miss DeVaine." Kerne spoke formally, with no mention of the kiss; he behaved as though nothing had happened. "I received a note from the King. He orders that you attend the library and assist young Kee Dala with research."

Anya placed her fork on her plate carefully. The shaking of her hands would surely betray her excitement at the thought of leaving his chambers. She briefly imagined summoning help, of finding a way to remove her collar . . .

"What are you thinking?" he demanded.

The command sliced through her and she replied instantly. "I'm looking forward to leaving this room, and you." Anya hated the way she acquiesced so easily now, her traitorous thoughts leaving her lips before she had time to clamp them shut.

Kerne dabbed his mouth gently with his linen cloth and observed Anya. She hated the way he stared at her, but now she defiantly looked up and held his gaze. To her satisfaction, she saw a flicker of surprise.

"You will not tell Prince Kee Dala about the collar. You will not discuss me or what occurs between us. You will assist in his research and each night will relay to me all conversations that you have. If he touches you, or so much as looks at you inappropriately, you will inform me, is that clear?"

Anya nodded, her fleeting thoughts of freedom melting.

"There will be no secret communications between the two of you, no notes, no ciphers, no cryptic comments."

She lowered her eyes. Kerne moved to stand behind her and she shuddered. She wanted to pray, but knew the pain she would suffer was too much. He bent down, lips by her ear. The closeness made her flinch. His body radiated no heat, but his whispered words were hot in her ear: "You belong to me, Anya. You will always be mine." He straightened, and cleared his throat. "I enjoyed our intimacy last night, Miss DeVaine. I expect that I shall require your services again this evening." He buttoned up his tunic and added casually: "One of my guards will collect you shortly and present you to the little prince. Remember the pain that will befall you should you defy me."

He left Anya to cry into her hands and wish for her freedom. When her tears dried, she went into Kerne's rooms where he had laid out her dress for the day. She washed her body and dressed in the clothing of his choosing, then smoothed the linen underskirts and picked up a green satin overdress. He knew her size perfectly.

As she lifted it from the table, a small envelope fell to the floor. As it unfolded in her shaking hands, a small scrawl could be seen, and she had to bring the note close to her face to read it, eyes sparkling with hope. Once read, she ripped the note into tiny pieces. The hearth was cold and the fragments would be obvious there. In frustration, she paced the apartments – there was nowhere she could hide the remnants. At last, she shoved them into her mouth, washing them down with cold tea.

With renewed vigour, she dressed and brushed out her long golden hair. The black collar sat above her clothes, out of place and conspicuous. She would have no answers for the prince if he inquired about it, it hardly looked like regular jewellery.

A knock at the door startled her. Cautiously, she opened it a crack and Small's comely face greeted her. "Miss, are you ready?" He smiled gently and she nodded

They walked in silence, through corridors lined with King's Guard; each one stared at her as she passed. As they reached the entrance to the library on the third floor, she took a deep breath and entered. Small began to follow, but paused by the door.

"I'm sorry, miss, but I'm not the one who is staying here today."

She looked at him in surprise and disappointment. Then she heard the voice she remembered from her cell, all the more memorable for its blend of cruelty and amusement.

"You and me are going to be very close all day." The beast of a guard grinned ferociously at her. She merely nodded in response.

"I'll be right outside, Miss Anya. Don't you worry about Donal here. He knows he's not to touch you, else Kerne will chop his hands off." Donal scowled at the younger man, flexing his fingers into a fist.

"Thank you, Small," she replied quietly and then looked up at the beast. "I will scream if you so much as look me inappropriately.

I suggest you sit by the door and observe from there." Donal hesitated, but relaxed his fists and barged past Small to the seat by the doors from which he glared at them both.

"Sorry, miss. I tried to be the one in the room, but the captain wouldn't allow it." He looked at her once more, then left the room, tripped by Donal as he passed.

The smell of old leather, ink, and parchment surrounded her, and she closed her eyes in bliss. She had spent so many happy hours in this room. Opening her eyes again, she saw a dark-haired figure hunched over one of the benches, absorbed in a text. She gently placed a hand on his shoulder and he turned around. A simple yet attractive face smiled up at her from under scruffy dark hair and the stubble of a few days' beard; the ring of the royal house of Algary glinted in the soft light.

"Prince Kee Dala?"

"Yes, but please, call me Dal." He took her hand and kissed it lightly, motioning for her to join him on the bench. She snatched her hand back fearfully and glanced at Donal who grinned and wagged his finger at her.

"I'm sorry, Miss DeVaine, it was wrong of me to touch you." He had such a gentle voice that Anya wanted to throw herself at him and beg for his help, but even the thought caused wisps of pain to snake through her.

"I'm sorry, Your Highness, I– I don't allow people to touch me," she replied. She sat and looked at him expectantly. "Captain Kerne informs me you require help with your research?"

"Oh yes, of course. Before we start, though, I wish to express my desire to help you—"

"No, please, we must not talk of me." Fighting the familiar burning of the Underworld, she touched her collar. "Understand?" Dal stared at the collar and nodded.

"I understand. In that case, Miss DeVaine, *I* require *your* help. I am after a copy of *The Precepts of War*. King Stirm informs me he has eleven of the twelve volumes. I want to research the rites of military leadership in Trithia in times of war."

"Perhaps it is best if you don't explain yourself to me."

He sighed and drummed his fingers on the table.

"That's rather lovely," she said, pointing at a pretty silver and gold ring on the little finger of his left hand.

He looked down and smiled. "It reminds me of a lady I had the pleasure of meeting. Unfortunately she left before I could apologise for making a fool of myself." He hesitated and again started to say something but, glancing at her collar, he shook his head. "Whilst you search for the volumes, I will research something else that has come to my attention."

"I'll try the top level. Most of the old war books are stored there, along with out-dated medical journals and the histories of the churches." She paused. "And please call me Anya."

Hours passed, each of them working on different levels of the library. Anya glanced over at Donal several times and wished she hadn't, for he watched her constantly. As she struggled with large tomes and coughed at the dust, she began to organise the writings. Humming to herself lightly as she went, she thought of Nathan. She wanted to pray for his safety, but the habit that was once so easy had been broken and she couldn't, the knot of pain increased at the mere thought. She wanted her gods, the warm comfortable feeling of their love.

"I've had lunch brought to the library, and Kingdom forbid we should eat when handling these treasures." Kee Dala approached her with a theatrical sweep of the arm.

"Thank you, Your Highness." She followed him down the spiral staircases.

"Dal," he repeated. "Have you had any luck?"

"I'm sorry Your . . . Dal, but the top level is a mess. I've been organising as I go, but I fear it will take a while."

"Good, anything to keep you away from your prison. However comfortable the interior maybe, it is still a prison, is it not?"

He had arranged for cold hams, breads and cheeses. As she sat the rich aroma of cocoa hit her. "Oh! You have drinking chocolate," she exclaimed happily, relieved that he hadn't brought tea. She had consumed so much tea with Kerne that it made her ill just thinking about it.

"Yes, I have a partiality to cocoa." He grinned. "Cocoa and wine, but, alas, I am trying to reduce my wine intake as I seem to make a fool of myself rather too often."

She allowed herself another small smile, piling the meat and bread onto her plate. This food was richer than that which Kerne brought to her, and she devoured it greedily.

"What brings you to Trithia, Dal? Why not the libraries of Lindor? And how did you get Stirm to agree to me helping you? He can be very . . . obstinate at times."

Dal flicked a glance at her collar. "I came to Trithia to celebrate Stirm's birthday on behalf of Algary. It wasn't until I was here that I decided to research Trithian ways and practises. I felt it would be beneficial for Algary to observe and report alternate ways of military life. I merely asked Stirm if he knew of a great scholar who could help me, and his first thoughts were of you. I asked, he obliged."

"I give thanks to the King then. I love this library. I spent many happy days buried in books whilst I lived within these walls."

They finished the meal and revelled in the deliciousness of the cocoa. It had been years since Anya had last had the drink, and she savoured each sip.

Donal approached, smirking. "Miss DeVaine, the captain wants you."

"I am to have Anya for as long as I wish, soldier. King's orders."

"I'm sorry, Your Highness, but the captain told me she is to return after luncheon. The captain renegotiated this agreement before breakfast. I do apologise you weren't informed." Donal sounded anything but apologetic, and Dal frowned at him, then glanced at Anya, softening his glare.

"This is unfortunate. I will find out what is going on." Dal went to touch her hand, but she drew away and he nodded. "Keep faith, Anya."

Donal accompanied her to the doors but made no effort to open them, watching smugly as she struggled with the heavy wood.

"Here, miss, let me." Small opened the doors wide and glared at Donal. "Where are you going?"

"The captain has asked me to return. My freedom was short lived."

"You're coming back tomorrow though, miss. Donal told you that, right?"

"I hadn't got that far," grumbled the big man. "Mornings with the prince, afternoons back with the captain."

Anya turned to Donal. "You are abominable, Donal. I will not have you escorting me. I shall discuss this with the captain this afternoon." She hoped the firmness of her voice was enough. The older soldier said no more. "Small will escort me. You are excused," she added, hoping she hadn't pushed it too far. A flicker of a grin crossed Small's lips. Donal hesitated, then lumbered away.

"Nicely done, miss."

She smiled and together they walked back to Kerne's rooms. She was always comfortable in Small's presence. He made no comment on her scars, never stared, and always showed her respect. Dal, too, had treated her with respect and care; he was unlike any royal she had ever met.

"Captain Kerne is inside, miss. Please . . . remain strong." He opened the door for her and she walked in. The captain sat at his dining table. He looked up as she entered and held her gaze.

"You may leave," he ordered Small. "Please sit down, Anya." His voice was soft, but she knew that meant nothing. She didn't move. "Sit *down*." The softness was there still, but its undertone made her jerk involuntarily and she moved towards the table. Kerne stood and gently pushed her chair in behind her, and then poured her tea.

Tea, again. Her stomach churned. She could still taste the cocoa and her wonderful meal with Dal. She didn't want tea.

"Tell me, did you enjoy the library?"

"Yes," she whispered.

"Did you enjoy the company of the little prince?"

"Yes."

"Did you enjoy the way he kissed your hand? Touched you with his filthy lips?" His voice grew harder and lower. "Answer me, Anya."

The fire started in her bones, which ached and throbbed in reply; she let the pain build and resisted for as long as she could before she blurted out: "Yes and yes!"

"I see." He was quiet for a long while. He sat sipping at his tea, scrutinising her. She could feel his eyes on her, devouring her. "Tell me everything you discussed and everything he said to you. Leave out nothing. Change no words and hide no expressions. I want to know every place he touched you, every look he gave you. If I find you have misled me, I shall be extremely displeased."

Her heart sank. She repeated her conversations with Dal, trying to gloss over the glances he gave her collar and the small ring he wore, but she couldn't. She saw Kerne smile as she struggled with the compulsion. His eyes danced and glinted with pleasure at her pain.

"Excellent. You are proving much more useful and efficient than my spies." He put his china cup down. "Drink your tea." She picked up her cup and swallowed the tea, washing with it the revulsion she felt for Kerne, and for herself. The smell of the tea sickened her. She hesitated and glanced at Kerne, staring at his hands.

"I intended to enjoy your company again this evening, Anya, but I shall be indisposed. So I have decided that I will experience your delights now."

She looked up fearfully at his masked expression and wished he showed at least a little emotion; it might somehow lessen her pain and humiliation. She opened her mouth to speak, but closed it again as she realised she didn't know how to express her desire.

"Speak, Anya. Tell me what you were thinking."

"I hate you," she said. "I hate what you've done to me, the coldness of your touch, your inhumanity. I have no desire for you. You are a monster."

She had said more than she intended and immediately regretted it. Biting her lower lip, she avoided his eyes.

"My little bird, my Anya, I own you, you are mine to do with as I please. Stirm betrayed you, but I have never lied to you. I will use you in whatever way it pleases me. I care not for your happiness or your desires, only my own."

Anya felt the sickness rise in her throat.

"Now, I wish to try again. There will be no tears this time, no cries, and no complaints. I want you to show me love, Anya. Today I will embrace you and you will give me nothing but tenderness in return." He stood and took her hand, guiding her to her feet. He leant in and kissed her hard on the lips. She started to pull away but the collar pinched her skin and sent the bolt of pain up her spine again. He pulled her closer and kissed her cheek, running his tongue along her skin. The nausea returned and she closed her dry eyes. She wanted to cry, to scream, but could not. There was nothing she could do, no way to escape him. She knew the harsh justice he handed out to those who had crossed him, had heard the stories of how he punished those who disobeyed his commands. Fear ruled her as much as he did.

His arms were hard, and he didn't relax in embracing her, so she shifted her weight.

"What are you doing?"

"Your arms hurt," she said.

He searched her eyes, his face impassive, but she felt his hold relax slightly. He raised an eyebrow at her questioningly and she nodded. He moved in again and pressed his lips against hers. He made no attempt to further the embrace, but she did, fighting her disgust and terror. The helplessness she had felt when Stirm forced himself on her was something she never wanted to experience again. A small amount of control, a small amount of self worth. This would be her decision. She put her arms around him, and his body tensed. He jerked away, breaking contact with her lips. She would be in control of this, not him.

"What are you doing?"

"Loving you the way you commanded," she replied, dead inside, but not removing her arms. He relaxed and moved to kiss her again, tenderly this time.

She closed her eyes – it was easier that way – and she imagined herself kissing someone else. *His* face filled her mind, the one she dreamed of. She reciprocated when he moved his tongue, gasping slightly as his hands moved to the small of her back. Her insides knotted and her stomach churned so fiercely she feared she might throw up. But no, she wouldn't allow him to see her pain or fear anymore. He mimicked their kiss from the previous night down to the tiniest detail, no originality at all. She realised then that he was a novice; she was the first person he had kissed. The thought allowed a small amount of pity to trickle, but as quickly as it came, she pushed it away in anger. Why should she feel sorry for him? His inexperience was not her concern, and certainly did not excuse his behaviour.

She couldn't fight, she couldn't run, couldn't scream or refuse. She had to accept and return his affections no matter what it cost her. Her hatred for him sparked inside her and spread around her body like liquid fire.

She ran her hand down his face, his skin as smooth as marble. He moved to deepen his kiss and pulled her closer – she couldn't take any more, and he slowly released her. His lips were red and his face flushed. Anya had no heat in her own skin, only the icy feeling of despair and loathing. He took her hands in his, and, staring at her face, started to lead her to his bed chambers.

She froze again and he frowned. He pulled at her hand firmly.

"Please, Kerne, no." She couldn't stop the tears now, and even with the pain the collar caused, allowed them to fall.

"I want you, Anya. I want you to love me."

She rooted herself to the spot, the fear of what was coming mixing with the smell of sulphur and the pain of the collar to overwhelm her. She collapsed, breaking free of his grasp.

Kerne said nothing as she writhed in agony. It ought to be easy, she knew, for her to give in and let him own her completely, but she couldn't. Not again. She needed to hold onto something. If she gave in, she was nothing, an inanimate object for him to possess and parade when it pleased him. She was *alive* and she *felt*.

No! I would rather die.

As she thought the words, she knew them to be true and relief mingled with the pain. To die would be the greatest escape. She would win. Kerne would have nothing more from her.

The collar tightened and fire circulated within her body, burning as though her blood was lava. She cried and cried for what seemed like an eternity, weeping with pain and happiness as she started to slip from consciousness, that feeling of lightness and emptiness she had experienced when Stirm sliced her returning. It was coming, and she wished it along with the speed of one thousand snow leopards. Eventually she heard his voice over the roaring in her ears.

"Stop! I rescind my command. I do not want your love today."

The pain started to subside, but fear remained, disappointment screamed.

No, just let me go!

She would be punished; he dragged her to her feet by her hair, his fury a thing of ice and snow, white lips, huge eyes, and she knew he was finally close to losing his calm façade.

"I thought you loved me, Anya. I told you to love me! You wanted me tender, you wanted me gentle, but instead you lie like all the others. You offer yourself, but when I want to take what's mine, you refuse." He wound her hair around his hand tightly, pulling at it from the roots.

"I can't."

The pain in her voice was clear, and knowing he would now not let her die, she hoped it would appeal to any shred of humanity this man had.

He yanked at her hair again. "Why won't you allow me what's mine? You are mine, body and soul!"

She continued to cry, but had no more words for this man. The pain inside exhausted her, and all she wanted was to sleep, for all this to end.

"Why don't you love me, Anya? Tell me! Tell me and I'll stop. I won't touch you again today and will allow you time in the library with the little prince." She sensed the desperation in his hurried words.

"Because you treat me like an animal. You collar me, demand affection, you expect me to *love* and want you intimately. How can any woman love a man like you? You're disgusting. You're nothing but an animal yourself! Your very touch makes me sick. I hate you, I despise you . . ." She broke off, sobbing, and without waiting reached up and twisted his hand away from her hair, slapping at his wrists and jerking her body way. He let go of her and stared.

He reached up and held the collar; she felt a surge of his energy, then the band snapped undone and fell into his hands. Instinctively she touched her neck. She had grown accustomed to the feel of it, and rolled her shoulders and neck in wonderment at the sense of freedom while watching him with distrusting eyes.

His voice was low when he finally spoke. "While we are together, I will remove the collar. When I leave, it will be replaced. If you try to cross me, I will place it back on and use you as I please. I will show no more mercy."

The thick cloud of the Underworld had lifted and the sweet warmth of the Kingdom rushed back into her. She felt the presence of her gods and they soothed her pain and anguish; she could almost hear them again, and their murmurs resonated throughout her body. She still couldn't run – he would find her and punish her – but she could pray.

He wrapped his arms around her, making her toes curl in disgust, but she allowed it.

I will beat you, and when I do, I will kill you.

The venom of her words caused tears to form anew. He was destroying her and everything she stood for. She was a medic, not a murderer, but his treatment of her made it impossible for her to think of anything but his demise.

The sympathy of the gods filled her, their sympathy, their understanding, but also their agreement flooded her senses. He let go and touched her scars with his hands, gentle but emotionless, and at his touch, his coldness wrapped around her own heart.

"Thank you, Anya."

She didn't reply. He went to pick up the collar but she touched his arm. "Please, I would like to pray," she said. He looked into her eyes and nodded.

"Five minutes."

She walked to the closed window and lifted the latch. At once he was by her side, placing his hand on hers. He looked at her with narrowed eyes and, after a few seconds, Anya realised why.

"I don't intend to jump. Suicide is sin and I would never enter the Kingdom. I merely wish to pray with the warmth of the sun on my face and the breeze in my hair. Alone. Away from you." Kerne removed his hand and nodded.

Stepping onto the small balcony, she closed her eyes and opened herself fully to the gods. They sang to her and she gave thanks and asked for guidance. It was then that *he* entered her mind, the one whose face she always pictured and dreamt of. He came to her, begged for her forgiveness for her pain. It had been so long since he had spoken to her and she wished she had more time. He gave her what strength he had left, and it was enough.

After a few minutes of silence, Anya turned and walked back into the room. Kerne stood with the collar his hand.

"Please, there is no need. I won't try to run or leave. Please don't." She wanted to maintain her control, her small amount of humanity. Without that, she was nothing.

He placed it around her neck. "I can't take that risk." The heat of his charm sealed the collar and the stench of the Underworld seeped into her very soul again, as though she was cut off from everything good.

"I repeat: you will not run, you will not scream, you will not try to escape or encourage others to help you escape. When outside this room, you will go straight to the library and help Prince Kee Dala. There will be no ambiguous or cryptic comments between the two of you. You will not discuss me or what happens here. Is that clear?"

Anya nodded and he turned and left the room. She ran to the attached bathing rooms and retched into the chamber pot over and over again. When she realised she couldn't throw up, she washed her body thoroughly, scrubbing all traces of Kerne and his touch from her skin.

They found Nathan in his rooms packing his belongings, Sheiva hovering in the background looking worried

"What's wrong?" Adley stopped and stroked the fae.

"Nathan's leaving us," said Sheiva with a sad mew.

"What?" Chaeli strode over to the bed. "You're leaving?" Nathan said nothing and continued to pack. "Answer me, damn it!" she cried wresting the pack from his hands. He didn't resist, but turned to face her. "Well? You're leaving me? Leaving us?"

"It's for the best. I don't want you in my head. Some things are private."

"I know I was wrong, but please, Nathan, don't go. Stay with us."

"Why?"

"What do you mean 'why'?"

"Why do you want me to stay? I am a liability, he's made that quite clear," said Nathan, throwing a resentful glance at Adley. "So has Mickalos. I bring despair wherever I go. You will always be at risk of the Underworld when I'm with you."

"If it wasn't for you, Nathan, I'd be dead by now or worse. I would never have made it into Trithia, or out again. Danven would still have me, and even if I had escaped, I would have emptied myself of all my power if you hadn't been there to give me yours." The warrior was silent. "Please come with us, just for now. If you still feel the same way in a few days, I won't stop you leaving. I truly am sorry for what I did. I won't pry again." Her hands were shaking and she passed him back his pack.

He stared out the window, not a muscle moving. "If, in three days, I feel the same, we will part ways."

"We really need to get going," said Adley from the doorway.

Chaeli touched Nathan's arm, then turned and sprinted back to her room. She grabbed her pack and stuffed in a change of clothes, accidentally taking some of the bedclothes with her. An envelope on fell to the floor by her feet; she opened it and a silver chain slipped into her fingers, a sparkling star dangling from it. Puzzled, she looked in the envelope and opened the little card within:

This reminded me of you. N

She let the chain run through her fingers. Where would he have got it from? She slipped the chain over her neck and hid the necklace under her shirt. As she left the room, she almost collided with Mickalos.

"Careful child, careful," he muttered. Chaeli apologised but the old man didn't seem to hear her. "You'd better be worth it, my girl. He's been through too much to be broken now."

"Worth what?"

"Worth losing his heart, his head, and his honour over. He is the greatest warrior on our side, not to mention the most loyal friend a man can have."

Adley.

"Chaeli, my time on this world is nearly up. I doubt we will meet again. Take care of him." He grasped her hands in his; they were as cold as ice.

"I will," she promised. He nodded and released her.

"There is much I wanted to tell you, but I fear time has beaten us," he said, accompanying her out to the front of the library. "In many ways, you're so much like your mother, Chaeli. Led by the heart and not the head." He looked thoughtful for a moment, as though lost in memory, but he quickly shook it off and patted her arm. "Come, let me escort you."

"You knew my mother? Why didn't you say? How? Wait . . ." she trailed off and stopped. "*How* did you know my mother? That was four hundred years ago."

"It was, but I remember her as though she stands before me today. Come now, we must get you out of here." He urged her on.

Both Nathan and Adley had packed their horses, and Sheiva had transformed into a stunning silver owl. Chaeli grinned at him and he blinked slowly back. Taking her bag silently, Nathan packed it onto her horse.

Adley grasped Mickalos's arms. "Old friend, I release you from your indenture. You are forgiven your past. The Kingdom welcomes you."

As he spoke these words, Chaeli felt the hair on the back of her neck stand on end. A gentle trickle of power blew on the air like a whisper, passed through them and away into the distance.

Mickalos laughed. "Thank you, Adley."

"Thank you." He kissed the old man on each cheek and held him close.

"Safe travels to you all!" the old man cried.

"Goodbye, my friend."

Adley led the horses from the library and towards the city gates whilst Sheiva flew overheard. He knew he would never see his friend again.

The streets were eerily quiet, the dimmed lamps casting indistinct shadows on the limestone, none of the bustle and laughter to which Chaeli had become accustomed. The air was thick, and a bitter smell travelled on the wind. She urged her horse to a trot to catch up to Adley. "This doesn't feel right."

"I know. Stay sharp."

Nathan appeared distracted and his eyes were glazed; he undid the top button on his leather doublet and scratched his neck and throat roughly.

"Nathan, are you all right?"

"Sorry, what?" He didn't look at her. "Can you feel that?"

"Feel what?"

"That pull. Something or someone is calling me by my power. The serpents are going wild, I can't stop them."

"Where is it coming from?

"A few streets away, but it's getting stronger." He held his bridle tight with one hand and ran the other through his hair. "It's here!" His eyes flew wide and alert. "They're here, Chaeli, you have to go! Go now, *NOW!*"

Adley shouted and fell hard to the ground as his horse reared up in fear, then clattered away down the street.

"Adley!" Chaeli screamed, sliding from her saddle. She ran to him, skidding to a halt by his side and desperately trying to drag him to his feet. There was nothing with them but the flickering of the shadows in the lamp light.

"No, go," Adley groaned barely able to move. "It's an ambush. Leave me."

She struggled and heaved, but when she at last managed to pull him to his feet, he groaned in pain. A sticky warm wetness covered her hands; he was bleeding heavily from his head.

"Sherai! Go, Chaeli, now! Run!"

She followed his gaze and saw a small veiled female standing on the wide street. She wore slitted red silk trousers that billowed with the wind, and a silk vest covered her breasts. The scent from the

The power of the strike caused Blue to stagger back, but he ducked and swept White's legs. But neither warrior would truly attack. The Watcher stalked around the arena, his eyes narrow.

Blue crouched, breathing hard and clutching a stone figurine tightly in his left hand as he watched his foe. His lips moved in a soundless whisper before he pressed the figurine to his lips.

White edged to the boundary of the arena and emptied a small leather pouch into his open palm. The Watcher followed, peering over White's hunched shoulders. Nestled in White's palm were a number of tiny ivory runes and figures. The warrior rattled them and threw them into the wet sand, then nodded to himself. He looked from the figures to Blue and then back again.

The Watcher frowned.

In his castle apartments, Dal bolted the door and sat at his desk, piles of gold coins, scrolls and letters scattered over the surface. Pulling the stopper from a crystal decanter, he swigged the liquor and began to read, pausing only to remove the silver and filigree ring and place it on the desk. Pressing his fingers to his temples, he cursed in frustration, then took out a fresh sheet of paper.

Hana giggled, a smile spreading across her face as Adyam chased her through the rose-lined courtyard. Her blood-red hair blazed behind her as she twisted and turned to avoid the young soldier's grasp. Adyam stopped, laughing, then stepped back into the shadows, disappearing into the darkness. Hana squealed, then stilled. She squinted and reached out to grab at the seemingly empty darkness. Her hands grasped his and she pulled Adyam toward her, throwing her arms around him. He kissed her on the top of the head as she pressed her flushed cheek against his chest. Her aura glowed a pearlescent opal colour, enveloping them both.

Anya sat in the chair by her bed, staring at the wall. Her eyes were red and swollen from weeping, and her hair hung loose and unbrushed. She apologised aloud, over and over, turning a small silver letter opener in her hands before finally slipping it down the front of her bodice.

Kerne stood back from the wood panelling that separated their rooms and replaced the notch of wood in the spyhole. As he walked past Anya's door, he paused with his hand on the knob, then chuckled and returned to his rooms. He stood at the window and looked down into the rose courtyard in time to see a kiss pressed to the top of a flame-bright head. His fingers pressed hard and white against the glass.

Kry'lla and Nishka stood behind the heavily pregnant Grand Maji as the warhosts of her realm converged. Bowing, the leaders of the clans laid gifts at her feet and crawled in deference to their gods. The Grand Maji stepped back and her son took her place on the golden platform. A roar of approval thundered in the air as she dubbed him Grand Warlord of the thousands of warriors below. Nishka and Kry'lla grinned and disappeared.

ABOUT THE AUTHOR

Sammy H. K. Smith lives in sunny Oxfordshire, UK, with her husband, her two big dogs and an army of cats. She works full-time for the police as a detective and writes when time allows. When her head isn't in a book or staring at her computer, she studies for her BA degree in Humanities with a specialism in Classical Studies.

A lover of fantasy and science fiction, she can be found watching re-runs of Battlestar Galactica (the new series!) and wishing she could pilot a viper. The H.K does not stand for 'Hunter Killer', regardless of what some people think.

Other Titles from Kristell Ink

Darkspire Reaches by C.N. Lesley

The wyvern has hunted for the young outcast all her life; a day will come when she must at last face him.

Abandoned as a sacrifice to the wyvern, a young girl is raised to fear the beast her adoptive clan believes meant to kill her. When the Emperor outlaws all magic, Raven is forced to flee from her home with her foster mother, for both are judged as witches. Now an outcast, she lives at the mercy of others, forever pursued by the wyvern as she searches for her rightful place in the world. Soon her life will change forever as she discovers the truth about herself.

A unique and unsettling romantic adventure about rejection and belonging.

Published March 2013

The Art of Forgetting: Rider by Joanne Hall

A young boy leaves his village to become a cavalryman with the famous King's Third regiment; in doing so he discovers both his past and his destiny.

Gifted and cursed with a unique memory, the foundling son of a notorious traitor, Rhodri joins an elite cavalry unit stationed in the harbour town of Northpoint. His training reveals his talents and brings him friendship, love and loss, and sexual awakening; struggling with his memories of his father who once ruled there, he begins to discover a sense of belonging. That is, until a face from the past reveals a secret that will change not only Rhodri's life but the fate of a nation. Then, on his first campaign, he is forced to face the extremes of war and his own nature.

This, the first part of The Art of Forgetting, is a gripping story about belonging and identity, set in a superbly imagined and complex world that is both harsh and beautiful.

Published June 2013

The Reluctant Prophet by Gillian O'Rourke

There's none so blind as she who can see . . .

Esther is blessed, and cursed, with a rare gift: the ability to see the fates of those around her. But when she escapes her peasant upbringing to become a priestess of the Order, she begins to realise how valuable her ability is among the power-hungry nobility, and what they are willing to do to possess it.

Haunted by the dark man of her father's warnings, and unable to see her own destiny, Esther is betrayed by those sworn to protect her. With eyes newly open to the harsh realities of her world, she embarks on a path that diverges from the plan the Gods have laid out. Now she must choose between sacrificing her own heart's blood, and risking a future that will turn the lands against each other in bloody war.

The Reluctant Prophet is the story of one woman who holds the fate of the world in her hands, when all she wishes for is a glimpse of her own happiness.

Published August 2013

Shadow Over Avalon by C.N. Lesley

Fortune twists in the strongest hands. This is no repeat; this is what happens next.

A man, once a legend who bound his soul to his sword as he lay dying, is now all but a boy nearing the end of his acolyte training. Stifled by life in the undersea city of Avalon, Arthur wants to fight side by side with the air-breathing Terrans, not spend his life as servant to the incorporeal sentient known as the Archive. Despite the restrictions put on him by Sanctuary, he is determined to help the surface-dwellers defeat the predators whose sole purpose is to ensure their own survival no matter the cost.

Published October 2013

The Art of Forgetting: Nomad by Joanne Hall

Friendship dies in the face of cruelty; new loyalties are forged, blood merged into new life . . .

In a single moment of defiance, driven by a rash act of compassion for a stranger, Rhodri turns his back on his unit, his country and his comrades in arms. Taken in by the Plains Hawk tribe, he finds compassion, love, and a new purpose for his unique memory. But just as he is beginning to accept his decision, an invasion from the east throws the tribe into chaos, and threatens to destroy the new life he has built.

Rhodri must rally the tribes to take on his former comrades, his former friends, and fight the forces of the crown he swore to protect—and the sister he has never known. Thrust into the role of leader, he must use the very lessons he learned in the King's Third against his closest friends, and his most bitter enemy.

Published May 2014

The Sea-Stone Sword by Joel Cornah

"Heroes are more than just stories, they're people. And people are complicated, people are strange. Nobody is a hero through and through, there's always something in them that'll turn sour. You'll learn it one day. There are no heroes, only villains who win."

Rob Sardan is going to be a legend, but the road to heroism is paved with temptation and deceit. Exiled to a distant and violent country, Rob is forced to fight his closest friends for survival, only to discover his mother's nemesis is still alive, and is determined to wipe out her family and all her allies. The only way the Pirate Lord, Mothar, can be stopped is with the Sea-Stone Sword – yet even the sword itself seems fickle, twisting Rob's quest in poisonous directions, blurring the line between hero and villain. Nobody is who they seem, and Rob can no longer trust even his own instincts.

Driven by dreams of glory, Rob sees only his future as a hero, not the dark path upon which he draws ever closer to infamy.

Published June 2014

The Book of Prophecy by Steven J. Guscott

In a world where technology and evolution has ground to a halt, Dragatu and his brothers are gifted with powers that will change their lives and their world, forever.

After the death of his father, Dragatu vowed that he would never give in, never give up, and never be weak. Strong, focussed and undeterred, he often ignored criticism and caution, and eventually convinced his townspeople to build a water source and expand. This set the wheels of change in motion, and soon The Creator intervened and released the untapped potential within the three brothers.

Gifted with extraordinary powers, balanced finely on choice and consequence, the brothers finally learn the meaning of sacrifice, and that strength comes in many forms.

Philosophy, pain, heartbreak and love. This is a book for those that enjoy their fantasy layered with strong characterisation.

Published August 2014

www.kristell-ink.com

Lightning Source UK Ltd.
Milton Keynes UK
UKOW04f0935110216

268154UK00002B/6/P